ADAM'S PEAK

ADAM'S PEAK

A Novel

Heather Burt

DUNDURN PRESS
TORONTO

Editor: Barry Jowett
Copy-editor: Andrea Waters
Design: Alison Carr
Printer: Webcom

Library and Archives Canada Cataloguing in Publication

Burt, Heather, 1965-

    Adam's peak / Heather Burt.

ISBN-13: 978-1-55002-646-7
ISBN-10: 1-55002-646-1

    I. Title.

PS8603.U785A64 2007   C813'.6   C2006-905755-9

1   2   3   4   5   10   09   08   07   06

Conseil des Arts
du Canada

Canada Council
for the Arts

Canadä

ONTARIO ARTS COUNCIL
CONSEIL DES ARTS DE L'ONTARIO

We acknowledge the support of the **Canada Council for the Arts** and the **Ontario Arts Council** for our publishing program. We also acknowledge the financial support of the **Government of Canada** through the **Book Publishing Industry Development Program** and **The Association for the Export of Canadian Books**, and the **Government of Ontario** through the **Ontario Book Publishers Tax Credit program** and the **Ontario Media Development Corporation**.

Care has been taken to trace the ownership of copyright material used in this book. The author and the publisher welcome any information enabling them to rectify any references or credits in subsequent editions.

J. Kirk Howard, President

Printed and bound in Canada
Printed on recycled paper
www.dundurn.com

Dundurn Press
3 Church Street, Suite 500
Toronto, Ontario, Canada
M5E 1M2

Gazelle Book Services Limited
White Cross Mills
High Town, Lancaster, England
LA1 4XS

Dundurn Press
2250 Military Road
Tonawanda, NY
U.S.A. 14150

For Paul

DECEMBER 1970

The whole family, it seems, is out of sorts. Mum now cries at the slightest thing — the mention of a holiday for which she'll be absent, the sight of tea pluckers in the hills — or sometimes for no reason at all. Aunty Mary follows Mum's cues, bursting out in supportive tears promptly and heartily. Susie creeps about, staying out of everyone's way, doing as she's told. Even Grandpa, proud host of the tea plantation, seems small and uncertain. Dad is behaving strangest of all — one minute playful and boisterous, rounding up the troops for a game of cricket; the next, wandering silently into the hills, not answering when Mum calls. At the moment, he and all the other grown-ups are out on the lawn, gloomily drinking their afternoon tea. From the cool shelter of Grandpa's verandah, Rudy watches them.

It's the usual group sitting around the low cane table, and yet nothing at all *seems* usual. Over the course of the weekend, the once ordinary events of a visit to Grandpa's tea plantation have been given special titles, each of them beginning with "The Last": The Last Tour of the Factory, The Last Milk Rice Breakfast, The Last Trip to the

Nuwara Eliya Market. And now, a cloud of stifling sadness hangs over The Last Afternoon Tea on the Lawn. Next week, there will be a last Christmas at Aunty Mary and Uncle Eugene's house, and by New Year's Day the Van Twest family will be carving a new life from the ice and snow of Canada (though Dad will be taking his tea expertise to an important job with the Red Rose Company). For a long time it seemed to Rudy that this new life was all anyone could talk about. But in these final days, the bubbling anticipation has gone flat and the word *Canada* has taken on a new, taboo meaning, like Uncle Eugene's illness. Something that shouldn't be talked about.

In contrast to the gloomy gathering on the lawn, the day is bright and airy, a welcome change from Colombo's heat. Mum is wearing her fancy turquoise sari, one last time, its gold embroidery gleaming in the afternoon sun. When she came outside for afternoon tea, Dad said she looked like she was off to a bloody Kandyan wedding, but Rudy noticed that he smiled proudly when he said it.

Scratching a new mosquito bite, Rudy turns his attention to an army of small red ants transporting the corpse of a cockroach across the polished cement floor. For a time, the collective strength and cooperation of the insects fascinates him, but as they disappear into a crevice, he heaves a sigh of boredom and squints out at his cousins, all older and all girls, talking endlessly in a far corner of the lawn. For the first time ever, he finds himself wishing for a brother his own age to play with, or even a younger one he could boss around. His mother has told him there'll be plenty of children on their street in Montreal, which makes him wish he were there already.

For a change of scenery, he goes into the bungalow. It's quiet and dark inside, and it takes a while for his eyes to adjust. Dragging his fingers along the wall, he goes to the sitting room in search of Susie, last seen giving the elephant figurines a ride on the turntable of the old gramophone. He's disappointed not to find her, as he hoped she would take him to look at the crocodile lamp in Grandpa's study. But on further consideration, he decides that a six-year-old who'll soon be going to school in Canada shouldn't need his sister's protection to look at a dead crocodile. He continues down the hallway, his bare feet making sticking sounds on the wooden floor, and pushes the study door open. The room is dusty and old-fashioned, but bright, its white walls ribbed with slats of sunlight from the louvred shutters. As his eyes readjust, Rudy scans his grandfather's things — the tall shelves crammed with leather-bound books, the framed certificates and photographs, the brass ashtray stand, and the mounds of documents on the massive desk. Finally, he zeroes in on the lamp.

The crocodile lamp is Grandpa's prize possession. It stands next to the fireplace, seemingly balanced on the curve of its tail, though a pair of metal supports drilled into the hind legs provides the real stability. When the lamp is on, the animal's ivory belly reflects the soft glow of the electric light bulb that has somehow been rigged to its head under a small khaki shade. Stunted forearms and chipped claws are frozen in a perpetual snatch, while the mouth is fixed in a toothy grimace. The eyes are glass and disappointingly artificial; still, the overall impression is one of terrific fierceness.

Facing the creature now, though, Rudy feels his family's cloud of sadness descend on him. It is The Last Meeting with the Crocodile. He isn't even particularly afraid, which only heightens the sadness. He touches the creature's shoulder and watches it teeter back and forth from one support to the other, more lamp than crocodile. He steps back, tries to be afraid. But it's useless. Somehow the fierce beast has been tamed.

He's about to leave the study when he notices, above the lamp, a framed black and white photograph. In it, two young men are standing against a low stone wall on either side of a bell, which hangs like a third head above them. Behind them, in the distance, are rolling hills. One of the men — too dark to be a Burgher — looks as stiff and lifeless as the crocodile lamp. He's dressed in black trousers and a long-sleeved white shirt. The other fellow, in light trousers and a polo shirt, is leaning away from the serious boy, not even looking at the camera. His eyes are fixed on something, or someone, off to the side, and he's laughing.

Absorbed in the two figures, wishing again that he had a brother to play with, Rudy doesn't immediately notice his grandfather in the doorway of the study, and he jumps when Grandpa asks him what he's doing. He glances at the crocodile then back up at the photograph.

"Who are those two people, Grandpa?"

His grandfather comes to stand beside him. Old-man smells of tobacco and shoe polish fill Rudy's nostrils. Grandpa points his pipestem at the serious-looking fellow.

"This chap is the best tea taster I've ever encountered."

"Does he still work here?" Rudy says, standing on tiptoe and craning his neck.

"No, son. He left a long time ago. Long before I became P.D. This was back when I was Tea Maker, in charge of the factory." Grandpa points again to the photograph. "Amitha Jayasuriya here was my best taster."

"What happened to him?" Rudy says.

"I had to let him go. He might have gone to another plantation." Grandpa emits a gravelly sound, like a sigh. "A terrible waste — but the planting life has lost the discipline it had under the British, Rudy. Mental and physical discipline. That's what it takes to make things run."

Sounds of laughter — Susie's and the girl cousins' — tumble through the shutters, beckoning, but for the moment Grandpa's strange remarks have the stronger hold.

"Who's the other man?" Rudy says.

"That's Ernie. He would have been seventeen or eighteen at that time."

Rudy wants to ask who Ernie is, but Grandpa has turned to his desk, where he's rummaging under papers, saying "I've got something here I want to read to you." Edging toward the window, Rudy catches a glimpse of bails and stumps being set up on the lawn.

"Are there mountains in the part of Canada you're going to?" Grandpa asks. He's leaning against his desk, flipping pages of a fat book with a black cover. His pipe lies on the green blotter, smouldering.

Of Canada, Rudy knows only that it will be cold. He shrugs.

"Well," Grandpa continues, "if there *are* any mountains, I can assure you they won't match up to this peak I'm going to tell you about." His palm slaps the open book. "Here it is. Come, Rudy. Sit here in the chair. I'm going to read you what I wrote the day after that photograph was taken. It might be a very long time before you have the opportunity to climb Adam's Peak for yourself, so listen closely. This is part of your history."

While his sister and cousins begin their cricket match, Rudy slips behind the desk and boosts himself into the padded leather seat. Grandpa stands next to the window, his oiled hair catching the sunlight. He runs the heel of his hand down the centre of the book then coughs into his fist.

"Seventh of February, nineteen forty-four," he begins. "Yesterday took Ernie on the annual pilgrimage to the summit of Adam's Peak. Alec peeved, but still too young to withstand the ordeal, I feel."

Rudy giggles at the mention of his father's name. Grandpa looks up, makes a sound close to a chuckle, then carries on reading.

"Jayasuriya made it known in his way that he wanted to join us. The chap was certainly deserving of a brief holiday, so I consented. Left early in the day, to be at the base for midnight, the summit by sunrise. The usual mob of devotees made progress slow, but we reached the final ascent in good time. Expected complaints from Ernie, but the boy surprised me this year and proved up to the challenge. Up top he and Jayasuriya went off to look at the footprint, while I repaired to my customary spot to witness the appearance of what I maintain to be the most spectacular vista in this entire country, perhaps the entire world. And here I find myself inspired to quote the words of James Emerson Tennent, who climbed the peak in the last century, before the advent of decent roads and other amenities."

Rudy stifles a yawn while his grandfather reads on with even greater authority.

"He writes: 'The panorama from the summit of Adam's Peak is, perhaps, the grandest in the world, as no other mountain, although surpassing it in altitude, presents the same unobstructed view over land and sea. Around it, to the north and east, the traveller looks down on the zone of lofty hills that encircle the Kandyan kingdom, whilst to the westward the eye is carried far over undulating plains, till in the purple distance the glitter of the sunbeams on the sea marks the line of the Indian Ocean.'"

Grandpa pauses, presumably to let the reading sink in. It sounds like a foreign language, but Rudy nods seriously, if only to nudge himself closer to the cricket game on the lawn.

"Moments before the sun lifted off of the horizon," Grandpa continues, "I went to find Ernie. Wanted him to grasp that the true grandeur of Adam's Peak has nothing to do with the bloody footprint of Buddha or Shiva or whatever the hell that slab of rock up there is said to be. The greatness of the peak lies in our ability to conquer it, and in so doing to conquer our own weaknesses. The view that Tennent describes is the reward we earn for attaining that goal. This is what I wanted Ernie to understand, but didn't I find —" Grandpa stops reading and coughs into his fist. "Yes, well, you get the idea, son. To climb Adam's Peak is to fight your own demons."

He closes the book. Rudy imagines a mountain overrun by armies of men doing battle with fearsome demons. Leading this battalion of the Good is his grandfather, silver hair shining in the rising sun. His eyes wander back to the photograph on the wall.

"Do you ring the bell when you win the fight?" he asks.

"What's that?" Grandpa says, then he smiles vaguely. "Well I don't know if the average Sinhalese chap would put it that way, but yes, that's one way of looking at it."

"Mum is Sinhalese, isn't she, Grandpa?"

"Mmm? Oh, yes. Your mother is high-class Sinhalese. From Kandy. On her mother's side."

The old man places his book on the desk and rests his fingers on the cover several seconds before reaching for his pipe.

"Why is it called Adam's Peak?" Rudy says. "Who's Adam?"

Grandpa taps the bowl of his pipe into his cupped palm, deposits the powdery mound into the ashtray. "The Adam from the Bible, of course. The British named the peak after him."

And with those words, the conversation ends. Grandpa waves Rudy off the chair and into the hallway. Following, he shuts the study door with a clunk.

Back out on the lawn, the cricket game has dissolved into squabbles, but the adults are ignoring the ruckus. Dad has set his chair aside from the others and is gazing out at the hilly landscape that surrounds Grandpa's property. He summons Rudy with a sideways tilt of his head. Rudy pulls a face but goes to his father, dragging the tops of his feet across the warm grass. He deposits himself next to the chair, where he silently proceeds to scavenge dirt from between his toes.

After a dreary length of silence, Dad finally clears his throat. "You missed our big news earlier," he says.

"What news? About Canada?" Rudy says, risking the forbidden word. "I know everything about that already."

Dad smiles. "Well, it's going to happen *in* Canada."

Rudy surrenders his toes to the grass. "What is it?"

"You're going to have a new little brother or sister. At the beginning of August."

Rudy looks up at his father, amazed. Never before has anything he's wished for come to him as quickly as this. Thoughts racing, he imagines himself leading his little brother on expeditions through the Canadian snow, and his whole being sharpens: he is to be an Older Brother, a role no less important in his mind than that of Tea Maker or Plantation Manager.

"We'll be getting him in Canada?" he says.

Dad, elbows resting on the arms of his chair, fingertips pressed together, frowns. "The baby is growing inside your mother's stomach. The doctor will take it out in August. And don't forget, it might be a girl. Susie has her heart set on a little sister."

This, Rudy knows, will not happen.

"Can I choose his name?" he says.

Dad rises slowly from the chair and presses his palms to his lower back, like an old man.

"And what name would you choose, Rudyard Alexander Van Twest?"

"Adam."

A telling smile curls one corner of Dad's mouth. "Adam," he repeats. "The first man ... the first of our family to be born in the new country." He takes Rudy's head in his hands and tousles his hair. "That's not a bad idea, son. We'll see what your mother thinks of it."

Over by the murunga tree, Aunty Sheryl is gathering everyone together for one Last Family Photograph. Rudy ducks away from his father's grasp and bounds across the lawn, arms flapping, to join the others.

AUGUST 1971

I t's a stifling day. They've been running through the sprinkler on the
front lawn, Clare and Emma and two of Emma's brothers, and now
they're sitting on the wet grass in their bathing suits, watching waves of
hot air ripple over Morgan Hill Road. Clare's new one-piece is light
blue and has a skirt like a ballerina's. She and Emma are sharing a package of Kool-Aid — dipping their fingers in the orange powder and
licking it off. A special treat. Only nothing feels special. It's the kind of
day when everything goes in slow motion and nothing ever *happens*.

But then, miraculously, as if God or someone has taken pity on
them, something does happen.

From the direction of the Boulevard, the Vantwests' car comes
speeding, really speeding, down Morgan Hill Road and into the driveway across the street with a squeal that slices the stale air. Excited, in
an uncertain kind of way, Clare sucks her finger while Emma and her
brothers shout.

"Whoa! He should get a speeding ticket for sure!"

"Whaddya think's goin' on? D'ya think he's drunk?"

Mr. Vantwest, the driver of the car, gets out and runs to the house.

"Hey, he left the car door open! Someone could steal it!"

"Who's gonna steal it? That's so dumb."

"He left the front door open too!"

"Maybe there's a burglar in the house, or a murderer, and his wife called him for help."

"She wouldn't call *him*, you retard. She'd call the police."

Determined not to say anything that might give Emma's brother reason to call *her* a retard, Clare sits in silence, staring at the house across the street, while the Skinner children keep talking.

"Mom thinks it's weird that people like them have a name like Vantwest. She says it's a Dutch name."

"So? What's weird about that?"

"Dutch people are *white*, like us."

"So how did people like them get a white name?"

"Mom says they probably intramarried. Their kids go to the Catholic school."

Clare wonders if Mrs. Skinner has ever been inside the Vantwests' house. She sells Amway stuff, so it's possible. Sometimes she comes to Clare's house with samples, but her own mother always says "No, thank you," then talks about something else.

"Hey," Emma begins, "did you know, at the Catholic school they have to — Oh, look!" She points across the street, where Mr. Vantwest is scooting his son and daughter out the front door. When Mrs. Vantwest appears behind them, Emma squeals. "Whoa! Look at that! I bet she's gonna have her baby!"

It seems Emma may be right. The enormous Mrs. Vantwest is leaning against her slender husband, and the two of them are slowly making their way to the car. Clare dips her finger in the Kool-Aid and sucks distractedly. Emma has told her how babies get out, and even what makes them start growing in the first place, but Clare has never really believed any of it, never believed that *she* could have come to the world that way. For if such horrible and outrageous things were true, then surely her mother would have told her. Now, though, she isn't sure what to think. She wonders if terrible secrets have been kept from her ... or if, perhaps, her mother would be as astonished as she herself was to hear Emma's explanations. The second possibility seems most likely; still, as Mrs. Vantwest reaches the car door, clutching her belly and squatting awkwardly, Clare looks away.

Off to the right, the Vantwests' son is hauling two small suitcases across the lawn. She fixes her eyes on him. He's a strange-looking boy, like an undersized grown-up, stiff and serious, with his legs poking out from a pair of school uniform shorts like two halves of a yardstick. He goes to Catholic school, whatever that is. To distract herself from Mrs. Vantwest, Clare wonders about the suitcases — what's in them, where the boy is going. She pretends one of them is for her, and that she and the Vantwest boy are going to run away from Morgan Hill Road on an adventure, like the Famous Five. They'll sneak off while Emma and her brothers are watching Mrs. Vantwest, and they'll go to the train station and sneak on a train. She licks her orange fingers. Then the Vantwest boy looks across the street, right at her it seems, and a terrible awkwardness comes over her. She wipes her hand on the wet grass. The Vantwest boy smiles. It looks like he's smiling at her, but that's impossible. It has to be one of Emma's brothers, or Emma herself. Clare gets up and walks back to the sprinkler, shaking out the skirt of her new bathing suit. Standing under the fan of water, she blocks off streams by covering the holes with her big toe.

I

March 26/96. The thermometer says 32°, but I don't believe it. It must be 37 at least. They've taken my portable fan for an assembly in the auditorium, and I have to keep the ceiling fan on low or it scatters the kids' stuff. The windows are open but it makes no difference. Sigh. If I'd never moved away from here, would I be comfortable in this wretched heat? I know, I know. It got hot where you and I grew up, but this is different. There's no winter here. I think my body underwent some sort of mutation over all those Canadian winters. That makes sense, doesn't it? Or am I just a born wimp? Hmm. I can see you smiling, Clare. You know the truth. First-class whiner and complainer, that's me, no? But my life is here now. Or it will be. I'm not going back. Where I *should* go is to the staff room (it has air con), but I'm not in the mood to social-ize. Anyway, the break's just about over. English 12 next. More essays coming in today — sigh again. Thank God for Easter holidays.

RUDY CLOSED HIS DIARY and glanced up at the clock. Wistfully he tried to imagine being *cold*, to conjure up the sensations of stinging cheeks and frozen nostril hairs, but a trickle of sweat meandering from his temple to his ear distracted him. Something *had* happened to him in his twenty-five-year absence. The heat in which he used to play cricket and hunt for snakes now tortured him. On particularly oppressive days, his hands and feet swelled up and he moved like an old man through the viscous air. The weight he'd put on from his aunt's cooking slowed him down all the more. And he sweated — unstoppable streams that pooled in any crease or depression, dripped from the hooked tip of his narrow nose, salted his lips and stung his eyes. As students began wandering in, he recalled the day he'd confiscated a crumpled drawing depicting a naked Mr. Vantwest (the maple leaf covering the nether regions gave it away) spraying sweat over the school flower beds. Embarrassed, but also amused — it was a damn good cartoon — he'd slipped the paper into his pocket and carried on with the lesson while wide-eyed glances darted back and forth across the room.

Today, however, he was quite certain his students wouldn't be taking any notice of him. The object of their attention would still be the new student, Kandasamy Selvarajah, now strolling toward the front desk of the middle row, explaining the correct use of the semicolon to a group of girls. Kanda wasn't an ordinary student. He was larger somehow, more *present*. He'd read more English literature than most of Rudy's colleagues and had no reservations about quoting Shakespeare or Milton to his bewildered classmates. He was the kind of pupil Rudy had fantasized about having back in Canada. But the reality was all wrong. The boy's presence in class — his confidence, his command of the lessons — had become irritating. Each time he raised his hand, Rudy felt his own hands clench. He expected to be challenged, to be revealed as a fool or an impostor. And yet, there was nothing concrete for him to complain about, even to himself.

The bell rang. Shirt sticking, drips of sweat trickling from his temples, Rudy took his place before the five rows of uniformed boys and girls, looked past Kanda, and said, "Good morning." As the buzz of conversation quieted, he mopped his face with his handkerchief. "We're going to start off with some of those exercises on identifying point of view," he began. "I think we got up to page sixty-five last time."

Textbooks were opened, pages flipped. When it seemed to Rudy that most of them were ready, he began reading the page sixty-five excerpt from *Robinson Crusoe*, his voice strangely crisp in the languid air. His students listened politely, not taking in a word of it, he was sure. With the exception of Kanda. By the end of the passage, not five minutes into the class, the boy's hand was up. Wiping his forehead, Rudy braced himself wearily against the possibilities — a comment on Defoe's racism, perhaps (though the selected excerpt was innocent enough), a question about the meaning of *distemper* ... or maybe that challenge he would be unable to answer. He lowered his eyes and met Kanda's stare.

"Yes?"

The boy hesitated a moment, then cleared his throat. "Are you feeling ill, sir?"

Around the room heads turned and eyes widened. Rudy coughed involuntarily. "What do you mean?"

"I was only wondering, sir, as you seem to be perspiring very heavily. I thought you might be ill."

If it was a joke, or an insult, the kid certainly had balls. Rudy mopped his face and studied his student. Kanda himself was tidy to a fault — navy tie knotted snugly around his white collar, black hair trimmed and gelled, spine straight, skin dry. *I'm not the impostor here*, his appearance insisted. Yet his expression was sympathetic. Not a hint of ridicule or sarcasm.

"I'm not sick, Kanda. I just don't handle the heat very well. Anymore. But thank you for your concern." He glanced at James Fernando, the caricaturist, and snickered in spite of himself. "You see, when I first came here, I applied for a job as a garden sprinkler," he said, folding his handkerchief into a neat square. "But I wasn't quite sweaty enough, so they made me a teacher instead."

While James shrank behind his desk, the others laughed. Rudy risked a wink. Then Kanda raised his hand again.

"I have an idea, sir. If we put the desks in a semicircle and you stood under the fan, you might be more comfortable."

Around the room there were murmurs of approval. Rudy dragged the folded handkerchief along his jaw. Finding no good reason not to take Kanda's suggestion, he nodded, and the boy stood up. It seemed that he intended to organize the desk-moving himself, and indeed he got right to it, directing his classmates, even reminding them not to scrape the furniture across the floor. "Lift it up, or it leaves marks," he said, his manner neither condescending nor bossy. When the brief chaos had subsided and the students were again seated, their desks forming a horseshoe that opened toward the front of the room, Rudy took his place under the ceiling fan. Chamika Heenatigala, seated closest to the regulator dial, got up and adjusted the speed to full. In the rush of cool air, Rudy's shirt pulled away from his skin, and his pores tightened in tiny, euphoric contractions. He pocketed his handkerchief, cleared his throat, and returned to the lesson with an awkward smile in Kanda's direction.

At the end of class, he called for the essays he'd assigned. There was a brief stampede at his desk, and when this had subsided, Kanda came up, paper in hand. "I hope this is acceptable, sir."

Rudy straightened the stack of essays on the desk. "I'm sure it'll be fine. Would you like me to consider it a practice run? I mean, I'll mark it, but we don't have to count it. You weren't here when I explained the assignment."

"I'd like you to count it, please."

Rudy nodded and took the essay. It occurred to him suddenly that he should thank his student for the new seating arrangement. In his head he fumbled with the words, but the longer he hesitated, the more lodged in his throat the message became, until it seemed that to cough it out would sound ridiculous. Just as Kanda was about to disappear out the classroom door, he called to him to enjoy his holiday, but the boy didn't seem to hear.

Rudy stared blankly at the door, then he lowered his eyes to the essay in his hand. The title, "A Defence of the Liberation Tigers of Tamil Eelam and Their Fight for a Tamil Homeland," made him frown. He'd asked his students to write argument essays, and predictably most of their chosen topics were banal. Kanda's topic challenged even more than his classroom manner did. At the same time,

Rudy felt his ambiguous antipathy toward the boy taking root in the unequivocal words. He checked the clock then added the paper to the pile.

∞

THE BUS HOME WAS CROWDED AND HOT. Arms and legs, shopping bundles and briefcases nibbled at the boundaries of the tiny space Rudy managed to secure on a padded vinyl seat behind the rear doorway. He eyed a bent woman hoisting herself through the door, clutching the skirt of her sari, and held his breath until another man offered his seat. Then he shut out the faces around him, leaned his head against the metal window frame, and began his hunt for the saints.

They were all along his route through the teeming city, painted plaster statues gazing at the hubbub from behind glass casings: brown-robed Anthonys, arrow-impaled Sebastians, anorexic Marys. Like the faith that had brought them to the island centuries before, these statues had acquired a local character as unremarkable as that of the fruit vendor tidying his mound of yellow coconuts on the sidewalk. Two saints shared a corner with a cross-legged Buddha; the Virgin herself greeted customers on their way to Ganesh Bookshop. One of the Anthonys, without the protection of a glass case, served as a perch for birds and was splattered with droppings. As a private game, a sort of meditation, Rudy counted them. His most recent tally had boosted the total from fourteen saints to seventeen. He was sure there were more, eluding him in obscure nooks and alcoves, but on this particular ride he lost track at the bookshop. Eyes fixed on the blue Virgin stationed a few metres from the shop's door, he thought of Clare Fraser, his sanctuary. He saw her solemn face watching over him, and he drifted. Unlike other visitants from his Morgan Hill past, she came to him unencumbered, provoking neither remorse nor irritation, though sometimes there was a vague pang of longing, like the echo of a desire he'd ceased to experience first-hand. He didn't mind forsaking his saint-hunt to be with her — her presence had the same calming effect — but when the bus jerked to an unexpected halt, he lost her as well.

It was a military checkpoint, or police. Rudy was never sure which was which. The men, dressed in khakis and carrying guns, represented a danger he couldn't quite manage to fear. Not from courage, certainly, or even indifference. Rather, it seemed to him that his years on Morgan Hill Road had left him with a thick, invisible shell that kept him separate, both from the danger and the fear. Mechanically he shouldered his knapsack and stepped out to the side of the road with everyone else. There was no shelter from the sun, but the ID check was carried out with reasonable efficiency, and the passengers soon filed back into the bus to reclaim their spots. Rudy searched his bag for Kanda's essay. If he couldn't fear the country's troubles as he should, he would at least acknowledge them in the abstract. He mopped his face and began to read.

> I have been studying in English medium schools because my parents believe that knowing English is the only way to have a good profession. I would prefer to study and work in my own language, but unfortunately, my language and my culture have a second-rate status in Sri Lanka. My people have been treated unfairly and abused. Therefore my thesis is that Tamil people must fight a war for their own Tamil homeland where they can make their own decisions.

The words were eerily familiar, challenging, but he read on.

> The Sri Lankan government has discriminated against Tamil people since the early days of independence. Tamils were denied the rights of citizenship; their language was denied an official status and their religions take second place to the favoured Buddhism. Early as 1957 Tamil people are suffering and dying at the hands of Sinhalese extremists. In 1983 in an unjustified reaction against a minor LTTE ambush, thousands of Tamil people had their homes, their businesses, and even their lives, destroyed.
>
> Today the government says that their soldiers are liberators of the Tamil people, but the people don't think of the

army as their liberators. Mr. Prabhakaran and the LTTE are the liberators. The army arrests and kills innocent people out in the countryside where their government can't watch over them. My uncle who is living in Trincomalee knows a girl who was attacked by army soldiers. She was walking early in the morning to see her brother to give him money from their father for his journey to Colombo. The girl was fourteen years old and she started to be a woman that month only. She passed a vegetated area and two soldiers pulled her off the road and put a cloth in her mouth so she would not scream. The soldiers did not take the money but they violated the girl. Now my uncle says this girl has no hope for the future. I have a sister who also is fourteen, I would do anything to protect her.

For a moment Rudy stopped reading and looked out the window — a flimsy show of respect for the unnamed girl, who, like the dangers of her country, remained stubbornly foreign to him. He thought uneasily of his own sister — how far would he go to protect *her?* — then he read the rest of Kanda's argument: his reasonable claims about the plight of Tamil refugees and the need for cultural and linguistic equality, his more dubious ones about the intentions of the LTTE and their leader, his predictions that the government's recent military offensive in Jaffna would fall on its face. There was plenty in the boy's essay that made sense, but when Rudy reached the end he sank into a silent, brooding rebuttal: *Do you really think the kind of violence the Tigers use can be justified, Kanda? Is the idea of a homogenous Tamil homeland even realistic? Would you want to live in such a place?* And so on. When he next looked out the bus window, the essay was rolled up tightly in his hand, and he'd missed his stop.

He got off at the junction of the rail line and Vaththe Mawatha — Garden Street, as some of the old Burgher residents persisted in calling it. There was still a winding half-kilometre to backtrack, but he went first to the shady front doorway of his aunt's church, across from the train station, to mop his face and breathe in the cool emptiness of the massive white sanctuary. In a few days the place would be chock full for Easter Mass, but for now it was starkly, marvellously vacant.

He considered resting awhile under one of the whirling ceiling fans, clearing his head of Kanda and everything else, but he was already late. He pulled off his tie, undid several buttons, and crossed the street.

Passing the station, he quickened his pace to get away from the mob of taxi drivers hovering around their Bajaj three-wheelers, but one fat-bellied driver stepped into his path immediately.

"Sixty rupees only, sir."

Rudy deked to the right. "No, thanks. I'll walk."

The driver kept pace with him. "Okay, okay. Fifty rupees. Good price."

"No."

"Okay, how much you want to pay?"

"Normal price."

"Fifty rupees is very good price for you, sir, but I'll give you forty-five. Last price."

Rudy stopped and sighed. "Look — I'm not a tourist. Give me the same price you'd give my aunt and I'll go with you. Otherwise forget it."

The driver held his stare a moment longer then shrugged and ambled back to his three-wheeler, refastening his plaid sarong in a neat fold and tuck. Rudy waved away a few more offers and finally slowed to a stroll. He was glad the taxi ride hadn't tempted him. There were other people out in the road — people who paid him no particular attention as they went about their business — and in that random, fleeting community, amid the tangled yards and airy bungalows of Vaththe Mawatha, he could believe that he really wasn't a tourist — that this uncomplicated world, the one he'd shared with his parents and Susie for six years, was still his.

Up the road, he stopped to buy a comb of bananas from the fruit stand. Apart from his own "Ayubowan," the transaction was conducted in silence, for the old fruit vendor spoke no English, and Rudy's Sinhala was still awful. He nodded his thanks and carried on to the top of Aunty Mary's lane, where he lifted a few flyers and envelopes from the mailbox then swung open the wooden gate. As he made his way down the narrow, overgrown path that led to his aunt's bungalow, he experienced a familiar flash of empathy for those outsiders who ardently insisted that his birthplace was so *exotic*. The short walk took him past feathery ferns, wide, waxy leaves, and whiffs of jasmine that made his head spin. Overhead, the pawpaw and mango trees were loaded, while underfoot, sticky brown fruit oozed from fallen tamarind pods. It *was* exotic, he had to admit, though he preferred to believe that his own attraction came from a sense that this tangle of tropical growth was part of him.

Outside the yellow bungalow he peered through the latticed cement wall into the sitting room, where the exoticism of the lane lost its integrity. The rattan and teak settee had cotton throw pillows from Ikea; the painted Sinhalese devil mask with bulging eyes and a hanging tongue looked down on plastic figurines of Jesus and Mary; the old gramophone sat next to the television from Singapore. The floor was polished red cement; the white walls were decorated with school photos and souvenir tea towels.

Faintly Rudy heard his aunt in the kitchen. He let himself in and sorted through the mail. There were two advertisements, a telephone bill, something from the bank, and a single letter, from his brother. He turned it over, looking for Aunty's name. Adam's letters were always to the two of them. "To Aunty Mary and Rudy," the envelopes always said, and inside would be short, chatty updates on his job at the campus bookstore, his swimming, his motorcycle, family goings-on, and other things of that sort. But this letter was addressed simply to "Rudy Vantwest." Frowning, Rudy folded the envelope in half and stuffed it in his trouser pocket.

In the kitchen, Aunty Mary was dusting Easter cookies with sugar. A kitten with matted orange fur had stationed itself at her feet, while a mob of tiny flies hovered over a jack fruit on the counter. Rudy deposited the bananas next to the jack fruit and kissed his aunt's cheek. She smoothed her cotton dress and patted the thick twist of silver-black hair at the back of her head.

"You're home late, son."

"Yeah. The bus was slow." He reached above her head for a glass.

"Want tea?"

"No, thanks. Water is fine."

"Ah, yes. My doctor is telling me I should drink more water. Very good for the health, isn't it. You'd like chicken for dinner?"

"Sure."

"I'll just finish this. It shouldn't be long."

"No hurry," he said distractedly. "I'll get started on my marking."

He filled his glass from a pitcher in the fridge, drained it, then went out back to wash at the well. Bathing at the stone well in the pink-gold light of late afternoon was one of those entitlements, like eating rice with his fingers or shitting in the outdoor toilet under a leafy canopy, that Rudy indulged in simply because it was not — could never be — part of his Canadian life. With renewed determination to distance himself from that life, he drew a pail of cool water dotted with dead leaves, emptied it into the plastic washtub, and rolled up his sleeves. A pair of mosquitoes — enormous brutes with long, dangling legs and abdomens — danced threateningly over the tub. He clapped them both dead, pried a bar of soap from the rim of the well, and scrubbed his hands and face. Completing the ritual, he emptied the tub over the dirt and shook his hands.

Adam's letter weighed heavily in his pocket as he returned to the sitting room and installed himself at his grandfather's desk. His knapsack was on the floor, Kanda's essay inside. It was a queer twist of fate, being confronted with both on the same day — though the coincidence didn't particularly surprise him. He reached down and unzipped his bag. He would start with the essay; the letter could wait.

Skimming Kanda's introduction, he put a check mark next to the thesis statement. (The boy had a thesis; two-thirds of the class wouldn't.) He made a few more check marks throughout the paper, circled some errors, then, turning to the back page, considered what comments to make. A further response had entered his mind, joining those he'd come up with earlier: *What if your sister got in the way of a Tiger attack, Kanda? What then?* But he couldn't write that — or anything else he'd come up with, for that matter.

He leaned back, and his gaze drifted up to the framed oil painting hanging above the desk. The painting, an awkward, immature work, apparently done by Uncle Ernie, had been in Aunty's house for as long as Rudy could remember. Its subject was Adam's Peak, the mountain his brother was named after, rendered as a dappled green oblong under a yellow sun. Despite the clumsiness of the brush strokes, the light on the peak showed a certain sensitivity to nature, while the surrounding hills cast convincing shadows on the landscape. At the summit of the oblong was a red pavilion. The lopsided building was too large for the scale of the painting, and it seemed to Rudy that the picture would be more effective without it.

As he sat pondering this, Aunty Mary emerged from the kitchen with a cup of tea.

"I thought you might like this since you are working."

He turned and sighed. His aunt's attentions embarrassed him — the cooking, the laundry, the cups of tea. He planned to move out, of course. Buy a house closer to the city, ship his belongings from Canada. But for now, for Aunty Mary, he was still a child. He took the cup and thanked her.

"How are your pupils doing?" she said.

"Oh, most of them are fine." He paused. "I just finished reading the new kid's essay. Seems he supports the Tigers."

"Aiyo." Aunty shook her head. "These Tigers only care about making trouble. You must explain to him."

Rudy looked down at the half-page on which his comments would be written. "There's nothing I can explain to him that he doesn't already know, Aunty. He believes that violence is the only option left for his cause."

Aunty frowned. "And why is a young man so worried about a cause like this? He has more important things to think about, no?"

Feeling oddly compelled to defend his student, Rudy shrugged and sipped his tea. "Kanda identifies himself mainly as a Tamil. He thinks his language and culture will be best served in an independent country."

"He is full of strange ideas then," Aunty said. "What's most important is our family, no? We should worry about those people, whether they are healthy and living a good life. Language and culture will look after themselves, isn't it."

Rudy opened his mouth then shrugged again. "You may be right."

"Do you think this Kanda is involved with the Tigers?"

"I doubt it. But who knows? The Tigers employ kids a hell of a lot younger than him."

"Ah, yes." Aunty shook her head. "They give machine guns to children. It's a sin."

Rudy gulped down most of his tea and stared at the back page of Kanda's essay. In the brief silence, the ticking of Grandpa's old clock and the thrum of the electric fan were strangely loud.

Then Aunty sighed. "I think our government is putting itself out on the murunga branch."

Rudy looked up, surprised. His aunt never discussed politics. "What do you mean?"

"Ah, it's an old expression. When someone is feeling very proud of himself, we say he is sitting on the murunga branch." She pulled a handkerchief from the pocket of her dress and shook it out. "As you know, the murunga is a very tall tree. It also has very brittle branches. You can climb high up in this tree, but then the branch breaks . . ." Her voice trailed off.

"And how does that relate to the government?"

Aunty wiped her forehead and cheekbones. "The government is feeling very proud these days. They believe that capturing Jaffna will put an end to all this fighting. But I think these Tigers will make sure the army's murunga branch comes crashing back to the ground."

"You and Kanda agree on that much," he said with a wry smile. "And Dad. What does he say? 'The Tamil man and the Sinhalese man will never get along. It's not in their nature.' Or some rubbish like that?"

His aunt stuffed the handkerchief back in her pocket. "Ah, no. You're right. We must be positive, isn't it. It's Easter." And on that, she turned and went back to the kitchen.

Rudy picked up his pen and composed his comments.

Kanda: Your essay is quite well organized and the prose is clear and engaging. There are some problems with grammar and punctuation, as marked, but they don't seriously detract from the success of your paper. The essay has a strong, attention-grabbing thesis, and you offer plenty of good evidence in support of it. The major way in which the paper could be improved would be to give some consideration to the best arguments in support of the other side. The most convincing arguments are often those that show they understand their opponents' position and can reasonably refute it. You have the potential to be an excellent writer. Keep up the good work.

It was a long way off what he wanted to write, but it would have to do. At the bottom of the page he wrote "B+" then reached for the rest of the essays in his knapsack. As he shifted position, Adam's letter crinkled in his pocket. He decided to save it till Aunty Mary had gone to bed.

∞

LATE THAT EVENING, after chicken dinner and more marking, Rudy slouched at the desk, tapping his pen against the cover of his diary. Mosquitoes hovered around him, but he was too tired to bother lighting a coil. Too tired to write, really, but it was something of a ritual, his nightly communication with Clare Fraser — begun on a cold Christmas day back home and carried out ever since. He told her about his afternoon, about reading Kanda's essay and missing his bus stop, then he left his diary in his bedroom and went to the shower shed in the backyard. The green plastic enclosure was dimly lit by a pair of bulbs fixed to the back wall of the house. Overhead the black sky was pierced with stars. Rudy hung his sarong over the door and turned on the water. It fell from the broad metal shower head, straight and heavy and warm, like a monsoon downpour. He backed into it, watching a rupee-sized spider scurry across the concrete floor, reached for the soap, and lathered his hands. Eyes closed, he masturbated with dull frustration, a desire for release of some kind. He thought of his ex-girlfriend Renée's muscular thighs and prodigious breasts, of the girl in Kanda's essay, walking by herself early in the morning, of Clare. He came easily. Relieved, if only temporarily, he rinsed off then stood still under the spray in the shower's green light. At the faint sound of the dining room clock striking eleven, he turned off the water and hurried to dry himself before the mosquitoes moved in.

In the bedroom he put on a T-shirt, an ancient souvenir from the Toronto Jazz Festival, with gaudy splashes of turquoise and pink. His sarong was covered in red and gold elephants.

"A real fashion plate you've become, machan," he heckled his reflection in the wardrobe mirror. Turning sideways, he sucked in his belly and straightened his shoulders, ran his fingers through his damp hair and cursed at the amount that came out. He considered doing some sit-ups while the air was cool, then he remembered Adam's letter.

He imagined what it would say.

I think we need to talk about our relationship, Rudy. I've tried to connect with you, but it hasn't really worked, has it. What have you got against me? I don't think I've deserved your coldness . . .

The more Rudy imagined, the more real the words became, until he felt he knew the contents of his brother's letter precisely. A vague memory came to him. He was twelve or so; Adam was still little. They'd built something together in the backyard. It was a rock sculpture of some kind, but it all fell apart. What he remembered most clearly was picking up one of the rocks and throwing it as hard as he could. But he couldn't recall what his target had been.

"Jesus Christ," he whispered.

Leaving the letter in his trouser pocket, he unknotted the mosquito net hanging over the bed. He made his way around the mattress, tucking the net underneath, leaving a small gap through which he finally crawled. Safe inside, he reached his hand out to switch off the bedside lamp then tucked in the rest of the net.

2

THROUGH A GAUZE OF CLOUDS Clare glimpsed the grey-white land-scape, cut through with ruler-straight roads and patched with rectangu-lar roofs. She leaned back in her seat and closed her eyes. On the head-phones Gilles Vigneault was singing "Mon Pays," but her mind wasn't on the music.

We can't ever really know anyone else, can we, she began.

Depends what you mean by know.

What life is really like for them, what they really think. It's impossible. We're all locked inside ourselves.

You mean you are, Clare.

Maybe. But I think it goes for everyone. We can imagine somebody else's life, but we'll never know for sure if we're right.

Yeah, well as far as that goes, who's to say we know ourselves any better? Who the hell is Clare Fraser?

Sometimes I think I know. When I'm back here, it's obvious. The question seems pointless.

The plane dipped gently, and the seatbelt sign chimed.

What made you think of this anyway?

I was thinking about my parents. What they were like when they were younger . . .

Their sex life you mean.

Emma. It's not that. It's nothing to do with that.

Oh, come on. You're dying to know if —

No, never mind. We're about to land.

∞

THE PEOPLE SURROUNDING CLARE and her mother in the arrivals hall had waiting faces — necks craning, eyes searching. The greeters hovered in heavy coats and clumpy boots, dripping dirty puddles of melted snow on the linoleum floor. The passengers streamed endlessly through the sliding security doors and around the luggage carousel, underdressed, burdened with parcels, a little dazed. Like camera flashes, faces lit up as searched-for parties or pieces of luggage were spotted, and gradually a uniform wave of satisfaction swept through the crowd. Beyond their superficial uniformity, however, the people in the crowd were, as always, unreadable, their circumstances unknowable. Even the most banal of exchanges with any one of them would involve infinite risks: a smile could be tactless; a comment about the weather could trigger terrible memories. How could one tell? Sensibly averting her eyes from these strangers' faces, Clare watched the assembly-line progress of suitcases rumbling from the chute and sliding into place on the carousel. In her head, the conversation with Emma competed with the hurried, desperate voice of Gilles Vigneault.

Go on, ask her.

I'll ask her in the car.

You're such a chicken.

Dans la blanche cérémonie, où la neige au vent se marie; Dans ce pays de poudrerie, mon père a fait bâtir maison.

I just got here.

You've only been gone three weeks. And it's just your mother. What are you worried about?

I'm not worried. But it is my mother. We don't talk about that stuff.

Et je m'en vais être fidèle, à sa manière, à son modèle.

Don't talk about it then. Just get a yes or a no.

I'll ask her, Emma. When the time's right.

You promise?

Mon pays ce n'est pas un pays, c'est l'hiver ...

She reached in front of her mother for her suitcase and hauled it awkwardly onto the luggage trolley. As they made their way out through the mob, she kept her eyes down. The conversation in her head drivelled on, a secret necessity, until they exited into the vast, frozen airport parking lot, where at last she relaxed her grip on the trolley and allowed herself to look around. Like her fellow passengers, she was underdressed — jeans, T-shirt, running shoes, rain jacket — but at home.

"It's a pity Easter's so early this year," her mother said. "It hardly seems the season for it."

"Mmm. You're right."

"Did you have a good flight, pet?"

"It was fine."

"Was the food all right?"

"Not too bad."

"Was there a movie?"

"Yeah. I didn't watch it."

She'd fallen asleep listening to *Traditions Québecoises* on the headphones. Leaning against the window she'd dreamed of a solitary man on a snowy plain. It could have been Gilles Vigneault — the man in the dream was singing — but he was wearing her father's overcoat. His grey hair blew wildly in a whistling gale that threatened to drown his voice completely. In her dream, Clare struggled to hear him but caught only meaningless fragments.

She paused to zip her jacket, and her mother took over the trolley and hurried on, the hemline of her skirt swaying in perfect alignment with that of her black wool coat, her coppery bob dancing over the collar. Clare followed. Shutting out Isobel Fraser's chit-chat, shutting out Emma, she searched the frigid air for her father. She'd been back home almost an hour; it was about time they spoke.

It must be a wee bit warmer in Vancouver these days, he said, predictably.

His voice was perfectly intact. He'd been gone so long (heart attack in the driveway, on his way to play golf) that many of the particulars of his existence could be difficult to retrieve. But the voice of

Alastair Fraser, no less real than it had been in life, lingered, indefinitely it seemed, in Clare's head.

You say that every time I go out there, Dad. Vancouver's warm and rainy, just like Scotland. You'd hate it.

Aye, I suppose I would. He spoke in the scant, reluctant way he'd always spoken, never uttering more than a sentence or two, a measured observation, a pellet of sensible advice. But only at home. *You'll be moving out there then, I suppose,* he said next, and Clare clenched her hands in her pockets.

I don't know. Maybe.

She'd been thinking about it. "It's time, Clare," the real Emma had insisted, just the night before. "You're stuck in a rut and it's not doing you or your mother any good. Listen to me: I've known you forever. It's fine to be close to your family, but there's a limit. You're thirty-one, for God's sake. I'll help you find work. I've got heaps of connections at the college." It all made sense. And Vancouver was a nice enough place — slower than Montreal, which suited Clare fine. Each time she visited, the idea of moving there gained appeal, until now, she realized, it was pressing inside her with just enough urgency that she could, perhaps, act on it.

She caught up to her mother at the trunk of the Oldsmobile.

"I think this old thing has had its last winter," Isobel said. "Time for something new."

Clare lifted her suitcase into the trunk. She'd never cared for the Oldsmobile, but as she climbed into the passenger seat, she felt a pang of regret that her father's sturdy blue car would be replaced.

Her mother started the engine and pumped the gas pedal. She set the heat on high and the CBC on low. Then she extracted a pack of Virginia Slims and a plastic lighter from her purse, pinched a long cigarette between her copper lips, and closed her eyes as she lit up. Clare frowned and cracked her window.

"When did you start smoking again, Ma?"

Isobel examined the cigarette between her fingers as if baffled by how it had come to be there. "Oh. I hardly ever. I decided to treat myself on my fiftieth, and I guess my body just remembered how much it enjoys them." She slid open the ashtray and squashed the cigarette into a mess of lipsticked butts, then she wrestled the gearshift into reverse.

The word *body*, coming from Isobel, sounded foreign and off-key.

Clare rubbed the car window with her fist, but in the waning afternoon light and the dirty snow of late winter, the world outside was hardly worth looking at. She stared at the dashboard. Inside her pockets, her hands clenched and her thumbs fretted her index fingers. The question, Emma's question, made her absurdly tense. It was pathetic. Her mother wouldn't care, and the answer would hardly change anything. There'd be the jolt of having her suspicion confirmed, of looking at a portrait she'd professed to know intimately and discovering in the corner something new and out of place. But aside from those small shocks, there'd be nothing remarkable. The answer to her question would be just another oblique reminder of something she already knew: in the social world, Clare Fraser was a failure. A bore. A mute, staring spinster from a different century.

Oh, for God's sake, the Emma in her head blurted. *Don't be so negative. I'm just being realistic.*

She removed her headband and shook her hair down in front of her face. Emma had suggested she colour it. Highlight the blond, or darken it all. It might look good, she had to admit, though surely people would see through the disguise. Her mother had been colouring for years, but the red had once been natural. Clare had her father's hair, his blue-grey eyes.

"So you had a good holiday?" Isobel said.

"Uh-huh."

"And how's our little Emma?"

Clare slid the headband back across her head. "Not so little. But she's fine. She's teaching voice this term."

"Oh, lovely. Does she ever miss Montreal? How long has she been in Vancouver now?"

"I don't think so. Almost six years."

"That long! Are you sure?"

"She left right after I moved back with you."

Isobel changed lanes without signalling. "Gordon Bennett! Does that mean it's been almost six years since your father ..."

"I guess so."

"Good lord."

Ask her now, Emma's voice urged. *While she's on the topic.*

She's remembering Dad's heart attack. It wouldn't be fair.

Fair-shmair. Your mother has dealt with his death just fine. You're the one who still has issues.

"And are the flowers out yet in Vancouver?" Isobel said, switching on the headlights.

"Uh-huh."

Clare closed her eyes and leaned back against the headrest. She could be lazy with her mother. Conversation for Isobel was a gliding over smooth surfaces, an avoidance of bumps and cracks. Her questions never challenged; they led directly into short, easy paths of response. Emma's questions, on the other hand, opened onto vast and frightening terrain. Politics, ethics, relationships, sex. Apart from the ones about sex, she didn't mind Emma's questions. Talking to Emma wasn't like talking to other people. It was the closest she came to the conversations in her own head. But on this last visit, Emma had been pushy on the sex thing. In her view, sex was a character-defining experience, a crucial element of one's humanity, and, having made this argument, she'd forced a blind date with the recently divorced director of the jazz studies program at her college. Not, she pointed out, that it would necessarily lead to anything at all. Just to get Clare in the swing of things.

They'd gone for coffee on the east side of town. The Jazz Studies Director had carried their cappuccinos to a table in the middle of the café, and as he sat down he smiled and said, "Emma tells me you're quite the pianist."

"Not as good as Emma," Clare had answered, her hands clenching under the table. A terrible answer — and not even true.

The Jazz Studies Director then raised his eyebrows. "So what was it that drew you to music?"

If he'd been a voice in her head, if he'd been Emma, she could have answered him, easily. But everything about him — his skin, his clothes, his raised eyebrows — was so real and physical, so *other,* that the space between them seemed gaping and uncrossable. He was terrifying in the way that all strangers, with their unpredictable words and boldness of existence, were terrifying.

"I'm not sure," she'd said, and sipped her coffee. "It just happened, I guess."

The date had ended with a handshake.

Emma had stifled her disappointment admirably. She suggested that Clare's social difficulties were a result of being born prematurely. "I'm serious," she said. "You came into the world before you were really ready, and now everything still overwhelms you." To Clare, this explanation missed the obvious. But then Emma hadn't known her father very well.

Her mother exited the highway onto St. Giles Boulevard. They passed the Provigo, the Chinese restaurant with the revolving red dragon, the shopping mall, and Emma's family's church, a building that looked more like a recreation centre than a place of worship. Just before Morgan Hill Road, Isobel swatted the turn signal, and Clare sensed the pattern of her life closing around her, tucking her inside of itself. It wasn't a terrible feeling; her life suited her in many ways. But if pressed, she'd have confessed that this particular life wasn't exactly what she'd imagined for herself.

The lights in the Fraser house, timer-controlled, were on, warm and welcoming. While Isobel put the car in the garage, Clare wandered to the end of the driveway to collect the empty garbage can. Across the street she saw shadows behind the Vantwests' living room curtains and recalled Emma's latest musings about Rudy.

"He always looked so exotic, don't you think?" Emma had said, wide-eyed. "He sort of intimidated me when we were teenagers, but I'd love to meet him now. Do you ever see him? Don't you think it would be amazing to have sex with someone like him?"

"What do you mean 'like him'?" Clare had said. But her friend just smiled knowingly.

Remember the day his brother was born? the Emma in her head now coaxed, as Clare, eyes still on the Vantwests' house, picked up the garbage bin.

Not as well as you.

It's kind of creepy to think about, but, God, that afternoon was the highlight of the whole summer.

I hardly remember anything. Just the car.

And one other image: Rudy Vantwest standing with two suitcases at the edge of his lawn, looking across the street at her. She might have imagined the suitcases; most of her childhood fantasies had involved packing up and running away on an adventure. But she remembered the scrawny legs and the squinting smile clearly — one of those use-less memories that hangs on for no apparent reason, even when more important things have drifted out of reach. She hadn't seen Rudy in years, she'd told Emma. He'd moved away; she didn't know where. And in any case, she'd felt like adding, if he *were* to appear on Morgan Hill Road one day, what would she possibly say to him?

She made her way back up the driveway, knees thudding against the plastic bin, which she left at the side of the house. Her mother was waiting at the front door with the suitcase. Reaching for it, Clare glanced back across the street.

"How well did you know Mrs. Vantwest?" she said.

Isobel's eyes followed. "Oh, not very well at all. She wasn't even here a full year, poor woman. Why do you ask, pet?"

"No reason. I was just thinking about the day Adam was born."

"Good lord, he must be finished high school by now."

"He's doing his M.A. at Concordia."

She blurted the information awkwardly, as if she'd had no right to be in possession of it. Adam had told her about his studies one morning on the train platform, after spotting her and coming over. Catching her off guard. A minute or so into the conversation, she'd lied about needing to pick up some bus tickets then hid around the station wall until the train came.

"Master's degree! I had no idea he was that sort," Isobel said. She unlocked the front door and swung it open. "Well, it's nice to know he's managed so well in spite of everything."

Inside the vestibule, the pattern of Clare's existence closed in tighter, more familiar, a little more oppressive. She sat on the clothing bench, a small, hinged church pew her father had salvaged, and as she yanked off her shoes, the Vantwests and their troubles disappeared under the weight of Alastair Fraser's presence. Inside the house, that presence was impossible to escape. Most of the furnishings came from

the store Alastair had managed for twenty-odd years, and he was in
those objects still, held there by an inertia that even death had been
unable to challenge completely. In vain Clare kept her eyes on the
vestibule floor, willing something to have changed in her absence. But
when at last she peered into the living room, it was the old pattern,
perfectly intact, that greeted her: blue floral print chesterfield, arms
jacketed in plastic sleeves; polished oak coffee table, never touched by
coffee cups; record player cabinet, weighted shut by a lead crystal
bowl, gigantic and empty; grey recliner; dormant fireplace. And under
it all, an unchanging sea of Wedgwood blue carpeting, the best
Alastair Fraser's store had to offer, stretching from wall to wall.

She lobbed her shoes across the vestibule, onto the rubber mat
where her mother's boots were already neatly stowed. Isobel was off
checking the answering machine. When she returned, she placed her
hand lightly on Clare's shoulder.

"I meant to tell you, pet. I'm planning on doing some redecorat-
ing in there."

Clare's eyes shot up. It was like that long-ago summer day — Mr.
Vantwest's car roaring down Morgan Hill Road.

"You're changing the living room?"

"Aye. I'm tired of the colour scheme. The carpet's awful. It's going
next week. And the furniture's really dated. There's a lovely yellow set
in the Ikea catalogue I'd like to have a look at tomorrow. You're welcome to come along, if you like."

"Oh. That's okay," Clare said distractedly. "Whatever you choose
is fine."

Once more she took in the living room, imagining naked floors
and sofas the colour of bananas. Then she picked up her suitcase and
started up the stairs with a vague, vexing sense that these renovations,
like the goings-on of the family across the street, weren't likely to make
much difference in the long run.

"There was a message from Emma," her mother called after her.
"Two, actually. She wants you to ring."

Clare left the suitcase on her bed and went straight through to her
studio. The piano and the bookshelves were dusty; the March issue of
National Geographic was still open on the loveseat, another relic from

Alastair's store. She sat at the piano, the same tired upright with spinning stool she'd been playing for years, and conjured a voice with which to escape. What she came up with was a fuzzy combination of the Jazz Studies Director and Rudy Vantwest, whose real voice she'd never actually heard.

I hear you're quite the pianist, he said.

She rested her fingers lightly on the keys and held them there a moment, letting the urgency of the touch, the desire of the one for the other, build. Then, taking hold of the signatures like a crutch — four-four time, key of E flat; precise, mathematical — she played.

I'm flattered. She's a great musician.

Have you ever done any performing?

Not really. I work at a music store. Waste of a degree, perhaps. I went into it thinking I'd be a music teacher, but that was a bad idea. Her notes meandered, like conversation over coffee. *Sometimes Emma and I played duets at her church, if you could call that a performance.*

Do you go to church?

No . . . the duets just gave us an excuse to practise there whenever we wanted. Well, whenever Emma wanted. I liked it, though . . . the church with no one in it.

She played the empty sanctuary, arranging details for this listener with Rudy Vantwest's face and a borrowed voice to appreciate — a chirpy phrase for the blond wood of the pews, something richer, more harmonic, for the thick burgundy carpet that flowed down the centre aisle. She played the glorious emptiness, the echoes.

Sometimes we'd just fool around. Pretend we were stars. Emma would give me a key, and I'd play . . . whatever I felt like. She'd sing along, following me. I guess that's how I learned to improvise.

As in jazz? You don't seem like a typical jazz person.

He would have to say this. Clare struck single notes, considering her response.

Not cool enough? Not passionate enough?

Well . . .

I don't love my music; I need it. We don't have to call it jazz. Actually, I'd prefer we didn't.

She changed key, embarking on a new progression, the notes agitated, uncertain.

The church was a completely different place on a Sunday morning, of course. I remember the first time Emma took me there. I was twelve or so. I didn't want to go, but I didn't know how to refuse. Everyone was so unbearably nice. They shook my hand and told me how happy they were to have me there, sharing the joy of life in Christ. Even Emma's brothers were nice. I hated it.

Was it one of those born-again, tongue-speaking places?

No ... nothing that weird. The actual service wasn't so bad; I didn't mind it at all ... except for the part when the pastor asked us to share the Light of God.

What happened?

Everyone started milling around aimlessly, hugging and shaking hands. Emma hugged me, then she wandered off. I stared at the floor and prayed that I'd be magically transported back to my own bedroom. Then this young woman tapped me on the shoulder and asked me if I'd accept the Light of God.

What'd you say?

Here the music became low, sheepish.

I said yes. I was mortified — and furious. Then I wondered if there was something wrong with me.

But if you don't share their beliefs ...

She paused.

I'm not sure I don't. I think there's a God out there. Or something. Fate maybe. I'm like my father, I guess. He thought all our dealings with God should be conducted in private. Even the Presbyterians were too demonstrative for him.

So whatever inspired you to play at that church?

That was much later. Emma and I were sharing an apartment. When she asked me to do it, she promised we could sit up front the whole time and not have to hug or shake hands with anyone. She kept her —

There was a knock. Clare stopped playing.

"Sorry to disturb you, pet," Isobel said, nudging the door open. "I was just wondering if you were hungry."

"Not really. No. Thanks."

The voice with Rudy Vantwest's face was gone, and suddenly it was Emma back in her head.

Ask her now! Come on, you promised.

Clare clenched her fists between her knees. "Can I ask you something, Ma?"

"Of course, pet. What is it?"

"Was I really premature?"

"What do you mean?"

She couldn't tell if her mother was flustered or angry or genuinely confused. "I mean was I really born early, or did you get pregnant before you and Dad were married?"

Isobel approached the piano slowly, rubbing her arms. She breathed in and straightened her shoulders. "Things were different back then, pet."

Clare nodded. She didn't need to hear any more.

Her mother traced a finger across the dusty piano top. "I should have said something a long time ago."

"It's okay. I figured it out."

She lowered the fallboard and stood up. She would go to her bedroom and unpack, maybe read a little or call Emma. It was still early in Vancouver. But her mother's eyes were fixed on her, following her.

"I should have told you, Clare. Are you —"

"It's fine. It's no big deal."

She picked up the *National Geographic*. At the doorway joining the studio and the bedroom, another question came to her — *Did you love Dad?* But at the sight of her mother absently running her sleeve across the piano top, she let it go. "I'm going to unpack," she said.

In the bedroom she unzipped her suitcase and tossed clothes into the laundry hamper until her mother's footsteps sounded on the creaky stairs. Then she went to the window and stared at the dark boughs of her father's favourite tree — the pine he'd brought with him from Scotland. His final resting place.

It was good we did it on Christmas. You always loved Christmas, didn't you ... the rituals anyway.

Oh, aye.

It's been six years already?

So it has.

What have I been doing?

Och. Carrying on.

Not even. I feel like I'm still standing out there in the snow with your ashes.

DECEMBER 1990

It's winter again. Christmas Day. Rudy has driven out from Toronto along with Susie and her family. Adam still lives at home. All in all, it's an ordinary Christmas — messier now that Sue and Mark have baby Zoë. Mum's absence no longer oppresses, as it did for so many years, though Dad still drinks too much arrack.

Rudy is at the kitchen table with the rest of the "children," browsing an old issue of the *Gazette* while his aunt makes Christmas lunch and his father listens to the Jim Reeves Christmas album in the living room — right hand anchored to his drink, left hand lazily tapping the armrest of his chair, more in time with his own thoughts, it seems, than with the music. Bundled up in her multiple cardigans, chopping away, Aunty tells stories of the old days on the tea estate. Adam's the only one paying any attention. He listens as a curious outsider would, tilting his head and widening his eyes, as if it were all fabulously exotic — as if peraheras and kavichchis and Peria Dorays were from a different planet. It's vaguely embarrassing, Rudy thinks, the way his brother fawns over things that should be ordinary to him. But then Adam has never been home; he's different from the rest of them.

"So, Aunty," he says, rocking back on two legs of his chair, hands clasped behind his head, "were there any problems between the Tamils and the Sinhalese back in those days?"

In the living room Dad coughs. Aunty keeps on chopping.

"Ah, not like they have now," she says. "Things were more peaceful then." She brushes loose strands of hair away from her face with the wrist of her chopping hand. "People got along better, isn't it."

Adam frowns. "Well, they made it *look* like they did. But I can totally understand why they got fed up — the Sinhalese *and* the Tamils. I mean, I'd wanna start fighting too if I had second-rate status in my own country. Wouldn't you?"

"Ah, maybe," Aunty says, without conviction.

Dad coughs again. Rudy and Susie exchange a glance, then Susie retreats to the heavy manual she has brought with her from Toronto: *An Introduction to American Sign Language*. As far as Rudy is concerned, Sri Lanka's problems aren't *real*. Real is another frozen Christmas with crappy gifts and too much food. It's Adam's larger-than-life presence. It's Susie and her husband finding out their tiny blue-eyed, black-haired kid is severely hearing impaired.

Watching his sister move her hands like pieces of newly acquired anatomy, Rudy senses a familiar impotence — a powerful but hopeless desire to be helpful, to be significant in some way. He remembers an afternoon, ages ago, in Aunty Mary's garden, when Susie leaned too far over the edge of the well and got stuck. For several long seconds, she teetered perilously atop the narrow stone wall, screaming, feet kicking in the air, before Rudy got to her and yanked her back down by the hem of her skirt. In his mind, he'd saved his sister's life, and for a brief, triumphant time he was her hero and protector. But he doubts Susie even remembers the incident. And in any case, it's no longer Rudy she calls for in her moments of crisis, but Adam.

Adam's interest in Sri Lankan politics seems to have fizzled. Whistling along with Jim Reeves, he slides his chair away from the table and slips into the living room, where he drops to the floor in front of Zoë, who's playing with a pile of *National Geographic* magazines.

"Whatcha got there?" he says, signing "Zoë," along with something Rudy doesn't recognize.

Zoë looks up and slaps the magazine on the floor in front of her. Adam blows a wave of hair out of his eyes.

"Cool picture," he says. "That's a woolly mammoth. It's like an elephant, only it's bigger and hairier. And those things coming out of its mouth are tusks." He exaggerates the signs for "big" and "hairy" and fingerspells "tusks." He starts to read from the magazine — "'The woolly mammoth ranged over North America, Asia, and Europe during the Pleistocene. It was —'" then interrupts himself. "Hey, Zoë, can you imagine if they used one of these things instead of a regular elephant in the Kandy Perahera? Wouldn't that be crazy?"

Rudy hears his father clear his throat, and his own body tenses.

"What are you expecting her to understand from all this?" Dad says, his voice deceptively mild. "Point to the picture and say 'elephant.'"

At the kitchen table Susie's eyes again catch Rudy's. Their father is the one member of the family who won't sign.

"I don't want her to learn anything from this," Adam says. "I just want her to know I'm interested in what she's looking at."

Dad doesn't answer. For a moment the only voice in the house is that of Jim Reeves, crooning the final verse of "Blue Christmas," his velvet melody pocked with record crackles that have become part of the music itself. Then Zoë laughs as Adam swoops her up off the floor and steers her like an airplane, through the kitchen and down the hallway, past the trophy room and the dining room, across the entrance hall, and back into the living room, where he deposits her with a fading whistle next to the pile of toys beneath the Christmas tree.

"Now, let's see what we have to play with here," he says. "Stuffed doll ... stuffed dog ... stuffed platypus ..." One by one, the toys fly over his shoulder. "Hey! Giant Lego! I believe this is from your Uncle Rudy. Hey, Uncle Rudy, wanna play Lego with me and Zoë?"

Rudy shakes out his paper and turns to a new page. His brother's invitation strikes him as a challenge.

"Uh, no thanks. You two go ahead."

He detects the shadow of disappointment that crosses Adam's face, and briefly he regrets his answer. But his regret muddles with irritation, and as Adam dumps the tub of Lego out on the floor, Rudy stares hard at the page before him, unable to make himself concentrate. He decides to go out.

Beside him Susie closes her book and begins straightening the clutter on the table.

"Mark and I are going to have a rest upstairs," she says. "Adam, would you mind watching Zoë?"

Outside, Rudy walks as far as the end of the driveway and leans back against the juniper tree stationed like a sentry at the corner of the lawn. The sky is low and grey; the air has that particular about-to-snow sharpness to it. He buries his hands in his pockets and inhales the cold. He doesn't really plan to walk any farther.

Stretching out to his left and right, Morgan Hill Road — *chemin de la Côte Morgan*, officially — is perfectly straight and, despite the name, flat. The snow on its front yards is still untrampled after the latest fall. Its houses, from the bricks of their living room levels to the aluminum siding strips of their bedroom levels, are ordered and straight. Most of them have their Christmas lights on, and these strings of lights, too, conform to the right-angle geometry of the street.

Rudy looks back at his father's sagging lights, the exception on the block. Complementing the red shutters and door, the bulbs are green and red, but the wires hang in loose arcs along the eaves and under the windows. "Like the lights at the Kandy Perahera," Adam apparently said when he put them up. Dad said they looked sloppy and apologized for them when Rudy and the others came home. "Kandy Perahera!" he huffed, shaking his head. "The boy has never even seen a perahera. The neighbours must think we're completely ignorant."

Rudy turns back to the street. "You should have been born in the old country, machan," he muses to his absent brother.

Rudy himself is tired of being Sri Lankan. Or, rather, of being *only* Sri Lankan — especially to women. His relationships follow a pattern as regular as the lines and angles of Morgan Hill Road. Currently it's Renée, who took the initiative and asked him out. At first, she found him exotic (that word he has grown to despise) and therefore incapable of being boring. And he, in the interest of boosting his desirability, became in her presence someone not quite himself, peppering his descriptions of "home" with tropical flavours and smells, using Sinhala words whose meanings had escaped him, admiring the contrast in their skin tones when they made love. It worked, for a while. Then Renée asked about his name, and on discovering he was neither Sinhalese nor Tamil, but a hybrid with European ancestors, began to find entirely ordinary faults in him. Soon, he's sure, they'll break up, and once again he'll vow not to take part in this embarrassing routine.

As if to assert his Canadianness, he crouches and scoops up some snow with his bare hands. It doesn't pack very well, but he manages to form a lumpy little ball, which he fires across the street at the Frasers' Oldsmobile. He crouches to scoop up more snow, but as he does so the Frasers' front door opens and Mrs. Fraser and her daughter come out. For an instant, Rudy worries they're going to bawl him out for hucking snowballs at their car, the way Mr. Fraser once did. But Mrs. Fraser and her daughter seem oblivious to his presence. Mr. Fraser himself — odd, sullen guy — is no longer around to care. Apparently his heart gave out on him in the summer.

Rudy straightens up slowly and leans back into the juniper, grateful that his jacket isn't far off the green of the bush. To step out into the street would probably call for a greeting — something he'd rather not bother with — so he stays where he is, waiting for the two women to get into the car and drive off. Curiously, though, they stay where they are, hovering by the front door, as if trying to decide where to go or what to do. Mrs. Fraser, in a fur-trimmed coat, is cradling something in one arm, gesturing toward the middle of the lawn with the other. Her daughter, Clare, looks frozen in a turtleneck and jeans. Her arms are folded across her middle and her head is bowed, long hair hiding her face.

Rudy hasn't seen Clare Fraser in years. In his time away from Morgan Hill Road, he's forgotten her, and only now, watching her like this, does he recall with an unexpected wave of nostalgia that she used to be a fixture in his life. He never spoke to her; they weren't friends. But she was regularly *there*, the girl across the street, about his age, a presence he could count on.

His mind begins to drift, until Clare and her mother walk out to the driveway. Rudy presses his body farther into the juniper. The

Christmassy smell fills his nostrils. "Come on, you two," he mutters. "I feel like an idiot here. Get in the car." Cupping his hands around his mouth and nose, he prepares to slip around the bush and back to the house. But then the scene across the street changes.

The two women march through the fresh snow to the pine tree in the middle of the lawn. Mrs. Fraser circles the tree, examining its branches, while Clare stares at the ground. Rudy squints at the thing cradled in Mrs. Fraser's arm, craning his neck to get a better view. It's a container of some kind, he guesses. Then, teetering into the shrub, he gets it: an *urn*.

"Jesus," he whispers.

He steadies himself then squats down, making his body as small as possible.

Mrs. Fraser says something. Clare's head is still down, her arms folded. If she answers, Rudy doesn't hear it. He imagines her heavy-hearted but restrained. He knows the feeling. She wants the whole thing to be over with, he imagines — and, for her sake, so does he. But Mrs. Fraser, fondling a branch of the pine tree with her free hand, seems to be in no hurry. Rudy shifts his weight. His knees are complaining, but to get up now is out of the question. Waiting, he notices that the Fraser house is the only one on the block without Christmas lights. Though reasonably well tended, the place wears a vacant stare of abandonment, as if, despite Mr. Fraser's grumpy manner, the house can't manage to look homey without him. Rudy knows little about the circumstances of his neighbour's death. Living in Toronto, he received only a sketchy account. But it occurs to him that even if he'd been living here on Morgan Hill Road, he'd not have known much more. For though the Frasers have lived across the street for as long as he can remember, the distance between their house and his own has proven itself, for no straightforward reason, to be unbridgeable.

Holding the brass urn in both hands now, Mrs. Fraser offers one side of it to her daughter, but Clare shakes her head. Her mother turns to face the pine tree then takes a step back. Rudy's eyes are fixed on the urn. He's never seen ashes before; he's heard there's more to them than one might expect. And indeed, when Mr. Fraser's remains spill out into the branches of the pine, onto the snow, upward in great, whitish gusts, their quantity is surprising.

That's what we amount to, Rudy tells himself, though he doesn't quite believe it.

Mrs. Fraser wraps her arm around her daughter's shoulders, and together they stand, facing the tree. It would be fitting, Rudy thinks, for the snow to start now. He searches the sky and in the absence of any climactic flakes tries to honour the Frasers' small, quiet ceremony with a memory of his mother's burial. It's an event that should have stuck, but all that comes to him of that muggy August afternoon is the car ride from the cemetery to the house: he and Susie in the back seat with a large 7-Up to share, baby Adam screeching on Aunty Mary's lap.

His knees are killing him. Seeing Clare retreat, head down, toward her house, he straightens up painfully, extracts himself from the juniper, and tramps back across his own yard. He's halfway to the steps when the front door opens a crack.

"Rudy! Lunch in ten minutes!" his aunt calls, loud enough to be heard several houses away.

Rudy groans into his collar. He could carry on to the house without looking back — he's almost there — but he stops and turns.

Mrs. Fraser is looking in his direction, clutching the empty urn. He expects her to ignore him, or dismiss him with a friendly wave. But instead she starts walking toward the road, her free arm out for balance, as if she's on a tightrope. Awkward and baffled, Rudy watches her for a few steps, then he backtracks across his yard.

"Rudy? I haven't seen you in ages."

The Scottish accent is a surprise. He'd forgotten it, along with other quirky things about Mrs. Fraser that used to captivate him in a confusingly sexual way when he was a kid — the fiery hair, the makeup, the pretty clothes. Though he understood her relationship to Clare, it was always difficult to imagine Isobel Fraser as a mother.

He pulls his right hand from his pocket and waves. "Hi, Mrs. Fraser. It's been a few years at least." The *Mrs. Fraser* sounds ridiculous; she can't be more than forty-five. But she doesn't correct him.

At the edge of the road he stops, while she, on her side, does the same. A sensible position, Rudy thinks. With Morgan Hill Road between them, it's easier to avoid the urn, not to mention the fact that in almost twenty years of living across the street from each other, he and his neighbour have almost never spoken.

"Is your family together for Christmas?" she says.

He's forgotten about Christmas. "Oh. Yeah. My sister and her family are here, and my aunt's out for her visit."

He wonders if she has any idea where his aunt is visiting *from* — if she even knows where the place is. Renée didn't, though she tried to hide it. But Mrs. Fraser, he sees, is smiling and nodding in a way that seems entirely genuine.

"Oh, that's lovely. I must say, I always envied your aunt every time she went back home. I've dreamed of going to that part of the world ever since I was a girl."

"Really?"

"Oh, aye. I think it would be marvellous. The lovely beaches, the temples ..."

Touristy stuff, he thinks, but still. It seems to him suddenly preposterous that Mrs. Fraser has never been inside his house, never had a cup of tea with his aunt. He takes a small step forward.

"You should go sometime."

"I should, shouldn't I. Well, maybe when things here are a bit more settled." She shifts the urn in her arms.

Grateful for the opening, Rudy clears his throat. "I was really sorry to hear about your husband. Is everything all ... I mean, is there anything ..."

She shakes her head. "Thank you, pet. It was a terrible shock, but we're managing quite well. It just takes time, doesn't it."

Pet, he repeats to himself, nodding. She's speaking to him as if for all these years the Vantwests and the Frasers have been regular neighbours. He glances back at his own house. Through the living room window he can make out his brother, tossing Zoë up in the air. Adam's build is slender, but he's a swimmer, lean and strong.

"I shouldn't keep you," Mrs. Fraser says. "I heard Mary calling you in."

"Yeah. I should probably go."

"Well, it was lovely chatting with you, Rudy."

"You too."

"You're still living in Toronto?"

"For a while anyway. I've got a teaching job in North York."

"Oh, that's wonderful! Well, best of luck with it."

"Thanks."

He wonders if he should wish her a Merry Christmas, but a final glance at the urn dismisses the idea. He waves again then turns and retraces his steps through the snow and up the concrete stairs to the front door. With his hand on the latch he looks back to see Mrs. Fraser disappear behind her own door. His eyes travel to the upstairs windows of the Fraser house, and there, in the middle window, he catches Clare Fraser's pale, pretty face, turning away from him then vanishing altogether. *Odd duck*, he thinks. And yet he watches a few seconds longer to see if she'll return. He wants her to — wants her to come back and just be there. But she doesn't. One last time he meets the vacant stare of the house across the street, then he goes inside.

Christmas lunch is almost ready. The counter is crowded with Aunty's special dishes, and the air is heavy with the competing smells of curry spices and turkey. While Aunty and Susie fuss over last-minute details, Dad and Mark drink arrack and talk hockey. Down on the floor, Zoë struggles with the lid of an empty Tupperware container. Adam is rummaging through a drawer; Jim Reeves is still singing. Rudy hovers in the archway between the kitchen and the living room, staring out the front window. In all the noise and confusion of his own house, it seems suddenly impossible that across the street Mrs. Fraser has just disposed of her husband's ashes. But she did. He was there. He could even say that, in a way, he was part of it.

"Found them!" Adam suddenly calls out. "Christmas oven mitts! I told you they were in here, Aunty."

"Very good, son. Now take the turkey out before it dries up."

Adam pulls on the mitts — ridiculous, ruffled things with reindeer on them — opens the oven door with a flourish, and slides out the rack on which the turkey pan sits. The bird is greeted with noisy enthusiasm. Adam lifts the pan and stands with it while Aunty Mary clears a patch of counter space and the others shuffle aside. Then, from the archway, Rudy sees Zoë race toward the oven on hands and knees. He guesses what she's going to do, but he's a kitchen's length away from her. His father is closest.

"Dad!" he shouts. "Get Zoë!"

Alec looks down, and as the baby's arms stretch upward, her eyes fixed on the oven rack, he calls to her.

"Zoë! Don't touch!"

Zoë's hands grasp the rack, and the kitchen is shaken by her scream. She topples over and strikes her head on the linoleum. Rudy winces.

Susie cries, "Oh my God!" and shoves past Aunty Mary to get to her wailing daughter. She gathers Zoë in her arms and struggles to open the child's clenched hands — calmly at first, but as Zoë's screams become more and more desperate, she snaps. "Dada, what were you thinking? She can't hear! She's — Oh God, never mind. Mark! Do something, for God's sake. Don't just stand there!"

Mark flounders. Aunty says, "Butter" and goes to the fridge.

Rudy is staring at the far kitchen door, through which his father has just disappeared, silently, unnoticed by the others. Startled back by his aunt's suggestion, he calls "No!" and heads for the sink. But his brother is way ahead of him. Throwing off the reindeer mitts, Adam crouches next to Susie with a bowl of water, into which he plunges the baby's hands. Zoë's screams taper off to sobs.

"Somebody get the bag of peas out of the freezer," Adam says. "She's getting a bump on her head."

Mark gets the peas and drops to his daughter's level, nudging Adam out of the way. Adam doesn't seem to mind. He offers to search for some first aid spray in the bathroom.

"Thanks, Addy," Susie calls after him. "And turn off the damn music, would you? It's driving me crazy."

Rudy steps aside to let his brother pass. Dad, he notices, hasn't reappeared. He knows where he is, of course, and as the commotion in the kitchen dies down he goes there, ambivalently.

From the trophy room, a shaft of lamplight cuts across the dim hallway. The small room is the place that houses Alec Vantwest's past — the cricket trophies and English literature classics from his days at Trinity College Kandy, the old black and white photos taken at Grandpa's tea estate, even a wooden tea chest, once used to ship family belongings from Colombo to Montreal. A puzzling room, Rudy thinks, given his father's aversion to the past, but on the other hand everything in the room is neatly shelved or framed, kept in its place, and it's possible to imagine that this museum-like containment is a comfort. At the moment, Alec, curator of the trophy room's artifacts, is sitting in the armchair next to the tea chest reading table, staring at the wall of photographs.

Rudy raises his hand to the half-open door then lowers it. He knows what will happen if he enters the trophy room with words of consolation. His father will rise from the chair and put a hand on his shoulder. He'll say, "Thank you, son," all the while looking not directly at Rudy but somewhere just off to the side, as if he were blind, or Rudy were invisible. Then he'll pour himself a drink, maybe offer Rudy one as well, and go to the bookshelves, where he'll examine the spines of his books with a show of great interest. And that will be that.

Seeing Aunty and Mark carrying dishes to the dining room, Rudy steps away from the door. He suspects it isn't sympathy or understanding his father wants — not his, anyway — and with this in mind he returns sullenly to the kitchen to help with the food.

At Christmas lunch he sits next to Mark. Dad has appeared, thankfully, though he had to be called to the table three times. Zoë seems fine. Seated in her high chair, she clutches a wet cloth in her hands and sucks on it. The turkey has been carved, the curries uncovered. The dining room is so cramped and the food so plentiful that the windows of the china cabinet are steamed up. In the living room, Jim Reeves has been replaced by Andy Williams.

"We should have a toast," says Aunty, last to take her place. "Who would like to do that? Adam?"

Adam nods and raises his glass of rosé. "I'd like to propose a toast to Aunty Mary, for carrying on the old traditions and for keeping our stomachs satisfied over the holidays. Merry Christmas!"

Rudy clinks his glass against Mark's, while underneath the table his right heel taps and his left hand forms a tight, aimless fist.

"And God bless us all," Aunty adds. "Now, eat, eat. The food will get cold."

Rudy drinks down half his glass. As he piles his plate, conversations begin around the table and the useless tension in his arm gradually subsides. He glances at his father and clears his throat.

"So, Dad, I hear Australia's set to wallop England in the test match."

"What's that? Oh, yes."

"Are you gonna watch?"

"Mmm? No, no."

"Do you think the English have had it in the cricketing world?"

"I suppose so."

Rudy catches his aunt's eye and shrugs. Aunty turns to her brother.

"Alec, you must tell me what you think of the beef. They didn't have all the proper spices at the supermarket. No mustard seed, only the powder. And no green chilis."

"I'm sure it's fine, Mary."

"Ah, but just fine isn't good enough. Try it and tell me."

"It's delicious. Same as always."

Suddenly, across the table from Rudy, Adam clinks his fork against his glass.

"I'd like to say something," he announces, "so that we can all enjoy our lunch more."

Turning to Dad, he continues. "About Zoë's accident. Dada, it wasn't your fault. I think you're feeling badly about what happened, but no one is blaming you. You didn't have time to grab her. It was an accident. Right, Susie?"

Susie nods. "Everything's fine, Dada. Little ones fall and burn themselves all the time."

Rudy watches his father uneasily. A public announcement isn't what he'd have wanted. He would feel trapped. But Adam has never understood how to deal with Dad.

His expression unchanged, Alec swallows then sets his fork on his plate. "I appreciate your concern, Adam. But I think the root of the accident was that the child was left unsupervised. She should have been with Susie."

At this, Susie's eyes widen. "Dada, I can't watch her every second! I was helping Aunty with dinner."

"And besides," Adam adds, "I was the one watching Zoë. Susie asked me to."

Rudy stares into his plate, willing his brother to shut up.

"It's just as I said," Dad answers. "Zoë should have been with *Susie*."

The reply — the particular emphasis on Susie — hangs over the table like the heavy clouds looming outside.

"What's that supposed to mean?" Adam says, his voice level.

Rudy shuts his eyes. If he had his brother's nerve, he'd speak up. "You know exactly what it means," he'd say. "You know precisely where this conversation is likely to end up, and you're going there anyway." Instead, he listens while Adam carries on.

"I don't get it, Dad. Are you saying I'm not capable of looking after Zoë? It's true I wasn't right with her when the accident happened, but I was holding the turkey for Aunty. I don't think it was any more my fault than it was yours."

Here it comes, Rudy thinks. He looks at his father, whose face is now set in an expression of solemn concern.

"I take full responsibility for not intercepting the child sooner, and I apologize to Susie for that." Dad nods in Susie's direction. "But we are talking about a handicapped child who needs to be watched at all times, and I am simply suggesting that her mother — or her father — is a better person for that role than a boy who —"

"Alec!" Aunty Mary cuts him off. "Don't spoil the lunch. You're feeling upset about Zoë's accident and you're blaming everyone else. The thing is over now. Don't think about it."

"Who what?" Adam insists.

Rudy catches the faint sound of a skating needle. His father doesn't answer. What could he say, really? That Zoë shouldn't be left in the care of a young man who blows off a biology scholarship in order to take up history? That a young man who goes for long motorcycle rides with another young man shouldn't be allowed to babysit? No. Observing the slight tremor in his father's hands as he runs his fingers along the edge of the table, Rudy detects an uneasiness. Dad would rather call it quits, go back to small talk. But Adam doesn't see this.

"What's this really about, Dad? Is it about my babysitting abilities, or the rest of my life?" When Dad fails to answer, he presses stubbornly on. "I know you're upset about my new plans, but I can't change them. I know I made the right decision. Biology just wasn't my thing. It's not what I'm meant to do." He pauses. "And if you're talking about my sexual orientation, that's not a choice. It's like Zoë's deafness."

The word *sexual* sends Aunty Mary into a panic. "Adam! Such talk! You and your father are spoiling the lunch. Look — everyone has stopped eating."

"What have your preferences to do with Zoë?" Dad finally says, frowning.

Adam turns to the high chair, where Zoë is sitting with one hand wrapped in the wet cloth, the other in her mouth. "Being deaf wasn't a choice for her," he says, shouts almost. "She was born that way. There's nothing she or any doctor can do about it. And lots of people in the deaf community say it's not even a real handicap anyway. It's the same with me. Should I spend my life trying to change things I can't change ... that I don't even *want* to change?"

While Adam talks on, firing questions that Dad doesn't answer, Rudy's eyes dart to his sister. Her chin is puckered. Mark, plucking absently at his beard, doesn't seem to notice. Certainly Adam doesn't. If he did, he'd apologize, but he's too wrapped up in his monologue. Under the table Rudy's hand once again clenches against his thigh. Nothing has changed. Adam is still the bawling baby in the front seat. And just as it was on that car ride home from the cemetery, his voice is amplified by Dad's brooding silence.

Finally, Aunty takes charge. "The food is getting cold," she says. "Adam, you talk about these things later. It's Christmas lunch and we're here to enjoy our meal and be kind to each other, isn't it."

Adam looks around the table. At the sight of Susie wiping her eyes, he deflates. "Oh crap. I'm sorry. I got carried away. Sue, I didn't mean to ..."

Susie smiles weakly. "It's okay. Let's just eat," she says, and goes back to feeding Zoë.

Dutifully, Rudy takes a forkful of rice. At the head of the table, Dad reaches for a pappadam. He breaks off a piece and places it on his tongue like a Eucharistic host. "Excellent meal, Mary," he says.

"Just like the old days." In his voice and posture there is a hint of resignation. The skin under his staring brown eyes is loose and tired.

⚭

LATE THAT NIGHT, Rudy finds his sister in the trophy room. The lights are out, and she's sitting cross-legged in Dad's chair.

"Are you okay?" he says from the doorway.

"Yeah. Fine. Just thinking."

"About this afternoon?"

"Sort of."

"Adam shouldn't have gone on like that."

Susie unfolds herself from her lotus position. "It's okay. What he was saying made perfect sense."

"Yeah, but . . ."

"No, really, Rudy. I'm not upset about anything Adam said." She comes into the hallway, where she lowers her voice. "He's been having a rough time with Dada lately. Coming out and everything. He needs our support."

Rudy nods. "It's late. I'm gonna hit the couch. I'll see you in the morning."

When his sister has disappeared up the stairs, he goes into the trophy room with his diary and turns on the light. He examines the photographs on the wall. His favourite was taken long ago at the summit of Adam's Peak. It's a black and white portrait of two young men standing on either side of an ancient bell. One of the men is a tea taster from Grandpa's estate. The other is Uncle Ernie. He leans in to get a better look at this uncle he has never met, the black sheep who left home and was rarely heard from again. He's a handsome fellow, more European in appearance than Dad, though the family resemblance is evident. The square jaw has resurfaced in Adam, along with the cheeky smile.

"Maybe a few other things as well," Rudy muses aloud. "Things that would have made you a real black sheep back then, eh, machan?"

Renée can't understand that he could have an uncle living somewhere in the world — Sri Lanka probably, though not necessarily — and yet have no particular desire to meet the man. He isn't entirely sure himself, but it seems to him just as logical to wonder why, apart from the indulgence of a mild curiosity, he *would* want to meet his uncle.

He sits in the armchair and opens his diary. Glancing out the trophy room window, he thinks of Clare Fraser. Though he can't actually see the Fraser house from the trophy room, he imagines her at her window, watchful and quietly receptive, just as she was the first time he ever really noticed her, standing under a sprinkler on a deathly hot August day. The opportunity will never arise, he is certain, but if Clare — the solemn, watchful creature behind the glass — were to ask him about his family, he wouldn't resent it. He would welcome her detached interest.

He dates the page and taps his pen. He writes "Hello, Clare" then pauses, considering the move he has just made. Strange ... silly even. But he carries on:

> I'm sitting in my father's trophy room, looking at the old photos. Uncle Ernie on Adam's Peak, Susie's first communion, Grandpa and his cook, the last family gathering on Grandpa's tea estate before we left for Canada, etc. etc. It was on that visit that I first learned who Ernie was. And so much else, of course. I don't remember most of the details, just the emotional extremes. How I started off bored and glum like everyone else and ended up ecstatically happy.

He stops writing. It seems he has opened a floodgate, or a vein. The release could fill an entire book, he suspects — all his frustration and guilt spilling onto pages previously devoted to straightforward records of dates and events. For the writing is suddenly different. He has a listener, an intercessor. A calm, detached presence to stand between him and all the confusion in his life. Pleased with the discovery but too tired to write any more, he closes his book, switches off the lamp, and gazes at the scattering of tiny snowflakes dancing outside the trophy room window.

B Y THE TIME SHE WOKE UP on Good Friday, the morning was almost gone. Sunlight peered around the blind, and the clock, half-hidden behind a half-read copy of the unabridged *Clarissa*, read eleven-something. Clare stared at the beige expanse of her ceiling and listened to the distant clatter of the dishwasher being unloaded and her mother's heels tapping back and forth across the kitchen floor. Her trip to Vancouver no longer existed. Not in the way these other things did — the beigeness of her room, the numbing familiarity of Isobel's kitchen noise. The pattern . . .

She got out of bed, untwisted her nightgown from around her hips, and raised the blind. It was a brilliant day — snow melting from branches and eaves in sparkling drips, the sky an unbroken blue. She leaned her forehead against the windowpane, and Morgan Hill Road rippled through the streams of water trickling down the glass. The street was empty.

Clare turned from the window and lifted her suitcase onto the bed to finish unpacking. She pulled out the gypsy skirt that she'd worn on her date with the Jazz Studies Director — too hippy-dippy, according to Emma — and the pink, low-cut sweater that Emma had convinced her to buy. Under the sweater, she discovered a slender parcel wrapped in yellow tissue paper. It was tied at either end with gold ribbon, and attached to one of the ribbons was a heart-shaped tag. Clare flipped it over and read: "To be used solo, or maybe with??? P.S. I got one for myself too!"

She yanked one of the ribbons. The thing inside tumbled out, alien and intrusive. Mortifying. It was translucent orange, phallic, attached by a cord to a dial switch. Clare turned it on, and it trembled in her hand. She adjusted the dial, and it writhed about like an exotic eel.

Emma —

What?

Did you actually think I'd use this thing?

She turned it off and stuffed it back in its paper. Then she wrapped the whole package in a T-shirt and looked around the room for a place to hide it. Riskier than throwing it out. If she were to be hit by a truck, someone — her mother, no doubt — would have to go through her belongings. But she'd noticed the price of these things in the shop Emma had dragged her to. As a compromise, she went to her closet and slipped the parcel under a pile of sweaters, away from the unaccommodating patterns of her life.

She knew what Emma would say: *You're sick of those patterns, Clare. They're killing you. You need to change.* And her diagnosis would be mostly correct. But not the cure.

Clare shut the closet door and snatched her bath towel from the back of a chair.

In the shower, though, Emma's gift haunted her, and she found herself locked in her body, inescapably physical: curves and sharp angles; stretches of skin with their particular geography of moles and creases and dark blond fuzz; the necessary back and forth of air; the building up, somewhere inside her, of her next period (useless sacrifice) and of other unspeakable things. She closed her eyes and shampooed her hair, fingers clawing at her scalp, massaging her cerebral existence back to life. But the thoughts that came to her were of her mother's revelation — Isobel and Alastair in some dark, secret place.

She lathered more vigorously. *It wasn't necessarily like that,* she told herself. Then, to Emma, to the intruder back in her closet: *I bet it was all planned. My mother probably set the whole thing up, so she could come to Canada. She was desperate to leave Scotland.* She tilted her head back under the spray. *It makes sense. My father was just like me.*

∞

DOWN IN THE KITCHEN, Isobel was leaning against the counter, drinking coffee and flipping through a recipe book.

"Did you sleep well?" she said, as Clare emptied the dishwasher.

"Too well. I should have set the alarm."

"Mmm. You'll want to be back on track before work starts up again. Tuesday is it?"

"Monday."

"Isn't that a holiday?"

"Not in retail. Our sale starts then."

"Oh!" Isobel took a swig of coffee. "Will the pianos be marked down?"

"Uh-huh."

"Why don't you treat yourself, pet? Surely with the staff discount you could get a wee grand, couldn't you? Or at least a proper bench."

"I don't know. The timing may not be right." Clare reached for a mug and studied its familiar, faded pattern of blue and white stripes, the worn chip on the rim. "I've been thinking about moving, maybe." She glanced up. "To Vancouver."

Her mother looked surprised, of course, but not terribly so.

"Vancouver! Were you making plans while you were out there, then?"

"No, not really. It's just an idea. I may not do it."

"No?" Isobel flipped a few pages then placed the book on the counter. "I would understand, pet," she said solemnly. "It's not that I wouldn't miss you ... but I know what it's like."

Clare didn't answer. If her mother had resisted, she could have argued the case for leaving, given it some impetus in her own head. Instead, she shut the dishwasher and went to the fridge, while Isobel talked on.

"Aye, I know what it's like, wanting a change," she said. "It's easier these days, don't you think? Being able to do what really suits you?"

"I don't know. I guess," Clare said, not turning around. She imagined her mother's look of exasperation, a look suggesting that mothers and daughters are supposed to share their feelings, and that she, Clare, was failing to pull her weight in this mutually disagreeable obligation.

"There weren't so many choices when your father and I were —" Isobel paused. "Could you hand me out the eggs please, pet?"

Clare gripped the fridge handle tighter. As she shifted items around, searching, she dared herself to phone up her boss and give her notice.

"I don't see any eggs."

"Oh, dammit, that's right," Isobel said. "I used the last of them. I wanted to try this quiche recipe, but I'll have to save it for another time."

Clare shut the fridge door and turned. "I'll go get some."

"Oh, don't worry about it, pet. I'd rather we —"

"It's okay. I need to go out."

"Are the stores even open? It's Good Friday."

"They'll be open."

She grabbed an apple from the fruit bowl and headed for the vestibule.

"The car may need gas," her mother called after her.

"It's okay. I'll walk."

Outside, the sun's glare was blinding. Keeping her eyes down, Clare got to the end of her driveway before she noticed the motorcycle in the driveway across the street. Adam Vantwest, in a black leather jacket and black jeans, was crouched next to it, polishing the front fender with a cloth. Clare veered away from him. It was bad timing on her part, but at least he couldn't see her. He was facing the stretch of Morgan Hill Road that led away from the Boulevard and seemed so absorbed in his work that for a moment she leaned into the Skinners' front hedge and watched him. Emma's voice urged her to say hello, but that, of course, was out of the question. From the safety of the hedge she observed his careful work, the gleam of the sun off the chrome, then she took a bite of her apple and headed in the direction of the Boulevard.

A new conversation with Emma had just begun when Adam's voice rang out behind her.

"Clare! Hi!"

She stopped short and dropped her apple in the slush. He would know she'd tried to slip past him. She kicked the apple aside and turned, clenching her hands.

"Hi. Sorry. I didn't recognize you." Implausible, but she guessed he'd let it go.

Adam straightened up and slid his sunglasses on top of his head. "I haven't seen you in ages. I thought maybe you moved."

"Oh. No. I've just been on holiday." She forced a smile.

"Lucky you. Did you go away?"

"Uh, yeah. I was visiting a friend in Vancouver."

"Vancouver!" He shook out the rag in his hand. "I'm so jealous! I was there a few years ago. It's such a great city. I'd love to go back."

Clare smiled stupidly then glanced back at her house with a vague, uncomfortable sensation that her father was watching her.

"So, what did you do while you were out there?" Adam said, wiping his hands on the rag, advancing toward her. His wavy black hair was gelled, and a diamond stud sparkled in his earlobe. He was ridiculously confident.

Clare stuffed her hands in her pockets and rubbed her index fingers with her thumbs.

"Oh, not much. I mean, not many tourist things. I was just hanging out, with a friend."

Hanging out. She sounded fifteen.

"That's cool. What does your friend do?"

"She teaches music at a college."

She knew how this would go. In moments, Adam would get bored. He'd say, *Well, I should let you go,* as if she were the one being kept against her will. He'd go back to his motorcycle, she'd resume her walk to the store, and only then would she think of a dozen interesting things to say about Emma's work.

But Adam nodded patiently, twirling the cloth rag like a lasso. "Music teacher, eh? How does she like that?"

Clare met his eyes, just long enough to notice their extraordinary colour — very light, greenish brown.

"Um, she loves it," she said. On an impulse, she added, "Emma's really passionate about her music," and the word *passionate* echoed strangely in her head.

"Is that the same Emma who used to live here? Emma Skinner?"

"Uh-huh. That's her."

Adam gave a knowing nod. "Well, that's great, about her music. It's not often someone gets to make a living doing what they really love. Know what I mean?"

She searched for a response — something interesting or intelligent or merely adequate — but nothing came.

"Yeah," she said. "You're right."

In the pause that followed, she expected him to go back to his motorcycle. He'd been more than neighbourly. But instead he stayed, twisting the rag into a tight cord. Clare looked down Morgan Hill Road in the direction of the Boulevard. She'd yet to ask Adam anything about himself.

"Are you going for a ride?" she said.

He glanced over at the motorcycle. "Yeah, I thought I might. It's such a great day. How about you? You going somewhere?"

"Just to the Provigo."

Adam turned back, studying her it seemed. "Would you like a ride?" he said.

The shocking words hung between them in the cold, clear air. Impossible words. She needed to tell him that he was mistaken. That she wasn't the kind of person who did such things. Her hands clenched tighter.

"You mean on the motorcycle?"

"Yeah. Have you ever ridden one?"

"No, but ... I'd better not. I don't —"

"I have an extra helmet you can use. My sister wears it."

Inside Clare's head a chorus of anonymous voices fired cautions.

"Are you worried about the roads?" Adam said. "'Cause I was out walking earlier, and the streets were mostly dry."

She shook her head. "No. The roads are fine."

He twisted the rag one more time, then released it, and the fabric sprang out. "It's something to try," he said. "There's this amazing sense of freedom you get on a bike, like you're in complete control. Know what I mean?"

The idea was absurd. The voices in her head became more belligerent. *You'll have to talk to him. You'll run out of things to say. If you get on the motorcycle, you'll have to touch him.* Again she looked back at her house and saw in its ordered bricks, in the vacant stare of its windows, her father's face. Above all the warnings in her head, Emma's voice spoke to her, clear and certain. *Go with him*, she said, and Clare turned away from the house.

Adam took a step backward. "I'm sorry. I don't mean to pressure you. I was just thinking that I don't really know you at all, and this might be a good chance to ... But I understand if you don't want —"

"I'll go," she said. "I want to." She heard the words but wasn't sure they'd come from her.

Adam's green-brown eyes searched hers, then he smiled and gave her a thumbs-up. "I'll get the helmets. You should put on a heavier jacket, though. Leather's best, if you've got it."

She didn't.

Adam frowned in thought, then he tucked the rag into his back pocket and took off his own jacket. "Here — take this. I've got something else I can wear. I'll be right back." He turned and jogged across the street. Halfway up his driveway, he stopped and called across to her. "The Provigo isn't very far. Would you like to take a ride along the lakeshore first?"

Clare clutched the jacket to her chest. "Sure."

"We can stay on quiet streets. I'll take it real easy."

"It's okay. Go the way you'd normally go." She kicked at a chunk of dead snow. *I've been taking quiet streets my whole life.*

When Adam had disappeared into his house, she slipped off her old ski jacket — the one she'd had since she was eighteen — and hooked it over the wrought iron lamppost at the foot of her drive. It would have to stay there. If she went inside to hang it up, she would lose her nerve altogether. And then, of course, there was the impossibility of telling her mother what she was doing. She slid her arms into the sleeves of Adam's jacket and let the weight of it settle on her shoulders. It had heavy seams and a satiny lining. The leather was wrinkled, cracked at the elbows, and it smelled like cologne. She fastened the zipper and looked down at her faded jeans and scuffed boots, wishing she could see the entire image — herself in Adam's jacket. She wished Emma could see her. *Look at this,* she wanted to say. *I can change.* She straightened her shoulders and adjusted her headband, while underneath Adam's jacket her heart raced.

∞

SOMEWHERE ALONG Lakeshore Road, he called to her over his shoulder, but his words were lost in the engine noise and the rushing air.

"PARDON?" she shouted.

"I SAID ARE YOU OKAY?"

"YES — I'M FINE."

"IT'S NOT TOO FAST?"

"NO."

Hands anchored against Adam's hips, body leaning with his, Clare laughed out loud. It was a brilliant spring day, and she was riding on the back of a motorcycle — *a motorcycle, Emma!* — with a man she hardly knew. This wasn't the old Clare Fraser. On this speeding motorcycle, she was someone else — a fate-defying force, mocking the grey stodginess of the stone mansions and churches that they passed. Tearing through the patterns. She turned to the expanse of water on her right, squeezed the padded seat with her thighs, and exulted in the noise, the air, the sparkling water and trees, and the tensed muscles of Adam's shoulders and back. Right there, so close. His replacement jacket was trimmed with metal studs and chains, and his helmet was gleaming black. He should have been terrifying — much more so than the Jazz Studies Director — but he wasn't. Re-emerging from his garage, he'd worn an expression so undemanding, and yet so *eager,* that Clare had felt her awkwardness begin to dissolve. And now, at such speed, so far away from Morgan Hill Road, it lost its grip altogether. She thought of the dullness and doubt in which she'd been foundering that very morning and laughed again. This outrageous, unexpected flight was the most thrilling thing she'd ever done, and she knew that if Adam were to keep going, as far as the Jacques Cartier Bridge, right off the island, she wouldn't protest.

But at a narrow crossroad he slowed the bike, turned left, and pulled over. Lifting his visor, he looked back over his shoulder. "There's a depanneur just there. Will that do?"

She nodded, and Adam shut off the engine. In the sudden stillness, Clare felt her real self — the person who didn't do these sorts of things, who needed to buy eggs and get home — catch up. She lowered herself clumsily to the ground and fumbled with the chinstrap of her helmet. She unzipped the jacket partway but didn't dare take it off.

A cowbell rang as they entered the small, cramped shop, which was unnaturally warm and smelled like tobacco and root vegetables. Passing by the front counter, Adam plucked two strings of red licorice from a plastic cylinder and handed one to Clare. The grocer, perched on a high stool, reading *La Presse*, took note over the rims of his glasses.

"I really like these little shops," Adam said through a mouthful of licorice. He was moving slowly down the canned goods aisle, his helmet dangling from one hand. "You get the feeling they know most of their customers. Everything's small scale. You don't get that at the Provigo."

Clare said, "Mmm, you're right" and wondered how he came up with such things. Clever, engaging things to keep the conversation going. It seemed so effortless for him — for most people, actually — that she wondered if she herself were missing some necessary hormone or gene. It wasn't that she didn't have ideas. Sometimes, as now, they even came to her right away. The words *indifferent service* and *generic atmosphere* were in her head, needing only the most rudimentary grammar to be transmitted. But as she imagined those words irretrievably leaving her mouth, the pathway between her brain and her vocal cords seized up. She took a bite of licorice and hugged the motorcycle helmet.

Near the end of the aisle, just above her head, she spotted a tin of Érablière Bélanger maple syrup and took it down.

"Aren't they the same Bélangers that live up the street?" she said. Pointless, but better than nothing.

Adam glanced at the tin. "I'm not sure. I don't really know them." He then looked at Clare, frowning, and waved the stub of his licorice in her direction. "You know, there's something I've been thinking."

She replaced the maple syrup and hugged the helmet tighter. She imagined what he was going to say: that he'd had enough of her boring contributions, and could she please, for God's sake, say something *interesting*.

"What's that?" She held her breath.

Adam hoisted his helmet and wrapped his arms loosely around it. "It's about our street, sort of. I was thinking — I've been living there almost twenty-five years now, and you know, I don't know a damn thing about any of my neighbours? Nothing important, anyway. It's pathetic." He paused, still frowning. "I'm kind of a hypocrite. I complain about how impersonal modern society is, but I don't do anything about it."

Clare exhaled. "I know what you mean. I mean, not that you're a — I meant myself." Her cheeks flushed. "Sorry, I didn't —"

"No, no. It's okay. I know what you're saying. I think we're thinking the same thing."

She was certain they weren't, but she returned his smile and let him go on.

"It's sort of the reason I offered you a ride. I know I've seen you a couple of times at the train station, and we've talked about the weather and stuff, but ... well ... you know."

She nodded. By tiny increments, the awkwardness was once again abating.

"So ..." Adam rocked back on his heels. "Obviously I don't expect you to divulge your whole life story on a trip to the grocery store. You don't have to tell me anything, obviously. We could just ... Let's see. We could ..." He looked around. "We could talk about maple syrup. Or I could lecture you on post-colonialism. Or tell you about my brother's involvement with the CIA." He shook his head. "No, wait a minute. I'm not supposed to talk about that."

Clare laughed. "What's your brother really doing?"

"Rudy? He went back to Sri Lanka. He got a teaching job at some snooty private school in Colombo."

Sri Lanka, she repeated to herself. *Near India?* There were political troubles of some sort there, but that was all she knew. They carried on to the dairy case at the back of the store.

"It must be a different life there," she said, and hoped the remark wasn't entirely banal.

"Yeah, I'm sure it is. I've never actually been ... but I've always wanted to. I think it would be a pretty intense experience, reconnecting with the roots. But you know how it is. Other things get in the way." He paused. "I need to go, though. You need to know where you come from to really figure out who you are. Know what I mean?"

Clare looked past Adam and nodded mechanically. She thought of her own family holiday to Stanwick, the town where her parents grew up. She'd been ten at the time, afflicted with early menstruation and monstrous awkwardness. They'd stayed with Aunty Jean, and in Clare's mind the cold, ugly flat and its gossipy occupant came to represent the whole of Scotland. She couldn't agree with Adam, not at all. Figuring out who she was, if there was anything left to figure out, surely had more to do with getting away from her roots than with reconnecting. But she couldn't explain this.

"Why did your family leave Sri Lanka?" she said.

Adam placed his helmet on the dirt-streaked linoleum floor and stuffed his hands in his pockets.

"Well, my dad will tell you they left because of the political strife."

The front door cowbell rang, and a man with a booming voice struck up a conversation with the grocer.

Adam rested one foot on his helmet. "That's what my father *says*, but I don't know." He lowered his own voice. "I think he wanted to escape Sri Lanka all right, but I don't think it was anything political that motivated him. He actually gets off on political crisis."

"Really?"

"Oh yeah. You remember referendum day, back in October? When all the Anglos around here were crapping themselves, thinking the country was falling apart?"

Clare nodded. She herself had spent the day considering the possibility of Quebec sovereignty giving her a legitimate reason for going to Vancouver.

"Well, you should've seen my dad. He was happy as Larry, sitting in front of the TV, watching the results seesaw back and forth. You would've thought he was watching a big cricket final." The cowbell rang again. Adam frowned. "God, I hope I'm not boring you. I was wanting to get to know *you* better, and here I am doing all the talking."

Clare shook her head. If she'd been the type of person to say such a thing, she would have told her neighbour that he was perhaps the most interesting person she'd ever spoken with.

"No, no. It's fine. I mean, it's really interesting. So, what do you think was the real reason your father wanted to leave?"

"Well ..." Adam jutted his jaw back and forth a few times. "I think it was something about Sri Lanka. You know, something older than the war, or more specific or something." He nodded to himself. "Take his choice to come to Montreal — instead of Toronto, I mean. My dad knew lots of people in Toronto who would've helped him get settled, but he refused to go there. My aunt says he wouldn't hear of it. Instead he comes here, where you're about as likely to find a Sri Lankan as — Well, how many Sri Lankans do you see around here?"

"Uh ..."

"Exactly. And when he filled out the immigration papers? He changed the spelling of our name. It used to be two words: Van — Twest. Now it's just one." Adam bent down and picked up his helmet. "I know those are just details, but I think they mean something."

Taking the helmet to be a cue, Clare opened the dairy case and reached for a carton of eggs. But Adam kept talking.

"My father grew up on a tea estate."

"Really?"

"Yeah. His father was the head honcho. I think they were quite well off, by Ceylon standards. Anyway, his sister — my aunt — always tells these fantastic stories, about the fancy parties they went to, the workings of the factory, the servants. It's great. But if I ask my dad about those days, he just gets edgy and strange." Adam reached out and took the eggs from Clare. "My guess is he was getting as far away as he could from that whole scene. Not that the political stuff was irrelevant. He really worries about my brother and my aunt. He worries about all of us." He shrugged and smiled. "It's kinda stuffy in here. Should we get going?"

Digesting this sudden glut of information, Clare followed Adam to the checkout, where he placed the eggs on the counter then took out his wallet.

"Et les deux réglisses aussi," he said to the grocer, in perfectly adequate French.

With a start, she realized he was about to pay for her eggs.

"Oh, no. Wait." She fished for her money.

Adam, however, shook his head. "No, let me. Next time Dad and I run out of eggs, I'll come over and get some from you. We can be real neighbours." He slid a twenty-dollar bill across the counter, and the wrinkled grocer stabbed a button on his cash register. Clare stared at the "Oui" sticker on the side of the register then glanced back at Adam, putting away his change, and smiled awkwardly.

Outside, the temperature had continued to rise, and the air smelled of springtime mud and thawing dog shit. As Adam helped her with her chinstrap, Clare studied the dark whiskers peeking out from his light brown cheeks and the flat, dark mole at the base of his throat.

"I'm thinking of moving to Vancouver," she blurted, pleased with the remark and the unexpected surge of confidence that prompted it.

Adam's eyes widened. "Wow! Big change!"

"Yeah. But I think I need it. It'll be good for me."

She readied herself to explain, somehow, *why* such a change would be good for her. Adam seemed, for a few seconds, to be considering what she'd said. Then he nodded.

"Yeah, I know what you mean. When I was in Vancouver for the Gay Games, I started thinking I could really make a life for myself out there. It's such a different scene." He put on his own helmet. "But I don't know. There's a lot keeping me here. What about your mom? You'd move that far away from her?"

It wasn't at all what she'd expected. It was possibly a criticism, though she wasn't sure.

"I haven't planned anything definite yet. It's just an idea."

"Yeah? Well, keep me posted."

They mounted the motorcycle. Adam advanced a few inches with his feet, then he looked back. "I thought I might take a ride up Mount Royal. Would you like to come?"

Clare stared down at the carton of eggs wedged between the two of them. "I need to get back," she said. "But thanks."

She regretted it, of course. Even before Adam dropped her off at the end of her driveway, she regretted her refusal, but there was no easy way to let him know she'd changed her mind. The parting didn't seem to be final, however. As she unzipped his jacket, he waved his hand dismissively. "Just hang on to it. I'll come by for it later," he said, smiling, then he sped away in the direction of the Boulevard.

∽

LYING IN BED THAT NIGHT, she tried to imagine Adam's eyes, but their colour had escaped her. She got up and raised the blind, and the bedroom flooded with the glare of the street lamp outside. It was past midnight, and it seemed that in the dead of night, winter had returned to Morgan Hill Road. "Like a patient etherized upon a table," Clare recited, though she couldn't remember where the line came from. Across the street, the Vantwests' house was dark. Adam hadn't been by yet for the jacket. It hung in Clare's closet, secret and exotic as the vibrator.

Wrapped in her bathrobe, she went to the studio and picked up the phone. She'd been trying Emma's number all evening, getting the answering machine every time. She'd wanted to tell her about the ride, but strangely the desire was waning. She sat on the loveseat with the receiver in her hand until the disconnect signal struck up its panicky alarm, then she hung up. Falling asleep was out of the question, so she crept downstairs, the sound of her steps muffled by the steady respirator-drone of the furnace. She went to the den and turned on the light.

Her father's presence here was unmistakable, especially at night. Clare remembered waking regularly as a child to the squeal of the swivel chair, the click of the desk lamp. She didn't know what her father did in his den in the middle of the night — it never occurred to her to find out — but she imagined that he just sat, and that in those moments of quiet sitting, he was more himself than at any other time.

From a crammed collection of buckled hardcover volumes on the bookshelf, she extracted Alastair's atlas. The dried glue of the spine

72

crackled when she opened it. Its pages were lumped together in musty parcels, weathered along their edges, though surprisingly unblemished inside. She turned first to the map of Canada at the front and eyed the distance from Montreal to Vancouver. It was at once too far and not far enough. Searching for her next target, she discovered that the book opened quite naturally to page seventy-two, where, next to the pale pink triangle of India, she found Ceylon. It was a tiny green drop, marked only with the capital city, Colombo, and a few other places. She pictured Rudy Vantwest lecturing to a group of uniformed students in a classroom furnished with teak desks and leather-bound books. Then she looked around at the furnishings of her father's den — Time-Life books, wall-to-wall carpeting, functional shelves. In this room, her ride on Adam's motorcycle seemed as distant and unreal as the country represented by that tiny green mark on page seventy-two. As irretrievable as the colour of Adam's eyes.

4

Rudy sat at his grandfather's desk with a stack of essays and his brother's letter. The essays, barring Kanda's, were tedious. Adam's letter needed a response, but he'd been stalling, grateful that the post office wouldn't be open for another couple of days. With a determined breath, he slid the thing out of its crumpled envelope and opened it for the hundredth time. It was written in red ink, in a large, loopy script.

Hey there Rudy,
Happy Easter big brother! What will you and Aunty be getting up to for the holiday? One thing I can say for sure is you'll be eating better than us! As Susie and I discovered at Christmas, we don't have a freakin' clue what we're doing when it comes to Sri Lankan culinary delights. Susie's pretty ho-hum about it all anyway. I hate to be the bearer of bad news, but she and Mark seem to be on the outs again. Yep. Rumour has it he'll be staying in Toronto for Easter, I think this may be the end of it. But anyway, S. and Z. are supposed to be here Friday night. It should cheer Dad up. Things between me and him have been up and down as usual. I

wonder sometimes if I should get a place of my own or maybe even get out of Montreal altogether. Sometimes I think it'd be best for me and Dad both, but as a professional student it's hard to give up the perks while I'm still working on my thesis. (Don't worry, I won't bore you with any more details on that front right now, although I have to say that Dad has developed quite a surprising interest in the post-colonial politics of Ceylon!) Anyway, my financial woes aren't the real issue re. moving out. The big thing is I wouldn't want Dad thinking I've abandoned him. He hates my "lifestyle" as he calls it, but he loves me. I don't mean this in a nasty way but I think Dad loves me most, in a way. Just the circumstances, you know. And despite everything, I love him. Me staying here with him and him not kicking me out is the way it gets acknowledged I guess. But I tell ya, it's murder sometimes. He's on this thing now where he tells me that if there's anything he did wrong in the past, could I just forgive him and try to get my life on track. Meaning: "convert" (or at least pretend I'm straight), finish the damn thesis, and get a real job. He gets almost choked up, and I feel so helpless. Sometimes I really do wish I could change for him but it's not gonna happen. And you know, even if it would have been possible for Dad to somehow influence the way I'd "turn out," it wouldn't have made any difference. The way I am has nothing to do with Dad. I'm the way I am because of Mum. I'm sure of it, Rudy. When she died, I became two people, her and me. It's the reason I feel so connected to her homeland, even though I've never been there, and it's the reason I have this feminine spirit I can't deny, not even for Dad. I assume other people are born gay or bi because of their genes, but it's different with me. It's like my body has two souls. Anyway Rudy, I hope you won't think I'm turning into some kind of wing-nut. I know my explanation would sound flaky to most people, but it makes perfect sense to me. I just wanted someone to know these things, and you being so far away makes it a bit easier, if you know what I mean. (Can you

imagine me trying to tell Dad that my queerness is a tribute to Mum?!?) Anyhow, sorry for getting deep on you. You and Aunty have a happy Easter, okay? Ciao, machan.
Adam
P.S. Write to Susie if you get a chance. She's pretty down in the dumps.
P.P.S. I love you.

He wished, in a twisted sort of way, that the letter had been what he'd expected. A resentful clearing of the air would have been easier. He would have understood his part and played it out dutifully. But this letter complicated everything. In a way it was more accusing than the one he'd anticipated. *I hold no grudges,* he imagined his brother thinking. *What's your problem?*

He wished he knew.

With another determined breath, he took a sheet of paper from the desk drawer and wrote quickly.

Dear Adam,
Thanks for your letter. I appreciate it. I know you're busy with the thesis and all, but what would you say to coming to S.L. for a visit? You must have research to do in this part of the world, no? It'll be my treat. Don't worry, my expenses here have been ridiculously low. (Although I've decided, just now actually, to find a place of my own over the Easter holiday.) We'll talk, okay?
Say hi to everyone for me.
Rudy
P.S. If you come soon, we can climb your peak before the season ends.

It seemed the right thing to do. He folded both letters, eyed the pile of unmarked essays wearily, then went to his room for his diary.

March 28, Saturday. Hey, Clare. So what are *you* getting up to this weekend? I like to imagine you reading, curled up in one of those window benches with a bunch of ruffly cushions and a cup of tea. I know, I'm sorry. You're probably out socializing with your friends, or painting Easter eggs with your kids. Me? Slouching around as usual. Listen, Clare, you wouldn't happen to know what went wrong between my brother and me, would you? Anything you noticed from over there on your side of the street? I keep trying to remember a certain summer day when I tried to be a decent big brother and fucked up completely. Adam and I built something out of stones, and I think I got pissed off or impatient or something and destroyed whatever it was we made (maybe even worse). I don't think that day was the cause of our lousy relationship, but it seems characteristic somehow. Anyway, I've invited Adam out here for a visit. Don't worry; I have no delusions that I'm going to make up for all the past problems and suddenly have a cozy, brotherly thing going with him. I really can't imagine what being with him would be like at all. We're almost strangers. I have an easier time imagining you coming out here to visit. But we'll see. God, Clare, what the hell happened to that feeling I had when I found out Mum was pregnant? I don't know. I may chicken out of inviting him. I *will* start looking for my own place and set-ting up my own life, though. It's about time, don't you think?

He closed the book and drummed its black cover with his fingers. He wondered what had become of his grandfather's diary, the one Grandpa had read from on the day of the big news. It had to be around somewhere still; Aunty had held on to junk of a much less sen-timental nature than that. But then again, if Dad had gotten his hands on it when he came back to settle Grandpa's affairs ...

Rudy went out to the front garden, where his aunt was hanging clothes on the line. He spotted a pair of his boxer shorts in the laun-dry basket and reached down to pluck them out.

"Hey, Aunty?" he said, pinning the shorts to the line. "Do you remember that diary Grandpa used to keep?"

Aunty Mary frowned, then nodded. "Yes, yes. He used to write in it about the plantation goings-on and whatnot, isn't it."

"That's the one." He took a T-shirt from the basket. "Any idea where it is?"

Again Aunty Mary paused. He thought she was trying to remember where the diary might be, but her answer suggested something else.

"Why do you ask, son?"

It was a fair enough question, though an odd one, coming from Aunty.

"I was just thinking about an entry he read out to me when I was little, and I thought I'd try to find it. About Adam's Peak."

"You want to read the diary?"

"Well ... yeah. If you have it. If it's okay." He suspected he'd intruded in some way — asked for a privilege he hadn't earned. But the idea that his grandfather might have written things that Aunty wanted to hide made him all the more curious.

Aunty nudged the laundry basket along with her foot then ran the back of her wrist across her forehead. "Let me finish this," she said, "then I'll find it."

Of the four books she found — for Grandpa had filled up that many volumes — the one Rudy remembered was a lot like his own. A little thicker and heavier — nevertheless, he half expected to open it up and see his own handwriting. At the same time, the book was secret and unsettling. The last time he'd seen it he'd been six years old. It had been with him in Grandpa's study, and it no doubt remembered the day perfectly. *I know who you are better than you do*, the diary seemed to say.

Perched on the edge of his aunt's bed, he opened the book somewhere near the middle. The writing looked to be done with a fountain pen, and in the script there was a preponderance of straight, almost vertical lines. Most of the entries were short — a telegraphic date, followed by three or four sentences of what Aunty had called plantation goings-on: yields, shipments, weather conditions, meetings with the assistant manager or the factory manager. Flipping the pages, however, Rudy noticed that a few of the entries went on a bit longer.

"It's what you were looking for?" Aunty said.

"This is it. Do you mind if I hang on to it for a few days?"

His aunt's manner had given the impression she was reluctant to hand over the diary at all, but to Rudy's surprise she said, "You keep it, son. Keep all of them. You seem to have an interest in this journal writing, isn't it. Best that they go to you." Then she shut the drawer the books had come from and dusted her palms, as if, having gone this far, she now wanted nothing more to do with the matter.

Rudy thanked her, then he took the diaries outside, to the bench under the jack fruit tree, which the sun hadn't yet reached. Selecting the black-covered diary that most interested him, he sat down and began his search. He found the entry quickly enough, and for a moment he simply stared at the fact of the date.

"Nineteen-forty-four," he whispered. "Shit. The war was still on."

And yet, it wasn't so much the date that moved him as the sudden jolt of connection to the six-year-old Rudy who'd first listened to the entry. With the strength of a long-lost smell, his grandfather's words yanked him back to the padded wooden chair in the study, the undersides of his thighs sticking to the cracked leather. He hadn't remembered anything very specific that his grandfather had said that day — just vague notions of the glory of the peak — but as he read, the words were magically familiar. So familiar that he imagined he would have noticed if any of them had been missing, or altered.

He read slowly, for the old man's writing wasn't easily legible, and when he got to the part that quoted James Emerson Tennent, he heard his grandfather's smoke-clawed voice reciting the audacious words of the colonial adventurer. Grandpa's own follow-up was just as audacious. Rudy read aloud, in concert with the voice in his head: "The greatness of the peak lies in our ability to conquer it, and in so doing, to conquer our own weaknesses. The view that Tennent describes is the reward we earn for attaining that goal. This is what I wanted Ernie to understand, but didn't I find the —" Here he stopped, just as his grandfather had. He backed up then read on silently.

This is what I wanted Ernie to understand, but didn't I find the bugger cavorting with a pair of village louts, the lot of them giggling and prattling away in Sinhalese like a mob of women at the market. I had a mind to swat some dignity into the boy but couldn't bear to draw any more attention to his behaviour. Can only be thankful the peak was overrun with ignorant villagers. Took a photo of Ernie and Jayasuriya under the bell, then made haste back down. In retrospect, Alec might have been the better companion after all.

Rudy's impulse to laugh at the silliness of the passage was tempered only by the fact that this old conflict was still simmering between his own father and brother. He liked to think Dad was a little less obnoxious than Grandpa, a little more tolerant — the Christmas of Zoë's accident had, after all, been the worst of it — but then Dad was from a slightly more tolerant generation. Rudy reread the passage. Unwittingly, his grandfather had given him the most interesting account of Uncle Ernie he'd ever had. He left the Adam's Peak entry to flip through the rest of the book, scanning its pages for other references to his uncle. He found nothing, however — scarcely a mention of Ernie's name. With the exception of brief, uninspired descriptions of holiday lunches, visitors from Colombo, occasional excursions to Kandy, the rest of the book was devoted to the daily business of the tea factory. It was a diary as removed from desires and opinions as Rudy's was steeped in them.

The next book, dated later than the first, contained more of the same. Rudy skimmed then stopped reading altogether. His shade was gone, and he was sweating. As a final gesture of interest, he flipped open the covers of the other diaries to check the dates. Tucked inside the front of one of these was a small envelope bearing Aunty Mary's name and address. Rudy glanced around the garden then lifted the envelope's flap and removed the sheet of notepaper inside.

Dear Mary,
Thank you for the opportunity to look at these. I'm sending them back with Simon and Louise. They're good chaps. You'll give them lunch, or tea, won't you?
Kind regards, Ernie.

Rudy slapped a mosquito that had been gorging itself, unnoticed, on his forearm.

The letter wasn't dated. But even if Uncle Ernie had borrowed the diaries right after Grandpa's death, it would mean the note was no more than ten years old. It would mean that Aunty Mary had been in contact with her brother long after he was said to have abandoned the family. And she'd kept it a secret — from Rudy anyway. He smiled at this secrecy. It gave him a thrill much like the one he'd gotten as a kid from the dual identities of Clark Kent and Peter Parker. And then there was Uncle Ernie — a real person. Someone with the quirk of calling a woman a "chap," with the cockiness to give his sister orders.

Rudy sat on the bench, contemplating how to ask his aunt about Uncle Ernie — wondering whether or not, and if so, how, to confess that he'd read the note — when it occurred to him, quite plainly, that Aunty had left Ernie's note in the diary on purpose. Recalling their conversation at the laundry line, he was sure of it. The note had been the source of her hesitation. She'd considered taking it out, he guessed, but by the time she promised to find the diaries, she'd decided to reveal all. Before he could convince himself otherwise, he went to the kitchen and leaned across the counter, where his aunt was chopping.

"Aunty, what ever happened to your brother Ernie?"

He braced himself for a repetition of the timeworn answer — Uncle Ernie left home as a young man, and we hardly heard from him again — but the moment his aunt looked up, he could tell she'd prepared something different. She set down her knife, pressed her lips together, and patted her hair.

"He is living near Kandy," she said.

Less than a day's drive away. He straightened up.

"Are you in contact with him?"

"We speak occasionally. He was in England for many years, but he retired and came home. He's an old man now." She spoke matter-of-factly, like a witness giving testimony.

"What was he doing in England?"

"He lived near London. He was a teacher."

Rudy frowned. "Uncle Ernie was a teacher? Why didn't you ever tell me?"

This, he knew, was an unfair question. Aunty hadn't told him anything at all about her brother; she'd obviously had her reasons. But the secrecy surrounding this now-real uncle was beginning to lose its appeal. Aunty said nothing, so he carried on.

"Does he ever come to Colombo? Why don't we see him?"

His aunt's expression left no doubt that the answers to such questions were difficult. Finally, she replied: "Ernie keeps to himself. He prefers it that way."

A new image, of Uncle Ernie as a bitter old man, wilfully estranged from his family, began to take shape. And, with it, Rudy's interest grew. "What would he think of me calling him up?" he said. His question surprised even himself. He'd never entertained more than a shred of interest in Uncle Ernie. Now, suddenly, he was thinking of calling the man, maybe even visiting him. The possibility that the visit might be resisted made the idea strangely more compelling.

Aunty wiped her hands on her apron. "I don't know what he would think, son. He believes that after so much time it's better to keep things the way they are. I don't agree with him, but those are his wishes."

Rudy raised one eyebrow in a manner he knew to be challenging. "Why are you telling me about him then?"

"Ah, well. I'm not young anymore. Someone needs to know about Ernie. Where he is living, who his neighbours are. I've written some of this information in the address book. Just in case." She resumed her chopping. "I've asked him many times to visit since you've been here, but Ernie is very shy. He likes to hear about the family from me." She shrugged. "What to do?"

Rudy recalled his grandfather's words. *Cavorting with village louts, giggling, prattling . . .* If Uncle Ernie had become shy in his old age, he certainly hadn't been that way as a young man. More likely, Aunty Mary was guilty of couching the prickly truth about her brother in comfortable language. Risking awkwardness, he pressed on.

"Why exactly did Ernie leave home, Aunty?"

This, clearly, was the most difficult question yet.

"Ah, son, it was a long time ago. I don't remember —"

"Sure you do." He made his voice patient, coaxing.

"Ernie was just ... a different chap," she finally said. "He didn't suit the planting life the way our father wanted him to. He was very artistic, but Dada had different plans for him. He wanted Ernie to be like him. Like all fathers, no?"

Once again, the story began to sound familiar. Rudy gave up. He didn't really need his aunt's version of the details — and Aunty, for her part, was clearly unwilling to give them.

"That painting of Adam's Peak was done by Ernie," she said after a pause. "He is very talented."

Up the lane a dog barked. Rudy wove plans in his head. Monday, he'd start looking for a place of his own — an apartment, closer to the city, or maybe a small house. Now that the decision was made, he was impatient to get started, to make up for lost time. He'd spend his evenings and weekends furnishing the place and settling in. Then, he would buy Adam's plane ticket. Adam wouldn't waffle; he was too impulsive. They would make their pilgrimage to the peak just before the season ended. And after the climb, they would go to Kandy.

"You'll come to Easter Mass tomorrow?" Aunty said.

Rudy locked his fingers and stretched his arms out in front of him. He imagined the crowds and the suffocating heat and sighed quietly. "Sure."

March 28, later. I don't really buy my aunt's line about all fathers wanting their sons to be like them. I mean, in a sense it's true, but I think it's the wrong angle. I think what parents care about is not exactly that their kids be like them, but simply that their kids *like* them, as people. But they're afraid to ask outright, so they go looking for clues. If the son or daughter seems to go for the same sorts of things as they do, it means they have common interests. It means that if the parent and the kid weren't tied by blood, and they happened to cross paths somehow anyway, they'd still have a relationship of some kind. My dad knows Adam loves him. I'm sure of that. But it's not enough for him. Instead of appreciating the fact that Adam (unlike yours truly) would do anything for him, drop anything and come running, just because he's family … instead of being goddamn thankful for that, he appreciates *me*. He sees my sensible career, my conservative clothes, my girlfriends, even my decision to come back here, and he thinks, "I don't need to feel guilty about him. He's the sort of fellow I could be friends with. He could be part of my life even if he weren't my son." And you know what? I understand him.

Somehow the afternoon had slipped away. He imagined Clare Fraser watching him as he wrote to her, repulsed perhaps by his laziness — his podge of belly and his unwashed hair, his Led Zeppelin T-shirt and ratty old Adidas shorts. Apart from wallowing in the past and writing letters to strangers, he'd done nothing. He was planted on his bed in the breeze of the fan, staring at the blue walls and sinking deeper and deeper into the underworld of his own thoughts. On the other hand, he'd made a decision. He'd uprooted himself from his aunt's house, and he was an afternoon closer to establishing himself the way he had intended. Perhaps Clare would understand the significance of this. Perhaps she'd allow him a day of laziness.

He slumped lower, letting his diary slide to the mattress. He imagined the moment he would spot Adam through the security gate at the airport — the strange awkwardness of sensing that the only thing connecting them at that moment would be blood. Not nearly as thick as it was rumoured to be, he feared.

He wasn't sure how long he'd been holding that moment, frozen, in his mind, when the telephone rang. Startled, he swung his legs off the bed then stopped as he heard Aunty Mary cross the living room. Her "Hello" was followed by a longish silence, and he knew somehow that the call was long-distance. Waiting for his aunt to speak again, he convinced himself it was Adam, fatefully in tune with his plan.

5

OVER THE PHONE, long-distance, Emma never seemed quite herself. Or maybe, Clare thought, it was that she seemed more completely herself — separated from Morgan Hill Road and its patterns, living her busy, independent Vancouver life. On the topic of Clare's
motorcycle ride with Adam Vantwest, she said all the right things, but
there was something in her tone, a hint of distraction, that suggested
it was no big deal.

"He's gay, right?" she said.

"I think so. Yeah."

"Too bad."

"It doesn't matter, Emma. He's way too young. And besides,
he's ..."

"What?"

"I don't know. Kind of ... impulsive, or something. But anyway,
it's irrelevant."

"Impulsive is exactly what you need."

"Emma."

"Okay, okay. So did you find the present I got you? I hid it in your
suitcase."

Clare, slouched on the loveseat in the studio, shut her eyes and rubbed her forehead. "I did. Sorry, I forgot to thank you. But you shouldn't have spent so much."

"Oh pshaw. Have you tried it yet?"

"Not yet." She straightened up and eyed the clock on the piano. It was late afternoon. More than a day had passed, but Adam hadn't yet come by for his jacket. "Listen — I'd better get going," she said. "Markus and I are going to a movie."

This was a lie. She rarely socialized with her boss anymore. His feelings had gotten in the way. Increasingly, over the year they'd been working together, she understood the ambiguities in his behaviour — the pauses, the hesitations, the incomplete gestures — to be signs of an unspeakable desire, *for her*, and the idea sat like a lump inside her, embarrassing and irritating. Reason told her that Markus was the kind of partner she was fated to be with — respectful, conservative, neither attractive nor ugly. A decent human being. But if Markus was fate's choice for her, she was determined to put up some resistance.

"Tell him you're quitting," Emma said. "Do it, Clare! I've already got a couple of possibilities lined up for you."

"Maybe. I'll see what kind of a mood he's in."

"What difference — Oh, shoot, I've got another call. Okay. Let me know. I'll talk to you later."

Emma didn't believe she'd leave her job; Clare could tell. She wasn't convinced herself. But as she hung up the phone, she forced herself to make a plan. Monday was the next time she would see Markus, the earliest opportunity. She would arrive a few minutes before her shift. Markus would be hanging around, maybe talking to Peter, the new part-timer who played in a band and had a pierced tongue. She would take him aside — not to his office, if she could help it — and she'd inform him, quietly and matter-of-factly, that she would be leaving. *This has been a really great job*, she would say, *but I'm moving to Vancouver.* Straightforward. And if she committed herself that far …

She took her hand off the phone and ran it through her hair, realizing she'd ended the call without telling Emma she'd become a brunette. It was a compromise: she'd chickened out of riding up Mount Royal with Adam, but she'd coloured her hair — an operation carried out secretly in the bathroom, with flimsy plastic gloves and a foul-smelling concoction she'd picked up at the drugstore. The colour was called "chestnut," and the results were surprising. Each time she passed a mirror, the strangeness of her reflection gave her a jolt of pleasure. In appearance at least, she'd tweaked the pattern, even if it was just a disguise. She imagined Adam showing up for his jacket and assuming she was the kind of person who did this sort of thing regularly.

But he hadn't shown up yet. Outside, it was already dark. Clare went to the window, as she had countless times already that day, to look for him. She didn't want to be caught off guard — the leather jacket was draped over the back of the loveseat, ready to be grabbed. More importantly, she didn't want her mother to answer the door, though at that particular moment it would have been impossible to get there before her. Isobel was in the living room, supervising the taking of measurements for the new carpeting. If anyone came to the door, she'd be right there. But as far as Clare could see, there was no one home at the Vantwests'.

She sat down at the piano and thunked a few chords. They sounded like the ash-blond Clare, so she tried again. Her right hand wandered about in B flat — darkly, chestnutly. Black, cologne-scented leather music. Her left was slow and sparse. She imagined the Jazz Studies Director sitting on her loveseat, his eyes half closed, bobbing his chin and saying there was an unusual something ... a certain, oh, tensile introspection to her delivery ... an implicitness in the voicings. It was the sort of thing a jazz person such as he would say. And secretly she'd find the comment silly and pretentious.

She stopped playing, pushed the stool back, and spun around lazily. When she'd passed Adam's jacket four or five times, she braked and changed direction. This time, she went faster. She leaned her head back and turned the studio upside down. As she whirled, the geography of the room — the window, the wall of books, the loveseat, the piano — became an unfamiliar jumble. She closed her eyes until the stool reached its lowest point and stopped. When she looked again, she was facing the window.

What if it doesn't work, Emma?
What if what doesn't work?

Going to Vancouver. I'll still be the same person, won't I?

That's up to you. If you're expecting the change of scenery to do it all for you, then no, it won't work.

But I can't stay here.

No. For God's sake, no. You're stuck in a perpetual adolescence there. It's pathetic.

She stood up and approached Adam's jacket, cautiously, as if it were Adam himself. He wouldn't be coming for it that evening. It was Saturday; he'd be out. She picked it up and slid her bare arms into the satiny sleeves. The fit was a little loose, but more intimate than before. She put her hands in the pockets. Then she crossed the studio to her bedroom, to the full-length mirror inside the closet door. The reflection she saw was astonishing. She'd known, the first time she wore Adam's jacket, that she looked different. But the person in the mirror was a stranger. She pulled off her headband and shook out her dark brown hair.

My God, Clare. Look at yourself. You're gorgeous.

She stared hard at her reflection.

But is it me, Emma? Could this ever be me?

She stood forever in front of the mirror, experimenting with infinite minute adjustments to her posture and clothes, shutting out the ivory walls, the almond duvet, the tidy beigeness of the whole room. Eventually, her gaze drifted from the mirror to the top shelf of the closet, the pile of sweaters that concealed Emma's gift. It needed to be thrown out, before her mother found it. She slid her hand under the bottom sweater and took down the over-wrapped parcel. Thief-like, she hid it inside Adam's jacket, then she locked the bedroom door. She pulled down the blind and turned on the stereo. Co-op Radio was playing something foreign — twangy, percussive, unpredictable. Sitting cross-legged on the bed, she unrolled the T-shirt then the tissue paper. The orange vibrator plopped onto the duvet, lolled there unabashedly, demanding her attention with its suggestive shape and unnatural colour. She picked it up and weighed the dense rubber in her palm, then she put it down again.

How do you expect me to have sex with a piece of plastic, Emma?

You're not having it with the vibrator. It's like I told you in the shop.

Tell me again.

You're having it with yourself. Or whomever. Use your imagination.

Like who? And don't say Markus.

I don't know. The motorcycle guy. Adam.

He's gay.

So what? You were attracted to him, weren't you?

She hugged her knees to her chest. The feeling *was* there, she supposed — the muffled twitching, the reaching for something unimaginable. They happened so rarely, these sensations, that when they did, she didn't know what to do with them. Emma talked about masturbation as if everyone did it, like breathing. But to Clare it seemed wrong. Not morally wrong, but wrong nonetheless. Pathetic, she guessed. It was something she couldn't explain to Emma. Or, rather, it was a secret she'd managed to keep from Emma: that even to herself, she was a virgin. Emma seemed incapable of imagining such a thing. She spoke of clitoral orgasms and G-spot orgasms, of getting herself off on Jacuzzi jets, as if any woman would understand exactly what she was talking about. As if *Clare* would understand. But Clare, listening quietly, nodding meaningfully, had pulled one over on her.

Once again she picked up the orange device. She leaned back against her pillows, and held the thing at eye level, between her index fingers. It was no more absurd, really, than an attraction to Adam. No more pathetic.

Tell me this, Emma: can't a person be happy, or fulfilled, or whatever you want to call it, without sex?

I suppose so, in theory. But I don't think that's you. I think you're afraid of it. Dealing with other people scares the hell out of you, and sex is the ultimate case of dealing with the Other.

Then isn't this thing just another way of not dealing with real people?

She wanted Emma to be stumped here, but it wouldn't be right. She pushed on.

The vibrator's different. It's not replacing sex with other people; it's helping you get in touch with yourself. Anyway, in your case, I think it's a prerequisite.

For what, Emma? There's a reasonably good chance I'm not ever going to have sex with anyone. Why can't I just forget it?

Oh, Clare. You've been obsessing over Adam Vantwest all day. And it isn't his charm or his intellect you're stuck on. Come on. You know what you've been thinking. His eyes ... what he'd be wearing when he came to get his jacket ...

And? Keep going. Those other things. The ones you try to ignore.

Oh God, Emma.

Think of the motorcycle ride. This is no different.

She switched on the vibrator and it trembled, its thrum nearly lost in the cryptic music coming from the stereo. She pictured the narrow, snaking alleyways of an Egyptian market. She'd never been to such a place, of course, but Emma had.

The motorcycle, Clare.

With glacial slowness, she undid her jeans. She placed the thrumming vibrator on her belly and wrapped Adam's jacket around it. Then she sat very still, staring at the triangle of space marked by the foot of her bed and the two speakers mounted at either end of the facing wall — the space occupied by the strange music. She closed her eyes and sank down, her destination still unimaginable. She was a groping foreigner, ignorant of the language.

It's too weird, Emma. I can hardly imagine myself as someone who has regular sex. How can I turn this thing into sex with Adam Vantwest?

Imagine it. You imagine other people all the time, Clare, but your idea of yourself is so narrow. Imagine touching him. Imagine him touching you. What do you want him to do? Figure it out.

She eyed the lamp on the bedside table.

Turn it off, said a new voice. It was Adam, even closer than Emma.

She switched off the light.

That's better. I'm here now.

And he was. His voice, in her head, was perfect; the green-brown eyes that had eluded her the night before came back to her in the darkness of her bedroom, beautiful and arresting. A reassurance ... but not entirely. For she'd hoped he would remain real to her. That he would come to her door for his jacket and challenge her again with his existence, give her another chance. Instead, here he was, part of her secret, pathetic inner world, offering to be whatever she wanted him to be.

You see, Emma. This is wrong. This isn't Adam.

Her argument was halfhearted. She opened her eyes and stared across the room at the stereo's green lights. The song was new, perhaps. A little slower, a breathy arrangement of tones, more than sharps, not quite flats, from which a graspable melody began to emerge. She slid the vibrator past the elastic of her underwear, between her thighs. In almost imperceptible rotations, she moved it. The wetness was mortifying — not just the sudden, slimy abundance of it, but the very word itself. It was one of those innocents, like *come*, that Emma's sex talk had destroyed. But her squeamishness gave way to other things. The vibrations were electric. The contact between the smooth plastic and that nub of her flesh she knew only by name radiated sizzles of sensation, like a birthday sparkler or a stick of cartoon dynamite. She was aware of the music, fluty and languorous, directing the motions of her hand, and she was aware of the moment at which her hand accelerated and left the music behind. But beyond these flimsy feats of consciousness, her body was shockingly in control — all screaming nerves and urgency, now reaching desperately for that end it still couldn't imagine. She set the vibrator on the bed and wrestled her jeans partway down her thighs, anxious that in the pause the sensations should wane. Then she rolled over, on top of the plastic device whose sudden power was both fearsome and ridiculous. She moved frantically, impatiently, pressing down, searching. She hugged the pillow to her chest, tighter and tighter.

When at last it was done, the otherworldly destination reached — and left behind so quickly — she fell onto her back and lay in the darkness, breathing hard.

She kept the light off, refusing for the moment to face the scene she had created. She imagined her dishevelled hair, her screwed-up jeans and limp underwear, the orange vibrator, glistening like some vile sea creature. And surrounding all of this: the beige pattern of her regular life. She sat up, sliding her arms out of Adam's jacket, and pulled her T-shirt over her head. Still in darkness, she bunched the shirt around the vibrator and stuffed the awkward parcel under her pillow. She'd deal with it later. First she needed a shower, a blast of hot, plain water to douse the confusions of her body. She peeled off the rest of her clothes and crossed the room to the laundry hamper. But as she fastened her bathrobe around her waist, the doorbell rang.

"Adam," she whispered into the darkness. "Shit."

She lunged for the overhead light switch and the room flooded with an indifferent glare. She flicked off the stereo. The conversation at the front door was distant and muffled, but she expected to hear her mother's voice any second, calling her down. There was no time to get dressed, to look the way she would need to look, so she snatched the jacket from the bed and shook it out. She would hand it to Isobel, to give to Adam, and that would be the end of it.

Isobel's call didn't come, however. Clare pressed her ear to the bedroom door and strained to hear her mother, or Adam, but the voices downstairs were low, concerned only with each other. It occurred to her then that her mother was chatting with Adam — hearing his version of the outing to the depanneur and wondering aloud why her daughter hadn't mentioned it. Turning the whole transcendent experience into a worthless piece of neighbourly conversation. Clare hung the jacket on the doorknob and looked around for something to wear. The choice didn't matter anymore. She pulled on her gypsy skirt and a baggy sweater, combed her fingers through her hair, and opened the door, determined to complete the handing-back as quickly as possible.

From the top of the stairs she saw that the carpet installers were still at work. One man crouched on the landing, taking measurements, while another scribbled on a notepad. They blocked the front doorway. Behind them, Isobel's voice sounded peculiarly hushed, and Clare wondered what she and Adam could possibly be talking about, what sort of intimacy the two of them could be cultivating. She dug her toes into the pile of her father's doomed carpeting and clenched the leather jacket in her hands. When the installers retreated to the living room, she started down the stairs.

Halfway there, her grip on the jacket relaxed. The visitor at the door was Emma's mother — which made infinitely more sense, at this time on a Saturday evening. Sheepish and relieved, Clare headed back up the stairs. Then Mrs. Skinner called to her.

"Oh, Clare, I didn't notice you there."

Clare turned to see her neighbour cock her head in a manner that suggested she was assessing the new hair colour.

"Hi, Joanne."

"Have you heard the awful news?" Mrs. Skinner said brightly. "Your mother hadn't."

In her fluorescent yellow ski vest, Joanne Skinner looked like part of an emergency crew, and Clare indulged fleeting thoughts that an actual crisis was underway — a fire or a hostage-taking, perhaps a bomb scare. She tossed Adam's jacket up the stairs and once again descended. The awful news would be no more earth-shattering than a postal strike or a late snow storm. Still, whatever it was, something was *happening*, and Clare noted vaguely that the idea of this excited her.

"I haven't heard anything. What is it?"

Mrs. Skinner glanced over her shoulder, out the open door, and touched her fingertips to her platinum curls. Turning back, she sighed. "The youngest Vantwest boy was in a motorcycle accident. Yesterday. They're not sure if he's going to come through."

Clare gripped the railing. "Adam?"

Mrs. Skinner nodded. "He skidded and ran into a van, just up here on the Boulevard. I was just telling your mother it's a miracle he's alive at all. But as I was saying, the prognosis isn't very good at the moment." She delivered her script at a measured pace, with theatrical gravity.

Clare's skin flushed hot. She pushed aside the monstrous fact that she had refused Adam's offer to continue their ride together and glanced at her mother, who'd started to say something.

"And it was only just the other day you and I were talking about him. Don't you remember, pet? It was the evening you came home." Isobel sounded confused, as if her recent acknowledgment of Adam should somehow have prevented what happened.

"He's at the General," Mrs. Skinner said. She had stepped inside the vestibule, and her hand now rested on the back of the clothing bench. But the front door remained open, and the hall was cold. In the living room, the carpet men were packing up. They'd caught the gist of the conversation, it seemed, for they moved with an exaggerated silence, their faces expressionless. Clare turned back to her neighbour.

"How did you find out?"

Mrs. Skinner eyed her meaningfully, as if, having discovered an unexpected source of curiosity, she was now relishing the power of her knowledge. "I saw the daughter this morning, on her way out to the hospital. She's back home for Easter. She was taking her little girl to stay with friends of the family, and I hadn't seen the little one in so long, I thought I should pop over and find out how she was doing. She doesn't speak very well, but she chatters away in sign language." Mrs. Skinner's voice was briefly cheerful, then she turned solemnly to Isobel. "That poor family has certainly had its share of tragedy. The mother, the little girl ... now *this*. I offered to help out any way I could, but it sounds like they have people in their own community they'd rather go to."

Clare frowned. "What do you mean 'their own community'?"

"Oh, I mean other East Indians," Mrs. Skinner said, with a hint of authority. "I think they're quite close-knit."

Clare looked down at her left hand, clutching the railing. "They're not from India," she said. "They're Sri Lankan."

There followed an uncertain silence, during which her contradiction hung uselessly in the air.

"Well, it's a very similar part of the world," Isobel finally said. "Joanne only meant that they have friends who share their culture."

Mrs. Skinner nodded gravely. Clare gripped the railing tighter. It was outrageous that this news should come to her in this way. Almost as outrageous as the news itself.

"A motorcycle accident has nothing to do with culture, Ma," she said.

She wasn't sure what she meant, and she wished immediately that she'd kept her mouth shut. For it seemed to her just then, unaccountably, that through this outrageous conversation her mother and Mrs. Skinner would gain access to her private world. That eventually, but inevitably, they would be led not only to the motorcycle ride she and Adam had shared but also, if she wasn't careful, to the bright orange device hidden under her pillow.

"I don't understand what you mean, pet," Isobel said.

"Nothing. It doesn't matter."

At that moment, the carpet installers, who'd been hovering at the living room entrance, excused themselves and ducked between Clare and her mother. "We'll see you next week, then," one of them said in a low voice, and Isobel, in response, smiled a warm, ordinary smile.

While her mother confirmed dates and times with the man who'd spoken, Clare turned and fled back upstairs.

"Your hair looks very nice," Mrs. Skinner called after her.

She pretended not to hear. At the top of the stairs she picked up Adam's jacket then returned to her bedroom, locking the door behind her. She turned off the light and stood with the jacket draped over her arms, repeating to herself the bald facts: Adam had invited her to go for a ride on his motorcycle, and on that same ride he'd possibly killed himself. She knew the sorts of things she was supposed to feel. But her response was confused and inappropriate — lacking proper sympathy for Adam and his family, proper terror and relief at her own fate. She leaned back against the door, and as she adjusted to the dark she saw the state of her bed. She closed her eyes, but the images in her head were just as chaotic. Adam's motorcycle, crumpled at the edge of the Boulevard; Joanne Skinner's fluorescent vest; hissing respirators; thrumming vibrators. She crossed the room and raised the blind.

Down in the street, the carpet installers' van had just pulled away, and moments later Mrs. Skinner slipped through a gap in the hedge to her own yard. Across Morgan Hill Road, the Vantwests' house was dark. There was a strange car in the driveway, probably belonging to Adam's sister, whose name Clare couldn't remember. Just as she hadn't remembered the sister's daughter, or the fact that the little girl was deaf. Clutching Adam's jacket to her chest, she pressed her forehead against the windowpane and stared at his house — an ordinary Morgan Hill house, so flawlessly embedded in the pattern of its surroundings that the quirks of its inhabitants could be ignored, forgotten about. But maybe not forever, she allowed.

She rubbed the window where it had fogged over and looked down at the pine tree in her own front yard. With sudden clarity, she remembered the ashes that she and her mother had scattered — their astonishing quantity, blustering through the boughs. She remembered her mother's cryptic "Thank you" as the final wisps of white dust disappeared into the snow ... her own suffocating sense that those ashes were now inside of her. And she saw Isobel at the edge of the road, cradling the urn like a bag of groceries and chatting with Rudy Vantwest, as if they were regular neighbours.

"What could you possibly have been talking about?" she whispered.

Downstairs, her mother's heels tapped furiously across the kitchen floor.

97

MAY 1964

Isobel turned on her side and felt a fresh surge down below. She reached under the covers and adjusted the thick padding then curled her legs up, securing the hot water bottle against her stomach. She called it her *stomach*, though she knew that that particular organ wasn't to blame. Stomachs were bland, pink, docile creatures that went about their business unnoticed, provided one fed them properly. The real culprit, whose very name repelled her, she imagined as an angry, nettled mass of plummy red, writhing inside of her, tearing at her flesh. For a few weeks each month it would lie still, mustering its energy and its wrath like the God of the Old Testament. Then, sometimes early, sometimes late, never truant, it would spend itself in a four-day fury, and she would bleed a sea that crested vermilion with thick purple clots and receded a rusty brown. In moments of sublime pain, she often imagined excising the villain inside with her mother's carving knife — enduring a single apocalyptic ordeal in order to free herself from this cyclical torture. This time, however, she closed her eyes and concentrated on retracting her entire being into a tiny space at the very top of her head. She imagined the conscious, insubstantial *essence* of herself peeling back from tissue and blood and bone and gathering in that minuscule space close to the surface, from which it could then escape her body altogether, until the perverse punishment had passed.

She took herself to New York. She'd never been there physically, but with intense concentration she managed to transport her conscious essence to the block of Fifth Avenue featured on her cousin Archie's latest postcard. And there, amid the noise and towering buildings, with Central Park just in sight, she detached herself from her pain. It was still there, of course, still horrible and vindictive, but it wasn't part of *her*. They were separate. She stood a while outside the elegant windows of Saks Fifth Avenue, admiring the handbags and hats, then took herself, place by place, to the sights featured on the rest of Archie's postcards: Greenwich Village, Times Square, the Metropolitan Opera House. Archie had immigrated to America, and the short, scribbled cards he occasionally sent to the McGuigan family evoked a world so exciting and so *new* that Isobel had taken to fantasizing about it even when she felt fine. Over the past several months, in fact, New York, though an ocean away, had begun to cast increasingly dark shadows over the narrow, familiar streets of her town. Even on cloudless spring Sundays, when the Stanwick churchyards and high street were at their peak of colour and cheer, she saw shadows and wondered how folk managed to live entire lives in such a place. Her quiet despair was something no one else understood, not even Margaret, her closest friend. Though she suspected Patrick would, if she tried to explain it to him.

The thought of Patrick Locke brought with it a violent cramp, and Isobel, wrenched from New York, wondered if she were being particularly punished for her recent encounters with her father's apprentice. Just a few days before, she and Patrick had gone to the pond with a bottle of whisky, and she'd allowed him to thrust his hand up her blouse and inside her brassiere. He'd gone at it from underneath, stretching the band uncomfortably. Worse, though, was his tongue — thick and hot and invasive — plundering her mouth. Confused, awkwardly aroused, annoyed by both responses, she'd pulled away, and

Patrick had laughed. He'd pointed out that she was eighteen years old and asked her if she'd been living in a convent, in reply to which Isobel lit a cigarette and informed him that she'd be nineteen in a month.

She rolled onto her back. The water bottle, now lukewarm inside its towel wrapping, pressed on her bladder, so she pushed it aside. The pain had spread itself thinner, around her lower back and down her thighs. There was a dreary predictability to these episodes: first the writhing beast, which no pills could tame, then the settling in and spreading out — calmer, but still crippling, as if the treacherous organ had grabbed hold of every muscle between her navel and her knees and was clenching as hard as it could. Eventually, paracetamol would relax the clenching enough that she could do other things. In another hour or so, she expected, she would hoist herself up, open the window above the bed, and have a cigarette. She'd wobble to the toilet to change her pad and brush her teeth. Then she would join her parents and Jean for tea. In the meantime, though, she would endure her punishment as she sometimes did when nothing else worked, by imagining she was giving birth — for the pain of that ordeal, Isobel was certain, could not be any worse.

∞

HER MOTHER SERVED OX TONGUE FOR TEA. Recalling again her rendezvous with Patrick Locke, Isobel poked feebly at her food.

"Are the pains still troubling you, pet?" her mother said.

"Mmm."

"I hope you'll be all right for the ceilidh tomorrow. Alastair's mum says he's keen to meet you again."

Jean giggled, and Isobel glared at her across the table. Sallow-faced, dull-witted, plain, her sister seemed a personification of everything Isobel despised about Stanwick. Alastair Fraser, the son of her mother's new friend from the Women's Guild, was another choice specimen. She'd met him during coffee hour after the Easter Sunday service. He wasn't a regular and he'd looked so awkward and out of place that Margaret's father, the minister at Stanwick Abbey, had asked Margaret and Isobel to go sit with him. But then

Margaret, who wasn't much good at small talk herself, had been called away, leaving Isobel alone with the fellow. He'd blushed furiously, even on his scalp where his blond hair was already thinning, and the only subject he'd seemed comfortable discussing was the knitwear factory where he'd been a foreman since 1960. He was very polite, though, which was something.

Isobel dug a pit in her mashed potatoes and filled it with peas. "He's too old, Mum."

"Oh, aye, there's no getting away from that," her mother said. "He's a grown man. But nobody's asking you to marry him."

Again Jean giggled; Isobel sawed her meat.

Musingly, their mother continued. "Aye, these are modern times. You girls are young, and *I* believe you should get to know as many lads as you can before you settle down with one." She glanced at her husband chewing silently across the table then turned to Isobel. "You might even decide to do higher studies, pet. Think of all the folk you'd meet there! Anyway, there *is* one nuisance with this Alastair, even if you *were* to fancy him."

"What?" Isobel said.

"Well ..." Her mother paused, dabbing at her cardigan with her serviette. "Mrs. Fraser tells me he's very likely away to America. Perhaps quite soon."

"Ooh, you should marry him, Izzy!" Jean squealed. "You could go to America, just like Archie! And I could visit you!"

"Don't be stupid," Isobel said.

"Enough o' that," her father muttered.

She gave up on her food and reached for the teapot, noticing for the first time the appalling dinginess of the crocheted brown cap it was bundled in. As she poured, she pictured Alastair Fraser walking down Fifth Avenue in his ill-fitting tweed jacket, and the image, though laughable, pricked her with envy.

"I don't even ken the man," she said, her voice even. "And how does his mother know he wants to meet me again?"

"Oh, we were just blethering about this and that at the Guild meeting," her mother said. "She's a *very* interesting woman, Mrs. Fraser. Apparently she used to be a Catholic. But she converted when she was your age, Isobel. Just because she fancied the idea." She paused again, waving a forkful of mashed potato lazily back and forth. "Imagine that — being one thing for all those years then just deciding one day you're going to be something else. I don't think I could —"

"But what about *Alastair?*" Jean interrupted, and for once Isobel was grateful for her sister's impertinence. "How does his mother know he fancies Isobel?"

"Aye, well," Mrs. McGuigan continued, "she happened to mention that Alastair was thinking of going to the ceilidh and that he wanted to know if Isobel would be there. She said it took the poor lad all evening to get his question out, *and* that he'd never have troubled himself if he wasn't smitten." She smiled teasingly, then ingested her hovering mashed potato and signalled Jean to sit up straight.

Isobel rested her teacup on her still-aching belly and pondered her mother's remarks. The idea of meeting as many men as she could, of sorting through roomfuls of them and enduring their groping hands and tongues in search of one who would satisfy her, was oppressive. Moreover, the task seemed impossible. A person such as Alastair Fraser could not possibly make her happy; she understood that clearly. But could *anyone*, she wondered. Did anyone have the power to make her one thing or another? She thought admiringly of Alastair's mother — deciding one day to become a Protestant, shaking off everything she'd been brought up with. She gulped her tea. It was bitterly strong, but it came from Darjeeling, somewhere on the other side of the earth. Repeating the magical-sounding name to herself, Isobel glanced at the cluttered sideboard, where her cousin's latest postcard had been deposited, and imagined herself boarding an ocean liner from a crowded, noisy port ... watching the trodden grey landscape of her homeland disappear over the horizon.

APRIL 1945

"We use only the tenderest of these leaves," said Alec's father, the Tea Maker, employing expert fingers to pluck two pale green leaves and a bud from the waist-high tea bush. "Can you see the difference between the mature leaves and the tender ones, Alec?"

Alec nodded and dragged the back of his hand across his forehead, setting off streams of sweat. The difference between the leaves was obvious and, to him, uninteresting. He was bored. He'd been desperate for Easter holidays to begin, but now, tedious as school was, he imagined being back there, where at least there were boys his age and cricket matches. Powerless to change anything, he blew his hair from his eyes and watched the tea pluckers, bobbing like mermaids in their sea of green. They moved along the rows of bushes, deep baskets harnessed to their backs, each woman carrying a long rod, which marked the lower extremity of the tender leaves by resting atop the sturdier mature ones.

The pluckers' husbands and brothers were labourers in the tea factory, a two-storey light green building that overlooked the hills.

During the cold August holidays, when banks of cloud swallowed the hill country, Alec would have his tea lessons in the shelter of the factory. He would follow his father up the metal stairs to the top floor, where the labourers emptied bags of leaves into the withering troughs, spreading them out with their lean, muscular arms.

"What happens during the withering, Alec?" the Tea Maker would ask.

"All of the water evaporates from the leaves," his son would reply, too well rehearsed in this unchanging script.

"And how many hours for the withering?"

"About twelve."

"What happens next?"

"Rolling, fermenting, heating, sifting, tasting, packing, shipping," Alec would recite — to which the reply could be any combination of "There's a good chap," "You've got a fine brain," "Keep it up," or "Wits, principles, and discipline: they'll take you far in this life, son."

From the withering troughs they would descend to the dim ground floor rooms, where machines loomed like beasts of war. Alec liked the rollers best. With a secret thrill he imagined evil Nazi officers feeding their prisoners through such contraptions then transporting the flattened bodies by conveyor belt into ovens like the ones used to arrest fermentation of the tea leaves. Of course, he knew better than to share these thoughts with his father, a man for whom tea making was sacred. Rollers were used for crushing withered tea leaves into small particles, breaking the cell walls to begin the process of fermentation. Conveyor belts carried the particles during fermentation, a delicate process, which would decide the flavour and colour of the finished tea. And factory ovens were operated not by hard-faced German soldiers but by placid labourers who followed the instructions of their superiors without question.

The status of labourers was one of the countless sources of conflict between Alec's brother, Ernie, and the Tea Maker. Gazing out over the green monotony, Alec recalled the lunch, a day or two earlier, when his father and Ernie had exchanged words on that very subject.

"Since the labourers actually *do* the work that produces the tea," Ernie had mused in his slow, contemplative manner, "wouldn't it be a good thing to involve them more fully in the cerebral side of things?"

Alec had understood little of his elder brother's comment, but his father's response, punctuated by a snort, was quite clear.

"You're not to involve yourself with those people or their concerns," he said. "I won't have you jeopardizing my career with your misplaced affections. Don't think such things go unnoticed, Ernie. At any rate, labour has no interest in the thinking side of this business. You'd only be putting ideas into their heads."

For the first time ever, Alec noticed in the set of his father's lips a tightness of worry, perhaps even fear.

"I'm telling you, Ernie," he went on, "one day you'll have sons of your own and then, I assure you, you'll understand my point of view. You're eighteen years old, almost a man. As long as you're living in my home, you'll respect the values and reputation of this family."

Ernie cleaned his plate with a stringhopper, said "Yes, Dada," and filled his mouth. The Tea Maker simmered through the remainder of the meal, speaking only once, to his wife, to demand how it was that her children had forgotten how to use cutlery.

That evening, he summoned Ernie to the sitting room for a talking-to. Alec and his sister hovered in the corridor, listening — Alec measuring the possibility of a *real* battle; Mary, diplomatic middle child, nervously chewing the end of her long plait in anticipation of the usual stalemate.

The voices behind the door were low but audible.

"I'll never understand you, Ernie," was the Tea Maker's opening remark, though the acid of his tone gave the impression that he indeed did understand Ernie. He just didn't approve. "You've been given every opportunity to make a damn fine life for yourself. Schooled at Trinity, introduced to important men. I'm telling you, you've got a planter's life being handed to you on a silver platter."

"I know, Dada. I'm grateful for the things you've given me."

"Then tell me, Ernie, why is it that you seem virtually indifferent to these opportunities? Go on, you're a clever fellow. Tell me why it is that when you've been brought up like the best of the English, you choose to behave like a simple labourer or a low-country Sinhalese?"

On previous occasions Ernie had been known to say that the English were no better than the Tamils or the Sinhalese, and that one day the country would be ruled by those very people his father so often criticized. But his response on this particular evening was, quite simply, that he chose to behave like Ernie Van Twest.

"And who the hell is Ernie Van Twest, then?" the Tea Maker goaded, his frustration at boiling point. "Is he someone who cares to make a decent life for himself?"

"Yes, Dada."

To the ears in the hallway, Ernie's reply was barely discernible through the closed door. The Tea Maker, however, boomed.

"Yes Dada, yes Dada! You nod your head and agree with me, but where will you be next time the P.D.'s sons come around to invite you to the club? No doubt, you'll be loafing about with your low-life friends, or hidden away painting pictures like a child."

"Yes, Dada. I mean, no. If you'd like me to go to the club, I'll go."

"That isn't the point, Ernie! Do you not see the problem with your attitude?"

The problem, as Alec saw it, was that there were two Ernies living in the bungalow beside the tea factory: the dapper, up-and-coming Ernie of the Tea Maker's imagination, and the real Ernie. In some ways, the former was more of a presence in the house than the latter. Listening to this lopsided battle of the Ernies, bored by a script he knew as well as the tea making scripts, Alec willed his brother to erupt, vowed silently to defend him even. But the real Ernie said nothing. In the silence that followed, Mary spat out her hair and opened the sitting room door.

There had been no mention of the matter since.

Wilting in the fierce April sun, Alec felt a familiar resentment toward his brother. Ernie's strangeness — his musings, his paintings, his chumminess with servants and villagers — served only to increase the Tea Maker's expectation that he, Alec, be a normal chap. Not that he wasn't normal. He was — a good cricketer, a reasonable student, a boy's boy, as adults sometimes called him. But the extra watchfulness weighed heavily on his shoulders. The presence of his sister was little consolation. One day she would marry, and her responsibilities to the Van Twest family would come to an end.

Alec kicked at the dirt pathway and turned to his father. "Dada," he ventured, interrupting the Tea Maker's briefing on soil fertilizers, "could a labourer ever become a manager? A P.D.?"

His father emitted a sound, part snort, part laugh, that told Alec his question was a stupid one.

"It won't happen during my time," the Tea Maker said. "These people are ignorant, Alec. A different breed. They're not suitable for education and social advancement the way we are. The British did well to go shopping for their labour in India. Provided you treat these people decently, they'll work for you and won't cause trouble." His eyes travelled to the distant hills of the neighbouring plantation. "But one must treat them decently."

Alec understood his father's allusion. Though just turned twelve, he knew something of the unmentionable scandal that had caused the labourers of the neighbouring plantation to descend upon the manager's bungalow with the intention of killing him. The man escaped, but his reputation was ruined — an upheaval that Alec found deliciously exciting. If his older brother wished for the estate labour to have more power as a matter of fairness, Alec wished it for the turmoil of it all. The idea of a lowly Tamil labourer bucking fate and rising to a position reserved exclusively for the British tickled him in a way he would have found difficult to explain. But his father's reply had dismissed the possibility, so he altered his course.

"Dada?"

"Yes?"

"Could a Tea Maker ever become a manager?"

Alec took pleasure in the slow smile that spread across his father's face. His father, the Tea Maker, was lord of the factory, the brain behind the labour. In his starched white shirt and dark pleated trousers, he answered with a dignity befitting his refined presence in the field.

"I have every intention of becoming a Peria Doray, Alec. These British won't be staying here forever. And when they go, the country will need reliable men to take their places. Educated Burghers, like us, Alec. In the British eyes, we're the next best thing." He mopped his face with a limp handkerchief. "But you and I know we're even better, don't we? We have their standard of education and upbringing, but we're part of this land. We know it better than any Englishman ever will."

Alec followed his father back to the factory along the red dirt path, gauging his pace to remain within the shelter of the Tea Maker's long shadow. At the weighing station next to the factory's front entrance, his father left him with directions to go home and check the short-wave for any news of the war. Alec watched the Tea Maker mount the iron staircase to the withering room, then he drifted around to the tasting room at the side of the factory, hoping to find Amitha.

Tea tasting was very serious work, and Amitha was no less serious about it than the other tasters. But unlike the others, he had a sense of humour. In the spartan white room where teas were assessed like fine wines, Amitha made faces. Examining the twist and cleanliness of the dry leaves, the brightness of the infusions, he would contort his lips like a chimpanzee. Or, after testing a steaming liquor with the vigorous slurps and swishes of a good taster, he might puff his round cheeks and cross his eyes before spitting into the tall refuse urn, while Alec, convulsed with laughter, would shrink to a quivering lump in the doorway.

At moments of such conspicuous silliness, Alec would laugh without hesitation. But he had to be cautious. Amitha was a clown, true, but his facial contortions and stark gestures didn't always signify humour. More often than not they were critical comments on the tea, questions or instructions for the other tasters. In the three years he'd been at the estate, Amitha had conveyed his undisputed expertise without ever uttering an intelligible word. The tea jargons of Sinhala, Tamil, and English were unknown to him. And so, in the little time it had taken for his reputation to blossom, the tasting room had become an almost wordless place, and the assessment of leaf, infusion, and liquor using hand signs and facial expressions became an accepted practice. Left index finger scratched across the right palm: too much stalk. Eyebrows raised: a sufficiently bright infusion. Right fist drawn across the left palm then stopped with a chopping motion: fermentation too short.

Virtually everyone on the plantation knew about Amitha's handicap, though they rarely acknowledged it. Alec, for his part, understood that his favourite taster couldn't hear properly. But he wasn't bothered by it — unlike Ernie, who once pointed out that deaf people in places like England and America could actually go to school and learn to have regular conversations using their hands. Ernie listened to

Amitha's strange animal grunts and felt pity; Alec didn't. As he saw it, Amitha was perfectly content with his lot in life. The fact that he couldn't carry on a conversation seemed of little consequence.

Alec stuck his head through the tasting room door, but Amitha wasn't there. The two tasters hovering over the refuse urn were sullen-faced and serious, and the frowns they projected in the direction of the door were not, Alec was quite certain, comments on the quality of the tea.

He considered going home to listen to the short-wave. Alec liked wars, and over the past three or four years he'd spent hours next to the radio, digesting tantalizing reports of air raids and dogfights, the D-Day invasion, and, best of all, the Allies' thrilling run-ins with the Japanese air force and navy, close enough to home to present a genuine and serious danger. But the war was growing old and flat. The Nazis had been all but trounced, and reports on the Japanese no longer prickled with the possibility of a comeback. Alec wished he were in England or France; at least they'd been bombed. He kicked the red dirt of his maddeningly tranquil homeland then followed the shade of the factory's wall to the backside of the building, searching for something of interest.

6

In his dream, Rudy is back on Morgan Hill Road. He's crouching in the bushes, watching Clare Fraser and her friends run through the sprinkler on the Frasers' front lawn. They're playing a complicated sort of cricket game. Clare is wearing a skirted swimsuit the colour of the sea, and the water curls over her as she bats. Rudy's mother, enormously pregnant with the brother he's been waiting for forever, is vacuuming the lawn.

"Rudy, don't be shy," she says. "Go and play with the other children. I'll be close, close."

He shakes his head, not simply because he's a grown man but rather because he has forgotten how to play cricket. He'll make a fool of himself.

The day is boiling, however, and the fan of water surging from the sprinkler suddenly doubles in size and cascades like a fountain. No longer intimidated, Rudy gets up and crosses the street. Clare greets him at the edge of her lawn. She's an adult now, and the neckline of her swimsuit plunges extravagantly between her breasts. She's dark, like a Sri Lankan, but Rudy knows she is Clare.

"Are you coming in?" she says. Her accent is Scottish.

His eyes meet hers. "Do you want me to?"

She nods. He's desperately aroused, but as he fumbles with his belt, he notices that across the street his parents and sister are now in a flurry of activity, packing the car as if for a long vacation. There's luggage all over the place. His mother waves to him.

"Rudy, come! It's time for you and your sister to go to the Pereiras'."

Clare eyes him uncertainly.

"They're my parents' friends," he mumbles. "I have to go. It's my damn brother."

He starts back across the street, but then he is at Mrs. Pereira's kitchen table with his father and sister, and everything is horribly real — more memory than dream.

Dad, sitting between Rudy and Susie, massages his forehead with his fingers. He inhales deeply, exhales loudly, then rests his palms on the table. "Your brother was born last night," he says. "He's strong and healthy."

Rudy stares down at his bowl of soggy cornflakes, trying to will himself away from the oppressively familiar scene.

"There were problems with the birth," Dad continues, wearily. "It was —"

"But you said the baby's okay," Susie interrupts, her voice a shaky whisper.

Dad looks at her, then at Rudy. When he finally answers, it is as if he has jumped from a cliff or a high diving board, hurtling straight-on, with no possibility of turning back. "The problems were with Mum. She suffered terrible bleeding after the baby came out. It was nighttime and there weren't enough doctors." Then, like a slap against a hard sheet of water: the news.

Rudy flinches. He struggles to remind himself that he already knew — that he has lived with this unthinkable announcement for years and has grown to accept it. But the room is suddenly full of noise, and he isn't certain whose death his father has just announced. Dad suddenly looks far too old for it to have been Mum's, and in any case they're no longer in the Pereiras' kitchen but in their own, with everyone exclaiming over Aunty's cooking.

Rudy shouts across the room to his father. "Dad! What did you just say?"

Dad doesn't hear, or pretends not to. The kitchen is becoming more and more crowded and chaotic, but Adam isn't there. Rudy turns in circles, searching for his brother, calling his name. Then he appears in the living room. Draped in a turquoise sari with gold embroidery, he looks strangely beautiful. He combs his fingers through his hair and smiles.

"Everything's okay, Rudy," he says.

Rudy gasps and laughs. "You're really okay? You're out of danger?"

"Yeah, sure."

Adam steps forward, arms outstretched. Rudy advances to hug his brother, but his father gets there first. Stroking Adam's cheek with his finger, Dad addresses the crowd of people in the kitchen.

"The baby will make everything better," he says. "Look — he has his mother's eyes."

Rudy crosses the living room to the window. Clare, a child again, is sitting alone on her front lawn, and he waves his arms, trying to get her attention.

∞

A BARKING DOG WOKE HIM. It wasn't yet dawn, and the room was still mercifully dark. For a second, maybe two, he lay in relaxed oblivion, before the news of the previous day once again hijacked his thoughts: *Adam crashed his motorcycle. He's in a coma.* No room for anything else. Rudy mashed his face into the pillow and tried to slip back into the shelter of his dream, but it was no use. The full weight of consciousness avalanched down on him, bringing with it all the impossible details of his father's phone call. A van on the Boulevard ... a patch of ice ... the General. Adam in a coma. What the hell was a coma, anyway, he wanted to know. He imagined his brother lying under the glare of hospital lamps, his vital signs registered in sharp peaks and blips on a screen next to him. He tried to picture Adam's face, but the one he saw was Kanda Selvarajah's, calm and tidy.

Though it wasn't yet six o'clock, Rudy rolled onto his back and threw off the sheet. He needed to get away from Aunty's house. If he went out for a few hours and separated himself from the crisis, things could happen. Dad could call and say that everything was okay, that

Adam had woken up. He'd be in the hospital a few days — broken collarbone, a cast on his arm, a beast of a headache — but fine. Rudy's life could return to the path it was on before, the one where he made decisions and choices, and those were the things that determined the shape of his days.

He yanked a section of the mosquito net from under the mattress and ducked out of his gauzy tent. As he fumbled in semi-darkness for the school clothes he'd left draped over a chair, his head throbbed dully — a budding hangover from the shots of arrack he'd downed before bed. His cotton shirt and trousers were hopelessly wrinkled and in need of a wash, but he buttoned and zipped nonetheless. With his face stubbled and the shirt left hanging out, the sloppiness would look deliberate. He checked his knapsack for his wallet and diary, then, thankful for the polished cement that didn't creak underfoot, he crossed the bungalow to the back garden.

A cat meowed as he stepped outside. He shooed it away, and the dim yard fell silent. Inside the shower enclosure, he brushed his teeth at a small tap sticking out of the shower pipe. Up and down in rapid, vigorous strokes, he worked his way around his mouth, increasingly aware of the stunning complexity of what he was doing. It was a remarkable feat, really — the transformation of an intention, an intangible thing, into a precise and concrete action. He wondered vaguely how it happened. He wondered how the hell he'd ever managed to ride a bicycle, or put together the bookshelves in his old apartment.

He spat into the drain on the cement floor.

"Goddammit, Adam."

He wished there were a God. Someone he could reason with, or cut a deal with. *Look*, he'd say, *my family's had more than its share, don't you think? I know we're not living in a Calcutta slum or anything. But relatively speaking? Could you just spare my father at least? I'll pick up the slack. Give me some hellish students, or malaria or something.* He stared into the drain. Of course, if there were a God, it was entirely possible that Adam's accident was a punishment — not Adam's punishment, but Rudy's. He'd been a lousy older brother. He'd blown countless opportunities, and God was fed up. *No more chances for you, asshole*, He was saying, and it wasn't hard to sympathize. Still, Rudy suspected that if there was indeed a being capable of reversing his circumstances, it wasn't a pissed-off Old Testament Jehovah. Rather, it was some version of Lady Fortune from the Dark Ages. Fickle, blind, and deaf.

He rinsed his mouth with a handful of water and shook out his toothbrush. Then he splashed his face, over and over, as if to sluice away the previous twenty-four hours. The water was cool and fresh, but inadequate. He wrenched the tap shut, then slipped back into the kitchen, where he scribbled a note to his aunt and swallowed three Aspirins. It was strange that Aunty wasn't up yet, but a relief. When he left the house again, he closed the front door noiselessly behind him. Desperate to be away, he jogged up the lane to Vaththe Mawatha.

The sun was up, but still timid, and the air was comfortable, not yet crowded with the noises and smells and stifling heat that the day would produce. Rudy walked in the shadows with his hands in his pockets, his untucked shirt bunched at his waist. It could have been an ideal morning. The train to the city would be empty, or nearly. The hoppers and tea at the shop near Fort Station would be fresh and hot, and there'd be an unoccupied bench, in the shade.

Nearing the main junction, he noticed that there was a surprising number of people out walking, all of them dressed up. A young man, whom Rudy recognized but couldn't name, waved from across the street.

"Happy Easter!"

He'd completely forgotten, of course. These people in their Sunday clothes were off to Easter Mass, and it occurred to him then that his aunt, too, had probably chosen the quiet dawn Mass over the more chaotic ordeal that would happen later in the morning. Rudy forced a smile and waved to his neighbour. Then he carried on to the train platform. As he purchased his ticket, the church bell issued an insistent chime, and for a moment he considered abandoning his plan and making a dash for St. Anne's. But then the rails thrummed, and the approaching train obliterated the call to worship. He boarded the last car and found a seat, far away from other passengers.

He dozed for much of the journey. When the train finally drifted into Fort Station, he woke from scattered dreams to find that his car had nearly filled. There were several families and groups of young men, everyone now talking loudly and gathering parcels. Directly across from Rudy was a backpacker, a woman with white-blond hair fastened in a thick plait. She was reading a guidebook that seemed to be in German, or maybe Dutch. Rudy glanced down at his own knapsack, with the maple leaf stitched next to the brand name, and guessed that the woman had sat near him deliberately. He looked like a traveller — grubby and tired.

The train squealed to a halt. Looking up from her book, the woman squinted out the window and frowned. Her expression suggested that she hadn't been here before, and that the vast, shadowy interior of Fort Station was to her mysterious and vaguely threatening. She reached across the enormous backpack perched on the seat next to her and crammed her guidebook into a side pocket. She had an astonishing number of pockets, Rudy noticed. Her tan trousers sported at least eight of them, and even her grey T-shirt had a zippered pocket across the front, like a kangaroo. She seemed entirely self-contained, as if everything she needed on her journey could find a place in one of her innumerable pockets.

Rudy stayed in his seat, waiting for the noisy day trippers to finish spilling out. The woman, he assumed, was waiting for the same thing. Her fingers played with the beaded choker around her neck, and Rudy imagined with envy the small worries crowding her mind: Would she find a taxi driver who wouldn't rip her off? Would the guest house she'd selected be clean enough? Would it have a room for her? Would this city prove to be what she'd expected, to have what she was looking for, or would it ultimately disappoint? She turned away from the window and her eyes met Rudy's. They both smiled — distracted, partial smiles.

When the aisle had cleared, the woman manoeuvred her backpack to the end of the bench. Rudy watched as she squatted and slipped her arms through the straps. He noticed the contour of her biceps and the strip of pale belly that appeared when she raised her arms. She straightened up and fastened the hip belt of her pack, smiling once more in Rudy's direction — more generously, he thought, as if she'd somehow understood something of his situation. He liked the idea, and it occurred to him that if it were possible — if such a thing could be requested of a stranger — he would ask the woman to go with him to the snack shop. He'd order tea and hoppers for the two of them, then he'd sit beside her on the bench, and together, not talking, they'd

watch the rush of city life, connected only by their shared train journey. But of course he couldn't ask such a thing from this woman.

He got up, shouldering his small knapsack.

"Are you from Canada?" the woman said.

Rudy hesitated. "Yes ... originally," he said. "Sort of. And you?"

"I'm from Denmark."

"Is this your first time in Colombo?"

He followed the woman down the narrow passage, his eyes fixed
on the collection of small flags she'd stitched to her backpack.

"No. I was here two weeks ago, then I went travelling in the
South." Her accent was almost English — just an occasional intona-
tion that rang peculiarly.

"And now? Are you staying in the city?"

"I thought I'd go to Adam's Peak. There's supposed to be a really
beautiful view from the top. Have you been there?"

Rudy swore silently to himself. "No. Not yet."

They'd left the train and were now standing on the empty platform. The families and groups of young men had hurried away, perhaps to board the train to Hatton, where it was possible to catch a bus
to the base of Adam's Peak.

The Danish woman eyed Rudy's knapsack. "Where are you
staying?"

"I live here," he answered, his tone more defensive than he'd
intended. "Out in the suburbs."

The woman's eyes widened. "So you moved here from Canada?"

"I was born here. My family immigrated when I was a kid, then I
moved back."

"Then you're an authentic Sri Lankan!" she exclaimed, and Rudy
detected in her expression a blossoming attraction, a predictable route
that their encounter could follow.

He frowned, then laughed. "I don't know what the hell I am." He
started walking, and the woman walked with him. "Do you need to
find a place to stay?" he said.

"I was going to get a room at Adam's Peak. My book says they
have some rest houses there, at the bottom. Do you know anything
about these places? Is it easy to get a room?"

He thought about lying — telling her the guest houses would be full by the time she got there, or that most of them had already shut down for the season. Heading away from the Hatton platform, toward the exit, he rubbed his stubbled chin.

"I'm not really sure," he finally said. "I've never been up there. But I know a place here in town that would store your backpack for you — it's safe — then you wouldn't have to schlep it along with you. You could just take a few things."

The woman considered this for a moment, and it seemed that once again there was an understanding between the two of them. His last comment, Rudy hoped the woman would infer, was an offer — to take her to a guest house, to tell her a story or two from his childhood, and, provided all went reasonably well, to have sex with her. By noon, she would have an authentic Sri Lankan experience she could take back to Denmark; he'd have escaped his own thoughts for a couple of hours. And, possibly, his father would have called.

"That sounds like a good idea," the woman said. "Where is this place?"

They agreed to walk the two or three kilometres to the family-run hotel on Slave Island. It belonged to the brother of one of Rudy's colleagues, a man he'd heard about but never met. Rudy offered to carry the woman's backpack, and to his surprise she accepted. He gave her his own bag and hoisted the backpack, grateful for the distraction of physical work. As they walked, he told her harmless stories of his grandfather's tea estate, of floating paper boats on the Kelaniya River, of rescuing his sister from the edge of Aunty's well. He started to tell her about school, and Kanda, then he stopped himself and asked the woman what she did back in Denmark. Physiotherapy, she said, though she'd just recently finished her training and hadn't yet found a position. She wondered if there were job opportunities in Canada, and Rudy said he didn't know.

When they arrived at the hotel, the woman looked at her watch and decided it would be best to postpone the rest of her journey till the next morning. She took a room and asked Rudy if he'd mind carrying her backpack up the stairs. He agreed, provided she'd let him use her shower. She said it was strange that the heat affected him so terribly, considering he was a native. Then she smiled.

The room was bare but clean, with white walls, a small window, and a pink mosquito net knotted over a pink single bed. Rudy came out of the bathroom with a scratchy pink towel around his waist. The woman had gone back downstairs for two bottles of orange Fanta, one of which she offered to him. He took it from her and sat at the end of the bed.

"I think I'll take a shower too," the woman said, and Rudy nodded.

She left the bathroom door half open as she showered, but he waited for her to come out. She didn't bother with a towel. Her wet hair hung almost to her waist and her skin and eyelashes glistened with drops of water. Her legs were covered in white-blond fuzz; her pubic hair was surprisingly dark. The woman took a swig of his Fanta then rested the bottle on the small wooden night table, the only other furniture in the room. He stood up, letting his towel drop to the floor, and cupped her breasts in his hands. They were large and soft, a long-lost pleasure that now excited him intensely. He wanted to be inside her right away, but he held back. He would come too soon, and then neither of them would get what they wanted. Gently he pulled her down onto the bed. She guided his fingers where she wanted, as if, sensing an inadequacy on his part, she was willing to compensate. In return, he was entirely accommodating when she commented on the darkness of his penis against her pale inner thigh and when she compared their lovemaking to a scene in one of Michael Ondaatje's poems. When at last he entered her, he even quoted a line from *The Cinnamon Peeler* — required reading for the A-level Literature exam.

But he didn't come. They tried a few different positions, but when the whole thing became a mechanical chore, they gave up. The woman assured him there was no need to feel embarrassed. An unnecessary remark, for as he lay on his back, staring at the white ceiling, he felt only an oppressive heaviness at the centre of his chest.

The woman sat up and began combing her fingers through her hair.

"Would you like to climb Adam's Peak with me tomorrow?" she said, as if there were no reason in the world that he shouldn't want to join her.

Rudy hesitated, wondering how to refuse. "I can't," he finally said. He suspected the woman would have accepted any reason, or even no reason at all, but he went on. "I'm waiting to do the climb with my brother. His name's Adam — after the peak, sort of. Neither of us has ever climbed it before, and we agreed to do it together." He paused. "Actually, I just suggested it recently, but I'm pretty sure he'll go along with it."

"Where is your brother now?" the woman said.

For the first time since his father's phone call, Rudy's eyes threatened to well up. He reached for his clothes, piled on the floor. "He's back in Montreal."

"He'll be coming here?"

"I don't know. I hope so." His voice was strained, robotic. "He was in a motorcycle accident on Friday. He's in the hospital."

He glanced at the woman in time to see her wince.

"My God, you must be so worried!" She hugged her knees to her chest and fixed her eyes on Rudy as he dressed. "Will you go back to see him?"

The question took him by surprise. The possibility of returning to Montreal hadn't occurred to him, but he knew, even as he pretended to grapple with the idea, that he wouldn't go.

"I don't think so," he eventually said. "Not at this point."

"But why not? Doesn't your family need you?"

The question was presumptuous, Rudy thought. At the same time, it begged an answer. *Did* his family need him? Would it make any difference at all if he were there? If Aunty Mary were to go back — and he suspected she would — Dad and Susie would be happier. Aunty would cook for them, and clean the house, and through these familiar domestic miracles, she'd impose a certain order on the chaos that had no doubt invaded their lives. But if he, Rudy, were to go back? What could he do that his aunt, or even some neighbour, wouldn't already have under control? There'd be an intangible benefit to his presence, he supposed, to having the whole family together. But it was a togetherness that would quickly become crowded. His father's epic brooding, Susie's anxiety, Aunty's stubborn faith — each would take up an inordinate amount of space, and Rudy, the impotent observer, would be squashed into further uselessness.

Slowly he did up his pants. The woman on the bed was still staring at him, expecting an answer.

"I don't think I could get leave from work," he said. "Unless things got worse."

The woman shook her head. "That's inhuman. What's more important, English class or your brother? Couldn't they find someone else to do your job?"

Rudy shrugged. If he were to be completely honest, his companion would no doubt think *him* inhuman. "Anyway," he said, "I'm sorry, but I can't go with you tomorrow. I'm probably a cad for being here with you now. I should have told you right off what was going on."

The woman got up from the bed and approached him. Her hair was half dry and smelled lemony; her brown nipples had softened and enlarged. She took both his hands in hers. "It's okay," she said. "Nobody should be alone at a time like this." She kissed his cheek, squeezed his hands, then crossed the room to her backpack and began rummaging for clothes. Buttoning his shirt, Rudy wondered if her next outfit would have as many pockets as the last. He'd been mistaken, perhaps, in imagining she was self-contained.

He left the guest house alone and wandered back in the direction of the train station, weaving through vendors' displays of pirated music and brand name rip-offs. On the traffic island at the junction of Chatham Street and Janadhipathi Mawatha — President Street — he paused to mop his face. The island was occupied by a clock tower, a squat, off-white structure with the queer distinction of being, according to Aunty Mary, a year older than Big Ben. Leaning against it, Rudy recalled the visit he and his aunt had made to the city shortly after his arrival. Aunty had been the acknowledged expert that day, navigating the maze of streets, pointing out landmarks, telling stories of Van Twests who'd come to Colombo on merchant ships at the start of the last century. But all Rudy had retained was the location of his bus stop and a useless fact about a clock tower on a traffic island. His brother would have paid more attention.

Squinting up at the clock face, which read ten past eleven, he remembered Easter lunch. Aunty would be completing her preparations, expecting him to show up. He glanced around for a public phone, but though he spotted one, he didn't bother calling. He was getting hungry, and more for that reason than any other he decided to go home.

On the train back to Wattala he tried to sleep again but couldn't. The scene of Adam's accident had finally worked its way into his consciousness. He saw the Boulevard, slushy and grey, under a low, grey sky ... the ugly strip malls and regimented parking lots ... the streams of indifferent traffic. He put himself on the motorcycle, behind his brother, his hands around Adam's waist. He imagined the engine's thrust, the outrageous speed, the knifelike air, and he wondered that he'd never taken such a ride before. Adam had asked him once. The motorcycle was brand new, and he was enthralled with it. "Just a short ride, Rudy," he'd said, pleading almost. "Come on, it's a blast!" But Rudy had refused. Not because he was afraid. As he recalled it now, he just hadn't felt like being with Adam, allowing himself to be governed by Adam's whims and desires. He tried to remember what he'd done that evening instead. Read the newspaper? Stared out the window? He had no idea. Of course, if he'd gone on the motorcycle, it would have been a big deal. The event might even, he thought now, have changed the course of things to come. But this was a pointless consideration.

Putting himself next in the driver's seat, Rudy played the collision in his mind, over and over, trying to get it right. He fine-tuned the sprays of grimy slush, the flashes of chrome, the violent clenching of the van's brakes. A minivan? A moving van? He didn't know. He considered all possible points of contact and the shocks that each would send through his body. When the muscles of his legs and trunk had begun to throb for real, he threw himself from the motorcycle. But at this point, his imagination failed him. It got him into the air but couldn't land him, couldn't conceive of the terrible impact that would decide everything. It seemed impossible to him then that his brother would survive. God or no, he was being punished.

As the train rumbled into his station, Rudy became nervous — butterflies in the stomach and a bursting bladder. He crossed the platform to the public toilet and held his breath as he urinated into a concrete trough, covered, like the walls of the stinking enclosure, with graffiti. Most of the messages were in Tamil or Sinhala, though someone had scribbled "Give peace a chance" in English. Back outside, he left the shade of the platform and walked in the direction of Vaththe Mawatha. Then he stopped. In his nervousness he was no longer hungry, and he wasn't ready to go home. Behind him, people were filing out of Aunty's church, and it was there that he headed, eyes fixed on the statue of Saint Anne gazing down from an alcove high on the church's façade.

He waited until the last stragglers had left, then he slipped through a side door into the cool, cavernous sanctuary. He moved sideways to the middle of a pew and sat down, positioning himself under a ceiling fan. Gentle pulses of air dried his face. He stared ahead at the plaster Jesus hanging behind the altar. The figure's contorted, pinkish form was stained with blobs of red at the usual places. A white plaster loincloth drooped precariously from the skeletal hips, but the eyes, taking no notice, were directed upward, to the building's rafters and fans. The expression was one of weary exasperation, indifference to whatever might be happening in the church below. Rudy imagined the eleven o'clock Mass — a few hundred people pouring out their compassion and thanks to a guy whose image suggested he didn't give a fuck — and wished, in spite of everything, that he'd been part of the ritual.

Across the sanctuary, next to the confessional booths, a door opened and a cleaning woman appeared. She walked silently, carrying a dustpan and a straw broom with a short stub of a handle. She was very thin, and her silvered hair was dressed in a long plait down her back. Working her way around the perimeter of the sanctuary, she bent over at regular intervals to sweep. Her equipment was hopelessly inadequate, but she moved quickly. When she reached the centre aisle she noticed Rudy and acknowledged him with a sideways tilt of her head and a fraction of a smile. Then she took the palloo of her faded turquoise sari and wiped her forehead.

Apart from its colour, the sari was nothing like his mother's special one, and the cleaning woman herself bore no resemblance. Still, witnessing the simple gesture, Rudy saw her — Mum, enormously pregnant, pushing the vacuum cleaner around the living room, stopping to mop her face and catch her breath. His last goddamn image of her. He remembered nothing of the car ride to the Pereiras' apartment. His mother must have kissed him goodbye and reminded him to be good, but he didn't remember that either. And then there were the infinite moments he'd never remember because they'd been stolen from him. Cold cloths and calamine when the chicken pox finally caught up to him in grade four, sympathy when he failed to make the junior basketball team ... As he always did when he began to mourn her in this way, he imagined how things would really have been. He told himself his mother would have suffocated him with her doting, like Aunty. She would have bragged inappropriately about his run-of-the-mill accomplishments and pestered him increasingly for a daughter-in-law and grandchildren. As she aged, she would have complained of varicose veins and high blood pressure and developed a swelling nostalgia for the past in the cavities of her heart. He would have loved her, of course, but their relationship would not have been central to his life. This is what he told himself — but still, he couldn't bear the sight of the cleaning woman in the turquoise sari.

He turned back to the plaster Jesus, muttered "Useless bastard," then checked his watch and wiped his eyes with the back of his hand. It was time to go home.

Outside, he noticed the Bajaj three-wheelers across the street and groaned. As he headed toward Vaththe Mawatha, the fat-bellied driver who'd accosted him the day he missed his bus stop again stepped forward.

"Sixty rupees only, sir."

Rudy walked on a few paces then stopped. "Fine," he answered, and the driver, showing no surprise, nodded, refastening his sarong. Rudy ducked into the back of the taxi while the driver installed himself in the front seat. After several vigorous revs of the engine, they rumbled off in the direction of Aunty Mary's lane.

7

CLARE APPROACHES THE RECEPTION DESK with a strange confidence. "I'm here to see Adam Vantwest. He was admitted on Friday."

The receptionist types something quickly then squints at her computer screen. "Are you a family member?"

"No, I'm a neighbour. But I was with him right before the accident."

"I'm afraid you have to be a family member."

"But that makes no sense," Clare says helplessly. Then she recognizes the woman. "Ma, it's me. Can't I see him?"

Her mother shakes her head. "No, pet. It's too dangerous."

"But why?"

"He might not be dressed. It's too dangerous."

Suddenly aware that her mother is barricaded inside her station, Clare marches off in the direction of Adam's room. Isobel, still insistent, calls after her, but her voice becomes more and more faint.

The corridor is long and the fluorescent lights flicker and buzz. Clare passes darkened rooms and realizes she doesn't know which is Adam's. Desperate now to find him, she braces herself to return to the reception desk. Then she spots a large index card, taped to the wall next to a door. Sloppily printed in black felt pen is the name "VAN TWEST." The door next to the card is slightly ajar. Clare pushes it open.

The room is dim and orangey, and Adam's sheet is a saffron brocade. The bed is unusually high. Standing at the foot of it, Clare cranes her neck to see Adam's face, but Adam bends his legs, just enough to block her view. She stands on tiptoe, trying to peer over his knees, then backs out into the corridor, but Adam's legs, draped in the saffron brocade, hide his face completely.

Across the hall is another room, a regular-looking hospital room, brightly lit, with its door open. Clare looks inside. In the one bed is her father, reading a book. He looks up and smiles.

"It's my wee cub!"

She runs to his bedside. "I can't believe it! Ma told me you had a heart attack."

"Oh, aye. That's what they call it to avoid confusion. But it was really a metamorphosis." He puts the book down on the bed. "It's not restricted to the heart, you see. It's more pervasive."

"Metamorphosis?"

"Aye. I'm lucky they caught it. It's like a coma, you see."

"So you're going to be all right?"

"Oh, they're not positive yet, but I'm down to just this one wee IV."

He holds up his left wrist, from which a tiny rubber tube snakes to a hanging bowl of clear liquid.

Clare laughs. "That's great! Does Ma know?"

"No, no. Not yet. That would have been too risky."

He's so easy to talk to. She wants to ask her father about his metamorphosis — it makes perfect sense, and she's surprised that the possibility has never occurred to her — but the hospital has suddenly become noisy and chaotic. There are voices and footsteps out in the corridor, heavy things being dropped.

∞

CLARE ROLLED ONTO HER BACK, woken by the carpet installers hauling in their equipment and getting on with the business of tearing up Alastair's Wedgwood blue carpeting. She reached for the remote control on the bedside table, pointed it at the stereo, and shut them out.

She tried to remember her dream. The part with her father was hopelessly fuzzy, but the image of Adam's room was clear. Not surprisingly. Several days had passed since the accident, and in that time she'd thought of little else. First there was the shocking matter of the thing having occurred on the very day she had been with Adam. The only time she'd ever been with him, in fact. Then there was the swarm of what-ifs buzzing about her head in an ever-multiplying cloud. The number of ridiculously simple ways she could have altered events was horrifying. And it wasn't just the matter of having refused his offer to ride up Mount Royal. Everything she'd said to him, or not said — about his family, about Vancouver, about Emma — seemed part of a necessary chain. Remove any one of those links, or add one, she thought, and the outcome would have been different. She'd convinced herself, more or less, that these what-ifs were irrelevant — Adam was still in a coma (though showing signs of improvement, according to Mrs. Skinner's reports), and she, Clare, was in her bedroom, about to get ready for work. But while Friday's events were now beyond her control, her power over things to come was dizzying. The future, previously distant and uncomplicated, something to be mulled over and planned at leisure, was now *close* — on the other side of the blind, behind the bedroom door — and its possibilities, its what-ifs, branched infinitely.

Most of them simply had to be ignored.

Clare stared at the blank ceiling a moment longer then got up. She went to the window and raised the blind. Mr. Vantwest's car was in the driveway, but all the curtains in the house were drawn.

What if I were to go over there and knock on the door?

You should have done it already. Emma's voice was terse and accusing. *You were probably the last person to talk to him before his accident.*

I don't think his family knows that.

Doesn't matter. You should still visit them.

There was no getting around this, it seemed. Isobel had taken a casserole across and left it outside the Vantwests' front door with a card, which Clare had signed. Joanne Skinner had kept herself updated somehow. But Clare had yet to cross the street. Like a spy, she'd kept track of her neighbours' movements from her bedroom window. She knew that Adam's sister and her little girl had left, and she'd witnessed the return of the aunt — Mr. Vantwest hauling two bulging suitcases from the car to the house, the aunt trailing behind in a summer dress and a ski jacket, carrying what looked to be bags of groceries. She'd watched for Rudy Vantwest, but he hadn't yet appeared.

What would I say to them?

Emma became exasperated. *That you're sorry to hear about Adam's accident. You want to know how he's doing. Is there anything you can do to help?*

It just sounds so phony.

It only — Look, Clare, *what makes you think the Vantwests are going to be paying special attention to what you say anyway? You're not that important to them.*

For a long time she stared at the house across the street.

I'll go tomorrow, she promised at last.

Eyeing the clock, she swore under her breath then flew to the closet. She imagined her next pay statement: docked for lateness resulting from long, inexplicable conversations with self. The real Emma would send her to a shrink.

∞

DOWNSTAIRS, THE HOUSE WAS A SHAMBLES. The living room furniture had disappeared — given away to the Skinners' niece, to make way for the Ikea things — and everything else had been shifted into the kitchen. Since their arrival, the installers had torn up the dining room carpet, and one of them was now tramping across the Wedgwood blue living room in muddy work boots with lolling tongues. The other man was chatting with Isobel in the hall, thoughtfully smoothing his wavy grey hair with one hand, while Isobel touched his other arm, just below the elbow, and laughed.

A complete shambles.

Clare slipped quietly out the front door. Hurrying to the station, she rehearsed her resignation speech, defying the terrors and uncertainties that Adam's accident had spawned. *Listen, Markus,* she would say. *I'm going to be moving to Vancouver. I've really enjoyed working here, but ...* She considered this and started again. *I wanted to give you enough notice, but I've decided I'm moving to Vancouver. I know some people there, and . . .* What had Adam said? *It's such a great city.* Again she paused. She'd never be able to muster up Adam's enthusiasm for the place. But he'd said something else as well, something about making a life for himself there. An appealing idea: making a life. Like making a casserole, or composing a song. *In Vancouver I think I could really . . . I need a change and I think maybe I could . . .* She marched past brown lawns patched with dirty snow and scraps of rubbish newly exposed by the thaw. *The thing is, Markus, I'd like to go somewhere different and see what happens.* Hardly convincing, but it would do.

At work, though, she was paralyzed by what-ifs. From behind the front counter, she concentrated on Markus's dull, sandy hair and grey pinstriped shirt, trying to push herself over the edge, but the paths that branched away from Markus and his music shop promised only plane crashes and botched job interviews and regret. When her boss joined her behind the counter and set about changing the paper roll in the calculator, Clare sighed quietly and resigned herself to another day in the pattern.

"So, I guess that band teacher decided to do her ordering through us," Markus said in his slow, meandering way.

"Really? That's great."

"So . . . would you mind being her contact person?"

"No. Sure. That's fine."

"Good. I mean, you know, that would be great if you could." He fed the new paper roll through the machine and tore off the end. He kept the crumpled scrap in his hand, as if unsure what to do with it. "So . . ." He cleared his throat. "We should catch up some time."

Clare dusted the glass counter with her sleeve and watched Peter tidy the rack of songbooks.

"Sure."

"Maybe some day after work . . . or . . . whenever you're free."

"Yeah. Sure."

She thought of Adam's invitation, so different from Markus's. Adam hadn't messed around with vague propositions. He hadn't said they *should* go for a ride *some day*. No — he'd looked her in the eye and asked her to go with him right that moment.

She stared out the front window at the passersby in sunglasses and unbuttoned coats and considered the fact that Adam Vantwest could not possibly be among them. He'd wanted to go to Sri Lanka, Clare recalled, and with a sudden recklessness she imagined going there for him. A ridiculous idea, of course, but for a moment she pictured herself walking along a tropical village road, absorbing exotic sights and sounds, which she would bring back to Adam. Then she turned to Markus.

"What are you doing this evening?"

"Tonight? I'm not sure. Why?"

"You were saying we should catch up. I thought we could go for dinner — tonight."

Markus raised his eyebrows and nodded. "Sure. That would be great."

∞

THE AMBIANCE OF THE RESTAURANT was too intimate — small candles on the tables, a haze of smoke from the bar, and, from hidden speakers, an adolescent voice moaning about love — but Markus seemed unaffected. Clare watched him unbutton his cuffs and neatly roll up his sleeves, exposing delicate, finely haired forearms. Twirling a carrot stick between her fingers, she met his bespectacled eyes.

"Have you ever heard of the Gay Games?" she said.

Markus raised his eyebrows and chuckled awkwardly. "Uh, I think so. Why do you ask?"

The truth was silly: to see if she could say it — *Gay Games* — like Adam had, so nonchalantly.

"I was just wondering what you thought of the idea."

"Of games for gay people? Oh, I don't know. I guess they're fine ... but ..."

"But ..."

"Well ... you know ... there's nothing really stopping them from entering the real Olympics, is there?"

Clare frowned. "There's nothing stopping them, but they couldn't really be themselves."

The idea sounded hokey and hippyish. At the same time it was unsettling. It conjured up a world in which having a *self* meant having sex. She bit her carrot stick with feigned conviction, while Markus picked the onions off his burger.

"Yeah, I see what you mean," he said at length. "I guess that makes sense."

There was more that could have been said, of course. If Emma had been there she'd have had plenty to say about the Gay Games. Certainly Adam would. But Clare turned to the small television set behind the bar, tuned to hockey, and gave up. Across the table, Markus floundered.

"So, uh ... what made you think of ..."

On the TV, a red-jerseyed player flew into the boards amid a great spraying of ice. The glass shook, the player lurched, then he skated off, back into the fray. She turned back to Markus. "My neighbour went to them. The Games."

"Oh. Is he ..."

"He was in a motorcycle accident on Friday."

"Whoa. Really? Is he okay?"

"Not exactly." She took a breath. "Apparently he's in a coma."

Markus winced. "*Scheisse.* Do they ... Do you know him very well?"

"Sort of." She paused long enough to catch the widening of Markus's eyes, the hint of astonishment that she should be connected with someone who rode a motorcycle and took part in Gay Games. Partly to shock him further, partly to release the pressure of her secret, she continued. "I went on the motorcycle with him that day. He dropped me off right before the accident."

Markus swallowed. "Good lord, Clare. Why would you — What made you go on a motorcycle?"

"Why wouldn't I?"

She looked straight at him, daring him to say that people like her don't do such things, hoping even that he *would* say it, so she could dispute the claim out loud.

"Well ... it's just that it's dangerous. And the roads are still quite bad." He took off his glasses and looked suddenly vulnerable and unfamiliar. "It could have been *you* who ..." He tugged agitatedly at his shirt and used the fabric to wipe his lenses.

She reached across the table and took one of his fries.

"It's okay," she said. "I don't think it's something I'll be doing regularly."

Markus nodded slowly, and for a moment the silence between them, usually a dead space into which any background noise could seep, took on a meaning of its own. Clare brushed her hair from her face and noticed that her cheeks were hot. She pressed her lips together. In an awkward, outrageous flash, she imagined Markus naked, standing before her — his slender torso (would it have hair?), his penis (what shape? what size?), the overwhelming strangeness of so much skin, all of it so close. Then Markus put on his glasses, and they turned to their food, and the conversation stumbled from the details of Adam's accident to Vancouver weather to the school music program for which Clare was to act as shop liaison.

After dinner, he offered to drive her home, and though she knew it would be best to refuse, she accepted. They drove in silence — the meaningless, moribund kind. Clare stared out the window, brooding, as the nighttime sights became increasingly, inexorably familiar. When they passed the Red Rose tea building on Côte de Liesse, its sign a fixture of the landscape for as long as she could remember, she leaned back and pretended to sleep until Markus's ancient Volkswagen pulled into her driveway.

"So ... which house is Adam's?" he said, shutting off the engine.

"Right there."

Clare unzipped her bag and hunted for her keys. Markus hung his hands over the crossbar of the steering wheel and hummed. This was the nature of his courtship: making it clear that he was available, in no hurry to rush off. Willing to sit, and maybe chat, indefinitely. The radio was on low, and Bill Evans was playing — of all things — "A Time for Love." Clare stole a glance at Markus's hands. His fingers were moving up and down in the air, playing along with the music. If he was suffering at all, if the awkward potential of the moment was weighing on him, it was impossible to tell. Silently she prodded him.

How long would it take you, Markus? If I stayed here — just sat here with you in your car — would you ever get up the nerve? Would you ever take your hand off the steering wheel and put it on my leg?

Though the awkwardness of such a thing would be excruciating, she wanted him to try. She wanted it to be possible. But Markus's fine-boned hands remained where they were, floating in time to the music. Clare pulled her keys from her bag.

"I haven't visited his family yet," she said. "Do you think I should?"

Markus shrugged. "I guess it sort of depends how well you know them."

"Not at all."

"Hmm. A card might be best."

"Yeah." She zipped her bag. "I should go in. Thanks a lot for the ride."

"Any time."

Inside, the synthetic smell of the new carpeting was potent. Clare left the lights off and went directly upstairs, where she heard the eleven o'clock news from behind her mother's bedroom door. She brushed her teeth and washed her face, then she locked herself in her room. Neatly and methodically, she undressed. She deposited her underwear, her tights, and her sweater in the laundry hamper, then she crossed the room to hang up her skirt. From the top shelf of the closet she took down Emma's gift and weighed it in her hand, examining its size and shape.

She crossed the room again and took a navy blue towel from the laundry hamper. There would be blood, she imagined. She kept the bedside lamp on and the stereo off. With the towel in place, she lay on her back, her legs arranged as if for a pelvic exam. The vibrator rubbed and chafed, but as she nudged it around cautiously, the surprising wetness returned. Eventually, confident she could accomplish her task efficiently, she took a breath and plunged the thing in. The pain was searing, horrible, but she wanted to be thorough. She manoeuvred the device back and forth a few times, until, unable to stand it any longer, she pulled it out and fell back on her pillow, flushed and a little queasy. When she'd recovered enough, she sat up and reached for the box of tissues on the bedside table. She was bleeding — not as much as she'd expected, but enough to suggest that her rite had been accomplished.

JUNE 1964

"**H**ave you ever read Ecclesiastes?" Margaret said. She was flopped on her bed, listening to a Bob Dylan record.

Isobel, sideways in Margaret's charity shop armchair, knees curled up to her chest, turned from the window. "No. Why?"

"It's really brilliant. I don't think my father has preached from it once, but I'm going to write all my sermons from it. It's about not being greedy or vain and just letting nature —" Margaret spun around to face the record player. "God! Isn't he *brilliant*?! He's a poet!"

Isobel felt a pang of jealousy. She didn't really care for Bob Dylan, but he was an American, which meant that she *should* fancy him. "I like his other record better," she said vaguely.

Margaret eyed her intently. "Is anything wrong, Isobel? You're sounding glum."

"I'm getting the curse again." She let her head fall backward and stared at the ceiling.

"It's not a curse," Margaret said gently. "It's natural."

"You'd call it a curse if you got pains like I do. *And,* it's only been three weeks since the last one. *Three weeks.* That's cursed."

"Maybe it's just mid-cycle pains. That happens sometimes."

Isobel scowled. "I'd rather be early."

"Are you bleeding?"

"Not yet. It takes a while to get started."

They listened to Bob Dylan till the song came to an end, then Margaret sat up. "Should we take Roddy out to the pond? They say walking helps."

Isobel slid her legs down to the floor and reached for her trainers. She knew nothing would alter the inevitable course of her torture, but a few hours outdoors would make the time in bed more bearable.

∞

THE POND — a glorified puddle, really — was out of town, at the crest of a gentle rise. They walked to it along a dirt path, the Biggars' spaniel zigzagging back and forth ahead of them, plunging his snout into clumps of vegetation. Margaret held the leather lead in her hand, slapping it against her thigh as she marched in front of Isobel. Although the air was cool, Margaret hadn't bothered with a jumper, and her blouse was knotted just above her navel, revealing a pale roll of midriff. She wasn't exactly fat, but with the exception of her enviably round breasts, her best features were above her neck — a head of dark curls, cheeks that dimpled deeply when she smiled, sparkling grey eyes. She was what Isobel's mother called an *intense* girl. Nothing was ever frivolous with Margaret. Her ideas, her conversations, her friendships — her one friendship, actually, with Isobel — were potent with meaning. It could be exhausting at times.

At the end of the path she stopped to catch her breath and smiled in a way that indicated a certain type of question was about to be asked.

"Yes?" Isobel prompted warily, and Margaret narrowed her eyes.

"So have you and Alastair kissed yet?"

Isobel looked off at the pond. She hadn't told Margaret about Patrick Locke and wished now that she'd kept quiet about Alastair. For Margaret's intense stare forced her suddenly to acknowledge the awkwardness of having seen the man four or five times without kissing him, or holding his hand, or even considering the possibility of either. During their outings, Alastair had talked about the knitwear factory mostly, and walked with his hands in his pockets. Occasionally he mentioned his plans to go to Montreal — not exactly America, but it was all the same to Isobel — and she'd listened, and fantasized, and gradually she began to notice tiny, invisible threads connecting her life to his. Yet the idea of actually touching Alastair Fraser was ludicrous — which provoked in her a vague irritation with Margaret for forcing the realization.

"Not really," she finally said. "No."

Margaret seemed relieved, which made sense. After all, she herself had never had a boyfriend. "I suppose it won't be long, though," she said.

Isobel headed for the tree next to the pond. "I suppose not."

They sat on the grass, backs against the broad trunk, while Roddy zigzagged and sniffed. The pond's surface was as blank and beckoning as a fresh sheet of paper. Margaret lobbed a stone.

"It seems strange — kissing."

Isobel thought of Patrick's tongue and the confusion of strange feelings it had provoked.

"Why?" she said, her tone indifferent.

Margaret lobbed another stone into the water. "It doesn't *mean* anything. Not like talking does. And why should it be lips? Why not noses, or chins, or something else?" She giggled. "All right, it *can* be something else, but at least that has a special purpose."

"It's not just lips," Isobel said testily, weighing a heavy stone in her hand. "I mean, they're connected to how you feel inside. It's all connected." She hoped Margaret would understand, for she could explain no further. She tossed the stone and watched the buckling of its ripples to the edge of the pond.

"I know. It's still strange though," Margaret said. "How are the cramps?"

"Still there."

"They say it's better after you have a baby."

"I don't want a baby," Isobel sighed.

Margaret plucked at the long grass. "I know a kind of massage that works. My cousin had me do it to her when she had bad pains."

"What do you mean *massage?*"

"With my fingers. I can make your uterus relax."

Isobel cringed at the word. *"How?"*

"It's easy. I just press on your middle in a certain way."

There was something not right about the proposition, but the idea that her friend might somehow be capable of taming the beast in her belly made Isobel eye Margaret's small, dirt-smudged hands with guarded optimism.

"It really works, what you do?"

"It worked for Pam. Go on — lie down and undo your trousers."

"Can't you do it through my trousers?"

Margaret rolled her eyes. "No, don't be daft. It's much better the other way. Anyway, it's only you and me."

Isobel chewed her bottom lip. She wished at times like this that Margaret would be more reserved, or that her openness would extend to more people. This privileged access imposed a kind of obligation that Isobel neither welcomed nor wished to impose in return. Still, the promise of relief made her comply. Awkwardly, as if she were walking backwards, she unzipped her blue jeans — real American ones — and lay down in the long grass. Roddy trotted up and hung his droopy ears and freckled muzzle over her face. Margaret shooed him away then knelt beside her and folded back the two flaps of denim. The tip of her tongue protruding in concentration, she pressed down with her fingers and began kneading small circles in Isobel's flesh through the thin blue cotton of her knickers.

"I hope you don't need to use the loo," she said, laughing.

Isobel mumbled "No," but she wasn't sure. She'd expected something like a doctor's prodding and poking, but this was different. She rolled her head to one side and fixed her eyes on the pond, where faint waves still rippled, like echoes of the strange new rippling sensation inside of her. In the distance, at the edge of her vision, were the grey-brown shapes of Stanwick's buildings, low and flat, except for the towers of the town clock and the abbey.

"Is it feeling better?" Margaret said.

"I'm not sure. Maybe."

"Let me try it this way."

Margaret slid her fingers down Isobel's cotton knickers, and the sudden touch of skin on skin was both electric and terrifying. Isobel closed her eyes to shut out the town. The rippling inside radiated throughout her, warming her, like the warm flush she got from Patrick's whisky. Faint smells of grass and sweat and dog fur hovered in the air, terrible and intoxicating. Vaguely she knew she must put an end to this awful pleasure, but it wasn't until the unexpected rush between her thighs — was she bleeding? had she wet herself? — that she bolted up and shoved Margaret's hands away.

"Jesus, Margaret!" she panted, zipping her jeans. "What were you doing?"

Margaret's eyes widened. "Helping you with your pains. What's wrong, Isobel?"

"You can't — It's not —" She turned to the pond, where Roddy was wading chest-high in the muck. "You can't *do* that."

"But I didn't ..." Margaret rubbed her palms down her thighs; the pale freckles on her chin pinched and quivered. "It didn't *mean* anything. I was only helping."

Isobel flung a stone into the pond. Roddy lumbered out and spluttered like an egg beater in the long grass. *It didn't mean anything,* she repeated to herself, seeing in her friend's bewilderment that Margaret hadn't understood at all, couldn't see that everything was horribly, inescapably connected. The creature inside her twisted and cramped. She looked past the town and imagined herself at the top of the Empire State Building — not her body, just her essence, by itself.

"I have to go," she said. "I think the bleeding's started."

8

LATE THE NEXT MORNING, Mr. Vantwest's car was again in his driveway. Before she could talk herself out of it, Clare slipped quietly down the stairs. She intended to leave unnoticed, but as she sat on the bench, pulling on her boots, her mother appeared.

"Doesn't the new carpeting just liven the whole place up?" she said.

Clare glanced up the stairs and into the empty living room at the fresh, rust-coloured floors.

"It looks good."

"Just wait — it'll be even better when the new furniture arrives." Isobel plucked at an edge of floral wallpaper. "This needs to go, too," she added, almost contemptuously. "The carpet fellow said he could recommend someone who does painting and wallpapering." As she spoke, she tore away tiny strips of paper, letting them flutter onto the bottom stair. "I'll have to ring Ted first. That's the carpet layer. I don't think he left me the fellow's phone number."

Clare rubbed a scuff mark on the toe of her boot and silently urged her mother to go away.

"Are you off anywhere special?" Isobel said.

She wanted to lie, but nothing came to her.

"I noticed the Vantwests are home," she said flatly. "I thought I'd go across and see how Adam's doing."

To her credit, Isobel betrayed no surprise. She tapped her index finger against her lips and leaned backward to look out the living room window.

"I've been meaning to make another casserole for them."

Clare stood and shook out the legs of her jeans. She was a little sore, but the bleeding seemed to have stopped. "I don't think they've been home much," she said. She needed to leave; her resolve was already failing. But her mother held her back.

"I think I'll go with you, Clare. If you don't mind. They'll wonder why I didn't come. And I do want to let them know I'm thinking about them."

Clare's hand dropped from the doorknob.

"Just let me change into a decent pair of slacks," her mother said, then she dashed up the stairs.

They left the house together under an overcast sky.

"I wish I'd made another casserole," Isobel said as they started up the Vantwests' driveway.

Clare hugged her arms across her chest. "It doesn't matter."

"Hmm. I suppose they might not eat that sort of thing."

There were lights on in the house, yet when Clare rang the bell, no one answered. She whispered, "Let's go," but her mother pressed her ear to the door and shook her head. "The bell didn't make much of a noise. It could be broken." She rapped loudly while Clare stared at the concrete landing. Moments later, hurried footsteps sounded on the other side. The deadbolt jiggled, and the door opened.

It was the aunt. She clutched a tea towel in one hand, and she was dressed in a manner that had more than once prompted Isobel to say she would love to take the woman shopping — shapeless yellow dress, pilled white cardigan, opaque caramel-coloured stockings. The plastic buttons that fastened down the front of her dress were strained across her middle.

For a second or two no one spoke. Then Isobel reached out and touched the aunt's sleeve.

"Mary. How are you? I hope we're not intruding."

The aunt brushed invisible strands of hair away from her forehead. "Ah, Mrs. Fraser. Thank you for the beautiful card. And the chicken. My niece and her daughter enjoyed that very much."

"Oh, you're very welcome. We just wanted to see how you're doing, if there's anything else we can —"

"It's very good of you all to visit." The aunt stepped back, wiping her hands on the tea towel. "Come in. Please."

Clare followed her mother into the Vantwests' tiled vestibule, suddenly moved by the significance of the event. She'd been looking across the street at this house her entire life, never entering, never catching more than shadows behind the drapes. And now she was inside. She entered humbly, vaguely expecting to be awed, though at first glance, there was nothing especially awesome about the Vantwests' private world.

"It's good this snow is finally melting, isn't it?" the aunt said.

Clare nodded awkwardly; her mother smiled.

"Oh, yes! Now let's just hope we don't get one of those spring storms and have to start all over again. It's always so discouraging when that happens."

"Ah, no. That would be too much." The aunt glanced over her shoulder, down the hall, then waved her tea towel toward the living room. "Come in, sit down."

Isobel slipped off her black wool jacket. "You're sure we're not disturbing you?"

"No, no. Alec will be here soon." The aunt took the jacket then checked the hall once more. "Come, come. Sit."

"Should I take off my shoes?" Clare said. As an opening, it was hopelessly inadequate. Adam's family deserved more from her, and as she met the aunt's eyes, she tried to convey something of what her words failed to deliver.

"Ah, no. Never mind your shoes. Come, sit."

She sat beside her mother on the worn burgundy chesterfield. Scanning the photographs on the record player cabinet next to her, she zeroed in on a faded school portrait of Adam. He looked about six or seven years old. He wore a paisley shirt with an enormous collar and a knitted V-neck vest. A curl of black hair jutted out defiantly above his right ear, and two teeth were missing from the cheeky grin he'd flashed the photographer. In the washed-out colours of the portrait, his eyes were a nondescript brown, nothing like the particular shade that Clare remembered.

"Those are the old school pictures," the aunt said. "Not all the years, but most of them."

Clare nodded and pretended to examine the other photos. She tried out a question in her head — *How is Adam doing, Mary?* — but the boldness of "Mary" seemed inappropriate, while the question itself suggested that Adam was simply out of touch — living in another city, busy with his studies. Then it struck her, numbingly, that perhaps the reason the Vantwests were home at all that morning was that Adam had died. She braced her clenched fists between her knees and stared at his high school graduation photo — the same cheeky grin. It made perfect, terrible sense: he'd died in the night, his family was in shock, and she and her mother had no business being in their home. There was nothing safe that could be said.

But Isobel managed.

"Mary, we were so shocked to hear about Adam's accident. How are you and your brother doing?"

Clare held her breath.

"We were shocked also," said the aunt. "But we are living one day at a time. There's nothing else to do, isn't it. The doctor says it's a miracle he is even alive, so we must thank God for that."

"Is his condition improving?" Clare said, exhaling, and again her words seemed inadequate.

The aunt lowered herself into an armchair opposite the chesterfield. "Oh yes, little by little. They think he is beginning to respond to their tests, but they still must call it a coma." She frowned. "We'll be happy when the doctors stop using that word. Much too serious, no?" With surprising agility, she stood up again. "You'll have some tea?"

Before they could answer, the aunt disappeared into the adjoining kitchen. As water ran and cups clattered, Clare followed her mother's quiet survey of the Vantwests' living room. Isobel's eyes wandered from the embroidered runner covering the coffee table, across the trampled beige carpet, to the elaborately carved sideboard. Her eyes, and Clare's, then landed on an astonishing item, butted against a bookcase. It was an upright crocodile, which, like a proverbial party drunkard, had a lampshade on its head. Isobel leaned toward Clare, but whatever remark she intended to whisper was cut off by a knock in the hallway.

"Alec!" Clare heard the aunt say. "Alec, we have guests for tea. Mrs. Fraser and her daughter. Come out and join us." There was no audible reply, and a few seconds later, the aunt spoke again, but not in English. This time, the hall door opened.

"I'm not available, Mary," Mr. Vantwest announced, making no attempt to muffle his voice. "I'll take my tea in here."

In the kitchen the kettle whistled. Clare's hands clenched tighter. Suddenly she was relieved beyond measure that her mother had come along. She glanced at Isobel, whose chin was directed toward the hall like an antenna, then she turned back to the outrageous lamp by the bookcase. Something about its imperfections suggested the thing was real. Real or not, though, its outrageousness seemed appropriate, a tangible emblem that all was not right in the Vantwest house. Clare kept her eyes on the creature until the aunt reappeared carrying a silver tray, which she set on the embroidered runner. The tea, strong and steaming, had already been poured into four gold-rimmed cups, and there was a matching plate of yellow cake.

"Alec is taking this hardest of all," the aunt said heavily. "I told him he should stay home today, and the doctor agreed with me. He said he will call us if there's any change. I tell Alec he should go outside, take a walk, go to church. His health is not so good anymore." She added milk to two of the cups, sugar to one, sloshing tea into the saucers as she stirred. "His doctor has told him he has diabetes. It's only mild, but if he doesn't look after himself, he'll have to take the needle."

Isobel cleared her throat and leaned forward to take one of the remaining cups. "Well, it certainly makes sense, doesn't it, that your brother would be terribly upset. He's certainly had more than his share of troubles." She turned to Clare. "We know what *some* of those troubles are like, don't we, pet?"

Clare looked down and reached for the tiny pitcher of milk.

The aunt lifted a cup and saucer from the tray. "I must take this to Alec," she said. "Please eat some cake." Then she disappeared down the hall.

Clare plucked the smallest slice of cake from the plate and took a bite. She and her mother didn't speak, and she worried that the Vantwests would suspect them of eavesdropping. Nevertheless, when a new bout of urgent whispering erupted in the hall, she strained to listen. The aunt's words were muffled, but it was clear she was distressed. Her brother's voice, which he'd lowered a little, came in calm fragments.

"This isn't — time, Mary — not interested — they — appreciate it if you would ask them —"

Clare stared at the crocodile lamp. She tried to imagine the man that Adam Vantwest had described in the depanneur. A complicated, tormented man, he'd suggested. But devoted to his family. The word *fierce* came to her — fiercely devoted, fierce as a crocodile. It was a word that had no place in the pattern of her own life, yet she repeated it to herself, rhythmically, as her thumb rubbed the rim of her saucer.

When the aunt returned, she stood in the middle of the living room and smoothed the front of her dress with her palms. Isobel rested her cup and saucer on the table.

"Perhaps we should go, Mary. It seems we've caught you at a bad time."

The aunt hesitated just long enough that the answer she couldn't manage verbally became apparent. Clare set her own cup on the table, and, following her mother's lead, stood up. For the first time, the aunt addressed her directly.

"You must come back another time. You're still living with your mother, no?"

"Maybe not for long," Isobel chirped. "She's thinking of moving out to Vancouver."

Clare gave a tight-lipped smile. The aunt cocked her head to one side.

"Ah, so far away. Just like Rudy."

"How *is* Rudy?" Isobel then said. "I haven't seen him in years."

"Oh, he is fine. Always working very hard for his pupils."

"He's a lovely lad. Give him my best when you speak to him."

As they filed out of the living room, Clare took a last look at the six-year-old Adam. His face was no longer cheeky but imploring.

Come on, Clare. You were the last person I spoke to that day. Tell them about our ride. Anything. Go on.

The aunt fetched Isobel's jacket from the closet. While Isobel slipped it on and plucked a bit of fluff from the lapel, Clare stood with her arms crossed and her right hand clenched. The opportunity would last only a few seconds, she knew, and it wasn't until the last possible instant that she cleared her throat and said, as if it were an afterthought, "I spoke to Adam before his accident. I was on my way to the store and he was cleaning his motorcycle."

The saying of it was a relief — but a fleeting one. Searching the aunt's eyes she wondered suddenly if the Vantwests already knew the whole story — if Adam, when he returned to his house for the extra helmet and jacket, had mentioned to his father where he was going, and with whom, and if Mr. Vantwest and his sister were now wondering bitterly how it was that Clare Fraser had managed to escape Adam's fate. Resenting her.

And yet what she detected in the aunt's expression was the same eager reassurance she'd seen in Adam.

"Ah, that's good. You both had a nice talk at that time?"

"Yes ... we did."

Clare glanced distractedly in the direction of the living room. There was so much more to say — about the ride along the lakeshore, and the conversation by the dairy case, about Adam paying for the eggs, and speaking French, and offering to take her up Mount Royal. More importantly there was her sense that these things had, in some still vague but significant way, affected her. Adam had changed her, she wanted to say. But her mother was watching her as attentively as the aunt. Isobel would notice that these weren't the kinds of things her daughter ever talked about, and the fact of her noticing would be intolerable.

"We didn't talk for long," she finally added. "He was telling me about Sri Lanka."

The aunt smiled. "Ah yes. He is always talking about Sri Lanka, isn't it?"

Her words implied a generous assumption that Clare Fraser was close enough to Adam to know the sorts of things he liked to talk about. Though the remark left her awkwardly nodding and looking down at the floor, she wished it were true. She wished her mother and Mr. Vantwest would leave and that she and the aunt could sit together, like neighbours, and talk about Adam.

Instead, the aunt patted her hair, and Isobel reached for the door latch.

"Please give our best to your brother," she said. "Tell him we were asking after him. And if there's anything we can do to help, Mary, don't hesitate to ring."

The aunt stretched her cardigan across her middle and shivered. "Alec is taking this very hard," she whispered. "He's not himself these days." She glanced down the hall, and Isobel, in response, reached out and squeezed her neighbour's hand.

The visit ended. When the door had closed behind them and they were halfway down the Vantwests' driveway, Isobel exhaled as if she'd been holding her breath.

"Well, *that* was a strange visit."

"I guess," Clare said.

"I just don't see — Well, I can understand the man being reluctant to socialize. But to send us away altogether?"

Clare took in the familiar lines and angles of her own house. Her mother had yet to make any changes to the exterior, and for the moment Alastair was still there, in the brickwork, the windows, the aluminum siding — still attentive, if nothing else.

"Maybe he just had the guts to do what most people in his situation want to do." She kicked a chunk of dry snow and it sprayed across her driveway. "Wouldn't you have loved to tell Joanne Skinner to get lost when she kept coming over here after Dad died?"

"Not really," Isobel said. "She was the one who got me out taking that accounting course. I'm not sure what I would have done otherwise."

Clare eyed her mother uncertainly then followed her into the house.

∞

THAT EVENING, EMMA CALLED. She talked for thirty minutes, her thoughts ramming into each other like a high-speed traffic pileup, before finally taking a breath.

"So, what's up with you?" she said.

Clare was lying on the loveseat, picking idly at its worn beige cushions. She'd said nothing to Emma about Adam's accident — nor had Emma's mother gotten around to it, apparently — and though she toyed with the possibility now, a desire to keep her connections with the Vantwests private held her back.

"My mother's been flirting with her carpet installer," she said instead.

Emma gasped theatrically. "You're kidding! Isobel Fraser is out on the scene?! That's amazing. But I told you she would, didn't I? So who's the guy? He's a furnace installer?"

"Carpet."

"That's wild. What's he like?"

"I don't know really. His name's Ted. He's sort of rugged, I guess." She paused. Then, to make up for hiding the real story, she added, "It's kind of weird, imagining my mother with someone other than my dad."

Emma became serious, her voice like a therapist's.

"It had to happen, Clare. Your mother's not ready to lead an old widow's life. She's really attractive, and I can really see her getting out there and exploring the possibilities. I know it must seem like she's replacing your dad, but — and don't get me wrong here; I really liked your dad — but I bet she's ready for some younger blood."

Clare twisted the telephone cord around her index finger and watched the tip turn pink. Emma's predictions about her mother were logical but wrong. The Isobel Fraser that Clare knew — the woman with whom most of Emma's world could not be shared — was not, despite the murky circumstances of her pregnancy, an explorer of that sort.

"Anyway," Emma continued, "I think you're dealing with two difficult issues here. The first one is having to acknowledge *again* that your dad is gone. And I totally sympathize with how hard that must be.

And the other one is having to face the fact that your mother is becoming sexually active while you're not. I know that sounds kind of brutal, but I don't mean it that way. It's a reversal of the old — Oh, crumb, I've got another call. Can you hold on for a sec?"

In the brief silence, Clare unwrapped her finger and massaged it. Emma's voice, when it returned, was buoyed by a sense of barely contained busyness.

"That was Linus. He's going out of town and we need to finalize the music for Thursday. I'm really sorry, Clare. Can I call you back in a few minutes?"

"Sure."

Clare hung up and placed the phone on the floor beside the loveseat. The mention of the Jazz Studies Director with whom she'd gone for coffee made her restless. She didn't want to hear the rest of Emma's analysis. It would be clinical and useless, and to avoid it she would say that things had changed.

Markus and I had sex, she tried. *We went out for dinner and shared a bottle of wine, and we both kind of lost our inhibitions. We went back to his apartment. It hurt a little. The wine helped. Yes, I had an orgasm.*

She started over, fine-tuning her scenario, but when she reached the return to Markus's apartment, which required considerable elaboration, the phone rang. She snatched up the receiver before her mother could answer downstairs.

"That was quick," she said.

There was a moment of silence, then a man's voice spoke, hesitant and formal.

"Is this Mrs. Fraser?"

Clare's hand tightened around the receiver. She imagined the caller was Ted.

"It's Clare. Her daughter. Sorry. I thought you were someone else."

"This is Alec Vantwest. I understand you came to my home this afternoon."

"Oh. Yes," she managed to answer, despite the thumping of her heart at the base of her throat.

Mr. Vantwest coughed. "I would like to apologize for my lack of hospitality today."

Clare swallowed. "It's okay, I —"

"I haven't been myself recently, but that's no excuse for rudeness. I'd be pleased if you and your mother would consider a return visit. Tomorrow afternoon, perhaps. We'll be at the hospital in the morning. Of course, if you have something else on your program —"

"I have to work tomorrow, but ..."

"Well, perhaps another day then."

"I'm off on Wednesday."

"All right then. Let's say four o'clock Wednesday?"

"Okay."

"We'll have tea. Mary will be here as well, of course."

"Of course. Thank you."

Mr. Vantwest ended the call with polite efficiency. Clare replaced the receiver and slowly unlocked her hand.

9

Monday (April something), 6 a.m. I spoke to my sister last night. It seems Adam's recovery isn't going to be the kind of clear-cut event I'd been waiting for. Some days he improves a little, others he plateaus. Technically he's not in a coma anymore (he got up to the magic number 15 on the Glasgow coma scale, whatever that means), but he doesn't sound much better either. Apparently it may be a long time before we know the final outcome. And then there's the broken arm and the fractured vertebra. They've got him braced in some kind of halo contraption to keep him from doing any more damage. "Picture a metal circle bolted to his head with four posts coming down," Sue said. Jesus Christ. In other words, my brother is quite seriously fucked up. Susie's feeling guilty about going back to Toronto, but I'm glad she did. It makes me feel like less of a shit. After all, if Susie, with her high-maintenance kid and crumbling marriage, could still manage to drop everything and be there for Dad and Adam, what would my excuse be? My aunt has gone back. Maybe you've seen her. That is, if you're still living on MHR. I realize that's not very likely, but I still imagine you there, looking out your window. Anyway, I'm finding her absence kind of strange. On the one hand, I feel a little like a kid who's just moved out on his own for the first time. I eat whatever I like, walk around the house naked etc. etc. Given the stuff going on with Adam, I wouldn't admit this to anyone else, but there's a part of me that's feeling pretty good. On the other hand, without my aunt here I feel kind of strange about being *here*, in Sri Lanka, at all. It's as if I'm suddenly a tourist, which is exactly what I didn't want when I came here. I've got a couple of cousins in Colombo, but I don't really know them, so they don't really count (neither does Uncle Ernie).

(Later, on the bus) It's my first day back at school today. I took a few days off after the news about Adam, and I've planned a risky lesson for my English twelves. Well, for one of them in particular. Wish me luck.

R UDY GLANCED UP FROM HIS WRITING in time to catch the first saint. He closed his diary and began his tally. He was out of practice, so he did just one side of the street, craning his neck to spot his targets through the morning busyness of Jampettah Mawatha. Outside Ganesh Bookshop a small mob of women blocked the glass-cased Virgin altogether, and at the church he saw only one statue where he thought there'd been two. But when the bus turned off the crowded street, he made a satisfied mental note of the eight saints he'd found then searched his knapsack for the lesson plan he'd written out the previous night.

It was scribbled on a grungy sheet of lined paper, and as he read over the reminders and fragments of ideas, he began to wonder if the lesson itself wasn't a bit shabby. It wasn't even English, or a bona fide lesson for that matter. He'd gotten away with such things back home, but the students in his current English 12 class would find the activity weird — with the possible exception of Kanda. Kanda might not think it weird, though he'd perhaps find it offensive. He'd know that it was a response to his essay, and that the entire activity had been designed for him, as a rebuttal. Rudy looked around at his fellow passengers, and for a moment he doubted his right to embark on the planned activity at all. He spoke neither Tamil nor Sinhala; he belonged, only loosely, to a mixed-bag ethnic group of no political or social significance; he was a Canadian working in a British-style school that the average Sri Lankan couldn't afford. In all sorts of ways, he was in no position to involve himself, even abstractly, in the country's troubled state of affairs. And yet, he reminded himself, these were just the sorts of limitations that Kanda would impose. Just the sort of thinking he hoped to rattle in his second period English class.

He got off the bus in front of the school and made his way directly to the air-conditioned teachers' lounge. There were a dozen or so staff members there, and a buzz of conversation and faint smells of hair tonic and Magi-board pens greeted Rudy as he slipped through the door at the back of the room. He took in the scene with sudden timidity. He'd missed three days of school, but it seemed he'd been away forever. In his absence, he imagined, this serious-looking crew in business shirts and owlish glasses, the odd sari, had functioned perfectly well without him, and once again, as on the bus, he felt himself to be an intruder. He stood at the back of the lounge, unnoticed, awkward, until Nisal Somapala, head of the math department, waved to him, and the feeling eased a little. He crossed the room to the table where Nisal sat flipping through a textbook.

"Van Twest!"

"Hey there," Rudy said, pulling out a chair.

"Feeling better, machan?"

Rudy hesitated. He'd told the headmaster he was sick, and the old gentleman himself had covered his classes. "Yeah, I'm okay. How about you?"

Nisal thumped his palm against the cover of his textbook. "Superb! I myself only returned yesterday. You remember, I attended the mathematics conference in New Delhi. This Professor Ahuja was really fantastic."

He held up the book, and Rudy noted the professor's name on the cover. He hadn't remembered that Nisal was going to a conference, hadn't paid much attention when he was told in the first place.

"That's great," he said. "What did he talk about?"

Nisal straightened in his chair. Though a few years older than Rudy, he had a young, pimple-spotted face, and it beamed now with youthful enthusiasm. "Fermat's theorem. You've heard of this?"

Rudy shook his head. "No clue."

"Oh, Van Twest, you're missing out. Gripping stuff, I tell you." He leaned forward, then the warning bell rang, cutting him off. "Ah well, better get to class," he said. "I'll tell you about it at break time."

Rudy said he looked forward to it and offered Nisal a corny salute. Then he shouldered his knapsack and went to the sink for a glass of water. Mrs. Da Silva, the school secretary, was rinsing her coffee cup. She turned and studied him through her thick, round glasses.

"You look thin," she said.

Rudy glanced down at his belt, which was indeed fastened two notches in from its usual spot. "It's good for me," he said, patting his belly the way his father always did after Sunday lunch. "Too many love handles."

Mrs. Da Silva smiled and frowned at the same time. "Love handles are good for you, I think."

He laughed uneasily. "I don't know ... maybe."

By the end of his first class his stomach was all nerves. He stood under the ceiling fan, reading over his limp page of notes while the year tens scuffled out of the room. The twelves wouldn't start arriving for another couple of minutes, and in that time he rehearsed his opening in his head.

We're going to try something a little different today. A debate, if you like. I actually got the idea from Kanda's last essay. It was better to acknowledge this right off, he'd decided. Let the boy know his choice of topic was appreciated. *We're going to talk about Sri Lanka's political conflicts. Every one of you is caught up in this mess in some way.* Was that too belligerent, he wondered. He tried softening his approach: *I'd be willing to bet that all of your families have been affected in some way by these conflicts. You listen to the opinions of the LTTE, the JVP, the government, your families and friends. And I'm sure you all have ideas of your own about how the problem should be resolved. We're going to talk about some possible solutions this morning.* He looked up to see Chamika Heenatigala deposit her books on a desk then slip back out into the corridor. *But we're going to combine our discussion with an exercise in point of view. I'm going to assign each of you a role, a point of view, which might, perhaps, differ from your own personal point of view.* Again he paused, pleased with the way he'd managed to tie the unorthodox activity to the regular course material. He imagined looking at Kanda at this moment, making eye contact, sussing out the boy's reaction. *I'll give you some time to come up with arguments that would correspond to that point of view, and then —*

Chamika returned, accompanied by a few other girls, and their conversation, though hardly rambunctious, broke his concentration. He scanned the back of his paper, on which he'd written out the names of his students, and beside each name a narrowly defined identity. He'd considered a few possibilities for Kanda — Muslim doctor, Buddhist monk, indigenous villager — but finally settled on the title now scribbled beside the boy's name: Sinhalese teacher.

Rudy folded the paper but kept it in his hand as more students filed into the room. A few acknowledged him with nods or smiles; James Fernando even asked if he was feeling better.

"Not too bad," Rudy said, looking over James's shoulder at the door. "Thanks."

"Will you return our essays today?"

"I think so. At the end of class."

"They were satisfactory?"

Rudy eyed his student more closely, forcing himself to pay attention. Despite everything he'd assumed about James when he confiscated the sprinkler caricature, the boy seemed genuinely keen to please him.

"They were fine. We'll talk about them later."

He glanced up at the clock. Kanda was generally one of the last to arrive, but today he was pushing it. Rudy went to his desk and flipped open his daybook. He then struck a contemplative pose — one hand buried in his pocket, the index finger of his other hand slowly tracing the lines of the page in front of him. For a moment the random page actually caught his attention. It was a lesson he'd been particularly proud of: "To be or not to be? How does *Hamlet* ultimately answer the question?" He'd written the words *existentialism* and *relationships* in block letters and circled them, though he could no longer remember precisely how he'd connected the two concepts.

The bell rang. He looked up and saw that Kanda's desk was still empty. On any other day, he would have been relieved. He would have marked an "a" next to Kanda's name in the attendance book and gotten on with things. But while there was every reason to assume that Kanda was absent, Rudy believed he'd show up, if only as a fateful rejection of the hope he still harboured that the boy would drop his class or move to another school. He strolled to the door and checked the corridor, but it too was empty. In his own classroom his students were settled, ready to listen to whatever he would choose to say to them. He returned to his desk, where he'd left the lesson outline. He could launch into the political debate as planned, but without Kanda, there was no point.

"Has anyone seen Kanda Selvarajah?" he said, keeping his tone casual.

His students looked at the empty desk, then at each other, shrugging and shaking their heads. Again Rudy checked the clock. He wanted to ask them to wait a couple of minutes but could think of no reasonable excuse for the request. Instead, he stalled.

"Well, it's good to be back. I'm sure you were in very capable hands with Dr. Muller. He's filled me in on what you covered last week. Does anyone have any questions about the work you did? Keats and Wordsworth, I believe it was?"

For several seconds the class sat mute and still. Then Sharmila Arumugan raised her hand partway, and Rudy called on her, glancing sideways at the clock.

"Will Dr. Muller's lessons be on the exam?"

"They'd be fair game," Rudy said. Under different circumstances he would have dropped the matter there; this time he stalled further. "Why do you ask?"

Sharmila gave him an awkward smile and waved her hand in front of her face. "I only was wondering."

"Okay. Are there any other questions?"

This time there was no response. He considered asking them what they'd learned about the Romantics, but Sharmila's question suggested that Headmaster Muller, not surprisingly, hadn't taught them much of anything. Rudy unfolded his lesson plan and headed for his spot under the ceiling fan, skimming the introduction as he walked, weighing his options. If Kanda were to show up within the next five minutes he wouldn't miss much. He'd still take part in the discussion, still be forced to consider his world from a different perspective. But he'd lose the full impact, the moment of eye contact, when the challenge to his ideas would be made clear and personal. Rudy folded the paper on which he'd made his notes and slid it inside his pocket. He turned slowly under the fan, surveying his students. Several shifted in their seats; James fiddled with his pen. A final glance at the clock told him he could wait no longer.

"A slight change of plans," he began, dryly. "I was going to return your essays at the end of class, but I think I'll give you some time to go over them right now. You're each going to do a rewrite based on the suggestions I've made in my comments. Remember that what I've commented on is the development of your argument — whether or not you've got a thesis, and how you go about proving it. The content of the argument doesn't really matter." He paused, facing Kanda's empty desk. "Let me correct that. Content does matter. It matters a lot. It's just not what I marked you on, this time." His words drifted away from him, insubstantial echoes of his thoughts. He sped up. "If my comments say to come and see me, please make sure you do."

He went to his desk and fished the students' essays from his knapsack. When everyone had set to work and he was left with Kanda's paper in his hand, he sat down heavily. He picked up a pen and turned to the last page, determined to say something more to the boy, but before he could begin, a line of students formed next to him.

"You asked me to see you, sir," said the first in line, holding out his essay, and Rudy recalled with a sigh that he'd given the same instruction to most of them.

He set aside Kanda's essay and took the one being offered him. The lineup at his desk persisted throughout the class, with several students returning more than once, and as he coached and coaxed and repeated explanations, he resigned himself to the idea that these dull but manageable essay-writing skills would be more beneficial — certainly more appreciated — than his half-baked political debate. It was an interesting idea, he consoled himself, but inappropriate. Maybe even outdated. There were many who believed the government had finally brought the Tamil situation under control.

About five minutes before the bell, he approved Rajan Sivamohan's thesis statement, wiped his face with his handkerchief, shook out his shirt, and began to anticipate the pot of strong coffee that Mrs. Da Silva would have ready in the teachers' lounge. He waited for Rajan to collect his papers and step aside, then, prompting himself to take one more student, maybe two, he directed his attention to the next in line.

It was Kanda.

"Sorry I'm late, sir," he announced. "I'll do the revision tonight."

Rudy gestured the boy and girl behind him back to their seats.

"Where have you been?" he said. He looked for a late slip but saw none.

"I didn't know you had returned. I would have come if I knew."

Rudy frowned. "What do you mean? You're supposed to be here whether I'm here or not."

Though he kept his voice low, it was terse and accusing. Kanda, however, didn't flinch.

"I came to Mr. Muller's class last week, but we only wasted our time. He thought you would be away another week, so I decided to study by myself."

"Dr. Muller had no reason for saying that," Rudy blurted, the inappropriateness of his own remark fuelling his irritation.

Kanda shrugged. "He said you didn't sound well."

"Never mind that; it's not important. So you cut class today?"

"I went to my first class. I missed this one only."

"You didn't think you'd be missing anything important?"

Again Kanda shrugged. "I assumed Dr. Muller would be here, and I didn't find his lessons helpful. We only listened to him reading the poems and talking about his studies at Cambridge." He held up a library book, *Essays on Romanticism*. "I was reading this, then I saw Dr. Muller in the library, so I came here."

Rudy massaged his forehead. He wished the content of their exchange could justify his anger. That a bright, motivated student should find the headmaster's lessons a waste of time made perfect sense. That he should bother teaching himself the material more than made up for his absence. Still, he couldn't let Kanda off the hook.

He checked the clock and turned to the class. "The bell's going to go any second. You can pack up your stuff, and I'll see you tomorrow. Essay rewrites are due Friday." He paused as the bell rang. To Kanda he then said, "Have a seat. You're spending the break in here."

Kanda held his gaze a moment longer then made his way silently through the clamour and sat down. The others eyed him as they passed but didn't speak to him. When the room had cleared, Rudy pushed his chair back and picked up Kanda's essay. The proper thing, he knew, would be to talk to the boy. To let him know in some subtle way that he understood, even sympathized. That his anger wasn't as banal or authoritarian as it seemed. And if he got that far, the next step would be to tell Kanda that he'd wanted him in class for a special reason, needed him there. Not just for the debate.

For an instant he saw his brother, and his hand clenched. Pretending to scan the essay, he crossed the room.

"I'd like you to work on your rewrite," he said blandly and placed the paper in front of Kanda. "You need to incorporate the suggestions I've made in my comments."

He returned to his desk, oppressed for the first time that morning by the intensity of the heat. He was sweating, and missing his coffee break, and though the situation was entirely his own doing, he blamed Kanda. He sat in front of his daybook and turned to Tuesday's page. In the block of space reserved for English 12, he wrote "Debate" and underlined it twice. He stared at the word, its bubbly shape evoking for him all the phony "real life" activities he used to concoct for his students in Toronto, then he crossed it out. Leaning back in his chair, he took the unused lesson plan from his pocket. He tore the paper into small pieces and released them over the metal rubbish bin like a handful of white petals.

Across the room, Kanda was staring out the window. It wasn't defiance, Rudy guessed — not yet — for he had a pen in one hand, while the other hand drummed a silent, regular beat on the edge of his desk. The silence was as oppressive as the languid air.

"Do you need any help?" Rudy ventured.

Kanda turned to him. "No, sir."

He mopped his face. Had it been any other student, he would have given the help whether it was wanted or not. Then, after assigning a couple of punitive homework exercises, he would have dismissed the offender early and hurried to the teachers' lounge for his coffee. But the comparison was hardly valid. No other student would have boycotted a class because he found it too easy. And no other student's absence, Rudy had to allow, would have bothered him at all in the first place.

He watched Kanda turn to a middle page of his essay and begin writing in the margin. *He showed up for me*, he then thought, and the realization filled him with sudden humility.

He stood and cleared his throat. "Hang on, Kanda. I'd like you to do something different."

Kanda looked up from his work. Rudy crossed the room and sat on the desk next to the boy's, affecting casualness.

"Your essay's fine the way it is, technically. You don't need to rewrite it. I want you to do a different essay." Kanda said nothing, so he carried on, awkwardly. "I think I wrote in my comments that it would be worthwhile considering the other side of the argument. In your case, that would most clearly be the Sinhalese side." Like the word *Canada*, so many years ago on Grandpa's tea estate, *Sinhalese* had a taboo ring in Kanda's presence. But still the boy said nothing. Rudy continued. "You've written an essay that begins to explain how you think the country's political tensions should be dealt with, and you've written it from a Tamil perspective. Well, from an LTTE perspective — which is fine. What I'd like you to do now is to write a similar kind of essay — how the country's problems should be solved — but from a Sinhalese perspective."

Kanda stared. Rudy wished he would complain, or argue — something, in any case, that he could respond to. He glanced at the essay, recalling his first reading of it — the desire it provoked in him to prove its author wrong — and realized he'd been counting on the classroom debate to do his work for him.

"Do you understand the assignment?" he said.

"Yes."

"Do you have any questions? Anything you want to talk about before you begin?"

"No."

Rudy lowered his feet to the floor. "Well, get a start on it then. You can leave in five minutes." He felt cowardly, pathetic. He took three steps toward his desk then turned around. "Actually, you can leave now. Turn it in on Friday."

Unhurried, Kanda collected his things and left. Rudy wandered to the open windows and rested his forearms on the wooden frame of one of the drawbridge-style panes. Below him, on the school's mani-cured lawn, several boys drifted, jostling each other distractedly as they walked. A few of them had clearly snuck past the gates at the start of the break, for they carried bags of chips and bottles of pop, badly hid-den inside their blazers. Eyeing the group directly under his window, Rudy considered sending them to the office, then he dismissed the idea, finding it suddenly offensive.

∽

THAT NIGHT HE DREAMED ABOUT KANDA. The boy appeared on Aunty's doorstep, demanding to be let in. He wore combat fatigues and spoke with a heavy accent. Rudy looked around frantically for his aunt, then remembered that she'd gone back to Montreal. Kanda ducked through the doorway — he was huge — and blew out a cloud of cigarette smoke that filled the sitting room (not really the sitting room, more a cave, with stone walls). In his thick-soled leather boots, he stalked across the floor to the painting of Adam's Peak. Like Kanda himself, the painting had grown enormous and terrifying. The mountain was a lurid scarlet, with a blazing orange sun overhead. Kanda frowned at it. "This is crap," he said, then he leaned back against the canvas and sank slowly to the floor. He was crying, blubbering snottily like a young child, and his body was no longer huge. Rudy crouched next to him and put his hand on the boy's shoulder until the crying subsided.

He woke at the edge of his bed. The sheets were damp, and as he rolled onto his back, the details of the dream rapidly evaporating, he felt only a vague sense of relief that he'd been sleeping alone.

10

Shortly before she and her mother were due at the Vantwests' for tea, Clare overheard Isobel on the phone with Ted, the carpet installer. The call lasted no more than five minutes and consisted, on Isobel's part, of a string of businesslike queries, mm-hms, and thank-yous. When it ended, Clare felt that a small but annoying weight had been lifted from her. She was flopped on the loveseat, reading *Clarissa*, but when the weight lifted, she sat up, restless, the walls of her studio too close. There were still what-ifs circling her head, but for the moment they seemed slow and benign. With a purposeful breath, she picked up her phone and dialed the music shop's number. Peter answered, and while he went to find Markus, Clare drummed her fingers against her thigh and tried to think well of her boss. For if Markus was incapable of asserting himself in the world, she reasoned, what did his failings have to do with her?

He came to the phone and cleared his throat. "Hello? Clare?"

"Hi. I hope I'm not interrupting you."

"No ... no. How are things?"

"Oh, fine."

"Have you had any news about your neighbour?"

He was very *decent*; she had to give him that.

"Not much. My mother and I are having tea with his family this afternoon."

"Really? Well, I guess they don't know me, but you could tell them I hope everything'll be okay. Or ..."

"Sure." Clare glanced at the massive novel beside her on the loveseat — over a thousand pages of Clarissa Harlowe's meditations and agonies, recommended by Markus. Anxious to be done with the call, she turned the book face down. "Listen, Markus, I was wondering if I could talk to you, on Friday. After I finish work."

"Friday?"

"If that's okay with you." Her hand clenched.

"Sure ... I'll be in tomorrow, if you ..."

"Friday would be better."

It was two days away — long enough to decide what she would say to him, not so long that the urgency to do something would fizzle.

"Uh, okay." He sounded puzzled. But he wouldn't press the matter. "So ... where would you like to talk?"

"Your office should be fine."

"Okay. Sure."

"Great. Well, I'd better get going. I'm due at the neighbours' soon."

"Okay. Well, have a good visit."

Clare slid one arm out of Adam's jacket. "I'll try."

∽

THEY LEFT AT FOUR, Isobel reporting as they crossed the street that she'd booked Ted's brother-in-law to repaint the entire house. Clare mumbled a reply, but her attention was on the Vantwests' front door.

This time, the aunt answered right away, smiling eagerly.

"Ah, it's good of you both to come back. Come in. Alec! Our guests are here."

Entering the vestibule, Clare looked down the hall at the door behind which Mr. Vantwest had sequestered himself the time before. It was wide open. The light in the room was promptly turned out, and Mr. Vantwest emerged, nudging his glasses up the bridge of his nose with his index finger. His navy cardigan and white polo shirt looked like part of a school uniform. His grey pants added to the effect, though they were a little too long and flopped over the sides of his corduroy slippers.

"Mrs. Fraser," he said, extending his hand to Isobel. "Thank you for coming. I must apologize to you for Sunday. I —"

Clare anticipated her mother's interruption.

"Please, call me Isobel. And please don't worry about the other day at all. It was perfectly understandable that you'd be ... distracted. We really should have called first, but we were so shocked to hear about Adam's accident."

"The boy loved his motorbike," Mr. Vantwest said flatly. "I suspect he was reckless with it. That is his character."

The words echoed in Clare's head. *That is his character.* An extraordinary thing to say. But, then, Mr. Vantwest seemed an extraordinary sort of man. He stepped aside as the aunt, offering Isobel a hanger, fired him a look.

"Tea will be ready soon," she said. "Alec, show these people in."

Mr. Vantwest extended his arm toward the living room. Then, as Clare and her mother seated themselves once again on the burgundy chesterfield, he stationed himself in front of them, hands clasped behind his back, and cleared his throat.

"I hope you won't be inconvenienced," he said, turning to Clare for the first time. "I realize the main purpose of your visit was to offer your sympathy, but I'd be grateful if we didn't discuss my son this afternoon. His condition is stable for now, and the doctors are hopeful. That's really all I can say." He offered no further explanation, and in the silence that followed he kept his eyes on Clare.

She clenched her hands between her knees. "It's okay. We can talk about something else."

Mr. Vantwest nodded, nudged his glasses, then sat down in the armchair opposite the chesterfield. "Well," he said, amicably, and the tension in the room gave way a little. "It's been some time since we last spoke." His attention was now back on Isobel, who, nodding emphatically, seemed ready to begin making up for that time.

"Too long, I'm afraid. Was it summer that I last saw you? I remember you were out front trimming that beautiful lilac of yours. Did it bloom well?"

Mr. Vantwest craned his neck toward the window behind the chesterfield. "Not bad. It should fare better this year. You should take some cuttings when the time comes. They give a good fragrance in the house." He crossed his legs and the corduroy slipper of his dangling foot dropped away from his heel. "Strong though," he added. "Too overpowering for some."

In the kitchen, cups and saucers clattered. Clare's eyes drifted to the photographs on the record player cabinet, to Adam in his jaunty mortarboard. *I'm in a coma and all you guys can talk about is lilac cuttings,* she imagined him saying.

The aunt came in, carrying her loaded silver tray, which she rested on the coffee table.

"There now," she said. "I heard you all talking about the lilac tree and I was reminded of those flowers. I don't think we have them in Sri Lanka. They're very exquisite, no?"

Clare glanced at the crocodile lamp and wondered how anything from a Morgan Hill front yard could seem exquisite in the Vantwests' eyes. Then she marvelled at the entire conversation, at the capacity of these neighbour-strangers to connect themselves, obligate themselves to each other, with the flimsiest of threads. Awaiting a suitable pause, she stirred her tea and prepared something to say. When the lilac exchange had more or less petered out, she turned to the aunt.

"What kinds of plants do you have in Sri Lanka?" she said.

The aunt handed her brother his cup. "Ah, my garden at home is quite lush," she began, spooning sugar into her own cup. "There is no flower bed like we have here, but I have several fruit trees. Mango, tamarind, banana, custard apple, jack fruit, of course."

"What do you mean 'of course'?" Mr. Vantwest said, his tone musing but subtly reproachful. "People in Canada wouldn't assume you have a jack tree." He got up for a slice of cake. "Even Sri Lankans wouldn't assume this."

"Alec, your sugar," the aunt said.

Mr. Vantwest made a low hissing noise and rested the cake on the edge of his saucer.

"I only meant," the aunt continued, "that the jack fruit is very useful. So many dishes we can make from that one fruit. Even the seeds are made into a delicious curry." She flapped her hand over her steaming tea. "If ever the troubles back home get so bad that I can't go to the shops, I know I can survive on my jack fruit. The rest is all surplus."

"It must be lovely having all those fruits right there," Isobel said, apparently taking no note of the troubles the aunt had mentioned.

Clare tried to imagine them herself. She scanned the photos on the record player cabinet, searching for hints, but with the exception of Rudy's graduation photo, in which he wore a dark, brooding expression, the faces in the pictures seemed to deny the existence, anywhere in their world, of troubles that could prevent an aging aunty from going to the shops.

She turned back to the conversation. Mr. Vantwest was asking her mother if she'd done any travelling.

"Europe?" he said. "The British Isles?"

Isobel laughed and rested her cup on her saucer. "I grew up in Scotland. A small town south of Glasgow."

Mr. Vantwest looked flustered. He slapped his brow and shook his head rapidly. "Of course, of course. I should have known that." Sighing, he added, "I see we're both a long way from home then."

"Oh, I don't think of the U.K. as home anymore," Isobel said. "I left at nineteen, and to tell you the truth, I was desperate to get out. I thought I'd suffocate if I stayed." She paused, sprinkling tiny cake crumbs into her cup. "There was probably a bit of teenage rebellion in me. But I haven't regretted anything."

"I've never had the opportunity to visit Britain," Mr. Vantwest said. "I've always wanted to. I find the history fascinating. You'd know more about it than I would, but I studied it quite extensively at school — medieval times, the Elizabethan period, Cromwell, the Restoration — really fascinating stuff. And of course we Sri Lankans owe a great deal to that country." He glanced at his sister. "Things weren't perfect under the English, but the place has virtually fallen apart since they left."

Again Isobel ignored the reference to trouble.

"Isn't it funny? Here you are fascinated by a place that used to bore me to tears. I remember finding the history so dull when I was in school, and the present day didn't seem any different. But I suppose I was only looking at my own small town."

She sipped her tea. Mr. Vantwest nodded his head to one side and picked at the velvet armrest of his chair. When no one else spoke, Isobel continued, more slowly, as if gauging the particular impact of each word.

"You know, the funnier thing, now that I think about it, is that when I was still in Britain, I used to dream about going to Ceylon." She paused. "That was the name back then, wasn't it?"

Mr. Vantwest said "Oh, yes" and smiled. Clare frowned. The idea was preposterous.

"It never came to pass, of course. But I do remember thinking what a lovely place it must be. I wouldn't have believed anyone from over there would want to go to Britain."

"Ah well," said Mr. Vantwest, "the grass is always greener somewhere else, as they say. I spent my boyhood on a tea estate, when I wasn't at school, and I never thought of it as anything special. It was just the place where we lived. But Canadians must find it a strange place to grow up."

"A tea estate?" Isobel seemed to savour the words. "How interesting. Did your family own it?"

"Own the estate? No, no. The English owned them back then. And managed them. My father ran the factory. Later on he became a manager, after the English had left."

The aunt interjected, addressing her remarks to Clare, as if to acknowledge that Isobel had been claimed by her brother. "It was a very interesting life, as your mother said. There was a whole society that revolved around the tea making. We had all sorts of fancy dress occasions — dinners, dances. Ah, you can't imagine what it was like back then!" Mr. Vantwest coughed and the aunt's expression became serious. "But naturally the tea was the most important thing. My brothers and I learned all about that process. There's much more to it than drying the leaves and putting them in a crate, isn't it. All the rolling and fermenting and heating and whatnot."

"I didn't know you had other siblings," Isobel said. "Are they still in Sri Lanka?"

"Only one other," Mr. Vantwest replied, straightening in his chair. "Bit of an odd duck. You'll have some more tea?"

The aunt got up to refill their cups. "Not odd, Alec," she said, and Mr. Vantwest grunted. The aunt carried on, still to Clare. "Our brother is very artistic. He used to paint such beautiful pictures. I have several of them at home. Some aren't suitable for hanging, but they're very skilfully done." She poured the tea with a strong, steady hand. "Our father wanted Ernie to follow the planting business, but in the end it was Alec who carried on the tradition."

Clare glanced at Mr. Vantwest, picking at the armrest of his chair, and was struck by an intuition that both surprised and impressed her. From Alec Vantwest she turned to the photograph of Adam.

This brother is the something your father wanted to get away from, isn't he?

The face in the photograph grinned. She was curious, but Mr. Vantwest seemed anxious for a change of topic, and Clare, for the moment, was his ally. Pinching the tiny china handle of her cup, she said, "Does the tea we're drinking come from Sri Lanka?"

Mr. Vantwest stopped picking and raised his own cup, as if in a toast. "Oh, yes. The very finest. Only the tenderest leaves and the bud are used. This particular batch is very fresh. I'd wager these leaves were plucked no more than two weeks ago. Mary brought them over with her. It was my one special request."

Clare nodded. She could think of nothing else to say but noticed that her mother, eyebrows raised, lips parted, was ready to launch herself back into the conversation.

"I've a question for you, Alec," she said, and Clare withdrew once again.

Isobel asked about the quality of the teas sold at the Provigo, and Mr. Vantwest offered in return an amiable condemnation of shoddy ingredients and lazy shortcuts. Isobel then recounted her memories of the Sunday afternoon tea ritual with her parents and sister, back in Scotland, while Mr. Vantwest nodded and sighed, adrift, it seemed, on the wave of Isobel's nostalgia. They spoke of Morgan Hill Road — all the terrible blizzards, the heat waves, the blackout that lasted for three days and had everyone in a panic over what to do with the contents of their freezers. They remembered, leaning forward in their enthusiasm, the winter that several Morgan Hill families got together at Carnaval time to build an ice castle on the Boswells' front yard.

"Wasn't that a fantastic thing!" Mr. Vantwest exclaimed.

"Oh yes, and the skill that went into it! All those passageways, and the stairs going up top. But Ken Boswell is an architect of some kind, isn't he?"

"Yes, yes. I think so."

Clare peeked out the window at the Boswells' front lawn. She too remembered the evening the ice castle was erected. She'd been twelve or thirteen, and she'd heard the neighbours' scattered, rowdy laughter through her bedroom window as she sat on her bed, reading. The Frasers had been invited, of course, but Alastair had dismissed the invitation, disapproved even. "They'll be up half the night drinking and carrying on, the lot o' them," he'd said, and Clare, listening to the vaguely frightening merriment down the street, had understood her father's objections. She couldn't remember what her mother had thought of it all, or what she'd done that night. The details that Isobel and Mr. Vantwest recalled suggested that the two of them had actually participated in the event together — impossible, of course.

Still, as the reminiscences piled up, the conversation began to intimate that Isobel Fraser and Alec Vantwest were friends. *Real neighbours,* as Adam had put it. They laughed easily, and no pause lasted longer than a second or two before one or the other launched into a new thought. They managed somehow to talk about their lives with no mention of their late spouses. The names weren't awkwardly avoided; it was rather as if Alastair Fraser and Sirima Vantwest had never really been part of that Morgan Hill existence in the first place — as if, in defiance of what fate had dealt them, Isobel and Alec had made an implicit agreement to reorganize their past.

Settled into this remade history, Mr. Vantwest nudged his glasses up the bridge of his nose and sighed. "The neighbourhood is changing, though," he said. "One of these days they'll start handing out tickets for speaking English in the street."

Isobel coughed quietly. "Oh, I don't imagine they could do *that.*" She paused. "It's silly, though, isn't it, our French-English situation?"

She used the term inclusively — *our* situation, Mr. Vantwest's and hers — and Mr. Vantwest nodded thoughtfully.

"That last referendum was too close for comfort," he said. "I can understand these people wanting to be treated properly, but what is the sense in insisting that everyone in a country speak the same language? If that's the way it's to be, we should take a big knife to the world and start hacking away. And when we're done, make sure every man stays in his own little compartment. It's ridiculous. To listen to some of these separatists, you'd think that to be a French-speaking Quebecker is the greatest thing on earth."

He set his cup and saucer on the floor beside the armchair, and the aunt immediately moved it to the coffee table. Clare listened more closely, at the same time trying to remember what Adam had said about his father's mood on referendum day. *Happy as a clam? Happy as* ... In any event, happy. He got off on that sort of thing, Adam had said. Yet the pique in Mr. Vantwest's voice suggested that the tensions of Quebec politics were not currently giving him much pleasure.

"It's the same mess in Sri Lanka," he continued. "Tamils wanting to carve up the country. I'm speaking about the rebels, of course. God knows the average Tamil man is as fed up with the fighting as the rest. But those Tigers, they carry on about their homeland as if it would be some kind of paradise, and all the troubles of the under-developed third world country would magically disappear." He looked at Clare, and she forced herself to hold his gaze. "But if you want to know the truth," he said, "I believe these people wouldn't know what to do with themselves if they had their homeland. As far as the rebels are concerned, I think the fight has become more important than the prize."

He sank back in his chair.

"Do you think there's hope?" Clare said. "That the conflict will end?"

Mr. Vantwest shrugged, as if out of steam. "Who's to say? Eventually the thing will run its course, I suppose. But you must forgive me. I get carried away on the subject. Mary will be accusing me of spoiling the conversation." He turned to his sister. "So there you are, Mary. I've made my apology."

The aunt shook her head and began gathering cups and saucers; Isobel said she certainly hoped the troubles would sort themselves out.

Clare wanted to protest, to tell Mr. Vantwest there was no need to apologize. She wanted to tell him that she knew something of his worries, that Adam had told her. Suddenly it was no longer the aunt she wanted to talk to about Adam. She imagined herself instead sitting with Mr. Vantwest in the room off the hallway, each of them unperturbed by silence, indifferent to pleasantries. Little by little, she would reveal the details of her conversation with Adam, and begin to fulfill her obligations to his family.

But such a thing was impossible.

"We should be off, pet," Isobel said, resting a hand on her daughter's knee.

Clare's leg tensed. She kept her eyes on Mr. Vantwest and rose from her seat when he did. But he was looking at Isobel, pressing his palms together.

"You must come again soon," he said. "Perhaps Mary would treat us to one of her special curries."

"Yes, yes," the aunt said. "We must do that soon."

Isobel agreed, of course, and they all made their way to the front door. With the meaningless exceptions of a thank you and a goodbye, Clare said nothing else. Her mother's "Do take care," delivered just before the Vantwests' door whispered shut behind them, carried a hint of impatience that was obvious to Clare, though she doubted Mr. Vantwest and his sister would have caught it. Isobel was full of her decorating plans, and as they crossed the street, she scolded herself for not having thought to get the painting done before the new carpeting went down.

⌒

EMMA CALLED LATER. Her mother had told her about Adam's accident, and when she'd finished reprimanding Clare for keeping it a secret, she insisted on a full debriefing and a promise of regular updates.

"Especially if his brother shows up," she said. "Are you *sure* you haven't seen him?"

172

"Positive."

Emma pondered this, then, mercifully, let it go. "Hey, speaking of sexy men," she said, "what's going on with your mom and the carpet guy?"

"Nothing. She was just being friendly."

"Now, come on, Clare. You're not just in denial?"

Clare twirled the phone cord impatiently. An image of her mother and Mr. Vantwest came to her, the two of them leaning forward in their seats, reminiscing. "Not about that," she said. "Anyway, Emma, I should go. I'm getting together with Markus."

"Again? What's going on with you two?"

"I'm not sure. Anyway, I'll talk to you later."

"Clare! What —"

She hung up quietly and went to the piano. She wouldn't be seeing Markus that night, but their Friday meeting now loomed a few hours closer. Something would happen then. It had to. She played random combinations of notes — childish crashings, the way she had before she knew how to play. She drifted to her bedroom, where she paced the carpeted floor and scowled at the beige walls. Then she went to her closet and reached under the pile of sweaters that concealed Emma's gift. At the first touch of the smooth, hard rubber, she snatched her hand back. But after a time she reached up again and took the thing down, scowling harder still. For though the thing in her hand was ugly and vile and lifeless, she'd been unable to throw it out. Worse, she'd been thinking about it.

Masturbation gets you in touch with your real self, the Emma in her head claimed expansively, more compelling than the one on the phone.

She studied her reflection in the closet mirror, searched it for signs of a *real self* hiding timidly inside.

Go on, Emma prompted. *You've got nothing else to do.*

"Fine," she whispered. Then she undressed and got into bed.

Her first attempt was clumsy, and a little painful, but she kept trying. She went about the whole business methodically, recalling Emma's descriptions, covering all the bases. She discovered that if she lay on top of the vibrator and moved a certain way, she reached the type of climax she'd experienced the first time — a frantic, ticklish explosion of feeling. And when she rolled over onto her back and inserted the device, another type happened — a deep, rolling wave that she struggled to ride for as long as she could. With the hesitant assistance of her fingers, she learned to combine the two. She achieved subtle variations using her pillow and her spinning piano stool, and in the shower she took the Water Pik down from its mount and experimented with the startling effects of its different settings. It was thrilling and bizarre, and a little unnerving, like discovering a brand new sense, or being possessed. But when at last, exorcised of the strange spirits, she tied her bathrobe around her waist and watched the steam clear from the mirror, the face she saw in the glass remained as familiar as before.

At least I tried, she said to herself, faintly relieved.

It was after midnight. She was wobbly and drained, but not sleepy. Her mother had gone to bed, so she crept downstairs, where the watery drone of the dishwasher muffled the sounds of her movements. In the kitchen she made a cup of tea from the small packet that Mr. Vantwest had given Isobel as they were leaving. Then she went to the empty living room and stood in the dark, staring at the darkened windows across the street. Eventually she crossed the hall to her father's den. She turned on the desk lamp and sat with the atlas in front of her.

As before, the cracked old book opened naturally to page seventy-two, but Clare flipped to the world map at the front. She pinned Vancouver with her index finger, then she traced a path westward across the pale blue Pacific Ocean. Emma had travelled for four months through Asia. Her postcards had detailed movie-like adventures: attending a democracy rally in Rangoon; modelling American clothes for a Taiwanese fashion magazine; having sex with an anthropology student in a tribal village in Borneo. She'd invited Clare to travel with her, but Clare had declined, and each time a postcard arrived from some new destination she'd been freshly assured that her decision was the right one.

Still, her finger slid farther west, until it came to rest on Ceylon.

Sri Lanka might be different. It's not completely foreign anymore.

Adam didn't respond, but she could imagine him listening. She turned back to page seventy-two.

Maybe I could go there for you, she tried. *Maybe this was the reason you took me on your motorcycle and told me those things.*

The dishwasher sighed to the end of its cycle. In the silence, Clare looked out the window next to the desk, but saw only her own reflection. She thought of Adam, hovering in his unimaginable state.

I'd have a reason for being there.

The fantasy no longer seemed silly, or impossible. She'd been inside Adam's house; she'd had tea with his father and aunt. Gathering the atlas into her lap, she saw herself wandering through tea estates and markets, ancient temples, villages, all of it a single confused image cobbled from *National Geographic* pictures and Rudyard Kipling stories — but compelling nonetheless. She imagined Mary Vantwest's garden, teeming with its exotic fruits, a chorus of tropical insects. She sipped her tea and ventured tentatively further. She would go to a travel agent downtown and ask for some brochures. Maybe pick up a passport application. Neither committed her to anything. Both could be accomplished over lunch on a workday.

The thought of work made her straighten in her chair. Was this what she would tell Markus on Friday? That she was travelling halfway around the world to visit a place she knew almost nothing about, on behalf of an acquaintance she knew scarcely any better? She looked down at the map of Ceylon, which stubbornly refused to evoke anything at all of the Vantwests or their world, then put the atlas back on the desk.

Am I kidding myself, Adam? When I wake up tomorrow is this whole idea going to seem stupid?

The foot she'd been sitting on was numb. She massaged it through pins and needles and stamped her bare sole on the carpeted floor. When the feeling returned, she clicked off the lamp, and Adam's voice came to her in the dark.

So, what are you going to do with your life? he said.

The tone of the question was lighter than the words themselves suggested — closer to *What would you like for dinner?* than anything philosophical — and Clare only shrugged. The particular quiet of her father's house, invulnerable to any of Isobel's remodelling, pressed down on her.

Well, you know you gotta shake things up, Adam then said, his voice mischievous and provocative. *Get back on the motorcycle. Finish that ride we started. Or even better: don't finish it. Just keep riding.*

How do I do that?

She looked out the window at the featureless night.

Doesn't really matter. Go to Vancouver. Play in a band. Go to Sri Lanka. Yeah, Sri Lanka would be good for you. Something really different.

Will you be there with me?

Sure. Yeah. I'll be there.

But would I really be doing it for you?

You can think of it that way, if you like.

She began a new question then stopped. It wouldn't happen in her head, this trip; she would be stern with herself. It would happen for real or not at all.

In the darkness she returned the atlas to the shelf. She knew she should get to bed, but she wasn't tired at all. It seemed she'd just woken up.

II

Thursday morning, at the start of Rudy's spare period, Kanda intercepted him at the door to the teachers' lounge.

"I have a letter for you, sir," the boy said, holding out a folded sheet of paper.

Rudy took the paper and noted the "Mr. Vantwest" written neatly on the outside in Kanda's hand. "Should I read it now?" he said.

Kanda nodded his head to one side. "At your convenience."

"I have a prep now," Rudy said, and Kanda nodded again, his manner suggesting he not only knew what Rudy was doing just then but, moreover, could detect the intensity of his teacher's curiosity.

The boy strolled off down the hall, and it wasn't until he'd disappeared around a corner that Rudy wished he'd asked him to wait. He entered the teachers' lounge, where a few stragglers were rinsing their cups before heading to class.

"Van Twest!" Nisal called as he hurried for the door. "I still haven't told you about Fermat's theorem."

"Oh. Right." Rudy struggled futilely to remember anything at all of the math story. "How about lunchtime?"

Nisal smiled. "Very good. I'll see you here."

Rudy made his way to a table at the back of the room, where he unfolded Kanda's letter.

Dear Mr. Vantwest,
I apologize but I cannot complete your assignment. I tried to write about Sri Lanka's problems from the viewpoint of someone else but it was not possible. What I mean is that I am able to write the essay, but it would not be true. I was born as a Tamil and that is what is true for me. I can listen to another man's point of view but I cannot experience it. I cannot write about this country's difficulties as a Sinhalese, but only as a Tamil pretending to be Sinhalese. I do not see a purpose to this. My impressions of the Sinhalese life will be influenced by my Tamil thinking and therefore will be incorrect. I believe you thought this essay would change my political ideas but I would not make important political decisions from this type of thinking. The assignment you gave is only fantasy. Every person is formed by his culture and his race, and that is how he should act in the world. You do not ask a gazelle to be a lion or to understand a lion's point of view. Human beings are no different. I am a Tamil, that is how I think and conduct myself. I do not dislike the Sinhalese. The gazelle does not dislike the lion but it will do what is necessary to survive in the lion's presence. I apologize again and I will accept a failing grade on this assignment.
Sincerely,
K. Selvarajah

Rudy folded the letter into a compact square and squeezed it in his hand. He got up and went to the window. Just outside the school's front gate, Kanda was leaning against a lamppost. His hands were in his pockets and he was scuffing the sole of his shoe into the sidewalk. He could have been on a study break. Most year twelves had that privilege. But they were expected to study in the library. Rudy slid Kanda's letter into his pocket. He wouldn't report the boy. He would talk to him, the way he should have before — perhaps let him turn his letter into an essay.

He was considering the possibilities when Kanda looked back over his shoulder, directly at the staff room window.

"You know exactly what I'm doing up here, don't you, you little bugger," Rudy whispered.

He motioned to the boy to come back inside, but instead Kanda stepped away from the post and strolled down the sidewalk. If he was playing hooky, he was doing so with an air of absolute confidence and nonchalance.

For a moment longer, Rudy stood staring, then he darted out of the staff room, down the silent hallway to the custodian's stairwell. He took the metal steps two at a time, the crash of his hard soles splintering the hush. At the base of the stairwell he paused to check his watch, then he left the building through a side door. As he crossed the lawn, he began to sweat. Still, he carried on to the front gate. He would find Kanda at one of the food stands outside. He'd buy the boy a soft drink, and they'd sit for a while and talk, unimpeded by the decorum of the school.

Outside the gate, traffic noise competed with the staccato monologue of a man selling lottery tickets from a booth. The sidewalk was crowded, and as Rudy scanned the unfamiliar faces gathered around the food stands, his plan began to lose momentum. His face now dripping, he reached into his pocket for his handkerchief then recalled that he'd left it on his desk to dry out from the morning commute. He swore under his breath and took a final look around. Kanda had had enough time to walk a couple of blocks at least. But then Rudy spotted him. He was a few metres beyond the lottery booth, at a bus halt. He stood a little back from the others who were waiting, drinking a Coke. Rudy looked back at the school and caught sight of a colleague lecturing at the front of a classroom. He moved away from the gate and sank back against the tall hedge that separated the school lawn from the street. His concern wasn't that he'd be spotted but that the scene at the window would draw him back to that world where teachers kept their distance. He wanted to talk to Kanda, was determined to do so, yet he knew that if he thought about it too much, he would end up trudging back to the staff room, setting the air con to high, and putting the kettle on for a cup of tea.

He took a few steps in the boy's direction then stopped as a Fort-bound bus lurched to a halt in front of the lottery booth, its passenger load overflowing from the doorways. Rudy watched Kanda drain his drink, hand the bottle to a nearby vendor, and squeeze through the front door of the bus. Behind the hedge, one of the primary grade teachers was settling her class on the lawn to read to them. The teacher's instructions and the children's chatter summoned Rudy back to school, but as he turned toward the gate, his right hand fished his pocket for change.

The bus pulled slowly away from the curb. Watching it, Rudy caught through a window the angular profile of a young man. It might have been Kanda; it might have been someone else. He wasn't sure. But for a crucial instant, as he stared, the young man was Adam. He bolted toward the street, dodging people on the sidewalk, then lunged blindly for the rear doorway of the bus. He got his foot onto the bottom step, and a conductor clamped his upper arm and pulled him in. As he manoeuvred himself into a sliver of standing room at the back, he craned his neck over the heads of the other passengers until he spotted Kanda, also standing, just behind the driver. The boy's navy blazer and snugly fastened necktie seemed a guarantee that he would be back at school in time for the next class, scheduled to start in a little over an hour. Trusting in this, Rudy took hold of the overhead rail with one hand and wiped his face on his sleeve.

The pointlessness of what he was doing soon became obvious, however. If he confronted Kanda now, he'd have to explain his presence — an impossibility — which left as the next best option simply following the boy, to see where he would go. It was stupid, but Rudy made no move to get off the bus. He leaned his forehead against his raised arm and looked down at a tiny girl in a yellow dress, planted on her mother's lap. The child's eyes were rimmed with kohl, and her ponytail sprayed like a fountain from the top of her head. Rudy smiled at her, and she buried her face in her mother's shoulder, peeking out at him from the corner of one eye. He thought of Zoë, still that small in his imagination, and Susie, to whom he still owed a letter. Then, afraid that he'd lose Kanda, he searched the boy out again and kept his eyes on him for the rest of the journey.

At Fort Station, the still-full bus reached its terminus, and pas-sengers spilled out into a commotion of vans, cars, and three-wheel-ers, all bickering for passage in intertwining lanes. Kanda jumped from the bus and headed for the steps of a pedestrian overpass. Rudy fol-lowed, far enough behind to remain unnoticed, close enough to study the boy's movements — the confident walk, the running of his fingers through his hair, the checking of his watch. They crossed the overpass and descended to the street. Kanda advanced at a steady pace, scanning the windows of travel agents and gem shops without obvious interest. He seemed to have a destination in mind, and as he walked on, Rudy's curiosity mounted.

They progressed deeper into the city's business district. Up ahead, Rudy saw the clock tower. In fifteen minutes he would be obliged to turn around and go back to school. For the moment, however, he kept up his pursuit. At the intersection of Chatham Street and Janadhipathi Mawatha, Kanda dodged cars and three-wheelers to reach the traffic island on which the clock tower stood. Rudy held back and watched. The boy paused with his back to the tower and took something resem-bling a business card from the pocket of his blazer. He studied the card then looked up, his gaze seeming to follow the straight line of Janadhipathi Mawatha to the Indian Ocean, a block away. Perhaps he had an appointment, Rudy considered. A job interview, maybe. He wiped his face and squinted at the taut strip of horizon where the ocean's steely surface met the pale sky. When he turned back to the clock tower, he saw that Kanda had crossed over to the other side. Rudy dart-ed to the traffic island and again into the road, directly into the path of a three-wheeler. The driver blasted his horn but yawned and scratched his belly as he came to a stop, inches away from Rudy's legs. Heart thumping, Rudy raised his hand to the man and jogged to the sidewalk.

Kanda was standing at a wooden shop stall, not far from the intersection, drinking another Coke. He'd removed his blazer and now carried it over one arm. Rudy ducked into the doorway of an office building. His spy persona was wearing thin. Either his student had an appointment or he was just wasting time and perhaps had no intention of returning to school at all. Still, Rudy stayed where he was, watching.

Business at the little stall was thriving. Around Kanda several men hung about, some of them in suits, others in sarongs. Kanda drained his Coke but remained at the stall, scanning newspapers on a rack. As he read, he blew strands of hair away from his face. He checked his watch and looked down the street. An appointment, Rudy concluded. He checked his own watch and resolved to leave in another minute or two.

Kanda now had his back to him. Rudy admired the boy's broad shoulders and narrow waist — swimmer's lines — and for the first time since the news of Adam's accident, he fell victim to impossible wishes. He wanted another chance. The day of the stone sculpture, the Christmas Zoë burned herself, all the other times he could have responded to Adam's offers of fraternity and didn't — he wanted them back. It struck him as he stared at the young man's torso that not once in his life had he ever hugged his brother. His reticence must have been positively glaring to have scared Adam off. Adam, the fellow who at his high school graduation had hugged *everyone* — friends, teachers, assholes who'd tormented him over the years — had ventured only affectionate punches or an arm around the shoulders with his older brother. Never a true embrace. After twenty-five years, Rudy had no idea what Adam's body felt like — the muscles of his back, the strength of his arms. And now ... He retreated into the shelter of the doorway and mashed his rolled-up shirt sleeve into his eyes. He stared at the ground for a long time then took a deep, measured breath, exhaled, and straightened up.

When he turned back to the wooden stall, Kanda was gone. Rudy squinted at the clock tower, mopped his face with his sleeve, and started walking, eyes lowered from the sun's glare. Several metres from the office building doorway, he became vaguely aware of a commotion behind him, angry noises from the direction of the shop stall. He paid it little attention until, like a hard kick in the gut, the sound of gunfire stopped him mid-step, and he whipped around. A truck was blocking the road, and men with rifles were barking orders over top of the vehicle. Around them people scattered, wide-eyed; traffic lurched and squealed. The rhythms of the street, of Rudy's own body, ran amok. But though his neck and arms bristled icily and his cheeks pricked hot, he insisted to himself that the armed men were police, or soldiers, and that everything would soon make sense. Despite the fresh rounds of gunfire down the street, the screams, and the electric sting of the air, he moved backward in slow motion, witnessing through his invisible protective shell.

Then he remembered his student. He scanned the mayhem and called out into the din.

"Kanda! Where are you?!"

The boy, wherever he was, couldn't have heard him, but he kept calling, turning circles on the spot while people clamoured past him.

On his second or third rotation, he saw a young man in a white shirt. His muscles tensed, ready to run, when a noise — a massive, magnificent blast, physical as a lunging beast — launched him backward. On his way to the ground, he collided with something heavy and hard; his head struck the pavement. He felt the hard thing fall against him. His vision became a psychedelic swirl. Then he passed out.

Hours, it seemed, elapsed.

The journey back to consciousness was peaceful, painless, and black. A floating through nothingness. His first murky thought was that he was dead, but he was unable to recall how such a thing had come to be. He was on his belly, and the surface beneath him was warm, like beach sand. His mouth curved in a fraction of a smile that brought with it the first stab of pain. He wasn't dead. Outside his body, around him and above him, things were moving in a silent, menacing tempest. He concentrated on the beach — warm sand, swimming with his father — but as the tempest outside his body jostled and chafed him, the scene began to fade.

He noticed the heat. The air seared his skin, while his organs burned from a fire somewhere inside of him. He attempted tiny movements — flexing his fingers, opening his mouth, bracing his legs against the hard, immovable weight on top of him — but each attempt triggered new agonies, so he lay still. He opened his eyes, but the confusing blur that greeted him made him shut them again immediately. In the dark silence of his head, memories flashed in concert with the flashes of hot pain. He'd been walking downtown — *but why?* There'd been guns, fighting maybe. There'd been a noise of such magnitude it had knocked him over, but now he heard nothing. The explosion — it had been an explosion, yes — had deafened him. Like Zoë. Again he opened his eyes.

Across the street, two cars lay like helpless turtles, tires in the air. Rudy blamed the strangeness of what he saw on the awkwardness of his position, wormlike on the road, but as the haze in his mind cleared, he realized, heart pounding against the pavement, that the impossible scene was real. Loose fires danced around him. Beneath clouds of smoke that choked the air, shards of glass speckled the street, their light fierce and beautiful. He shifted his head to squint at things far- ther on. Up ahead, the skeleton of an office building spewed black smoke and flames. Whatever the building had housed was beyond repair. Rudy watched the hopeless ministrations of the few soldiers and civilians scuttling about the periphery then turned his attention to his own predicament. Though his shirt was stained with the blood of a gash across his forearm, the fire within him was radiating from his hips. He hoisted the throbbing weight of his head and looked over his shoulder. An empty three-wheeler lay on its side, its metal chassis col- lapsed over the lower half of his body. Next to the three-wheeler was the crumpled form of the driver. The man's eyes were closed, his skin an inhuman grey, and a dribble of red navigated his stubbled jowls — but his shoulders rose and fell defiantly.

To ease the tidal wave of nausea that swept over him, Rudy low- ered his head to the hot pavement. He talked to himself out loud, though at first he was still deaf.

"You're alive. Keep breathing. Still alive. Breathe ..."

Dull and distant, the sounds of his own voice began to reach him. He talked on, louder, coaxing meaning from the buzz between his ears.

"You were walking downtown. You looked at the clock. It was ..."

An army truck pulled up nearby, its tires pulverizing the shards of glass on the road. A pair of soldiers in khaki uniforms stepped down from the truck then stood, not moving, for several seconds. Rudy talked on.

"What were you doing there? Why are you —? That woman ... Kristina."

He remembered the Danish physiotherapist. He'd been with her. He remembered the guest house room and the bottle of Fanta they'd shared. Desperately he gathered together the facts of their encounter, but the more focused that one event became in his mind, the more chaotic was everything else. He needed order. As the uniformed men ran off, he began to recite — "Our Father, who art in Heaven ... hallowed be ... Thy kingdom come; Thy will be done, on Earth. Give us ... forgive us our trespasses ... Hail Mary, mother of ... full of grace" — but his garbled prayers were comfortless. He closed his eyes and imagined a quiet suburban street, a young girl standing under a sprinkler, her long, wet hair plastered to her shoulders, her skirted swimsuit a balmy aquamarine. He fixed the image of the nymph-like girl in his mind and managed, for a time, to detach himself from the chaos around him, to retrieve a moment of peace and painlessness under the girl's calm stare.

When he opened his eyes again he saw two soldiers gently depositing a young man on the road in the shade of the army truck. The young man wore a white shirt and grey trousers. Rudy lifted his head and squinted at the motionless figure, then he remembered what he had been doing in the city. He braced his forearms and lifted his shoulders.

"Oh Christ, machan. Is that you?"

He strained against the weight of the three-wheeler, but the vehicle gripped him tighter.

One of the soldiers was standing by the truck, shouting orders that reached Rudy like muted percussion. Rudy called to the man in English, then in Sinhala, panicking, in his confusion, when his shouts seemed to him nothing more than whispers. The soldier, however, darted a look in his direction and sprinted over. His polished boots stopped inches from Rudy's face. With a whistle, he signalled to someone Rudy couldn't see, and soon after, the weight of the three-wheeler began to shift. As the vehicle was righted, new fires coursed down his legs. Clenching his fists, he focused again on the figure by the truck.

"Can you help me get to that boy over there?" he shouted at the legs around him. "I need to see if he's okay. He's my — I need to see him."

One soldier ran off. The other crouched next to the wounded taxi driver, pressing two fingers to the man's jowl. "The ambulance will come soon," he said, then he stood and jogged away.

Rudy lifted his torso, supporting its weight on his forearms. His pelvis screamed, though the intensity of the pain served to dull the throbbing of his shoulder and head and the sting along his gashed arm. He fixed his eyes on the young man in the shade of the truck. Then, with agonizing slowness, he began to haul his lower half across the pavement, his arms awkwardly doing the work of legs, every inch of progress a marathon of exertion. He stopped often and brushed the glass out of his path so he could rest his cheek on the ground. People moved around him, some of them running into the maelstrom to help, others hobbling away from it, bloody and stunned. More soldiers had arrived, their tidy uniforms an incongruous sight. They carried the limp forms of those too injured to walk and deposited them in the shade of the army truck. Rudy was grateful he could scarcely hear, and began to wish he couldn't see. But he needed to get to the boy.

When at last he neared the truck, he shifted his course to move around the strangers who lay in his way: a pair of businessmen; a woman in a bloodstained pink blouse; another woman, with grey-streaked hair falling out of its bun. He'd begun to sense, with a creeping, prickling flush of horror, that the six or seven people lying in the shade were dead, or close to it. There was no pain in their battered faces, no trace of feeling at all. They could have passed for synthetic dummies, fashioned from some realistic, but not quite perfect, material. It might have been possible to dismiss them altogether — he desperately wanted to — if it weren't for Kanda. If Kanda were to be alive when he reached him, then these grim bodies on the pavement had to be real. On some level, he had to be responsible for them as well.

A foot or so away from the boy, he stopped, closed his eyes, and lowered his cheek to the ground. He imagined looking down at his student's face and seeing the same expressionless, rubbery features that signalled the strangers' fates. In his mind he saw the confident, intelligent young man lying senseless on the pavement, and the image filled him with a panicky dread that reached far beyond the pandemonium of Janadhipathi Mawatha.

He lifted his head and struggled forward with his arms. The street began to spin. Though he was virtually prone on the ground, he felt he would fall. He groped a few more inches and forced his eyes to focus. It wasn't Kanda. The fellow looked nothing at all like Kanda, and for an instant Rudy wondered who it was he'd been following through the city. His head throbbed. With what felt like the last of his strength, he pushed away from the line of bodies and flattened himself on the spinning ground.

Sometime later — he'd lost all track of time — he felt a hand rest gently on his shoulder, and he opened his eyes.

"You are Mr. Van Twest, no?"

Rudy lifted his head and looked up at the man crouching next to him — a doctor, or a paramedic of some kind, with a bald head and round spectacles.

"My son is a pupil at your school." The man smiled briefly. "He loves everything American, and he says you're from America." His expression became serious. "I think you need a doctor, sir. I saw you trying to get away. Leg is broken, maybe?"

Rudy noticed that his hearing had improved. When the man's hand slipped away from his shoulder, he raised himself onto his forearms.

"What happened here?"

The man ran his palm across his bald head and surveyed the destruction. "Hatred," he said. "So much hatred." He looked down at Rudy. "But as I was saying, sir, you must go to the hospital. The orders are to take only the really serious ones now, but I think we can find a place for you." He reached out and patted Rudy's shoulder. "Special case."

Rudy hesitated then nodded. "Thank you, Mr. ...?"

"Wettasinghe. My son is Viraj."

"I remember him," Rudy lied.

"Ah, good!" Again the man's smile was fleeting. "Tell me, Mr. Van Twest. You didn't have any of the children with you this morning? Was it a school outing?"

He thought of Kanda, still unaccounted for.

"No. I had a spare period, and I came downtown to do some errands."

Mr. Wettasinghe shook his head. "Terrible luck you had today, sir. But the worst is over. I'll come back with the stretcher." He assumed an air of authority. "You must stay where you are, Mr. Van Twest. No more crawling around. The hospital will be very busy, so the sooner you're getting there, the better."

Mr. Wettasinghe jogged off in the direction of an ambulance that had pulled up in front of the clock tower. Rudy turned away from the bodies on the pavement and rested his head on his uninjured arm. Something crinkled inside his pocket — Kanda's letter. He struggled to remember its content. Something about lions and gazelles and survival of the fittest. He tried to remember more, but what came to him instead was an image of the boy standing on the traffic island in the middle of President Street, looking out at the fragile calm, checking his watch. And a glib voice.

The Tigers employ kids a hell of a lot younger than Kanda.

The idea was unthinkable. He pushed it away.

In a final attempt to shut out the chaos all around him and the fires in his own body, he imagined himself with Clare Fraser on a slow, swaying train ride through the hill country of his grandfather's tea estate.

APRIL 1945

The back of the tea factory was the area where the men stacked wood and fed the fires for the ovens that dried the fermented tea leaves. As the previous day had been a poya day, no plucking had been done, and the ovens were not yet needed. Alec rounded the corner of the factory, thinking that in the absence of any workers he would snitch some wood and ease his boredom by building something. He stopped short, however, for leaning against the factory wall were his brother and another man, the latter blocked almost entirely by Ernie. The two of them looked as if they were locked in an important conference. Alec retreated behind the side wall and peered around the corner. He stood on tiptoe, craning his neck, and saw that the other man was Amitha. He and Ernie were facing each other, and for a moment Alec strained to hear what they were talking about, until he remembered that Amitha couldn't talk — a source of confusion, for what was the point of loafing about with someone who couldn't talk? Alec wondered briefly if the tea taster might be giving one of his comic performances, but he was far too still for that. And besides, Ernie wasn't laughing.

Restless, but having nothing better to do, Alec scuffed his shoe in the dirt and watched his brother with his usual mixture of resentment and admiration. For while Ernie's tendency to loaf about with factory workers was a nuisance, even Alec could not deny there was a great deal about him to be admired: the strength of his long limbs; his easy command of words and ideas; his ability to fit in with all manner of people, even the stylish, club-going young men he preferred to avoid. In many ways, barring the painting and the poetry-writing, Ernie was a more suitable man-of-the-house than their father was. For although their father had an important job and commanded respect, he lacked a mysterious but important something that Ernie clearly possessed. The word that seemed best to describe this something — a word that Alec had heard one of his father's friends use in reference to Ernie — was *charisma*. Ernie had charisma. It was something that Alec had attempted occasionally to project, smiling a certain way, entering rooms as if they were his own private domain, but he had no way of knowing if his efforts had been at all successful, or even noticed.

Ernie lit a cigarette and passed it to Amitha, then he lit one for himself. As the two smoked, Alec began to sense in the interaction something of which, he was quite certain, his father would not approve. Yet he couldn't say precisely what it was. Nor did he fully understand why his father would disapprove. Other than the obvious and, for Ernie, ordinary transgressions of loafing about with a factory employee and mucking up his white shirt on the grimy factory wall, the actions that Alec observed were frustratingly innocent. There was something not right, however, something out of the ordinary, and he found himself, as he had during the Tea Maker's recent lecture, willing his brother to do something, anything, that could be construed as an active declaration of the war that had been brewing for quite some time now.

The strength of his own will took Alec by surprise.

With casual defiance, Ernie tossed his unfinished cigarette through the open door of the wood stove — a seemingly trivial thing but nonetheless criminal, Alec was certain, for tea making was a delicate process. Anything could throw it off or contaminate it, even petty intruders like Ernie's cigarette. It wouldn't be tattling to mention the offence in passing, or, even better, to ask their father whether or not it was permissible to throw rubbish in the wood stove; this was, after all, something a Tea Maker needed to know about. Expecting his brother to be on his way any second, Alec scurried back to the front of the factory then turned and retraced his steps, so that when he and Ernie crossed paths it would look accidental. And he did want to cross paths. For even though he was going to cause trouble for his brother, it occurred to him that Ernie might be in a mood to take him to Nuwara Eliya in the car and entertain him with funny or scandalous stories. But Alec made it all the way back to his starting point without meeting his brother.

He peered around the corner of the building again and saw that Ernie and Amitha had shifted position. Ernie was now slouched back against the factory wall; Amitha's palms were pressed to the wall, on either side of Ernie's head, and his legs were straddling Ernie's. Ernie was making hand signs, like the sort that got made in the tasting room, and Amitha was watching. Alec scowled. He hammered the toe of his shoe into the dirt then took a step forward, intending to break up the bizarre interaction. Instead of carrying on, though, he stopped short, as if a barrier stood between him and the two young men. There was no barrier, however, and his reluctance only frustrated him further. Something told him he should march up to Ernie and insist they drive to Nuwara Eliya. For his brother's own good, this something at the back of his mind said, Alec should pull him away. But he remained where he was, unable to act.

Then Amitha laughed, a low, off-key sort of laugh, and Alec looked more closely. Ernie's fingers were laced together in another hand sign. Amitha lowered one of his own hands from the wall and took hold of Ernie's thumb. Carefully he manipulated its position, then he switched to the wrist of Ernie's other hand and moved it, too. A lesson, it seemed. Ernie had attempted one of the tea taster's hand signs and made Amitha laugh when he did it wrong. Now Amitha was correcting him. The explanation was both straightforward and entirely insufficient, and Alec was suddenly afraid to keep watching. He turned away and marched off in the direction of the P.D.'s bungalow, frowning intensely.

At the mouth of the long dirt drive that led to the road, he stopped and surveyed his calm surroundings helplessly. He wanted desperately to be playing cricket — to have a solid bat in his hands and the promise of a perfect, biting crack of contact to dislodge the baffling scene in his head. Eyeing the distance to the road, he assumed a batsman's stance and swung at the air. Then he ran.

It was well over a wicket's length to the end of the drive, but when he reached the road, he turned left and kept going, in the direction of Nuwara Eliya. He was no longer Alec Van Twest the school cricket champion, however; he was a British soldier, just landed in France, and the entire world was counting on virtuous, fearless men like him to run out the evil Nazis. He ran faster, in spite of the heat. Then he modified his story. The Nazis had retreated back across Europe, into Asia, and were now infiltrating Ceylon with the help of the Japanese. They were planning to reorganize in the hill country, where they thought only ignorant peasants lived (though they were in for a rude awakening). At that very moment, Nazis and Japs were closing in on Nuwara Eliya, and a citizens' alert had been issued. All able-bodied males were being called upon to help fight. Alec wiped his forehead on his sleeve. The other boys his age had been instructed to stay home, but he, Alec Van Twest, was an exception; his remarkable abilities had been noticed. He was brilliant: he'd learned everything there was to know about tea making and would probably be appointed P.D. as soon as he came of age. He was stealthy: he'd been spying on factory intruders, and rumour had it he was on the verge of an arrest. He was strong and fast. Most importantly, he had charisma — an often-ignored but crucial quality. Some men pretended to possess it, but they were fakes and impostors and weren't to be trusted.

Alec's soles rattled against the hard pavement, and he wished he were wearing his tennis shoes. Soldiers didn't wear tennis shoes, of course, but then soldiers didn't generally run long distances on paved roads under the April sun. A few yards up the Normandy beach and into the safety of a village — what could be easier? The road to Nuwara Eliya, on the other hand, was miles long. It was winding and much hillier than it ever seemed in the car. Alec looked over his shoulder and was both impressed and vaguely anxious to see that the P.D.'s bungalow had disappeared. He ran on, but in his isolation the futility of what he was doing became more and more apparent. At the sight of a fruit stand up ahead, he slowed to a jog, then a walk. His chest heaved and sweat streamed down his face and back. For a moment he couldn't remember what had brought him out on this ridiculous marathon in the first place, but when the scene behind the tea factory came back to him, as confusing as before, Alec feared it would be impossible to get rid of.

He picked up a long, thin branch from the side of the road and whipped it through the weeds growing next to the pavement. He whipped the mercilessly hot air. Then he whipped the outstretched palms of several invisible Nazis. He was about to strike at his brother, for refusing to take him to Nuwara Eliya, when his attention shifted to Amitha and found there a surprisingly fitting target. He pictured the uneducated, unspeaking tea taster leaning over his brother and lashed out with his whip. The stick whistled through the air, and for a second or two the figure in his mind lurched in pain. Then it resumed its position, as if nothing had happened, and Alec was forced to lash out again. Over and over he repeated the process, sweating and grunting, until some people in the back of a passing lorry pointed at him and laughed. Scowling, he threw his whip at the lorry, but the branch flopped unceremoniously to the pavement.

Now just a few yards from the fruit stand, Alec dug in his trouser pockets and came up with enough coins to buy a coconut. There were plenty of drinks in the icebox at home, but the cool, sweet water of a king coconut was the least the world owed him on this infernal day. The fruit vendor was alone at his stand, and as Alec approached him he silently rehearsed his request in Sinhala. It was a habit he'd acquired from his brother, who insisted it was rude always to speak English to shopkeepers and labourers. Right before the carefully chosen words left Alec's mouth, however, he swallowed them back. For through a muddy but powerful logic, the fruit vendor became, suddenly, an enemy, no less deserving of his contempt than Amitha. The two were no different, really, for they both belonged to that tribe of men lurking silently in shadows all over the country, waiting to take over. Both the Tea Maker and Ernie had suggested as much. But while Alec had previously found the prospect of such a takeover exciting, he now recoiled from it, ashamed that he'd done nothing as yet to combat it.

"One coconut," he said, in the haughtiest, most disdainful tone he could muster.

"Some fruit too?" the man said. "Nice rambutan? Banana?"

"No."

The fruit vendor lopped off the top of a fat yellow coconut and offered the bulky drink to Alec. Wordlessly Alec handed over his money then went to sit under a nearby tree, his back against the trunk, his legs splayed. He tipped the coconut, took a few gulps, and stared. Before him was a swooping, sprawling valley of tea, rolling waves of green, dotted here and there with crimson-flowered trees. Far below him a river sparkled, and on the other side of the valley waterfalls rushed down craggy cliffs. The beauty of the scene was so astonishing he wondered how it was that he hadn't ever noticed it, and he sat in a kind of awe. But it didn't last.

Once again the factory scene came back to him, more disturbing than before, and, with it, a vague recollection of a schoolyard conversation with Rohan and Peter. It was then that Alec had learned there are men who do *it* with other men. "Homos," they were called. Lunatics, perverts. "Up the arsehole!" Rohan had hissed, and the three of them nearly exploded. It was funny at the time, in the way that disgusting things were funny, but now the idea filled Alec with horror. He saw Amitha's hand touching his brother's, his face and shoulders leaning closer, and the source of his uneasiness became clear: the tea taster was a threat. A far more dangerous one than any ordinary labourer or fruit vendor could be, because his true nature was hidden. And though Alec didn't quite believe that his brother would be gullible enough to succumb entirely to Amitha's evil, Ernie was, as their father often said, too easily influenced by other people.

His thoughts now far away from the valley before him, Alec imagined a third Ernie, a secret one, taking up residence in his home, joining the Tea Maker's fantasy Ernie and the Ernie who painted pictures and occasionally took his brother on drives into town. It couldn't work, surely. For even if this new Ernie were a decent chap — and such a thing was clearly impossible — the house would be too crowded.

Alec drained his coconut, and the fruit vendor came over to slice the shell in half. Alec took the halves and scraped the pulp from the inside using a wedge of shell hacked off by the man. When he'd finished eating, he pitched the coconut husks, one at a time, as hard as he could, down into the valley. Then he slumped back against the tree and stared out again at the vast sea of green. He would stay there forever, he thought — or at least a very long time. He would make everyone back home frantic with worry — even the P.D., but especially Ernie, who would have a guilty conscience to begin with and would promise to renounce his sins if only Alec could be found. But within minutes he was restless and his backside was sore. He was still miles from Nuwara Eliya — impossible to get there and back before dinner. And besides, there would be nothing to do in town by himself.

Sullenly he stood up, brushed the dirt from his trousers, and set off down the road. He'd walked several yards when the enemy fruit vendor called to him, and Alec turned, just in time to catch a fat rambutan, drilled at him with terrific accuracy. He looked up, confused, impressed, and a little frightened.

"Good catch!" the fruit vendor called.

Alec hesitated, then called back, "Nandri!" — unsure in his confusion whether he'd thanked the man in Sinhala or Tamil.

As he walked, he examined the rambutan. It was like a sea urchin, pale green spines sprouting from its thick, pink skin. Alec pierced the skin with his thumbnail and tore it away from the pearly fruit, which plopped into his hand, firm and round as a hard-boiled egg. He'd eaten hundreds of these things before, but, just as he had ignored the spectacular beauty of the valley, so too, he realized, had he failed to appreciate the extraordinary weirdness of the rambutan. The whole world, now that he thought about it, was weird and unpredictable. He tossed away the rambutan's empty skin and bit into the fruit. Along with the sweet flesh were tenacious fragments of the woody seed, which marred the fruit's texture, but not enough to make him spit it out.

12

F RIDAY MORNING, on the train, Clare studied the thick, glossy travel booklets she'd collected Thursday during her lunch break. The books described tours to various parts of the world, and each featured a page or two of itineraries with names like "Coconuts, Tea, and Kandy" and "Exploring Buddha's Island." Unlike her father's dated atlas, the books had photos — images carefully selected to seduce, no doubt, but irrefutably real nonetheless. The pictures gave substance to her fuzzy imaginings, and she savoured them as her city-bound train chugged through the flat west-island landscape. She placed herself in these improved scenes, and the person she saw, strolling breezily in sandals and a bright pink sarong, chestnut hair tied in a loose knot under a wide-brimmed hat, seemed an ideal of Clare Fraser.

At work, she tried to be more practical. Hovering in the guitar section while a teenage boy tested one Fender after another, she forced herself to confront those features of her project that would, sooner or later, threaten to scare her off. She wasn't afraid for her safety. Sri Lanka's political strife was distant and unreal. Her real fear was of regular people, and the necessity of confronting those people every day, relying on them for basic necessities. She could imagine what Emma would say — not the real Emma, perhaps, but certainly the other one: *You deal with strangers every time you come to work, Clare. Not very well, mind you, but you manage. Horrible things aren't going to happen just because you've left home. You could —*

But before she could finish, Adam's voice interrupted. *You could be walking down the Boulevard tomorrow and be hit by a truck,* he said, clearly delighted with the irony of his remark. Then he became serious, kind. *You don't need to worry. I'll be there with you.*

She allowed him to reassure her. To tell her that people would be friendly and helpful, that neither she nor her luggage would get lost, that toilets would be plentiful and easy to locate, and that she'd come down with nothing more debilitating than a cold. Satisfied for the moment, she turned her attention to her customer, who'd run into difficulty.

"Try an E flat," she said, and the boy's body relaxed visibly as his song lurched ahead.

At the start of her lunch break, she walked to the passport office to pick up an application. On the way back, she stopped at a photography studio, and a dark-haired man with a thick mustache and a heavy accent took her photo. Peering through the viewfinder and gesturing with his enormous hands, he directed her to move a little to the right, to lift her chin, to sit tall. As he dried the prints with a hair dryer, he nodded, satisfied. "Very nice," he said. "Very beautiful." Clare smiled awkwardly, but as she walked back to work, she told herself that perhaps travel could be that easy, and her step quickened with the sensation that her trip had already started.

After lunch, when business was slow and Markus was in his office doing paperwork, she sat at the front counter and began filling out the application. The form gave her a queer, almost joyful, confidence. Inside the designated boxes, she supplied the first few facts — FRASER; CLARE JEAN; 14 • 03 • 1965; MONTREAL — delighted both with the certainty of the bold block letters and numbers and with her government's willingness to be satisfied with such a primitive account of who she was.

She was in the process of converting her height to centimetres when Peter slipped behind the counter. He rested his forearms on the glass and ran his silver tongue stud across his teeth a few times.

"Whatcha doing?"

Clare folded the application. "I thought I'd see if anything needs reordering in the books."

Peter jutted his chin in the direction of the form. "Is that for a passport?"

"Uh-huh."

"Are you going away again?"

Clare bit her bottom lip. She glanced in the direction of Markus's office, and when Peter leaned in, she said, "I think so."

"That's great. Where to?"

"Sri Lanka."

Peter raised his eyebrows. "*Très* cool. Do you know anyone there?"

"Sort of. Yeah. I'll be going with a friend who's from there."

Again Peter's tongue clicked over his teeth. "Hey, that's kind of a coincidence. I think I heard something on the radio this morning about Sri Lanka. I missed most of it, but it sounded like there was drama of some kind. Know anything about it?"

Clare shrugged. "I haven't heard anything."

"You should ask your friend."

A woman entered the store, and Peter drifted off to help her. Clare tapped the edge of the folded passport application against the counter. She really did need to speak to the Vantwests — for information, yes, but more importantly for their approval. She went to the staff room to put away the application and for the rest of the afternoon flipped distractedly through racks of songbooks, searching for a reasonable excuse to show up at Adam's house once again.

By the time she'd resigned herself to the frightening necessity of simply going across the street and presenting her plan outright, her shift was almost over. She completed the order form she'd been working on, then, charging herself to go straight to the Vantwests' from work, she collected her things from the staff room and left.

Stepping off the train, she was still determined. She walked purposefully from the station, rehearsing her lines. She would tell Mr. Vantwest and his sister that Adam had inspired her plan, that she'd been wanting to travel and he had given her a direction. Which was true, in a sense. But as she veered off Whitmore Drive onto Morgan Hill Road, the pattern of her existence tightened around her, holding her back. She looked down at the pavement and urged herself on, but when she reached the foot of the Vantwests' driveway and lifted her eyes to their sad, solemn house her determination failed, and she hurried to her own front door, suddenly afraid that her moment of hesitation had been noticed.

Inside, her mother was checking her reflection in the hallway mirror, fluffing her hair and pressing her lips together.

"I'm just off to the shops," Isobel announced. "You haven't by chance seen Ray Skinner's measuring tape, have you? Joanne thought he might have left it here when he was helping us move the furniture."

Clare sighed and shook her head. She started heavily up the stairs, the same chorus of anonymous voices that had warned her against the motorcycle ride now attacking her fears. In a feeble show of persistence, she paused halfway and turned back to her mother.

"Has Joanne heard anything more about Adam?" she said.

If there were good news, she would go across the street.

"She didn't mention anything." Isobel slid her spring coat out of the dry cleaner's wrapping. "But, you know, I've been thinking. It was lovely of Mr. Vantwest to invite us for dinner, but before we do that, I'd like to have him and Mary over here. It would be a nice break for them. Maybe next week sometime, after the painting's done and the new furniture's in."

Clare considered this while her mother scrutinized her coat under the vestibule light. Presenting her travel plans in her own house, with her mother listening, would be too awkward, surely. She wasn't even certain she would want to take part in this neighbourly get-together, whose primary purpose would be to christen the new living room furniture. But still ...

Slowly she climbed two more stairs then turned again. "I'll go over and invite them if you like."

Isobel looked up. "I suppose you could do that, pet. I was thinking I'd give them a call later on, but an invitation in person might be nicer. Should we suggest a date?"

"Tuesday?"

Minutes later, from the window of her studio, Clare watched the Oldsmobile reverse into Morgan Hill Road. She needed to leave before her mother returned, but she went first to the piano and sat down. With mounting confidence, she played her conversation with the Vantwests. The greeting — quick and light, a little Baroque. *How are you? I hope I'm not interrupting.* The dinner invitation — ordered and predictable, a march. *My mother and I were wondering ...* Ta-dum, ta-dum, ta-dum. Adam — the bridge, the segue into the unpredictable. *We talked about Sri Lanka. I've actually been thinking I might ...* She improvised, stepping gently but surely from phrase to phrase. *It sounds like a beautiful place, so different from here. I'd appreciate any advice you could give me. We could talk more when you come* — She stopped, lifted her fingers from the keys, and lowered the fallboard.

"Okay," she said aloud.

From her closet shelf she took down a burgundy sweatshirt with "Concordia" stitched in white across the front. She put it on then reached out and ran her fingers down the sleeve of Adam's leather jacket. In her search for a reason to show up at the Vantwests', the jacket hadn't occurred to her at all. It was the perfect excuse. Not even an excuse really — a responsibility. She slid it off the hanger. It still carried a faint smell of Adam's cologne. But she couldn't imagine giving it up — not yet. She hugged the heavy leather then put it back on its hanger.

Between her own house and the Vantwests' she kept her arms crossed and clutched her keys tightly in one hand. The journey across the street, though she'd made it twice, hadn't become any easier. At the front door, allowing no time for second thoughts, she held her breath, unclenched her hand, and rang the bell. She expected the aunt, but Mr. Vantwest answered.

Clare smiled. "Hi, I hope I'm not ..." She hesitated, for Mr. Vantwest seemed not to know her. He stared blankly, then his gaze travelled past her, settling on the Fraser house, and he gave a small nod of recognition.

"Hello. Hello," he said.

Something was wrong. Mr. Vantwest's speech was slack, his eyes glazed. He looked ill. Clare wished, suddenly and desperately, for the aunt to appear, but there was no sign of her. Behind Mr. Vantwest, the house was oppressively quiet.

"I, uh ... I came to see if ..." She forced herself ahead. "My mother and I were wondering if you and Mary would like to come for dinner. On Tuesday."

He said nothing. Though Clare had smelled the evidence when he answered the door, it wasn't until that lumbering moment of silence that she realized Mr. Vantwest was drunk. Not completely pie-eyed, as Isobel would say, but not himself. He frowned in an apparent effort to understand what she'd proposed, while she, wretched and ashamed on his behalf, clenched her hands and shifted her gaze to the mailbox next to the door.

The rhythm of her plan was lost. The whole idea had been preposterous, and she wondered what on earth she'd been thinking. The man's son was in the hospital, in what condition she couldn't say, and there she was, a shy, stupid stranger, expecting to engage him in a friendly conversation about her travel plans. Even the dinner invitation seemed inappropriate. And now, she had to extricate herself from a monstrously awkward scenario that she herself had created.

"Uh, you could let us know tomorrow ... or whenever." She retreated to the stairs. "It doesn't really —"

"Come in," Mr. Vantwest said. "Please."

Clare froze, one hand gripping the iron rail.

"I don't want to disturb you. I just came over to ask about —"

"Please come in."

His words, though slack, were insistent. Half-convinced he would yell at her if she refused, Clare released the rail and stepped past him into the house. Mr. Vantwest closed the door then shuffled to the living room, where he sank into his armchair. Clare sat on the edge of the chesterfield, placed her keys on the coffee table, and clamped her hands between her knees. It was the very circumstance she'd wished for on her last visit: she and Mr. Vantwest alone. But it was all wrong.

"Is Mary here?" she said.

"She's gone shopping. Insisted on walking."

His voice was tired. The thinning hair combed across his scalp was askew. On a low stool next to the armchair, Clare noticed the glass of clear drink, nearly empty. Mr. Vantwest reached for it but retracted his hand at the last instant.

"There was a bombing in Colombo yesterday," he said. "An office building. Dozens killed. Hundreds injured."

His announcement crushed the awkwardness. A full, flattening blow, just like that.

"My God. What happened? Who —"

"Suicide bombers. They drove a truck through the front door and blew the place to smithereens." He spoke with mock enthusiasm then fell serious. "These people have no regard for human life. No thought as to the ramifications of what they do." He crossed his legs; he uncrossed them. "Bloody idiots. Did they think there would be only government sympathizers in that building? Only Sinhalese? They kill off even their own kind."

Again he reached for his glass and this time took a drink. Watching him, Clare remembered Rudy.

"Your son. In Colombo. Is he — ?"

"He's lucky," Mr. Vantwest said, cryptically, swirling his drink. "I expect fate to be entirely vindictive, but occasionally it surprises me."

"Sorry. I don't understand."

Mr. Vantwest drained his glass. "You'll have a drink? There's whisky, sherry, arrack ..."

Clare glanced at the photograph of Adam, then at the crocodile lamp. "Whisky. Please."

"Water? Ice?"

"No, thank you."

"Straight up? Good."

Mr. Vantwest disappeared down the hall. Eyes fixed on the lamp, Clare repeated the shocking news to herself: a bombing in Colombo. An event she now had reason to care about. She got up and crossed the room to where the crocodile stood. She ran her fingers along the rough, dry skin of the creature's outstretched foreleg. The lamp teetered, and she pulled her hand away. From down the hall came sounds of clinking and pouring. Again she recalled her wish to sit with Mr. Vantwest in his own territory, on his own terms. Hands clenched, she followed him into the study.

He looked up as she entered. He was bent over a small tea service trolley, replacing the cap of a whisky bottle. In front of him were two glasses.

"You would prefer to sit in here?" he said. "Please, take a seat." He gestured to a leather armchair.

Clare looked around the room. There was a desk, but its chair was piled with laundry. "But there's nowhere else," she said. "Where will you sit?"

Mr. Vantwest handed her a glass then used his slippered foot to move a wooden crate that sat upended next to the armchair. His balance was off, and he stumbled, mumbling "Dammit" under his breath. When the crate was in place, he sat on it, facing Clare, and again motioned to her to take the armchair. She forced a smile and did as he requested.

"To your health," he said, raising his glass.

Clare sipped her whisky. It stung her eyes and burned her tongue. Mr. Vantwest, perched on his crate, crossed one leg over the other and took a long swig. Neither spoke. Clare took in the books and trophies crowding the shelves, the photographs on the wall, the dark, threadbare rug covering most of the carpeted floor. On a lower shelf she saw the spine of an atlas not unlike her father's. The crate on which Mr. Vantwest sat was stamped with the words *Strathclyde Estate* and *Colombo* in black ink.

A bombing in Colombo; hundreds injured.

The information refused to stick. Colombo was a speck on page seventy-two, a boulevard of pristine colonial architecture from the Adventures Abroad brochure. She struggled to imagine the ravaged office building, but the ruins of her travel plans were more immediate, more disheartening.

"That's terrible about the bomb," she said.

Mr. Vantwest nodded. "Terrible. Yes. Unless, of course, one simply places it in the natural course of things." His drunken voice meandered, but he was strikingly coherent. "You seem surprised. But think about it. When natural disaster strikes — an earthquake, a flood — we all say how tragic it is. But in our hearts we know that earthquakes and floods are part of nature's way. We mourn the losses, but we don't condemn nature for doing what it must."

"But that's nature. Terrorists are people."

"Terrorists are nature. Nature, fate, destiny — call it what you will. There are cycles of action and reaction that govern the human world, just as they govern the natural world." He drank down most of his whisky. "You see, people do things to each other — good things, bad things — and destiny arranges for those actions to be suitably answered."

Clare met his eyes. "But you said yourself, those bomb victims came from all different sides. Innocent people ended up dying."

Mr. Vantwest shrugged, in a manner that suggested the point was not so important. "We never know a man's whole story, do we? At any rate, I've become a fatalist, and I can't help thinking that Fate singles out certain of us for special treatment. If others happen to get in the way, they're no different from those poor devils who get swept away in the flood." He held his glass in front of his face, tipping it this way and that, then lowered it. "But what you say is true. Innocent people suffered in that attack. It was the work of sinister minds."

She didn't understand him, not completely, but his voice was oddly comforting. She turned to the photographs on the wall beside her. The nearest was a black and white portrait of a group of people on a lawn. The adults were seated in chairs or standing; the children were on the ground. There was a tree to one side of the group and a stately white bungalow with latticed trim behind them. No one was smiling.

"That was taken before we came to Canada," Mr. Vantwest said. "On my father's tea plantation."

Clare leaned closer. An older man with a pipe in his hand she assumed to be Mr. Vantwest's father. Mr. Vantwest was in the photo, young and handsome. Seated cross-legged in front of him was Rudy, half of his face screwed up in a squint. The stick-like legs that Clare remembered protruded from the same schoolboy shorts. One of the women was unmistakably Mary, a little slimmer, in a flowered dress. The woman enthroned in the centre wore a lavish sari and a jewelled necklace. This had to be Mrs. Vantwest. More than any of the others, she suited the stately bungalow.

Clare glanced at Mr. Vantwest. *Your wife was beautiful,* she wanted to say. But his feelings about the photograph were unreadable.

"Was the tea plantation near Colombo?" she said instead.

"Hmm? What's that? Oh, no. Up in the hill country." Mr. Vantwest studied the portrait a few seconds more, then, tilting his glass toward the lettering on Clare's sweatshirt, he said, "You've studied psychology? At university?"

At this abrupt shift, she recalled Adam's observation that his father didn't like talking about the old days. Thankfully, he didn't seem annoyed.

"Uh, no. My degree was in music."

"No matter. It's part of your generation to analyze the psyche. Tell me, what do you think it is that causes homosexuality?"

He posed his question without a trace of discomfort. Every syllable of the word *homosexuality* was given due articulation and emphasis. He then added, "Are the causes in the upbringing, or is a person simply born with those characteristics, like he's born with a particular eye colour?"

Already flushed from the whisky, Clare imagined her face shading to the deep red of Mr. Vantwest's carpet.

"I'm not sure. I guess it makes sense that it would be biological."

Surely it was biology that had been acting on her recently.

"I don't agree with you completely," Mr. Vantwest said. "Whatever caused my youngest son to be homosexual — he is homosexual, you know — was most certainly decided before his birth, but I don't believe biology was to blame." He was making no sense. But Clare nodded, and he continued. "For a long time I believed it was something he could get over. I thought he'd been manipulated by the people he spent time with. I thought he could be a regular boy, if he'd just set his mind to it. But I was wrong."

He finished his drink and shot an inquiring glance at Clare's glass. She shook her head. As Mr. Vantwest crossed the room to fix himself another, he hummed. Clare noticed that a lower button of his light blue shirt had come undone, revealing a white undershirt. He screwed the cap back on a bottle of colourless liquor and again raised his glass.

"My son was made the way he was by Fate," he then announced.

Clare said nothing, and, for once, it seemed to her that silence was best. She drank to the toast — if that's what it was — and Mr. Vantwest came to stand between the wooden crate and the armchair, facing the photographs on the wall. He pointed to a fuzzy, cracked photo of two young men standing on either side of a hanging bell.

"My brother," he said.

Ernie. The odd duck.

"My son is the spitting image of him. You can't tell from the photograph. The quality is poor, and Ernie isn't looking at the camera."

Clare scrutinized the image. The way she and Mr. Vantwest were positioned, each looking at the photograph, made it suddenly possible to talk freely. "Is Adam like your brother in other ways?" she said, risking the loaded question.

"Perhaps. I never knew my brother well. It only matters that my son reminds me of him." He coughed. "You see, for many years now, ever since I was a boy, Fate has kept its eye on me. Every aspect of my life is part of its scheme, its revenge — my wife's death, my granddaughter's handicap, my son. Especially my son. This incident in Colombo is just the latest." He sighed wearily then laughed, just as wearily. "I'm a bloody Shakespearean hero. I've made my mistake, and now there's no escaping Fate. I thought it would have relented long ago, but no."

Did he even know she was there, Clare wondered. Or had she become an inside voice for him, prompting and responding where necessary, but otherwise unreal? She imagined that these things Mr. Vantwest was sharing had never been uttered to anyone else, that he might even be on the verge of a confession of some kind. But before the words of his last sentence had settled, a key scratched obtrusively at the front door, followed by sounds of rustling bags.

"Mary," Mr. Vantwest announced dryly.

The aunt was back. Having hoped she'd appear at the start of the visit, Clare was now disappointed. She set her empty glass on the wooden crate and stood up.

"Alec?" the aunt called, louder than necessary. "Alec? Are you here?"

She came to the door of the study, Provigo bags in her hands. Her look of surprise was entirely justified. But its cause was not what Clare expected.

"Ah! This is such a coincidence!" the aunt exclaimed. "I was just with your mother. We saw each other at the shop, and she drove me home."

"Oh, well, I just came over to invite you —"

"Ah, yes. Your mother very kindly invited us to dinner on Tuesday, but we have already arranged to visit the Pereiras that day. Isn't that right, Alec?" She glanced at her brother, and the shadow of a frown crossed her face. "But I told her we would come another time. Maybe the following Saturday."

Mr. Vantwest placed his glass on the wooden crate, next to Clare's, and refastened his undone button. Clare wondered what the aunt would make of this. The possible connotations gave her a sudden rush of panic. "Next Saturday would be fine," she blurted. "That's why I came over, to invite you both for dinner."

"Dinner with the Pereiras has not been confirmed," Mr. Vantwest then said, sloppily, ambiguously, and the aunt's frown settled in. She eyed the glasses on the crate and shook her head.

"Alec! What is this? Only last week the doctor was telling you you mustn't drink. You're eating too much sugar already, and now you are going to kill yourself with arrack. Is that what you want to do?"

The awkwardness returned. Clare stared at the floor and braced herself, certain that Mr. Vantwest would explode. But his reply was calm, nonchalant even.

"The doctor's instructions were to restrict myself to an occasional drink. That is the limit I'm exceeding, Mary. And if I wanted to kill myself, I'd be more efficient about it."

The aunt gasped; Mr. Vantwest sighed.

"You needn't worry, Mary. I have no intention of muddling with God's plan for me." He turned to Clare. "Thank you for the dinner invitation. If a week Saturday suits your mother, we'd be happy to come then. Assuming, of course, that things at the hospital are progressing as they should."

Clare nodded. "Of course. I should get going. Excuse me."

She slipped through the study door, past the aunt. She felt tipsy and hot and wanted only to be outside in the cool, deserted street. But as she reached the front door, she remembered her keys, still on the coffee table, and had to turn back. Mr. Vantwest was behind her. "My keys are in there," she said, and he stepped aside to let her pass. From the kitchen came sounds of grocery bags being rummaged through. As

Clare retrieved her keys, she saw Mr. Vantwest pick up a photo from the record player cabinet.

He studied it briefly then looked up. "I was very demanding of him. Even when he was a little boy, but especially later. It's no surprise he wanted to get away."

"Rudy?" Clare said.

Mr. Vantwest seemed confused. Then he nodded. "Ah, Rudy too, perhaps. No doubt. Rudy too. But I was speaking of Adam." He held the photograph out for Clare to see. It was a high school shot, grade nine or ten.

"I'm sorry. It was just that you mentioned him wanting to get away, and I thought ..."

"No need to apologize." Mr. Vantwest replaced the photo. "Your assumption is quite correct. My two eldest have run off in their own ways. I only wish the youngest had taken the same route as his sister and brother. But he has always been over-dramatic."

Clare frowned. Conscious of the aunt in the kitchen, she whispered. "You think it was deliberate, what he did?"

She didn't believe it herself. The Adam she'd spoken to that day hadn't been suicidal, surely. She began to wonder, as she had on her first visit, if Mr. Vantwest knew all about her motorcycle ride with Adam, and if he were now searching for insights, laying out his greatest fear in the hope that she would quash it. Her right hand clenched, and her keys dug into her palm. But Mr. Vantwest shook his head.

"The crash was not deliberate, no. But the recklessness was. I have tried to instill in the boy my principles and values — a sense of responsibility — and his way of escaping my influence has been to lead a reckless life. I should have compromised earlier on perhaps. But, as I was saying, this is all part of my fate."

Clare braced herself for the confession Mr. Vantwest had seemed ready to make earlier, but none came. "It sounds like you only wanted what was best for him," she said. It was a useless remark — banal, presumptuous — but safe.

Mr. Vantwest shrugged. "That's true. What father doesn't want the best for his child? But there's a limit, of course." He slid his thumb and index finger up the bridge of his nose, dislodging his glasses, and rubbed his eyes vigorously. He then blinked three times in succession, screwing up his eyes and opening them wide. "Yes, there's a limit to what one's affections will endure. My son generally puts up a good front, but I'll wager he thinks I'm an awful bastard. Probably thinks I dislike him."

His voice had become fainter, as if he were again speaking to himself. In Clare's head, Adam's voice was full of urgency.

He's wrong, Clare. I know he loves me. And I love him. You could see that. I don't think he's a bastard. Tell him that you talked to me. Tell him —

But her throat tightened. She opened her mouth and tried to force something out, but the constriction was real and physical, and the words stuck in her esophagus. With each second that passed, they lodged themselves deeper and deeper, until she was sure that if she somehow managed to force them out, they would rattle insincerely, as jarring as the clatter coming from the kitchen.

She looked out the living room window at her own house. "I'm sorry," she finally said.

Mr. Vantwest held up his hand, his manner suddenly formal. "Please. You must excuse me. I've had too much to drink, and I'm afraid I've imposed on you."

Clare shook her head and said, "No, not at all," but her opportunity had passed. Mr. Vantwest made for the door, reiterating his acceptance of the dinner invitation — a dinner that Clare was now quite certain she would not be attending.

APRIL 1945

A lec sat cross-legged on the living room floor, in a wedge of afternoon light, pretending to read *David Copperfield* while he waited for his father to come home. The air had cooled down, but the house was oppressively quiet. At regular intervals he turned pages, to generate some noise and movement, but also to give himself the impression that he had better things to do than sit on the floor waiting for his father.

When at last the Tea Maker's voice sounded in the hallway, Alec's heart began to pound. Moments later, his father came into the living room, lighting his pipe as he walked, and settled himself regally in the chair by the window.

"What's that you're reading, son?" he said.

Alec held up the book, displaying the front cover.

"Dickens. Your mother will be pleased. Is that one of her first editions?"

Alec shook his head.

"Well, if it is, don't let her catch you taking it outside."

He closed the book and sat up straight. "Dada?"

"Yes?"

"This afternoon I saw —"

Just then, Mary came into the room carrying a cup and saucer with both hands. The cup jiggled threateningly as she walked, so that it was a relief when she finally set the saucer down on the small table next to her father. Alec waited anxiously for his sister to leave, but instead she deposited herself on the cushioned kavichchi and began picking at a thread in the hem of her skirt.

"Yes, Alec?" the Tea Maker prompted, lifting the saucer, his tone mildly impatient. "This morning you saw?"

Alec shot a desperate glance in the direction of the kavichchi. Then he swallowed hard and carried on.

"Dada, today I saw Ernie and Amitha doing love things behind the factory."

The Tea Maker's grey eyes bore into him with such fierceness that Alec wondered if he himself would be the one to receive a scolding. He turned to Mary, who had dropped the hem of her skirt and was firing him a look of disbelief and disgust. Her open mouth formed a neat, dark oval, but no words came out. For a protracted moment, the three Van Twests sat in a charged silence.

The fact that Mary didn't seem to believe the accusation proved immaterial, for it soon became clear to Alec that his father did. The Tea Maker placed his cup and saucer back on the table and sat up in a manner that accentuated his considerable height. His sideways glance suggested that he thought Mary should leave but that he wouldn't bother insisting on it. He spoke softly and slowly.

"Tell me what you saw, Alec."

Alec stared at the dark floorboards. Suddenly truth seemed a supple thing. What he'd witnessed behind the factory didn't *need* to be described the way he'd described it. Walking home from the fruit stand, he'd been solidly convinced of his interpretation — he believed it still, more or less — but now other versions, ignored or dismissed, clamoured for his attention, threatening to complicate matters. In his mind he tried to recall the details of the interaction between his brother and the tea taster, but the scene had gone fuzzy, like an out-of-focus pho-tograph. He wanted certainty and clearness, and he could see from his father's expression that he had the power to impose both. It was thrilling and dizzying.

"Alec. What did you see?"

Eyes still fixed on the grain of the floorboards, Alec moulded his truth.

"Ernie was — Amitha and Ernie were holding hands. Like boy and girl."

At this, Mary rediscovered her voice.

"Alec! You're making up stories! I think they were only shaking hands."

The Tea Maker ignored her, and Alec saw that in his father's mind the scene he had described was entirely plausible.

"What else, Alec? Was there anything else?"

Again he imagined the strange scene — Amitha's fingers touching Ernie's — only this time the picture was clear; it had a definite mean-ing, for he had given it one. There was more he could say, about the way Ernie and Amitha were standing, about Amitha's laugh, but he bit his lip and shook his head.

When Ernie came home that evening, Alec and Mary were sent to their rooms. Seated on the floor of the bedroom he shared with his brother, Alec listened at the door for the argument he'd been expecting for months. The crucial battle, in which, despite what he'd witnessed that afternoon, and despite his desire that Ernie be set right, he still felt a particular sympathy for his brother. But nothing, it seemed, was happening. The house was once again oppressively silent. Alec attacked his fingernails with his teeth. He wondered if Ernie had somehow managed to explain his actions, and if he, Alec, would be the one in trouble after all. Strangely, he began to hope that this would be the case, and that he'd be given a punishment of gruelling physical labour that would occupy him until the holidays ended.

It seemed to him he'd been waiting for days when he heard his mother scurry down the hallway, sniffing loudly. Alec hugged his legs and leaned his head against the door. Then he heard his father.

"And how are you planning to put food in your mouth?"

"I have friends. They'll help me."

The Tea Maker and Ernie were in the hallway, just outside Alec's door.

"Your friends are willing to feed someone with an appetite like yours and no money?"

To this there was no answer.

"And what about Sunday afternoon?" The Tea Maker sounded exasperated but resigned.

"Sunday afternoon?"

"The McIntyres are coming for tea. You were to meet their daughter Sirima. That was the whole point of the invitation. What do you want me to tell them now?"

"Dada, this isn't a good time for me to be courting young ladies. Don't you agree?"

"It seems to me that spending time with young ladies is precisely what you need."

"Dada, I'm not —" Ernie sighed. "Introduce Sirima to Alec. She's closer to his age, and she'll prefer him anyway." There was a long pause before Ernie spoke again, his voice imploring. "Please don't make Amitha go. He doesn't have —"

The Tea Maker cleared his throat officiously. "Jayasuriya left two hours ago."

Little by little, Alec began to see what he'd done. His body leaden with responsibility, he crawled to his bed and lay on his side, head pounding. When his brother came in, he pretended to be asleep. He watched through his eyelashes as Ernie changed his shirt and trousers, combed his hair at the mirror, then left, closing the door behind him.

13

CLARE LEFT THE VANTWESTS' house and walked in the direction of the Boulevard. The sun hung low and lazy; the maple buds were fat. It was a perfectly pleasant early spring evening, in which the fragrant air, the soft light, and the sturdy brick and aluminum houses seemed, like the photographs in the Vantwests' living room, to deny the existence of anything, anywhere, that might contradict such pleasantness.

At the corner of the Boulevard and Morgan Hill Road there was a pair of newspaper boxes. Clare rummaged change from her pockets and bought a copy of the *Gazette*. The news from Colombo was on the front page, along with a photo. "Blast in Sri Lanka Kills 60, Injures 1,400," the headline read. She studied the photograph, in which four men — office workers, according to the caption — were running, arms bent, legs mid-stride, through a street filled with debris. They looked absurd, running in their white business shirts and ties through the obstacle course of rubbish. One of the men had an enormous belly and probably hadn't run in years. The young man in the foreground looked fit enough, but his shirt was splattered with blood and he was holding a cloth up to his forehead. Clare thought of Rudy and studied the injured man's face more closely. There was a resemblance, but Mr. Vantwest had said Rudy was lucky. She skimmed the article below the photograph — things about Tamil Tiger rebels and a truck packed with explosives — then she folded the newspaper and turned back down her street.

There was no one out, with the exception of Mr. Carroll pulling into his driveway in his blue Reliant. Mrs. Carroll, Clare imagined, would be inside, making dinner — pork chops or chicken casserole, or something like that. The radio would be tuned to *The World at Six*, which would probably lead with the bombing in Colombo, though not necessarily. Clare watched Mr. Carroll get out of his car and head for his brown and white split-level house, briefcase in hand. Only moments earlier it had seemed inconceivable that the Vantwests' homeland could be falling apart while Morgan Hill Road basked in its pleasantness. Now it seemed to her that this pleasantness was dangerously volatile, and that the pattern of her life could not possibly hold.

As Mr. Carroll unlocked his front door, Clare held her breath and imagined his house blowing up in his face. She waited for the deafening noise and flying debris and clouds of smoke. Hoped for them even. She was at the edge of the Boswells' front lawn, and she imagined all the neighbours running out to join her at the sound of the blast — a bizarre re-enactment of the time they'd all gathered to build an ice castle during Carnaval. But Mr. Carroll disappeared quietly behind his door, leaving Clare alone in the street.

She carried on to her own house. In the narrow, shadowy space between the Skinners' property and the Frasers', she leaned against the brick chimney to think. She needed to do something. If the Sri Lanka plan was dead, she had to go somewhere else. Anywhere — it didn't really matter. Within reason. She recalled her awful, awkward family holiday in Scotland and realized that with the exception of trips to Vancouver she hadn't been away since. The Sri Lanka plan had been too much, too ambitious, but the impulse to escape made sense. She would do that much. Like a teenager fresh out of high school, she would leave the patterns of her Morgan Hill life.

Pull up your roots, the chorus in her head chimed.

Do your own thing.

Find yourself.

The words were empty and crass. They trivialized the terrible urgency mounting inside her, so she shut them out and turned to the matter of where to go. Europe had been Emma's first destination — backpacking, taking the train from city to city, staying in *pensions* and hostels. It would do. In an instant her decision was made, and she realized with a calming confidence that she would go through with it. She walked around to the front of the house, hardly noticing the lights on in the living room across the street.

Inside, she heard her mother on the kitchen phone.

"I think that's her just coming in now," Isobel said. "Clare! Telephone! It's Markus, from the shop."

She frowned. Markus never called. Never once in the time they'd known each other had he called. As she ran upstairs to her studio, she imagined him finally, after long and arduous soul-searching, working up the nerve to reveal his feelings. Or, perhaps, experiencing an epiphany of some kind. She dropped her newspaper on the floor, flopped on the loveseat, and picked up the phone. She would let him down easy.

"Hello? Markus?"

"Oh, hi," he said, and it was clear that no epiphany had occurred. "Is everything okay, Clare?"

"Everything's fine. What's up?"

"Didn't you want to talk to me after work?"

"About what?" she said. Then she remembered. Her telephone call to Markus seemed ages ago, when all she'd hoped to do was tell him she was moving to Vancouver. "Oh God, Markus. I'm sorry. I forgot. I was distracted all day. I was —" She glanced at the *Gazette*, its front page picture facing up on the floor. "I'm really sorry."

"It's okay. Don't worry about it."

Clare picked at the loveseat's tweedy armrest. Now that she'd shaken up her own life, Markus's impotence was more exasperating than ever.

"Are you still at the shop?" she said. "I hope you didn't wait around for me."

"I'm just clearing some paperwork. I thought you might have gone out on an errand or something."

"No ..."

He seemed to be waiting for more, but she punished him with a dull silence.

"So ... what did you want to talk about?" he finally said. "I mean, you don't have to tell me now, if you'd rather ..."

"No, it's fine." Again Clare glanced at the newspaper photo. "I'm planning another trip."

"Oh. Really?" Markus took shelter in his employer voice. "When are you thinking of going?"

"I'm not sure exactly. May, June. But listen, Markus, I know you can't give me any more holiday time. That's not why I'm telling you." She clenched her left hand and rubbed her index finger with her thumb. "I'm actually planning to leave the shop."

"To resign, you mean?"

"Yes."

"So you can go on a trip?"

"Yes."

"I don't know, Clare. I don't really think you need to leave. It's just that ..." The employer gave way to the repressed lover.

"It's not just the trip. I need to do something different with my life." *There.* She'd said it.

"Well ... so ... where are you going?"

She sat up straighter. "Europe." The word was sharp and convincing, completely different from the fuzzy foreignness of Sri Lanka.

"Really? How long — I mean, you could always come back."

"I'm not sure how long I'll be gone. But really, Markus, I don't think I'll be back."

In the silence she imagined him absorbing this.

"Um ... okay. So, uh ... what are you planning to do there?"

"Travel around." She improvised. "I'll start with France and Spain. At least I can handle the languages there."

"Do you think you'll go to Germany?"

What Markus really wanted to say and just couldn't get out, she knew, was that he *hoped* she'd visit Germany, for him. She was tempted to punish him again, to say she had no intention of visiting his homeland. Then an image came to her: Markus showing her around the small Bavarian town where he was born, speaking German with shopkeepers and the old people on park benches, wearing hiking shorts and Birkenstocks. The same decent, dependable Markus, but *different.*

"I might. It would depend."

"Oh?"

Her thoughts raced ahead. Surely if they got away from the shop, away from Montreal and the small but significant patterns they'd established with each other, they could each be different. Things could happen.

"If I knew someone there ... you know, someone who knew the language and stuff, I might."

"Hmm. Yeah. That makes sense," Markus said, his voice even, his feelings couched. But wanting her to continue. Yes ... definitely wanting her to ask.

Clare stared at the *Gazette* photo, the businessmen running, dazed. She could do this. After her encounter with Alec Vantwest, she could handle this. It was only Markus after all.

"So ... Markus," she said, "would you be interested in going with me?"

She imagined him looking up at the calendar over his desk — sketches and biographies of famous composers; April was Beethoven — and assuring himself, with mounting excitement, that he could find his way to taking some time off.

"You could call Terry," she said, to help him along. "She's always offering to come back if we need her."

Markus made a curious sound, something like a dreaming child's sigh. "That's a great offer, Clare," he said, "but I think I'll have to pass."

If she'd thought about it an instant longer, she would have given up. But she went on without thinking. "Is the timing bad? We could go later in the summer, or even the fall."

Again Markus made his strange sound, and Clare realized, too late, what it meant.

"Well ... no. It's not the timing. I guess it's just not really something I feel like doing."

Not something I feel like doing. An impossible answer. She wanted to shake him, to wake him up. But she'd already humiliated herself.

Worse than that, she'd glimpsed a possibility that had never, in all the time she'd known Markus, occurred to her: maybe he simply wasn't interested. Wasn't attracted to her after all ... felt as blasé toward her as his behaviour suggested.

"Oh. No problem," she said. "It was just something that came to me when you mentioned Germany."

"Oh ... yeah. Well, that makes sense. I guess I'm just not into going back there anymore."

Queasily she suffered Markus's tedious explanations and mortifying apology. She muttered an official resignation, and when Markus knotted himself up in speculations over the difficulty of replacing her, she rescued him. "I'll stay till you get someone else trained," she said. Then Peter interrupted, panicking over a cash register glitch, and Markus was gone.

∞

LONG AFTER THE CONVERSATION had ended, Clare remained slumped on the loveseat. She'd read two of Clarissa Harlowe's letters then closed the massive volume without marking the page. The sun had gone down on the picture from Colombo, and the room was dark.

At the sound of pots clanging in the kitchen, she went downstairs. There were tins of spaghetti and a styrofoam tray of chicken breasts on the kitchen counter, onions frying on the stove. Isobel was rummaging through the gadget drawer. Clare stood in the doorway, straddling the strip of wood that separated the new carpeting from the kitchen linoleum. The white door frame was pencilled with height marks: 18 mos.; 2 yrs. 3 mos.; 2 yrs. 8 mos.; 3 yrs. 11 mos. The last mark — 10 years and 5 months: 5'4"!! — Clare had done herself, ridiculously proud of having grown. Positioning herself against the door frame, she reached for the pencil on the telephone table and scratched a new line, about two inches above the previous one. She turned and studied the mark, considering its finality. As she reached up to write her age, the pencil slipped from her fingers and fell onto the linoleum.

Isobel looked over her shoulder. Can opener in hand, she closed the gadget drawer with a sharp hip check.

"There you are, pet. Guess who I ran into at the grocery store?"

"Who?"

"Mary. From across the street. I asked about dinner on Tuesday, but it seems they have another invitation that night." She set to work opening a tin. "Anyway, did you get a chance to pop over there? Have you heard what happened to Rudy?"

"Rudy? No."

"Apparently he was caught in the middle of a *terrorist attack.*"

"What?"

"He'll be all right, fortunately. But there was a bombing in the city where he lives, and a taxi drove right into him in all the commotion. Can you *imagine?*"

Clare bent down to pick up the pencil. Fleetingly she saw the stick-like boy who'd watched her from across the street with suitcases in his hands. She saw Mr. Vantwest's weary face. *Rudy too,* he'd said. *Rudy too.* "He's lucky," she murmured distantly. Her mother frowned, so she added, "that it wasn't worse."

"Oh, aye. You're right, pet." Isobel set aside the first tin and started on another. "We just never know what's going to happen, do we. Even here. I suppose it's best that way. But when something like this happens ..." Her voice was strangely heavy. "Oh, I asked Mary how Adam is doing, and she said he's improving, so that's a relief." She took a paring knife and poked the plastic wrap covering the chicken. "That poor family."

Clare scribbled "31 yrs." on the door frame then turned back to her mother.

"I'm going to Europe."

Isobel spun around, wide-eyed. The Vancouver announcement hadn't surprised her as much, it seemed. Before she could answer, Clare forged ahead.

"I haven't booked anything yet. I probably won't go till June. I quit my job and I just want to go somewhere and think about what to do next."

Her mother nodded slowly. "That sounds lovely, pet." She rested the knife on the counter. "Will you visit the U.K.?"

"I don't know. I haven't thought about it."

Isobel turned off the stove element and extracted a pack of cigarettes from her apron pocket. She plucked one out and held it between
her fingers then returned it to the packet, shaking her head.

"Can we have a wee talk about something, Clare?" she said, and
Clare, flustered to find that her stomach was knotting and her hands
shaking, crossed the kitchen to the table.

JUNE 1964

When she reached the chemist's shop below the flat that Patrick
Locke shared with his mother, Isobel's lungs were heaving and her
blouse was pasted to her back. She'd run from the pond, partly out of
fear that the bleeding had indeed started, but more as a means of
extracting herself from the suffocating closeness of her encounter
with Margaret. She opened the heavy black door next to the chemist's
and mounted the stairs slowly, wondering if it mightn't be better just
to carry on home. But Patrick was standing in the doorway of his flat.

"I saw you from the window," he said.

Isobel forced a smile. "Can I use your loo?"

Patrick stepped back. "Go on in. Mum's out."

She squeezed past him and locked herself in the lavatory. There
was no blood yet, just a whitish stain of a sort she'd had before. She
scrubbed it with a damp flannel and it vanished. Calmer now, she used
the toilet, re-tied the ponytail at the side of her head, and splashed
cool water on her cheeks, which were redder than her hair.

She found Patrick in the kitchen, stuffing a small kit bag.

"Haven't seen you in a while," he said. "Where've you been?"

In all the fuss at the pond, she'd managed to forget her courtship with Alastair Fraser, but now it came back to her, more troublesome than ever.

"Oh. Nowhere. Helping my mother."

Patrick rubbed his bristled chin and nodded. "Shall we take a wee walk out to your pond?"

Isobel took a slow breath. She didn't want to return to the pond. She didn't particularly want to be with her father's apprentice. But there was nothing else, it seemed.

"All right," she said wearily, and Patrick stuffed a bottle of Bell's whisky into the bag.

They walked the high street in silence, Isobel lagging half a step behind, her arms crossed, her eyes on the ground. At the edge of town she sighed a sigh of resignation and stuffed her hands in the back pockets of her jeans.

"Did you hear Ringo Starr collapsed and had to be hospitalized?" she said, for something to say.

"Serves him right," Patrick sniggered.

"Why?"

"Because he's a Sassenach."

"Because he's *English?*"

"Aye. His lot have had more than their share. Let them all rot in hospital."

He marched into the half-dead vegetation spilling across the path that would lead them to the pond. Isobel hung back an instant then followed uncertainly.

"Which lot?" she said.

Patrick turned and waited. "It disnae do your head in, Isobel, that your country's governed by folk who're nothing like you?"

"The English?"

"Aye."

Isobel plucked a rush leaning limply across the path. She squeezed it, and water ran down her thumb. "I don't think Stanwick folk are anything like me," she said solemnly. It was the first time she'd expressed the idea aloud, and the sound of it both startled and impressed her. She tossed the rush aside, wishing it were a weightier thing. "Anyway, Ringo can't help it if he's English."

Patrick smiled. "Aye, I suppose he has enough worries getting by with that hooter of his."

"Talk about the pot calling the kettle," Isobel muttered.

They reached the pond's clearing, and she eyed the place nervously — the surrounding trees, the turbid water. Patrick wrapped his hand around her wrist and pulled her forward. At the edge of the pond, he held his boot over the water's surface, as if preparing to step out onto it.

"Have you ever thought about where this water goes, Isobel?"

"What if I say it goes to England?"

His mouth curved in an enigmatic smile, but he said nothing. Isobel crouched to dip her hands.

"I know this pond feeds the stream," she said. "And the stream ends up in the Clyde River, and that ends up in the Firth of Clyde. Some of this pond water might go all the way to the Atlantic Ocean." She hesitated. "Maybe some of it will wash up on a beach in America. Wouldn't that be something?"

Patrick stepped back into the tall grass. Against the pinkish-blue sky, he cut an imposing if slightly scruffy figure.

"Aye, it would."

He went to the tree, unzipped his kit bag, and pulled out a blanket, which he spread over the lumpy ground, over the very spot where Isobel had stretched out earlier.

"Come sit and have a wee dram," he said, uncapping the bottle.

Isobel sat down and wrapped her arms around her knees. The cramps were still there, but bearable. She reached for the bottle and took a drink, basting the inside of her mouth until its surfaces burned then numbed. Patrick extracted a limp cigarette and a book of matches from his pocket, pinched the cigarette between his lips, and cupped his hands to light it. He leaned back against the tree, exhaling a grey-white cloud.

"I envy that water," he said.

Isobel held back a laugh. "What do you mean?"

"It travels," he said, intensely serious. "It goes places. You said yourself, this pond water could end up in America. It could go anywhere." He took a puff then passed the cigarette to Isobel. "That's what I envy. That freedom. I'm sure your dad could give me a grand working life, Isobel, but what I really want is to experience other places. Do you understand what I mean?"

"I know," she said. "I'd do anything to go to America. I think about it every day."

She took a puff, then another drink.

"It wouldn't be America for me," Patrick said. "I want to see the exotic places of the world. China, India, Ceylon ..."

"Ceylon is a lovely name," Isobel mused. "Very romantic," she then added, awkwardly, for it wasn't the sort of thing she was in the habit of saying.

Patrick took back the cigarette, and Isobel carried on drinking. It was like the lobbing of stones into the pond — a metronome to the conversation.

"We could go together," Patrick said. "Ceylon."

If he'd looked at her when he said it, she might have believed him. But his eyes were fixed on the end of his cigarette as he rolled a fragile point of ash against a stone he'd picked up from the ground.

"And what would we do there?" she said.

"I don't know. That's the beauty of it, you see. Anything is possible."

Isobel recapped the whisky bottle and swung it back and forth in front of the distant outline of her too-familiar town. She imagined herself on a gently tossing ship, a glimpse of tropical green on the horizon.

"Let's go then," she said.

Patrick coughed. "When?"

"Now. Tomorrow."

She felt his unshaven chin on her neck.

"I cannae arrange it for tomorrow, Isobel, but we'll go." He took a last puff then stubbed the cigarette on the stone. "In the meantime there's another place we could go," he said, his voice strangely quiet, almost breathless. "If you fancy it."

The whisky bottle slipped from Isobel's hand, landing with a thud and a slosh, then rolled out of reach toward the pond. She wasn't sure what he meant, but as he fumbled with the top button of her blouse, the heel of his rough, square hand pushing against her breast, she once again felt the strange rippling inside, the same alien surge. She would rather have talked with him about Ceylon. She repeated the name to herself, imagined her ship drawing closer, and as Patrick nestled in and pulled the blanket over their bodies she fixed her mind on the green horizon.

∞

BY THE TIME THE AWKWARD ACT WAS DONE and she'd sacrificed her blue knickers to wipe up the ambiguous blood, the sun had dipped low. Patrick lit another cigarette and shook the match violently. Isobel leaned back against the tree, the blanket tight around her shoulders.

"I can't go home like this," she said. "I'm drunk and I look a mess. They'll murder me."

Patrick brushed her cheek with his finger. "You can tidy up at my place. Mum won't say anything."

They set off back to town in silence. Wearily Isobel staggered down the path, heavy with the sense that she was no longer alone in herself. That her treacherous body was not only occupied by strange forces but that those forces had tangled her up in other lives, lives she could know only in their clumsy, messy, physical manifestations. She wanted to vomit up the entire day, or shit it out — anything to relieve her essential self of its burdens. Halfway to the road she thought she might indeed spew, and she stumbled into a knot of shrubs and doubled over. But though she heaved and coughed, nothing came up. She glanced over her shoulder at Patrick, hovering uselessly on the path, then she thought of Alastair, of life with Alastair, and allowed herself to consider, as she'd not yet done, that it might be ideal. She would be paired up — something that only girls with serious plans, like Margaret, could easily forego. Yet at the same time she'd be free, for Alastair Fraser would not invade her. Nor would he excite those strange forces inside her. He would take her away from Stanwick, far from its confusions and commitments, and he would let her be. Life *with* him would be dull — duller, perhaps, than life in Stanwick — but unlike life in Stanwick, life with Alastair would not be all-consuming. They would live side by side in a quiet flat, and outside that small, quiet space would be the city. Montreal. Not as big as New York, but big enough. A place where she could walk down her street and not know a soul ... where anything could happen.

14

Rudy lay on his bed, propped against pillows, in the air stream of the fan. Next to him his empty lunch dishes were piled on a tray, attracting flies. In the three weeks that had passed since the events on President Street he'd grown accustomed to doing nothing. The migrations of insects across the floor, the rhythms of cousin Bernadette's chopping and sweeping, the shifting light and shadows across the painting of Adam's Peak, which he'd asked Bernadette to hang on his bedroom wall ... these things occupied him for hours. The causes of his inertia weren't straightforwardly medical, of course. But in the light of consciousness he could pretend.

Sleep was a different story. Gory, apocalyptic images came to him in his dreams and were stubbornly slow to dissolve when he woke, heart pounding, at the edge of the bed. Even worse were the pursuits. Night after night, he followed slender young men through labyrinths of endless complexity — city streets, parkades, school corridors — repeatedly glimpsing but never catching his quarry. Sometimes he'd get close enough that his dream-self would cry out breathlessly in hope and relief. Desperately he'd lunge at the young man, but whatever he managed to grab onto — a sneaker, a sleeve — would slip off into his hand, and he'd cry out again. If he didn't wake himself up, he would lurch dizzily, utterly lost in his maze, struggling to stay upright.

He'd had no news of Kanda. Headmaster Muller had paid a visit to the hospital, but the subject of the boy hadn't come up. Muller talked of Cambridge the whole time, and in any case Rudy wasn't ready; he allowed no news to be good news. And now, in the dull tranquility of Aunty Mary's bungalow, he allowed himself to forget what had happened on President Street that day, or, rather, to speak of it — to Bernadette, to the neighbours who occasionally dropped by — as if it were a thing apart. It was only when Bernadette would leave him to go home to her family, only as he imagined his cousin's bus ride through the outskirts of the city, the stop at the supermarket that she frequently made, the walk from the market to her house, that the bomb would re-explode in his imagination.

Bernadette, Aunty Sheryl's eldest daughter, had been summoned by Aunty Mary. For the first ten days or so she'd stayed full-time, a live-in nurse and housekeeper. Now she spent two or three hours every couple of days, cleaning (Rudy couldn't imagine what, for he hardly left his bedroom), filling the refrigerator with portions from her own family's meals, or cooking up fresh lunches, violently spiced, which she served to him on a tray. At first he hadn't thought to refuse her help. It became obvious to him as soon as he left the hospital that hobbling to the bathroom on his crutches would mark the limit of his independence. But as his condition improved, and he ventured to think about matters other than his own injuries, Bernadette's presence began to baffle and embarrass him.

She came in for the lunch tray. She was thirty-five or thirty-six, a once-slender woman who'd gone through three pregnancies and apparently retained a few pounds from each. She had thick, layered hair that fell to her shoulders, a broad, full-lipped smile, and a penchant for tight-fitting T-shirts and jeans. The latter was the main source of Rudy's embarrassment. Despite his pains and terrors, he harboured fantasies of peeling away his cousin's clothes, squeezing her breasts, running his hands down her hips. Fucking her. He'd tried to convince himself that the fantasy was a product of circumstance and that he would have lusted after any reasonably attractive woman who came to look after him and who gave him jasmine-scented sponge baths, as Bernadette had done. He told himself it was the dual transgression of adultery and borderline incest that was turning him on. But the truth wasn't so easy. He'd never been with a Sri Lankan woman before — he found her exotic.

"How was the lunch?" she said, leaning over him for the tray.

Rudy stared at the gold sequined flowers on the front of her T-shirt. "Delicious."

"Not too spicy?"

"Yes. But don't worry. I'm building up my tolerance."

Bernadette shook her head, and the hoops in her ears danced back and forth. "You should tell me when it's too much. I'm always forgetting you've been away from our food for so long."

She headed for the door, but Rudy, restless and bored, summoned her back with the only conversation starter he could muster.

"Hey, Bernadette? Do you remember when we used to call you Bernie?"

She turned. "Oh, God! No one has called me that in years!" Giggling, she set the tray on a chair. "I used to hate that name so much, but now I'm doing the same thing with my own kids." She numbered them off on her fingers. "Rashelle is Shelly, Angelo is Angie, Dominic is Nicky. Crazy, no?"

Rudy shrugged. "Not really. Seems affectionate to me."

Bernadette flashed him a smile. "You're right. I should have understood that when I was little. You all weren't being mean when you called me Bernie. I hope my children understand that." Suddenly her eyes widened. "Oh, this is a coincidence!"

"What?"

"The kids in your family are girl-boy-boy and so are mine! Isn't that strange?"

He didn't think it was much of anything, but he smiled and said, "Uh-huh." The conversation was bordering on pointlessness, and although he suspected Bernadette would have been willing to carry on with it, he hoisted himself up on the pillows and gave his cousin what he hoped was a meaningful look.

"So, tell me, Bernadette. Why on earth were you willing to come and take care of me like this? We haven't seen each other in eons; I'm practically a stranger to you."

Bernadette shook her head; she seemed embarrassed. "It was no trouble, Rudy. There's another girl at work who was able to take my cases when you were just out of hospital, and Lionel has been spending more time with the children."

For a moment Rudy said nothing. He was mortified to learn that Bernadette had a job — one with Cases, whom she'd abandoned for his sake. To ask her now where she worked, after spending nearly a month in her company, would be hopelessly awkward, so he pushed on.

"I know you've been able to make arrangements — and I can't tell you how grateful I am — but what I don't get is why you would do it, for me. Like I said, I'm a stranger. I was expecting to hire someone."

Bernadette frowned. "You're not a stranger, Rudy."

"Virtually."

"No, no. Mama is always telling me what's happening with you and Susie and Adam. She and your Aunty Mary talk frequently. It's not the same as speaking to you in person, but I always know the important events."

"You know the important events in a lot of people's lives," he said, "but would you put your own life on hold for them?"

Bernadette wagged her finger at him. "You're family. That's different."

"I guess."

He felt suddenly as if he were arguing with his aunt — as if he and his cousin were speaking different languages. He pictured her out on his grandfather's lawn with the other girl cousins and wondered how far back the division could be traced. It struck him that growing up in Sri Lanka might have made him an altogether different person, and the idea of this other-Rudy who never came to be was unsettling. He slumped back against the wall. Bernadette picked up the tray and balanced it on her hip while her free hand collected a towel and a pair of shorts from the foot of the bed.

"Any more washing?" she said.

"Don't worry about it. Please." He scratched furiously at a mosquito bite on his thigh. "I've got plenty of clean stuff left."

"It's no worry. I just put your things in with ours."

"Just *leave* it," he snapped, startling himself. There followed a moment of hot silence. Then he met Bernadette's eyes and his core began to tremble. "Oh God, I'm sorry," he whispered. "I can't believe I did that."

She came to him solemnly. "It's all right. Better this happens while you're awake, no?"

"While I'm —" He sighed. "You know about the dreams?"

"It's not important." Bernadette brushed his hair from his forehead, a patient, maternal gesture. "Any more washing?"

Rudy pointed his chin in surrender. "There's a couple of T-shirts over there. Thanks."

He watched her as she crouched down for the shirts, keeping her upper body straight, geisha-like, so as not to upset the dishes on the tray. Gradually the fear and shame in his gut were tempered by a dull throb of desire. He didn't share Bernadette's sense of cousinship, wasn't worthy of it really, but he promised himself he'd ask Aunty Mary, next time she called, to fill him in on the important facts of cousin Bernie's life.

At the doorway, she turned back to him. "Your friend from school is still coming this afternoon?"

"Nisal? Yes."

"I'll leave after washing up then." She fixed her eyes on him. "Remember what the doctor said. Off your feet as much as possible. You overdid it last week."

Rudy made a shallow bow. When Bernadette had disappeared into the kitchen, he reached for the bottle of painkillers on the bedside table.

His collision with the three-wheeler in the wake of the explosion had cracked his pelvis and left him with a map of bruises, vaguely resembling Britain, so the nurses had told him, across his lower back. He'd suffered a mild concussion, which had been the cause of greatest concern initially, but it was the pelvic injury that was keeping him bedridden. He remembered little of the ambulance ride or of his arrival at the hospital. Thanks, he suspected, to Mr. Wettasinghe's interventions, he'd been promptly examined, then delivered from the pandemonium of the emergency room to a quiet ward occupied by elderly men with chronic ailments. The room was stale and monastic; the nurses wore starched white dresses and pointed caps. Spaced out on morphine, he slept for many hours between the cool, papery sheets, waking only occasionally to the ministrations of his nurse.

Early the next morning, he asked to be wheeled to the telephone down the hall, where he placed a collect call to his father. It was the first task he'd attempted since hauling himself across the pavement, and the limitations of his body surprised him. His arm immediately grew sore holding the receiver; his foggy mind struggled to remember the phone number. When his father answered, the familiar voice was jarring.

"So, you're fine, son," he said. "We were concerned when we heard the news of that bloody bombing, but I told Mary you would have been in school."

Rudy inhaled. "Actually, Dad, I was in the city. I saw it happen." A predictable silence followed. "They had to take me to the hospital." He tried to sound alert, alive. "I have a cracked pelvis, but it's not serious. I'm okay. I'll be home in a couple of days."

"You're coming home?" Alec said.

Again Rudy took a breath. "I mean Wattala home. Aunty's place. But, Dad, tell Aunty she doesn't need to come back for me. I'm fine."

"Broken pelvis, you say? What happened?" In the background Rudy could hear his aunt, her own frantic questions going unanswered as Alec pressed him further. "What were you doing in the city? It was a school day, no?"

"*Cracked* pelvis, Dad. A three-wheeler bumped into me." He paused. "I was on a prep. I went downtown to do some errands."

"My God. Not both of you," his father muttered.

"Both of who?" Rudy said, then he understood. He softened his voice. "It's okay, Dad. I'm not badly hurt. I'll be fine." His nurse was leaning against the wall, examining her fingernails. He turned away from her. "They're just being extra-cautious with me, 'cause I'm a foreigner. I guess it looks bad that I was caught up in this."

The conversation shifted briefly to the details of the event, then Rudy spoke to his aunt. His lies to her weren't too extravagant: yes, he could walk; just a small limp and a few bruises; he'd be back at work soon. When Aunty sent Bernadette to visit him in the hospital, he was found out, of course, but Bernadette had made it clear she had everything under control.

As his cousin washed the lunch dishes, Rudy's thoughts drifted from his own hospital stay to Susie's maternity ward quarters, the last hospital room he'd suffered before his recent ordeal. He remembered sitting in the vinyl armchair at the foot of the bed, holding the baby and staring with a vague mournfulness at his sister. For it seemed just then that Susie, her long hair mussed, dark circles under her eyes, had become a different person. A mother, a stranger. Even Dad and Adam had seemed different. Somehow the pink-faced, crazy-haired baby in Rudy's arms had changed them all, shifted their very identities, and Rudy had found himself stupidly resenting the tiny creature for the imposition.

He owed his sister a letter. "Write to Susie when you get the chance," Adam had instructed, generously implying that the only thing interfering with the writing of such a letter was busyness. Adam himself used to call Susie every few days, just to check in. *Used to.* Staring at the ceiling, Rudy fought off images of the frightening hospital paraphernalia that was keeping his brother alive and composed feeble apologies in his head. Then Bernadette returned.

"Wake up, sleepyhead," she called from the bedroom doorway. "You have company."

Rudy roused himself and squinted. Nisal had arrived. It was time to be Van Twest, the English teacher.

Smiling awkwardly, Nisal ducked past Bernadette and approached the bed, almost on tiptoe. "Apologies for being early," he said. "How are you?"

"Not bad. Getting there." Rudy gestured toward the chair next to his bed. "Have a seat."

While Nisal got himself settled, Bernadette brought in two glasses of iced tea then announced again that she was leaving. Rudy said, "Be careful," and she shooed him with a flap of her hand, smiling her broad smile.

Nisal loosened his tie. "I wanted to come sooner, but my son and daughter have had school holidays, and ..."

"Don't worry. I wasn't very good company before anyway."

The math teacher winced slightly. "Terrible business this is, Van Twest. We were so shocked."

"Yeah, I was pretty shocked too, I tell you." Rudy laughed, trying to ease the fellow's nervousness. "Not the sort of thing you expect to happen on a walk in the city. Or I guess I should say it's not the sort of thing *I* expect."

"Muller said you were going to the bank. Is that right?"

"Sort of. I was kind of wandering."

"You saw the whole thing?"

"Not really. I was walking the other way. Then I heard the guns."

Nisal shook his head and made a whistling sound. "And then ...? What happened? Big Bang sort of thing?"

Rudy met his colleague's eyes. "It was big."

Squeamishly, he ventured back to the fateful scene, aware that the time had come to ask about Kanda. The urgency of his nightmares was suddenly with him, and his conscious mind prepared for an end to the chase. He gave himself the news: *Listen, Van Twest. I hate to break this to you, but you weren't the only one from school out in the city that day. Muller didn't want to upset you when he visited the hospital.* He glanced at the painting of Adam's Peak and cleared his throat.

"So, anyway ... how did the term finish off?"

"Oh, very good." Nisal relaxed in his chair and sipped his drink. "The heat was getting pretty bad by the end, but we soldiered through."

"Did that genius kid in grade nine get any more hundreds?"

"Pradeep? Oh, yes. That chap gets nothing but perfect scores! Keeps me on my toes."

"Amazing." Rudy shook his head. "Hey, you teach the Selvarajah boy, don't you? Kanda?" Behind the casual demeanour, his heart was pounding.

"Oh yes," Nisal replied. "Also a bright boy."

There was no sign in the math teacher's face that anything was wrong, but Rudy had to be sure.

"He missed his last English class before I went out of commission. It was really unusual. I was just wondering if he was around for the end of term."

Nisal's forehead pinched briefly. "Yes — I'm certain he was there. Hasn't missed any math classes."

Rudy slumped back against the pillows and closed his eyes.

"Everything all right?" his colleague said.

He struggled to focus. "Yes. Fine. It's just the heat."

Nisal nudged the fan cage toward him. "You know, I just now remembered. The Selvarajah boy was asking about you. Yes, I think he was worried about you, Van Twest."

Rudy forced a smile. "Worried about having Muller assign his term grade probably."

"No, no. He was very concerned. I'm sure of it."

Again Rudy smiled, a smile of gratitude that wasn't altogether deceitful, but his thoughts were unruly. Now that he had it, this information about Kanda wanted mulling over. But Nisal had travelled more than an hour by train to see him. Shoving aside the brood of questions clamouring for his attention, he sat up straight.

"So ... you still need to tell me about that math theory."

"Fermat's theorem?"

Rudy had no idea, but he nodded. "Yeah, that's it. I've been waiting to hear it."

For an instant his colleague eyed him suspiciously, then he smiled and slipped into the kind of enthusiasm that succeeded in convincing teenagers math could be worthwhile. "Well, to begin with, Van Twest, it's the story *about* the theorem that you'd find most interesting. A real character drama. This Fermat, for instance, was not even a professional mathematician."

While Nisal talked cheerfully about the seventeenth-century French lawyer setting out the proof of a dull-sounding mathematical idea then running out of space in his notebook, leaving behind a mystery that took generations to solve, Rudy half-listened and, despite his attempts not to, thought about Kanda.

He hadn't been hurt; he'd returned to school. In a sense, the pursuit was over. Yet the reason for his excursion to the city remained a mystery. Once more Rudy saw the boy standing on the traffic island. Was he on his way to an innocent appointment? Or playing hooky? Or was it something else? And Rudy himself: had he simply been a victim of the same circumstantial flukes that had acted on every other person who'd found himself on President Street that morning? In his distracted state of mind, had he followed a young man who simply looked like Kanda? Or had he been lured away? Despite the heat, he shivered. He thought of Kanda's letter, its subtly chastising tone. Had the boy intended to teach him a lesson? And if so, just how severe a lesson? The most extreme possibility seemed preposterous, but he had to allow that his Morgan Hill years had perhaps rendered him incapable of seeing certain things.

He was pondering this, tormenting himself with barely imaginable scenarios, when someone knocked at the front door.

"More visitors?" Nisal said, breaking off from his story.

Rudy shrugged. "No idea." He was inclined to ignore the knock.

They sat in silence for a moment, then Nisal jumped to his feet. "Sorry, machan! I forgot about your injury. I'll answer it."

"No, you don't need —" Rudy began, but his friend was already at the bedroom door. "If it's one of the neighbours, tell them I'm asleep," he called out in a raspy whisper, then he sank back against his pillow.

Waiting for Nisal to return, he listened to the faint rustle of vegetation outside his bedroom window and tried to forget his student. He fantasized that the visitor at the door was Clare. Aunty had told him that she'd shown up at his father's house, once with her mother and once alone. The solitary visit in particular made him jealous, for in his imagination Clare Fraser belonged to him. She received all his rants and uncertainties and pains, and he was unwilling to share her. He'd recoiled from the image of her chatting with his father and his aunt in their Morgan Hill living room, and now, to combat the violation even further, he indulged the fantasy that Clare had come to see him. She'd heard about his injuries and was worried about him. Any moment now she would appear in the doorway, a fairy-like figure (Nisal would have slipped away), and they would acknowledge each other without words. She would cross the room and sit next to him on the bed, their bodies barely touching. He would tell her about his failures, and she would absolve him with a light touch of her hand. Eventually they would be naked. But there'd be no undressing, no coarse grappling with buttons or zips. It would just happen. And then —

He heard Nisal's voice and was jolted back by the realization that his friend had been gone quite a long time. There was another voice, too — a man's — and the two were speaking Sinhala. Rudy considered the possibilities. A neighbour? Another colleague? More likely, it was the "special doctor" the woman next door kept threatening to send over. Rudy began rapidly devising excuses not to be examined by the quack when the thought struck him, chillingly, that the visitor was someone associated with Kanda.

His thoughts flew off, worlds away from Morgan Hill Road.

The boy had been involved somehow in the attack. He'd had a role to play — something he needed to do at the clock tower, a signal of some kind. He knew he'd been followed, that Rudy had seen him, and he'd spoken to his superiors.

Rudy's muscles clenched. His heart thundered. He was back on Janadhipathi Mawatha, in the prickling interval between the gunshots and the bomb. If not for his injuries, he would have bolted for the back door. Instead he sat, frozen, grateful that Bernadette was long gone, insisting to himself that whatever was about to happen to him was only fair. He'd been sheltered too long.

Nisal appeared in the doorway first.

"You have a surprise visitor," he announced, his manner strangely formal. "I should be leaving anyway. There's a train at two o'clock."

The surprise visitor had changed the atmosphere of the house. Though Rudy couldn't yet see the man, he was conscious of the commanding presence, the foreignness and fearsomeness of Kanda's world. The air prickled with uncertainty.

"Thanks for coming, Nisal," he said.

"My pleasure. Thank you for the drink." He waved. "Get well soon."

Nisal turned and took his leave of the visitor standing behind him. The man stepped forward into the doorway. He was silver-haired, slender, and had fairer skin than Rudy had anticipated. He wore a white shirt, with a bulge in the breast pocket, and grey trousers.

"Rudyard. May I come in?" he said, and instantly Kanda's world evaporated.

Rudy nodded. "Yes. Of course."

"I don't imagine you recognize me." The visitor approached the bed. His face, though old, was unmistakable. Glaringly recognizable. They shook hands, and Rudy's heart continued to race. "I'm Ernest Van Twest," the man said. "Your father's brother."

Rudy nodded. "Uncle."

Uncle Ernie lowered himself slowly into the chair by the bed, his green-brown eyes surveying the room, resting only briefly on his own painting. Rudy stared, conscious that his near-reverential silence could go on only so long, and that he would have only trivial questions with which to break it. *How are you? How was the trip from Kandy? When did you arrive?* But Ernie spoke first.

"I apologize for showing up unannounced. Mary has been ringing me from Canada, trying to get me over here." He said this matter-of-factly, and it was impossible to tell how he felt about his sister's requests. "I had some business in the city, so I thought I'd kill two birds with one stone, if you'll pardon the expression." He glanced over his shoulder, toward the bedroom door. "I hope I wasn't interrupting anything private ... with your friend."

The obvious implications of Uncle Ernie's remark took Rudy by surprise. Yet they made sense. To Ernie, he was a blank slate.

"No, no," he said. "Nisal's a colleague. He just came by to see how I was doing." He was about to add *He had to get back to his wife,* but he stopped himself.

"Very nice chap," Ernie said, and Rudy nodded. "Yeah. He's a lovely guy."

Uncle Ernie crossed one leg over the other and smiled tentatively. "Yes, well, your aunt is terrified you're on death's doorstep, you know. Said you tried to pretty matters up for her."

Rudy shrugged. "I didn't want to worry her. She's had a lot to deal with."

He wondered how much Ernie knew of the family's troubles, how much he cared, if at all. He should have been asking about Adam, it seemed. Adam, more than anyone, he should have cared about.

"Hmm. Not a bad idea," Ernie said. He reached into his bulging shirt pocket and took out a pipe, a box of matches, and a small pouch of tobacco. "At any rate," he added, "it doesn't seem you fared too badly."

He added a pinch of tobacco to the bowl of his pipe, tamped it, and struck a match. Each time his lips parted around the stem, they made a faint "p" and wisps of smoke escaped from his mouth. Watching the familiar ritual, Rudy sank into the dry, heavy, old-man smell that used to hang in his grandfather's study. He glanced at the stack of books on his bedside table, among them his grandfather's diary, and recalled his plan to visit Uncle Ernie — the fleeting eagerness to know his lost relative. There were curiosities he'd been impatient to satisfy, gaps he'd wanted to fill, but now he could hardly think of one.

When the pipe was lit to his satisfaction, Uncle Ernie shook the match and tossed it through the open louvres of the bedroom window. Then he rested his right elbow in his left palm and pointed the pipe stem in Rudy's direction.

"So, you've come back. Is this permanent?"

Rudy shrugged again. "I think so. That's the plan anyway." He anchored himself with his hands and raised his right buttock off the mattress to relieve the dull throb in his pelvis. Returning gingerly to his former position, he added, "I'll be moving from here, though. As soon as I'm mobile again, I'll start looking for my own place."

Ernie nodded absently. "Ah, yes. Well, that makes sense."

"Something closer to the city, I thought."

Uncle Ernie didn't answer. He was again surveying the room.

Rudy fidgeted with his watch strap. "Are there any areas of Colombo you'd recommend?"

"Colombo? I hardly know the place." Ernie's eyes were now on his painting. "Do you recognize that mountain, Rudyard?"

"Rudy. Everyone calls me Rudy."

"Yes? Yes, I imagine Kipling has finally gone out of fashion. Good thing."

"It's Adam's Peak. Sri Pada. You painted it in 1946."

"That long ago?" Ernie rubbed his collarbone through the open neck of his shirt. "Probably the last time I climbed the thing as well. Have you been up?"

"No ... not yet."

"Ah, well, you must do it. It's rather spectacular. If you begin the climb at midnight, you reach the top by sunrise." Uncle Ernie closed one eye and traced an ascent in the air with the stem of his pipe. "It's a magnificent view up there," he said, stabbing his imaginary summit. "The season will be done soon for this year, but there's still time. You could —" He looked down at Rudy and lowered his hand. "Well, I gather climbing is out of the question for you just now, isn't it."

Again Rudy eyed his grandfather's diary. He remembered Grandpa's words — *cavorting, giggling, prattling* — and tried to connect them to this newfound uncle. To mention the diary at all was a gamble, he suspected, but in the aftermath of his earlier fears he felt bold.

"I've read about one of your climbs, in Grandpa's diary," he said. "Aunty Mary passed it on to me."

Uncle Ernie sucked on his pipe and nodded calmly as he exhaled. "How interesting. I wonder which time that was."

"My father wanted to go along, but Grandpa thought he was too young."

"Hmm. Yes. I remember Alec threw a hell of a tantrum every year. It was terribly important to him to be included on that expedition. He wanted to do everything I did. Typical of the younger brother, really. I expect he could have managed the climb. He was an athletic chap."

This description of his father as a tag-along little brother echoed uncomfortably in Rudy's head. For a moment he saw Adam, bawling over the remains of a stone sculpture in the backyard. He shifted his position.

"Can I make you a cup of tea, Uncle? I need to get up and move around a little."

Uncle Ernie waved his free hand in front of his face. "No. I'm afraid I can't stomach the stuff. Very inconvenient when I was living in Britain, but there you are."

Very inconvenient when you were living on a tea estate, Rudy thought, but in response he only nodded.

"In any case," Ernie said, "I should be on my way. I'll let Mary know you're perfectly fine." He stood up slowly, hesitating midway. "You *are* fine, I take it? Managing all right?"

"Uh, yeah. Just fine."

"Very good. I'll be off then."

Uncle Ernie emptied his pipe out the window. Rudy shimmied to the edge of the bed, lowered his legs to the floor, and reached for his crutches. Launching himself up, he teetered between opposing urges — on the one hand, to hold the old man back as long as he could, and on the other, to get rid of him as soon as possible. The visit, as it was, seemed either incomplete or a waste of time.

He followed his uncle out of the bedroom. As they neared the front door, and the choice of either planning to see each other again or saying a final farewell became imminent, Rudy silently reproached his aunt for forcing the visit. If he'd had some warning, he could have prepared. For one thing, he wouldn't have seen Ernie alone; he would have arranged for Bernadette to be with him. She would have welcomed her mother's cousin with all the warmth she would accord any family member, and at the end of the visit, she would have seen Uncle Ernie off with strict orders to stay in touch and an invitation to an upcoming birthday party or Sunday lunch. But Rudy had nothing to offer.

At the door, Ernie extended his bony hand. "It was a pleasure to meet you, Rudy."

"You too, Uncle."

"Take care of that hip."

"I will."

Uncle Ernie opened the door and stepped outside, and suddenly the balance of Rudy's teetering was thrown off. He lacked Bernadette's resources, but for an instant he discovered her will.

"How long will you be in town?" he said.

Ernie looked toward the lane. "Not long. Another day or two."

At the risk of sounding like a jilted lover, Rudy blurted his next question: "Will I see you again?"

"I'm afraid not this time," Ernie said. Then he turned back. "It isn't absolutely necessary that Sri Pada be climbed during the season. When you're feeling up to it, why don't you and I make the journey?"

The tension that had seized Rudy's body earlier hadn't really gone away, but it eased off now. He sank his full weight onto the crutches and nodded.

"Sure. I'd like that."

April 29, Wednesday. Hi, Clare. So you *are* still on MHR. I'm not sure how to feel about that. There's something too real about it, I guess. Especially lately. I've been avoiding thinking about home. I got a call from Dad (the serious calls always come from him), and it seems Adam's had a setback. He developed a clot that went to his lungs and fucked up his breathing. I asked Dad if I should come home (knowing full well I'm in no condition to do so), and he said there'd be no point right now. Adam's stable, he said, but he isn't "himself." No kidding. Susie sent me an article she dug up on the stages of brain injury recovery (the "Rancho Los Amigos" scale — sounds like a fucking vacation resort), and she highlighted some of the stuff she's noticed in Adam: inattention, aggression, incoherence, irritability, self-centredness, vague recognition of people, etc. Jesus, that sounds like *me.* I think I prefer the Glasgow scale. I don't know, I just don't know. The doctors keep telling Dad and Aunty they have to wait, and that it may be a long time before they know the long-term effects. We (the family that is) are supposed to carry on with our lives as normally as possible, they say. It's a wonder Aunty hasn't hauled off and belted one of them yet. In a twisted sort of way, I'm glad that I can't carry on with my normal life yet. I can imagine I'm keeping up a vigil here in my bed, useless as it is. But when I can walk again, I'm going to go on a pilgrimage.

15

O<small>N THE STIFLING TRAIN RIDE</small> from the city, Clare read her tattered copy of *The Jungle Books*, hearing her father's voice, the way it sounded when he first read her the stories so long ago. Deep and authoritative. But when she reached the part where Mowgli appears, naked, at the wolves' cave, it was her mother she remembered, and the awkward bed-time conversation that had followed Alastair's reading of the strange passage. She'd been lying in the dark thinking about it, wanting to know where *she* came from, wondering if she herself, like Mowgli, had turned up out of nowhere (not naked, though). More importantly, she'd wanted confirmation that, despite what she'd witnessed across the street at the Vantwests' just a few days before, Emma's explanation of where babies came from was fantasy. "How did I come to you and Daddy?" she'd asked anxiously, but her mother's surprising uncertain-ty meant that she had to explain herself further. "Emma says she knows where I come from, but I don't believe her." More uncertainty: "What did Emma say, pet?" Horrible awkwardness; sheet pulled up over her face. "She says I came from your stomach." Then the aston-ishing reply, delivered quietly and gravely. "Aye, that's right. Well, near my stomach. A separate place, where babies grow."

Fanning herself with the plastic folder containing her plane ticket, Clare wondered now what sort of awkwardness her mother must have endured that evening in the face of the unanswerable question. *How did I come to you and Daddy?* A few years later, Isobel had bought her a book that explained the biology in simple words and cartoon pictures, and Clare had assumed over the years that her mother was simply uptight, conventionally prim and Scottish. Part of her believed it still, in spite of everything.

Her stop was approaching. Clare put the ticket folder in her bag and knotted her hair in a sloppy bun. Through the window, trees and houses and lampposts whizzed past, then slowed, then finally fixed themselves into the pattern that once had accommodated her so readily. She stepped off the train and into the sun. The air hissed with the razor-like spray shooting from sprinklers across the station building's narrow strip of lawn. Shouldering her bag, Clare headed for the parking lot, which stretched away from the tracks and was lined with shady trees. The hissing persisted — cicadas, probably, but Clare attributed the noise to something else. Behind its quiet, patterned façade, her west-island suburb was hissing with secrets. Not the delightful secrets of classic novels, though — the kind which, the moment they're uncovered, serve to clear up confusion and restore the proper order of things. No — these secrets revealed instead that the lives behind the tidy lawns and façades were messy. Over the years, Clare had caught occasional glimpses of that messiness: the nervous breakdown that confined Denise Carroll to her house for months; Ken Boswell's retarded brother, said to be living in a special home in Verdun; Philip Skinner's bedwetting problem, which prevented him from going to camp in grade seven. And now: Alastair and Isobel Fraser's marriage of convenience.

Isobel hadn't described it in those terms, of course. In her words, she'd been taken advantage of by her father's apprentice, and Alastair, whom she was fond of, came to her rescue. "Nowadays young women are smarter, not so easily taken in," she'd said. "Not that he was a bad person — just a typical young man. And I was just very naive." At that point she'd reached across the kitchen table and placed her hand over Clare's. "But I got a wonderful daughter from my foolishness, and a fine, caring husband. So the story has a happy ending." And for thirty-one years she'd kept that story to herself — for Alastair's sake at first, then out of habit, then, finally, from a fear that by revealing the truth, she'd be playing God.

In a patch of shade Clare shook out her hair and searched her bag for an elastic band. She hummed an improvised tune, a diversion from her compulsion to repeat to herself, yet again, that her father was not her father — an idea that left her with the dizzying sensation that she was without substance, in danger of vaporizing on the spot. She told herself it was exactly what she'd wanted — an excuse to jettison the influences of her past once and for all — but she'd envisioned a letting go much different from this. She'd imagined slipping unnoticed out of the pattern of her life and drifting fatefully toward her authentic self, that elusive thing she'd expected to locate in a Paris café or on a train between Barcelona and Madrid. She'd never meant to forfeit her place altogether. When she'd imagined bombs exploding on Morgan Hill Road, it was never her own home that vanished.

"He'll always be your father, pet," Isobel had said — what else could she say? But to Clare the words were hollow and mocking.

On the evening she'd found out, she'd gone to her studio and sat at the piano, trying to reclaim him. The music had been his idea, his gift, offered during the trip to Stanwick. He'd understood her then, she supposed, understood her loneliness and boredom, if not her physical afflictions. But though she played her childhood songs, simple melodies her father had enjoyed, and even the same piece she'd been attempting on Aunty Jean's piano when Alastair made his offer, she couldn't find *him* — only her mother, who, now that Clare thought about it, had been nervous and agitated their entire time in Stanwick. Understandably, of course — it was her first time back.

She found an elastic, the one that held together the folder from the travel agent, and as she set about retying her hair, a car pulled up next to her. Clare glanced sideways and saw Joanne Skinner leaning across her passenger seat to roll down the window.

"Good timing," she said. "I'll give you a lift."

Excuses came easily. She had some shopping to do; she felt like walking. But the heat was oppressive, and the ride with Mrs. Skinner wouldn't be long.

"Thanks," she said, opening the car door. "It's really hot."

"Tell me about it!" Mrs. Skinner huffed. "I was just dropping David off at the train. He has an interview for a summer job, and his shirt's already soaked, poor guy."

Mrs. Skinner's bare arms were angry pink, and they jiggled as she pulled a U-turn at the end of the parking lot and headed for the exit.

"What sort of job is it?" Clare said.

"Oh, just waiting tables. He's not too keen on being a waiter, but the restaurant's on that street where all the tourists go, so he's expecting good tips. What on earth is the name of that street? The one with all the outside tables. I haven't been downtown in ages."

"Prince Arthur?"

"Prince Arthur ... Prince Arthur. I think you're right. I'll have to ask David again. Is that near your store?"

They stopped at a light, and Clare glanced inside her bag at the folder containing her plane ticket.

"Not too far. But it won't be my store much longer."

Mrs. Skinner darted a look to her right. "What's this? Are you leaving your job?"

"Uh-huh."

"Don't tell me Emma's finally talked you into going to Vancouver!"

"I'm not sure. Maybe. I'm planning to travel a bit first."

"Really? Well!"

Clare smiled feebly then looked away. She hadn't told Emma anything — about her job, or her father, or the plane ticket that was tucked inside her bag, real and nonrefundable — but now here she was, revealing her plans to Emma's mother as easily as she'd talked about the weather. The omissions seemed unfaithful, though they hadn't before. Her conversations with Emma had their particular way of unfolding, and the idea of rerouting one of those conversations with announcements like hers, however important, had paralyzed her more than usual. Which was probably, Clare now considered, the very predicament her mother had been in for the past three decades.

The light changed, and Mrs. Skinner turned onto the Boulevard, nodding to herself. "So, are you going to become another one of these third-world backpackers?" she said, with a levity that seemed forced.

"No. I'm not really into that."

Mrs. Skinner smiled. "Oh, I know what you mean! You wouldn't catch me traipsing off to the places that daughter of mine goes. The stranger the better seems to be her policy." They rode in silence for a while, past the shopping plaza and the Dairy Queen, then Mrs. Skinner said, "So where *will* you be going?"

"My flight's to London. I'm not sure where I'll go from there."

She would have to call Emma and tell her everything.

"The fancy-free approach! You're brave!" Mrs. Skinner signalled right and slowed the car, though they were still more than a block from Morgan Hill Road. "I must say, I like having everything booked before I leave. I find I just enjoy myself more that way. But ... *chacun son goût*, as they say. Do you think you'll go to Ireland? I only ask because Ray has a cousin there, in Galway, and I'm sure she'd be happy to put you up if you needed a place to stay."

Clare resisted an urge to reach for the door handle right away. "I don't think so. I'll probably head for France."

"Well, let us know if you change your mind. When did you say you're leaving?"

"Next Friday."

"They'll miss you at the music store, I bet." Mrs. Skinner smiled, then lowered her voice. "Emma tells me you've been seeing quite a bit of your boss lately."

Clare clenched the straps of her bag. "That's news to me."

She knew she'd regret her answer later on. She'd wish she had laughed off the remark, or simply acknowledged, matter-of-factly, that her boss was a nice man and a friend. But the idea of Emma and Joanne Skinner discussing her relationship prospects over the phone made her stupid.

"Oh. Well ..." Mrs. Skinner fumbled, "she only meant that the two of you seem to get along well outside of work."

They were now on Morgan Hill Road, and neither said anything as they drifted slowly to the Skinners' driveway. Just before making her final turn, however, Mrs. Skinner looked past Clare at the Vantwests' house and exhaled in a manner that suggested something between exasperation and pity.

"Adam still isn't himself. His sister was in town last week, and she was saying he's been stuck at a level six on the recovery scale for some time now. Or maybe it was a level five."

Clare had been ignoring the Vantwests — she'd had enough to think about, after all — but she made herself look at their house and pay attention to Mrs. Skinner's news. *Level six?* Was that worse than level five or better, she wondered. And what level had he been at the afternoon his sister telephoned to say that her father and aunt wouldn't be able to make it for dinner? Adam had had a setback, she'd said, and they needed to be at the hospital. In the wake of this news, Isobel had taken another casserole across the street, but Clare hadn't gone along. She'd moved Adam's jacket to the back of her closet, and gradually the Vantwests' existence had slipped away, back behind their living room drapes, with surprising ease.

But now Mrs. Skinner was talking about recovery levels.

"It sounds just awful. Apparently he talks to them, but he just isn't *there*. Mentally. He thrashes around and swears a lot, Susan was saying." She shifted the car into park and turned off the ignition. "I hate to say it, but it sounds like things were easier on them when he was completely out of it."

"He thrashes?" The word stuck in Clare's head. She'd imagined Adam asleep. Bandaged probably, and frail, but still *Adam.*

Mrs. Skinner rolled up her window slowly. "When he's frustrated. Susan says it's as if he's fighting to come back, but it's just terribly slow. And he's still in that brace — a halo, I think they call it." She turned to Clare and again lowered her voice. "The nurses have to do *everything* for him."

Clearly Mrs. Skinner was willing to elaborate on the embarrassing limitations of Adam's personal care, but Clare ignored the offer.

"Do they think he'll ever be normal again?" she said. Another problem word.

"Heaven knows. It sounds like they just have to wait and see. I know I'd be beside myself."

Back in her own house, Clare called to her mother but got no answer. She opened the front door again — the new Toyota was in the driveway — then she went from room to room. On the dryer there was a fresh pile of folded towels; next to the phone, a handwritten message — "Clare, call Marielle from work." The day's mail lay open on the kitchen table, and several plastic baskets of strawberries occupied the counter. After she'd checked upstairs and scanned the backyard, Clare went to the living room and sat on the plump new sofa, facing the window. She looked out at the Vantwests' house and decided that her mother was there. Isobel had gone to the Vantwests' with some strawberries and was at that moment listening sympathetically to the aunt's account of Adam's condition, which would most certainly be free of words like *thrashing*.

Clare ran her hand across the nubby yellow upholstery and breathed in its synthetic smell. Surrounded by varnished pine shelving (most of it empty), glass tables, and space-age lamps, she had the impression of being in a display room. Everything just so. She shook off her sandals and dug her feet into the rust-coloured carpeting. There were things to do — booking a hotel in London; calling Marielle about her family's cottage in France, which would be free for a week in July; talking to Emma — but she sat in the strange, lifeless living room and thought about Adam in his hospital room, fighting to come back.

Back where, though? she wondered. In the depanneur, Adam had told her he wanted to get back to his roots. To Sri Lanka. The fact that he'd never been there in the first place seemed a contradiction at the time, but now she wasn't sure. She imagined him struggling against his restraints — white sheets, IV, halo — and battling distance and darkness to get to this place he'd never been but felt connected to nonetheless. Thrashing to get there.

Again the extravagant desire to do it for him came over her. But she knew she couldn't. It wasn't the foreignness of the destination that was preventing her right now, or the danger, or even the fact that her connection to Adam and his family had virtually dissolved. The barrier right now was Patrick Locke. A name, with no more substance than the map on page seventy-two of Alastair's atlas. Her mother had lost track of him entirely, could scarcely remember what he looked like, and suspected he was no longer in Scotland. He was keen on travelling, she'd said. When Clare pushed her for more details, Isobel had added that he had a blacksmith's handshake — a strange thing for her to have remarked on, but then again, under the circumstances, handshakes had been manageable, whereas a simple mention of hands — "He had strong hands," for instance — had the potential to sink the conversation in awkwardness. "The physical part of a marriage just isn't as important as people make it out to be" was the closest Isobel came, in the entire disagreeable exchange, to an acknowledgment of sex. Brushing invisible crumbs from the placemat in front of her, she'd seemed determined to present her story and its characters as tidily and concisely as possible. Of the hard facts of her biological father's existence, Clare knew only that he had lived at one time on the Stanwick high street, over a pharmacy, that he'd worked for Papa McGuigan, and that if he hadn't died in the meantime, he'd be fifty-three years old. According to Isobel, he knew nothing of Clare. There wasn't a thread of connection between them. Still, it was plain to her that travelling to the place of Adam Vantwest's roots while Patrick Locke remained a mystery would be wrong.

She closed her eyes and put herself back in the depanneur with Adam. *You'd tell me to go looking for him, wouldn't you?* she began. *You'd say I have to reconnect with my roots.* But before the Adam in her head could answer, she heard footsteps in the hall. She opened her eyes, and her mother appeared at the living room entrance, dressed in her denim housework slacks and cradling Alastair's hole-in-one trophy in her arms.

"I thought I heard you come in," she said.

Clare wriggled her feet back into her shoes. "Where were you?"

"Down in the basement. Sorting through some bits and pieces in the storage room." She crossed the living room and placed Alastair's trophy on a shelf. "I thought I'd bring this up here."

The trophy was a brass "1," about six inches tall, with a golf-ball-sized hole in it, mounted on a dark wood base. It was ugly and tacky, and Isobel had apparently interrupted her strawberry hulling to retrieve it from the basement.

"It wasn't in here before," Clare said.

Isobel stepped back to examine the thing then shifted it slightly to the left. "No, I know. Your father didn't want it out. He said it was fool's luck he got it in the first place. But I think it should be displayed, at least for a little while."

On the new pine shelf, the trophy looked especially ridiculous. The entire room was ridiculous. Clare stood up and shook out her skirt.

Her mother turned to her. "So what have you been up to, pet? Just relaxing?"

"Figuring out what I need to do," she said vaguely.

"Gordon Bennett, I keep forgetting. You're away next week. Did you see that message from Marielle? That would be lovely if you could stay at her house."

"Uh-huh."

"Do you think you'll visit some other parts of France?"

Clare eyed her mother's denim work slacks. "I suppose."

"You'll have to see Paris. Don't you think? It would be a shame to go all that way and not see Paris."

She rubbed her fingers across the rough metal shade of the new reading lamp then crossed her arms and clenched her hands. "What difference does it make?"

Isobel frowned only slightly. "I'm not sure what you mean, pet. I was only suggesting it would be a pity not to see Paris, especially with your interest in the arts."

The clenching spread up Clare's arms and across her shoulders. But it wasn't awkwardness. She imagined crossing the room and pulling down the empty pine shelves, sending them sprawling. For an instant she imagined wielding the metal lamp like a sledgehammer and smashing the glass tabletops. To smithereens. She stared down at the plump yellow sofa with sudden vengeance. Then she turned to her mother.

"How did you carry on for all those years as if everything was fine?"

"Carry on? What are you trying to say, Clare?" There was a flash of anger in Isobel's eyes, and for this Clare was grateful.

"Back in Stanwick. You had your whole life ahead of you. You could've done whatever you wanted."

"I was nineteen. Everyone has their whole —"

"You were dating the apprentice blacksmith. *Fucking* him." The word was explosive.

"Clare —"

"Then all of a sudden you were married to a guy who didn't particularly interest you and playing Susie Homemaker in a dreary suburb! That wasn't the life you'd imagined for yourself. How did you behave as if it was?"

Isobel marched toward the window, where the chesterfield used to be, then stopped. "Your assumptions aren't all correct, Clare." She shook her head. "My life with Alastair was — It was just fine."

"But it wasn't ..." Her voice faded. "It wasn't what you would have *chosen.*"

Isobel rubbed the back of her left hand. She looked out the window, and for a moment it seemed she had nothing more to say. Then she turned back to Clare.

"It all worked out for the best," she said.

Outside the window, across the street, a car pulled into the Vantwests' driveway. Clare looked away.

"I want to find Patrick Locke," she said.

The decision and the announcement came at the same time, and in the silence that followed, she kept her eyes nervously fixed on her mother.

"It occurred to me you might want to do that," Isobel finally said. She sat down at one end of the sofa, and Clare knew, in the absence of any word or gesture, that she was being invited to sit as well. But she stayed where she was. "I have no idea where he is, pet," her mother sighed. "I'd be surprised if he's still in Stanwick. Like I was saying, he wanted to travel."

Clearly, Isobel didn't want her old lover to be tracked down. But her resistance was flimsy. Anything stronger, Clare suspected, would require a venturing into territory that had been deliberately and carefully avoided for so long. *I don't want you to go looking for him because he's part of a past I'll never have again. I'm afraid he'll tell you things about me I've never told you myself. I told him I wouldn't get pregnant; he'd feel betrayed.* The kinds of things Clare and her mother never discussed.

Clare shrugged. "I might not find him, but I want to try. I'll go to Stanwick and ask around."

"Aunty Jean's not in Stanwick anymore, you remember. She moved to Aberdeen."

"I know. I wouldn't have stayed with her anyway. I'll find a hotel or something."

Isobel nodded slowly, a signal that despite the necessary limitations of their conversation, they could at least share an acknowledgment that Aunty Jean was insufferable. "There's a nice wee bed and breakfast you could try. Your father and I stayed there on our last visit." Again she rubbed the back of her hand. Then she dropped it to her lap. "He might not be what you're expecting, Clare. He doesn't …" Her voice trailed off.

"I'm not expecting anything. I just want to know who he is. I just … want to know."

"Well, pet, I'm not sure what to say. I guess it's up to you to decide what's best. You're an adult now."

Clare headed for the clothing bench, where she'd left her bag when she came in. At the foot of the stairs she felt her mother's hand against her back, lightly, barely there.

"I wonder if you'd mind looking someone else up for me while you're there," Isobel said. "An old friend I haven't seen in a long time."

Clare hoisted her bag to her shoulder. She had no intention of contacting any long-lost friends, but she nodded and started up the stairs.

"That would be really wonderful," Isobel called after her. "I'm sure you'll like her. I'll write and let her know you're coming."

At the top of the staircase, she thought about protesting. But as she turned and was confronted by the steep, gaping distance between herself and her mother, a prospect more troubling than that of afternoon tea with one of Isobel's old school friends kept her silent. It was remarkable, really, that the idea hadn't come to her earlier, the very moment Isobel revealed the truth of her past. What did she say? *I realized I was expecting, and it was like the world had been pulled out from under my feet.* Clare stared down at her mother, crouching to pluck some foreign thing from the new carpet.

"You never wanted to be anyone's mother, did you?" she whispered, and in response Isobel straightened up and disappeared down the hall.

Clare went to her studio. There was so much to do, but she stood in the middle of the room, staring at the loveseat. It was nothing like the new yellow sofa. It was tweedy and beige, a little scruffy. A reject from her father's store. She'd looked at it every day for as long as she could remember but had scarcely ever noticed it. The fat, upholstered buttons, the stiff skirting. This ugly, unobtrusive piece of furniture was a mystery.

From a tin can container on her bookshelf, she took a pair of scissors and crossed the room. She leaned over her loveseat, staring into its blank button-eyes, clenching the scissors like a dagger. Then she stabbed its dense, beige back, again and again. The glimpses of its insides spurred her on. She opened the scissors, gleamingly sharp, and slashed the length of it, just above the buttons. A ragged, thready wound opened up; dingy foam sprang out. But still she wanted to know more. She ripped and slashed, thrashing through the back of the loveseat until she reached wood and staples and stiff white fabric that looked like a cocoon. She yanked out handfuls of stuffing and flung them behind her, hurled the beige cushions against the studio door. She attacked the arms and the silky, quilted surface that covered the springs. She dug right through to the floor, where she discovered a Red Rose Tea rabbit figurine. It was covered in dust and one ear was chipped. She dropped the scissors and squeezed the tiny rabbit in her hand. Then she slumped on her piano stool and spun, around and around, her breathing shallow and fierce.

JULY 1975

Aunty Jean's flat is ugly and cold. The rooms have fake fireplaces, but Aunty Jean doesn't like them to be on because they waste electricity, and because it's summer. Her tiny bathroom is all pink — the sink, the toilet, the tub, the shaggy bath mat and seat cover, the mildewy tiles, the crocheted cap over the extra toilet roll, and the cracked bars of soap that smell like dead flowers.

When Clare used the toilet the morning after they arrived, the pink paper turned red. At first she was confused. Then she realized what it was. Emma's warnings came back to her: "It probably won't happen till you're twelve, but you better make sure you've got your own supplies," she'd said knowingly. "Your mom's had an operation, so she doesn't use that stuff anymore." Frantically Clare searched Aunty Jean's cramped bathroom closet and found a box of pads with long, inexplicable tails. They didn't stay in place, however, and her mother noticed and asked her in an urgent whisper if she needed to take a trip to the chemist. Clare looked at the floor, confused again. On the walk to the drugstore, in the same urgent whisper, Mum asked if she had any pain. Clare said no, for her mother's odd expression suggested she'd be disappointed, and even angry, if the answer were yes. The lie wasn't a serious one, and in any case the queer pains she was feeling were easier to bear than the awkwardness of the conversation, which was nothing at all like the cheerful mother-daughter chat in the book Clare had read about periods and babies.

It's four days later now. The bleeding has almost stopped, and the cramps. But her parents are having a disagreement. They've never fought, or even argued, and what they're doing right now in the kitchen can't really be called either of those things. Still, it's uncomfortable. Clare sits in the dark, ugly lounge, rereading her old copy of *The Jungle Books* and wishing, to her own surprise, that she'd gone with Aunty Jean to the Safeway.

"I just don't see what the purpose would be," her mother says. There's a long silence, then she adds, "We've lost touch."

Another silence, then her father speaks. "What if we see her in the town?"

"We're away to Paisley on Sunday. We won't see her."

"What about *him*?"

Clare has no idea who they're talking about. It seems there are people her father wants to see, but her mother doesn't want to see them. Which is strange. Usually it's the other way around.

"No." Mum's voice is quiet but firm. "That wasn't the purpose of this holiday. We're here to see family."

"Aye."

"Alastair. He doesn't even … It wouldn't be right."

"Is it right the other way?"

"I don't know," Clare's mother says, then she mutters something that Clare can't make out. "And at any rate we're not likely to find him in Stanwick."

Despite her mother's certainty that these strangers won't be seen, it seems to Clare that they are *already* in Aunty Jean's flat, invading the place and demanding that she pay attention to them. In an effort to shut them out, she focuses on her book — the part where Father Wolf discovers Mowgli, the man-cub, outside his cave. *Directly in front of him*, she reads, *holding on by a low branch, stood a naked brown baby who could just walk — as soft and as dimpled a little atom as ever came to a wolf's cave at night. He looked up into Father Wolf's face, and laughed.* Distractedly she reads the passage again. She still can't quite believe that the author used the word *naked* to describe Mowgli, or that her own father would have said the word when he first read her the story. But what strikes her most now is the image of the little boy — the one in her mind, for the book has only crude sketches. Because he's brown, and because he has no mother, he reminds her suddenly of the boy across the street, back home. As she ponders this, her picture of Mowgli transforms and sharpens. He is older now, and he's wearing navy blue school uniform shorts and a light blue shirt — much easier to picture than nakedness. Instead of a tree branch, he's holding a small suitcase. Clare puts herself in the picture, in the place of the wolves. She stares at the boy and stares, until it seems that she's actually *inside* him, and that they've become the same person, all alone in the jungle.

The disagreement between her parents seems to be over. They're talking about the trip to Paisley and the teenage cousins that Clare has to meet. Her mother is certain they'll all get along, because the cousins are girls and like to read, but Clare knows it will be awkward and embarrassing. She crosses the lounge to Aunty Jean's piano and perches on the stool. For four days, all she has done on the piano stool is spin. Now she faces the keys and studies their precise pattern of black and white. With her right hand she tries them out, first one at a time, then in pairs and threes. Some combinations sound like chandeliers or secret passageways; others are like a traffic jam. There's a sheet of music in front of her, but the only part of it that makes any sense, though not much, is the title: "Minuet in G." She scans the notes on the page and plays randomly with her right hand, imagining that she's following the music.

Some time later, her father comes into the lounge and stands by the window. She doesn't mind him being there. Unlike Mum, he hasn't taken to looking at her suspiciously or asking her how she feels. Instead he stands with his hands in the pockets of his grey corduroys and looks out at the stone building across the street. Eventually he turns to the piano and quietly clears his throat.

"Would you fancy learning to play?" he says.

Clare presses her hands between her knees. "How?"

"There's a lady at the store who teaches. Mrs. Aroutian. You've met her."

Mrs. Aroutian works in the back office. She's plump and friendly and has a collection of Red Rose Tea animals on her desk.

"I'd take piano lessons from her?"

"Aye. If you fancy it. If it doesn't suit you, you can stop."

"We don't have a piano."

"That could be arranged."

Clare spins. She closes her eyes and imagines herself on a stage, in front of an enormous audience. But she can't see any faces; they're all in the dark, like at the school Christmas concert. She herself is hidden behind her piano, which is tall, like this one of Aunty Jean's. The only sign people have that she's there at all is her music. A kind of music they've never heard before. They sit in their rows, silent and invisible, and hope she'll go on playing forever.

When the piano stool comes to a stop, she's facing her father. He's looking out the window, his hands in his pockets.

"Okay," she says.

Her father winks. "There's my girl."

AUGUST 1976

It's the lull after eleven o'clock Mass, that Sunday-slow time when, church clothes shed, sins forgiven, everything feels lighter. Rudy takes his new library book, *Robinson Crusoe*, to the living room, where Susie has stretched the hallway telephone cord so that she and her best friend can both listen to the Beach Boys album playing on the record player. Rudy can't actually read with the music playing. The book is an excuse for him to sit near his sister, listening to the giggles and mysterious codes of her conversation. He sits sideways in the armchair, tapping his bare foot against the shoulder of Grandpa's crocodile lamp, shipped over after Grandpa went into the old people's home, and the crocodile teeters back and forth to the beat of "Help Me Rhonda." In a mood of Sunday lenience, Dad hasn't complained about the volume of the music. He's in the trophy room, listening to a baseball game. Aunty Mary is wanting to make lunch, but Adam is in her way.

"Rudy!" she calls from the kitchen. "Come look after your brother."

Guessing from his aunt's tone that complaint would be useless, Rudy stifles a whine and goes to the kitchen, where he finds his brother kneeling on the floor, directing a G.I. Joe action figure up the oven door.

"Come on, Adam," he commands. "We're going out."

Leaving his doll on the floor, Adam bounds ahead of Rudy, through the laundry room to the back door, like a puppy anticipating a walk. A puppy, in Rudy's opinion, would be better than a brother. At least he'd know what to *do* with a dog. Out in the backyard, however, the question of what to do with Adam leaves him baffled. Babysitting has always been Susie's department. She's good at it, but as Rudy goes through his sister's repertoire in his mind, he scowls. School and Doctor are boring, and dress-up skits with Mum's old dresses or Susie's outgrown ballet costumes are out of the question. He scrutinizes his brother, a wide-eyed imp in yellow shorts and a Cookie Monster T-shirt, and gives up.

"Go play in your pool," he says, then dashes back to the living room for his book, praying Adam won't bawl.

He doesn't. Back on the patio, Rudy installs himself in the long recliner and opens his book while his brother sets out an armada of plastic toys in the inflatable wading pool. Content to be a surveillance officer, he opens *Robinson Crusoe* to reread what he missed while listening to Susie's phone conversation. The shipwrecked man has built a fantastic shelter all by himself, but now he's just sitting around, thinking — boring things about God's providence. The book is harder than Rudy anticipated when he signed it out. Put off by words like *iniquity* and *repine*, he looks up often to watch his brother and eventually abandons the reading altogether.

Out on the lawn, Adam has filled his plastic pail with water from the pool and is walking lopsidedly toward the flower bed, spilling and splashing along the way. "Use the watering can if you wanna water them!" Rudy calls, but Adam ignores him. He sits down next to the stone retaining wall that borders the flower bed and begins scooping dirt into his pail, stirring the sloppy mixture with one hand. He digs far down, eventually burying his entire arm to collect the last handfuls. As he digs and stirs, globs of mud stain his yellow shorts. Rudy imagines the fuss Aunty Mary will make, but as he watches, the temptation to feel the mud flow through his own fingers becomes overwhelming. He leaves his book on the chair and crosses the lawn, spikes of freshly mown grass pricking the soles of his feet.

Crouching beside Adam, he immerses his hands in the pail. The mud is a thick, cool mixture of greyish clay and black soil.

"What are you gonna do with this?" he says.

"Build something," his brother answers, matter-of-factly.

While Rudy wipes his hands on the grass, Adam turns to the pile of flattish stones left over from the retaining wall and begins sorting them. Aunty Mary has been nagging Dad to get rid of the stones ever since he built the wall, on a whim, in early summer. But Dad's interest in anything to do with the flower bed seems to have dwindled, and the stones, as a result, have become playthings.

With an air of confidence and expertise that Rudy finds surprising, Adam selects several stones from the pile, weighing them in his hands and tracing the uneven textures and bands of colour with his fingers. When his collection is complete, he squats next to it, pointy knees aimed skyward, and experiments with different structures, each one vaguely resembling the human-like figures built by Eskimos in the Arctic. Rudy watches, tempted once again to join in, but the intensity of his brother's concentration makes him hold back. Finally, Adam settles on a design. He dismantles the model then sets to work fixing the stones in place with the gluey mud. He spreads it thickly on the surfaces to be cemented, occasionally massaging his forehead with his fingers. As he works, his face and hair and the Cookie Monster on his shirt disappear behind grey-brown splashes and smears. The sculpture, when finished, is as high as Rudy's knees. It has a mysterious look, he thinks — as if it were alive. A silent, solitary observer.

Adam backs away from his work, wearing a critical frown, then turns and skips across the lawn to the sandbox. Rudy returns to the chair on the patio, glancing up now and again from his book to admire the stone sculpture. Only when his father appears at the laundry room door to call the boys for lunch does he begin to worry about his brother's muddiness. As Adam jumps out of the sandbox, calling "Look, Dada! Look!" Rudy braces himself against a scolding. But Dad just laughs. Dressed in his weekend clothes — white shorts and a plaid, short-sleeved shirt — he looks unusually relaxed. His strong, spindly legs are tanned very dark; his calloused feet are immune to the baking hot patio.

"Look at *you*," he says, taking Adam's head in his hands like a supermarket melon, ruffling the mucky hair. "You've been playing in the mud, just like your dada used to do." With a wink in Rudy's direction, he adds, "I noticed your big brother was in on the fun, too. Good, good. I remember the mud we used to get —"

He seems to be on the verge of telling a story, but Adam, squirming out of his grasp, interrupts. "Dada! Look! I built a Chinese warrior like the one we saw on TV!" He bounces up and down like a Superball, while Rudy squints at the stone sculpture, re-imagining it as one of the famous terra cotta soldiers dug up by archaeologists in China.

Dad looks in the direction Adam is pointing, but Rudy can tell his father isn't really paying attention. His eyes drift back to the little boy, studying him, examining him, in that curious manner he often has. It's a special kind of attention, never accorded to Susie or, Rudy is certain, to himself.

"Very good, son. Very good," Dad says, then he steps back. "We'd better get you out of these things or you'll have your aunty to answer to."

Dad tows Adam by the forearm into the shade of the patio umbrella, where he strips the boy down to his brand new, ready-for-kindergarten underpants. Further invigorated in his near-nakedness, Adam bounces into the house, while Dad shakes out the muddy clothes and drapes them over his arm with a long, contemplative "Hmmm." Rudy, detecting the signs of a father-son talk, folds the corner of his page and gets up. A lecture from Dad on this flat, hot Sunday afternoon would be almost as tedious as Robinson Crusoe's worries about the future of his soul. But Dad comes over and places a firm hand on his shoulder, preventing escape. For several seconds he says nothing, while Rudy, feigning preoccupation, tries to hold his balance standing on the outside edges of his feet.

"I know your brother's young," Dad eventually says, "but it pleas-es me when you spend time with him. He needs to spend more time doing boy things, if you know what I mean." What Dad means is that Adam is a sissy, Rudy thinks. But he says nothing. "I was thinking that perhaps Adam could join you and the Heaney boys for baseball or street hockey one of these days," his father continues.

The Heaneys are the only other boys in the neighbourhood who go to his school. They're stocky and foul-mouthed, and they insist that only girls go to the public library for something to do.

"He's too little, Dad," Rudy protests, forsaking his balance. "Besides, he doesn't like sports. He'd just get in the way."

Dad's shoulder grip tightens. "A brother is a valuable thing, Rudy. Someday you'll wish you'd spent more time with Adam. He looks up to you, you know."

It's the sort of remark that can't be argued with. Still, Rudy ducks defiantly from his father's arm. "I should talk to *your* brother. I bet he'd agree with me. Little brothers are a pain."

"My brother and I had very little to do with each other," Dad says, his tone peculiar. "That's why I'm telling you these things."

Frowning, Rudy tries to remember a story his grandfather once told him about Uncle Ernie — something about climbing a mountain. An important, beautiful mountain. But the memory has slipped out of reach, if it was ever real to begin with.

Inside the house, Aunty Mary's voice rises, questioning Adam's state of undress in her usual tone of exasperation. Lunch, Rudy guesses, will be late. He plants his feet in the patches of shade offered by a pair of potted azaleas and clasps his hands behind his head. A drop of sweat trickles down his side from his armpit.

"Where is your brother anyway?" he says. "Why don't we ever see him?"

Dad reaches down for Adam's muddy shoes. "He left home as a young man," he says stiffly. "He might have left Ceylon."

Pondering this, Rudy corrects his father absently. "Sri Lanka, Dad. They changed the name. Remember?"

Dad smiles. "Why do I need to remember? I have a son who knows everything. He's going to be a very wise teacher one day."

Rudy makes a face. "I'm gonna be an archaeologist," he says, and Dad tousles his hair.

After lunch, giving in to his father's wishes, Rudy suggests to Adam that the two of them go back outside to check on the warrior sculpture. Adam, dressed and clean, beams with an enthusiasm that Rudy finds both heartening and embarrassing. He watches his brother slide down from his chair and bolt toward the back door, only to be intercepted by Aunty Mary's washcloth. Observing the struggle that takes Aunty and Adam from the kitchen sink to the laundry room in an exchange of physical and verbal tugs — "You didn't eat any Jell-O." "Don't want any." "Stand still; your face isn't clean yet." "Yes it is." "Do you need to use the toilet?" "No!" "Put your shoes on!" — Rudy is struck by a realization that thanks to his brother he himself has been spared the worst of Aunty Mary's suffocating attentions. Of course, if it weren't for Adam, he then thinks, Aunty Mary wouldn't need to be here. But this latter thought is confusing and frightening, and he pushes it away.

In the laundry room, Adam slides his feet back into his muddy sneakers then slaps open the screen door. "Come on, Rudy!" he calls over the metallic squeal. "Hurry! Do you think it'll be dry yet?"

Rudy strides importantly to the laundry room and follows his brother outside.

Halfway across the lawn, however, Adam comes to an abrupt halt. "It's wrecked!" he cries. "It's all wrecked!"

Rudy carries on with deliberate calm. He reaches the sculpture and sees that two of Adam's stones, presumably the head and one of the arms, have toppled to the grass. Adam comes up behind, his face a crumpled mess of tears and flecks of yellow gravy that escaped Aunty's washcloth.

"It's wrecked," he repeats through his sobs.

Rudy crouches beside his brother, like a grown-up would. He places a hand on Adam's quivering shoulder. "No, it's not," he says. "We can fix this. Don't cry. We'll just mix up some more mud and stick these back on." Basking in his newfound maturity, he reaches for one of the stones with further consolations — "No problem, men; this'll be a cinch" — then he freezes as Adam kicks the warrior.

The remaining arm lands next to Rudy with a soft thud. He scowls, incredulous, as his brother moves in for another go.

"Adam! What're you doing?! Stop that!"

Still crouching, he lunges to protect what's left of the warrior, but a vigorous kick knocks him back. In the seconds it takes him to stand, his brother, sniffing and grunting, sends stones and dried mud flying across the grass. When nothing remains of his sculpture, Adam stops. His face, though still messy, is no longer distressed. Rudy clenches his hands to keep them from smacking his brother.

"You idiot!" he squeaks. "We could have fixed it! Why do you have to be such a baby?"

Adam doesn't answer. His big-brother maturity hopelessly deflated, Rudy picks up a stone and fires it at the wooden fence as hard as he can. The crack of the impact makes Adam gasp. Rudy holds his breath, waiting for more tears — theatrical wails that will bring Aunty Mary out to the boy's defense, maybe even Dad and Susie, too. But Adam stays quiet. Bending for another stone, Rudy glances at his brother and notices then the stream running down Adam's leg into his sneaker.

"Adam ..." he groans.

The boy's expression, when he looks up, is one of surprise — a wide-eyed innocence suggesting he has no idea how this came to happen.

Rudy turns to the house and hollers. "Aunty! Adam needs another pair of shorts!" Then he snatches his book from the patio chair and goes inside.

Upstairs, he flops on his bed. He tries to read, but stupid, sissy tears blur his vision. He wipes them furiously with one hand, holding the book open with the other. But it's no use. He gets up and goes to the bedroom window, sniffing. Across the street, Clare Fraser is skipping in her driveway. Not fast, but she keeps going as if she'll never stop. She's wearing cut-offs, and Rudy feels a new pang of irritation that his aunt still refuses to let him wear jeans, never mind cut-offs. The irritation doesn't last, though. Mesmerized by the rhythm of Clare Fraser's skipping, he stares out the window and his breathing calms.

In time his thoughts drift back to the talk with his father, the stuff about Uncle Ernie, and he remembers, like a lightning flash in his brain, the subject of his grandfather's story. Adam's Peak. Of course. The mountain Grandpa climbed with Uncle Ernie was called Adam's Peak. The place where people go to conquer their weaknesses.

Rudy closes his eyes and concentrates, until he can just about see the magnificent landscape in his mind — acres of untamed jungle, treacherous rivers and cliffs. He sees himself, all alone at the top of the mountain. He's the only one who's made it; everyone else has turned back or died. And now flood waters have risen almost to the summit, stranding him. But he doesn't care. He's built himself a fantastic shelter, and he has everything he needs.

16

"**Y**OU'RE SURE YOU'RE UP FOR THIS, Rudy?" Uncle Ernie tapped clots of red dirt from his shoes with the end of his walking stick.

Rudy wasn't sure. For the first time in months he was cold. It was July, long past the season of pilgrimages, and Adam's Peak, a deserted ghost-world, was blanketed in thick layers of dark cloud and mist. Shops at the base of the peak, a kilometre or so behind them, were abandoned; an enormous reclining Buddha with painted orange robes and sultry curves stared past them vacantly.

He massaged his hip. It didn't hurt, though it was stiff. "I'm up for it," he said. "Let's push on."

The red dirt path of the initial approach cut across tea hills, glossy from a recent rain. Uncle Ernie, carrying a plastic shopping bag of necessities — a water bottle, a package of biscuits, tobacco — took the lead. Though they were utterly alone at the moment, they'd been passed earlier on by a pair of teenagers, a brother and sister, from Scarborough of all places, out visiting their relatives. The two kids, proverbially bright-eyed and bushy-tailed, had slowed down to chat for a minute or so before dashing off again, the girl's Toronto Blue Jays T-shirt quickly disappearing into the mist. It was mid-afternoon already

— too late for a recent invalid and an old man to be setting out, really. They'd planned to begin much earlier, but finding a room for the night, in a shabby guest house ten kilometres from the peak, had taken longer than they'd anticipated, and Uncle Ernie's car had slouched asthmatically through the hill country, less fit than its passengers. An intelligent person would turn back, Rudy suspected — go for dinner, and try again in the morning. But he walked on stubbornly, conscious that he'd have only himself to blame if they ran into trouble.

Ahead of them, the clouds masked any sign of the pathway or the summit. Across the valley to his right, Rudy caught a glimpse of narrow waterfalls rushing down a hillside, but minutes later those too disappeared, and his world was reduced to the immediate surroundings: beads of water on tea leaves; pebbles lodged in the cakey dirt; scuff marks on Uncle Ernie's loafers, ridiculously unsuited to climbing.

"Do you know the significance of this peak, Rudy?" Uncle Ernie said, breaking the awkward silence in which they'd been walking.

"I know my grandfather's version."

"Ah, yes. Well, there are other versions. The Sinhalese, for example, believe that Lord Buddha came here during his lifetime and left an imprint of his foot before leaving. Hence the name *Sri Pada* — holy footprint. In the case of Hindus, the footprint belongs to Lord Shiva. Mind your step here." He paused to navigate a patch of smooth, wet rocks. "The Muslims believe that Adam spent a few years in exile up here — not such a terrible place for it, if you ask me — and I suppose the Christians claim something of that sort." He pulled a handkerchief from his pocket and wiped his forehead. "So there you are. Something for everyone."

"Too bad the same doesn't apply to the whole country," Rudy grumbled, though his complaint wasn't altogether heartfelt. In the eerie solitude, with the path gradually steepening and his hip beginning quietly to complain, the conflicts of Sri Lanka seemed to him, as in the old days, distant and unreal. But Uncle Ernie snatched at the remark.

"The country's a different story, Rudy. It's not so simple. Things would be fine and dandy if we'd gotten off on the right foot after independence, but the government has been botching up from the start." He spoke slowly but deliberately, the measured planting of his walking stick complementing the rhythm of his words. "And they're realizing too late what sort of seeds they've been sowing in the Tamil people. These people have been exploited and excluded, and they've had enough. Just like your Frenchies, no?"

Rudy frowned then shrugged. "I suppose."

Again he searched the sky for a hint of the summit. Uncle Ernie had assured him that those pilgrims who took the whole night to ascend were either unfit or drunk, or slowed down by the majority who were. But the summit of the peak, unknown to him outside of his uncle's painting, remained concealed behind the mass of thickening forest and threatening cloud. It was strange weather — humid enough that beads of moisture collected on the outside of his sweatshirt, but penetratingly cold. He lowered his eyes to the dirt path and conjured up memories of outdoor jazz and women in short dresses, until Uncle Ernie, his own passions mounting, dispelled the images.

"I'm telling you, Rudy," he exclaimed, "I'm not a supporter of violence — never have been — but I sympathize with these Tamils. Just as I sympathized with the Sinhalese when the British were here. There comes a time when self-government becomes necessary, and if those with the power to do something about it refuse to take action, well, we end up with calamities like the one you had the misfortune to be caught in."

They passed a small plaster Buddha on a stone pedestal, and Rudy wondered absently if he should start a tally.

"But just how small a group should be able to govern itself, Uncle?" he said, his tone deliberately musing, as if this were the first time he'd considered the matter. "And what's supposed to happen to all the non-Tamils in a so-called Tamil homeland? Or all the Van Twests — or the Frasers — in an independent Quebec?" Fleetingly he saw Clare at the top of Mount Royal on a summer day, looking out at her city with beatific calm, and he sighed quietly. "People move around and mix themselves up so much these days. I don't think it makes any sense to define your country by language or ethnic background or ..." His voice trailed off into uncertainty.

The argument was the same one he had wanted to make to Kanda but never did. Never would, probably. Though he'd been back at work several weeks, seeing Kanda most days, he'd avoided the boy. It was easier that way. His first day back, he'd caught sight of him chumming around with a group of other students, none of them Tamil, and the idea that Kanda could have been involved in the events on President Street seemed once again, conveniently, impossible. He still had the boy's letter but hadn't bothered acknowledging it.

Uncle Ernie stopped. Leaning on his walking stick, he raised one palm skyward. "Rain," he announced then resumed his slow, steady gait. In the general dripping of the vegetation and dampness of the air, Rudy hadn't noticed, but it was indeed beginning to rain. He slid his knapsack from his shoulders and pulled out a black nylon jacket. Uncle Ernie, well-protected in a heavy pullover of army-green wool, lifted his plastic shopping bag and wagged his index finger in the air.

"You mustn't misunderstand me, Rudy, when I speak of homelands. I'm not saying we should allow all the green-eyed, English-speaking Burghers with Dutch ancestors to declare a homeland on the outskirts of Colombo. As you say, it makes no sense. All those things — language, race, religion, and whatnot — those are the least interesting aspects of who we are. They're just meaningless circumstances. But I'm telling you, it's precisely those sorts of circumstances that have been used against the Tamil people. It's a bloody mess, and the government should give the buggers whatever autonomy they want. Or expect to keep having their country bombed to bits."

Rudy kicked a stone off the path. He expected Kanda would have something to say to Uncle Ernie about the meaninglessness of language and whatnot.

"Let's take a rest up ahead, Uncle," he said.

The path had widened, and they'd reached a broad stairway bisected by a row of lampposts, the lamps unlit. The clouded sky was so close, so low, it seemed they would climb straight into it. Heavy raindrops dotted Rudy's khaki trousers and streamed down the sleeves of his jacket. A menacing ache gripped his right buttock and hip. As he took hold of a post and hauled himself forward, he thought of Adam, hovering in some transitional world not unlike this one. Yet close somehow, capable of spurring him on.

At the top of the stairway the ground flattened to a red earth terrace housing an enormous, bulbous stupa, its white surface barely distinguishable from the clouds behind it. Around its base, a few feet from the ground, were alcoves, each one sheltering a seated Buddha — a dozen of them at least. The top of the structure slimmed to a gold pin that pierced the sky. Rudy stared briefly at the lonely stupa then took off his pack and went to lean between two of the alcoves. An overhang sheltered him from the rain; his uncle remained out on the packed earth terrace, getting wet.

Rummaging for his water bottle, he recalled Aunty Mary's attempts to talk him out of the climb. The subjects of her warnings, issued over the phone, had been impressive: snakes, bandits, wild animals. Even worse, she'd seemed to think, was the solitude, the idea that they'd be completely alone on their pilgrimage. Rudy, for his part, had imagined with a wave of horror the kind of target that Adam's Peak would offer at the height of the pilgrimage season, but he'd stifled the thought immediately and listened dutifully to his aunt. "You must wait until the next season," she'd said, and when he insisted that that was out of the question, she pleaded with him to take a guide. "Ernie is an old man," she'd said. "He doesn't know the peak as well as he says he does."

Rudy had dismissed her suggestions, even laughed at her fears, but now he wasn't so sure. Adam's Peak, out of season, was indeed an inhospitable place, and the cold sea of mist most certainly held dangers of one kind or another. Impatient to be done with the whole thing, he called across the terrace.

"How much longer would you say, Uncle?"

Uncle Ernie, gazing about in a manner that suggested Aunty's judgments of him were quite correct, crossed the terrace to the shelter of the stupa. His silver hair was plastered to his forehead. He wiped it to one side then checked his watch.

"We've been at it approximately one hour. I estimate we'll be getting up top in another two." He kicked a stone at a scrawny dog that had appeared from nowhere, sniffing hungrily. "Poor bugger," he said. "Probably hasn't had a decent meal since the season ended. He'd get fat then, I'm telling you." Again he surveyed the surroundings. "You should see it, Rudy. January, February, this path is chock-a-block with pilgrims. You're held back by the mob. Not like today. The only thing slowing us down now is our own aches and pains." He looked up. "Perhaps this weather, if it persists."

Listening to the slap of the rain against the earthen terrace, the rustle of it through the trees, Rudy made rough calculations in his head. At the rate they were going, there was little chance they'd make it back down before dark. They didn't have a flashlight; they needed to turn around. But he couldn't make himself do it — could only lean back and contemplate the situation abstractly, as if there were nothing to be done. As if he were back on President Street, held there by forces beyond his control. He took a gulp of water and offered the bottle to his uncle.

"We could do with something stronger," Uncle Ernie muttered, but he took a long swig nonetheless. "You do these sorts of excursions often in Canada?" he then said, handing the bottle back. "Braving the elements, like the explorers?"

"Hardly," Rudy laughed. "I work out in a swanky gym with TVs and a coffee bar. The only emergency supply I've got is a Visa card."

Uncle Ernie nodded seriously. "Hmm, I'm afraid my knowledge of Canada is outdated. But in that case, why didn't you wait for the new season? Much less trouble climbing then, no?"

Rudy thought of reminding his uncle that it was he, Ernie, who'd suggested climbing Adam's Peak out of season, but he held back. The handwritten note he'd received, inviting him to travel to Hatton for an excursion to the peak, had been an immeasurable relief. He'd accepted without hesitation, in part because the brevity and awkwardness of his last visit with Uncle Ernie had tormented him. But also, of course, because of Adam.

On the train ride to Hatton, it was his obligation to Adam that kept him sane. Just minutes out of Fort Station, a stranger had approached Rudy's seat, carrying a bulky radio. The man slid the radio onto the crowded overhead rack, then he disappeared. As the train rumbled out of the city, Rudy's gaze travelled compulsively upward, and the junky old machine acquired a terrifying power. More than once he was sure he heard the sound of ticking, and he stumbled to the open doorway each time to gasp for air. He searched without success for another seat. When the conductor passed by, he pointed out the abandoned radio and pleaded for its removal, but the man merely shrugged and carried on. So he closed his eyes, massaged his sweating forehead, and concentrated on Adam. He was making this pilgrimage for his brother. If he was risking his life, it was for Adam — though at the conclusion of the journey, the stranger came back and reclaimed the radio, acknowledging Rudy with a cordial nod.

He took a mouthful of water and considered explaining to his uncle why he couldn't possibly wait until the new season to climb Adam's Peak. But the thought dissolved, unuttered.

"I'm not sure I'll be here next season," he said instead.

His answer echoed vexingly in his head. It was just something to say, but in saying it he recognized that it was in him — the possibility of leaving.

"You'll go back to Canada?" Uncle Ernie said.

Chilled from having stood around too long, Rudy put the water bottle back in his bag and stepped away from the stupa, shaking his arms at his sides. It was ridiculous, this weather.

"I don't have any plans to go back. I just meant that stuff like this shouldn't be put off. You never know what'll happen, right?"

Uncle Ernie nodded his chin to one side and rubbed his palms together briskly. Watching him, Rudy felt suddenly selfish and inconsiderate. His uncle was an old man. His eyes were pouched, his hands gnarled; he used a walking stick. He should have been spending the afternoon in his cottage overlooking Kandy Lake, painting pictures and smoking his pipe.

The image broke Rudy's inertia.

"Actually, Uncle, why don't we turn around?" he said. "We're gonna get soaked, and it'll be dark by the time we get back to the car. We could try again tomorrow, or some other time."

He expected hearty accord, but instead Uncle Ernie gave a contemptuous snort.

"Nonsense!" The old man took up his stick and set off across the terrace at a vigorous pace. "We've come this far, Rudy," he called over his shoulder through the veil of mist. "As you say, there's no telling what tomorrow will bring. *Carpe diem!* The path continues over here."

"Stubborn old bugger," Rudy muttered. Then, shouldering his knapsack, he jogged to catch up, his pelvis jolting painfully each time his feet struck the sodden red earth.

17

It was july, but the air in Stanwick was cool, the sky overcast. The town was not at all as Clare remembered it. Or, rather, her feelings about it weren't. She liked the grim stone architecture — soot-black-ened, indestructible buildings, mutely observing town life as they'd been doing for hundreds of years. And she liked the queer pairings of those ancient buildings with the modern conveniences they now housed: a video rental shop, a therapeutic massage clinic, a mobile phone service centre, a juice bar — all closed, as it was Sunday. There were also, of course, venerable old businesses, like the gloomy knitwear shop that had been in the same location since Queen Victoria's silver jubilee, and Hobbs and Sons Chemists, est. 1921, against whose front window Clare now leaned. But aside from herself, tingling with the knowledge that Patrick Locke had once lived in the flat directly above her, the people passing up and down the sidewalks of Stanwick High Street seemed oblivious to the weight of history all around them.

Checking her watch, Clare calculated the time in Vancouver and crossed the street to the phone box next to the pub. An elderly woman beat her to it, so she stood outside, staring up at the windows of Patrick's flat and revisiting her mother's revelation.

There's something I need to tell you about Alastair and me, she'd said, fingers twisting her wedding band, eyes on the placemat in front of her.

What is it?

A glance up, a deep breath.

It's ... He and I weren't ... Let me see. He wasn't ...

He wasn't my real father.

Oh, Clare.

The woman in the phone box raised her voice. "No, I didn't! You'll have to tell me."

Who was it?

A man I knew in Stanwick. His name was Patrick. He was my father's apprentice.

Did Dad know?

A merciless question. Twenty-five years of marriage and fatherhood on the line. More twisting of the wedding band.

Yes. He knew.

"Every day! She's a bizzum, that one."

But you never told me.

Cruel?

Everything we do has consequences, pet. And then with something like this ...

How could I know?

"— just said to her, 'Listen, Mary, you'll have to do something about that. You can't let it go on.'"

Why are you telling me now?

I always expected I would, if ... Well, you were asking about the timing, when you came back from Vancouver, and then there was your holiday. And the Vantwests. That's what did it in the end. I thought, if anything ever happened to me ...

The Vantwests. In the end it was the Vantwests. Strangers.

The woman in the booth, noticing Clare, pursed her mouth and reached for her handbag. "Listen, I need to go now, Janet," she said. "There's a lady wanting to use the phone." She exited the booth with a greeting of "Chilly morning," then crossed the street. Clare shut herself inside the Plexiglas box. She'd promised Emma she would call, but in the cool, Sunday-morning quietness of this faraway place, she wished she hadn't. She wanted nothing from beyond the vault of low, grey clouds to touch her.

Of course, if she'd said nothing to Emma about her father, the phone call wouldn't have been demanded. But she'd allowed herself to get carried away, seduced by the idea of possessing something that Emma found extraordinary, something that had actually shut her up and rendered her fumbling and awkward, if only for a few seconds. And the penalty for this brief moment of authority was the telephone call. Reading from the back of her phone card, she pressed an endless string of numbers, and when the intrusive ringing finally began, she turned to the solemn, mute buildings of the high street with a strange desire to be among them.

Emma answered almost immediately.

"Well? Don't keep me in suspense. Have you found anything out?"

"No."

"Nothing?"

"It wasn't as if the chances were good. It was a long shot."

"You've checked the phone books and asked around and everything?"

"As much as I'm going to."

"You mean you're giving up?"

Clare hesitated. There was a hint of compassion in Emma's disappointment, a suggestion that she wanted Patrick Locke to be found for Clare's own sake.

"Just for now. I don't want to spend my whole trip on a wild goose chase."

"No ... but this is important. I know you're not looking for a father substitute, Clare, but still. It's *important*."

"People spend years doing these kinds of searches, Emma. I'll write some letters when I get home. It'll be better that way."

"I don't get it," Emma said, and it was clear that she didn't. "You're already there. If I were you, I wouldn't give up till I found him."

Clare clenched the receiver tighter. "But you're not me."

For a moment neither spoke. The phone line crackled faintly.

"So when are you going to France?" Emma said at last.

"In a few days."

There was another silence. Then they talked about France, and Marielle's family's cottage in Normandy, and the weather. Then Emma said it was late and she needed to get to bed. She spoke in the kind of tone that gets used at airports — a tone of resignation, of desire to be out of that unnatural, useless space, even if it means separation. At the end of the call, Clare stood with her hand on the receiver and a dull, empty-ish feeling inside. Then she noticed the teenage girls waiting outside the phone box, cigarettes hanging limply from their mouths, and she stepped out into the cool morning, where the feeling began gradually to subside. She hunted out the rectangular tower of Stanwick Abbey and headed in that direction. Her mother's friend Margaret would be preaching in the abbey chapel at ten o'clock.

It was something of a cop-out, this going to church. She wasn't interested in the service, or in meeting Margaret Biggar — a New Agey, hippy type, according to Isobel. Still, on Clare's first visit to the phone box next to the pub, when it had come down to actually lifting the receiver and dialing one of the two numbers she had copied from the directory, Margaret's had been the easier choice by far. Whether or not she would get around to the other, Clare couldn't yet say. For the time being, there were Stanwick's buildings and streets, the flat above the chemist's shop, the rolling countryside with its stone fences and shaggy cows, and the service at the abbey. Enough to occupy her.

She turned off the high street onto a narrow cobbled road, which seemed to lead to the abbey. In her loose white blouse and her gypsy skirt, she imagined herself a nun from some medieval order, setting off on a pilgrimage. The image, so far removed from the embarrassing displays of the Skinners' church, gave her a jolt of smug satisfaction, and as she walked she dismissed her mother's warnings about Margaret Biggar's New Agey–ness and orchestrated in her mind the kind of solemn, droning mass that belonged in a church like Stanwick Abbey. She hadn't been inside the church yet, had only glimpsed its stone tower from the lower part of town. But the tower itself, stern and symmetrical, promised a no-nonsense place, where no one would hug and no one would ask her to share the Light of God.

The road gave way to a wide, hummocky lawn, where the abbey stood, magnificent in its enormity and its solitude. Clare leaned against a gnarled tree and admired the deep arches and sprawling buttresses, the masonry of unimaginable age. She watched the ant-like procession of people making their way toward a side entrance, then she crossed the lawn and joined the line. Inside the massive sanctuary she squinted and shivered. The rose window behind the altar admitted only a suggestion of light, while the stony maw overhead seemed to swallow all warmth. As she made her way up the centre aisle to the chapel, just off the transept, she felt a pang of regret that the service would not be held here in the abbey proper. She imagined sitting in an empty pew at the back and contemplating the implications of the remaining phone number she carried on a slip of paper in her bag. The number was no guarantee, of course. There was only one P. Locke in the directory, and if it turned out not to be him, then the story she'd told Emma would be true. Her search could take years. But for now she allowed herself to believe that the P. Locke on Farrell Road was the one she was after, and that an hour of contemplation in a grim stone sanctuary could prepare her to meet him.

The chapel, however, was nothing like the abbey. Its walls were white plaster; the seating consisted of a dozen or so rows of straight-backed chairs. The lectern-style pulpit was flanked by flag standards, and the modest stained-glass window behind the piano featured an art deco crucifixion. It was far from ideal, but it would do. Clare sat near the back, and as the seats around her filled she studied the program and flipped through the hymn book. A woman sat next to her with a friendly nod, to which Clare responded with a smile.

At ten o'clock a black-robed pianist took his place and arranged sheets of music while the congregation scuffled and coughed itself to order. There was a moment of silent anticipation, then the pianist leaned forward and began the processional hymn. Reverend Margaret Biggar, enormously fat, with round, ruddy cheeks and a mass of silver and black hair, ambled down the aisle in a tent-like white cassock and purple stole and took her place behind the pulpit, her arrival perfectly synchronized with the piano's lusty final chords. She nodded in the direction of the pianist then turned to the congregation. "Good morning and welcome to St. Giles Chapel," she said, her voice low and businesslike. "We come together this morning to share and celebrate the word of God and the teachings of his son, Jesus Christ. I can see we have some visitors this morning, so a special welcome to you."

Clare clenched the hymn book in her lap, but no one paid her any attention.

Margaret grasped the sides of the pulpit. In the same businesslike manner, she marched through the prayers of Adoration and Confession, and when she reached the Lord's Prayer, her voice slipped into the background, and the congregation took up the familiar recitation with Calvinistic fervour. Clare searched the minister's voice and gestures for hints of New Agey–ness and concluded finally that Isobel couldn't really have known the woman all that well. If Margaret had known Patrick, the visit to her church might still have been worthwhile. A bridge of sorts. But according to Isobel, the two had never met. Clare glanced at her watch and sank back in her chair. In the shift from prayers to Bible readings, she imagined the pointless exchange that awaited her after the service. Then, blocking out the proceedings altogether, she improvised something better — she and Margaret at the chapel entrance, the rest of the congregation off drinking tea and coffee in the hall. Patrick Locke on the horizon.

You must be Isobel's daughter! Margaret would exclaim. *I thought I recognized you. You have your mother's smile. It's lovely to meet you.*

You too. I enjoyed the service.

Oh, well, it wasn't one of my better ones, I'm afraid. Like I was saying when you rang, I've been preparing for this conference in Edinburgh, and I've just had no time for my work here.

I hope I didn't interrupt you when I called.

No, no, not at all. I'm sorry I had to run off so quickly. But the conference work's all done now. So, are you going to join us for coffee in the hall?

She'd be obliged to ask this.

Well . . .

You're most welcome, but I also want to have you over for lunch. Are you free?

Sure. That would be great.

She would skip coffee in the hall and instead go to the bakery to buy pastries for dessert. She'd arrive at Margaret's home — one of those narrow stone dwellings on the street leading to the abbey, the one with the bright red door and plants in the windows — and lunch would be just about ready. Margaret would reminisce about her friendship with Isobel.

Your mother was always very popular at school. Got along with everyone. We didn't spend much time together, but she was always good fun when we did.

What would you do together?

Clare hadn't the faintest idea what her mother would have done with her girlfriends here in Stanwick, but she gave Margaret a long reply nonetheless: schoolwork (Isobel was a whiz at math), strolling the high street, browsing the fashion magazines, listening to Beatles records (of which Isobel had saved a few). When she'd exhausted the possibilities and polished her own contributions, she considered at length the crucial segue: *Did you ever meet her father's apprentice? Do you remember her spending time with a Patrick Locke? Are any of her other friends still in Stanwick?* In the end, she gave the transition to Margaret.

Oh, and on a Saturday afternoon, a group of us would always watch the lads playing rugby. You must have seen the rugby field on your way here.

I think so. Did you know any of the players?

A few of them, aye.

Any boyfriends? She'd smile.

Oh, I think your mother had one or two. Not from the team, though.

At this point she would try hard to appear casual.

Do you remember her going around with a Patrick Locke? Her father's apprentice? Patrick Locke?

Just before she met my father.

Aye — it was only for a wee while, I think. She never mentioned it. She could be secretive that way. But I do remember him.

"What was he like?"

"Pardon?"

Clare jerked straight in her chair. The pianist was playing; the offering was being collected. The woman next to her had whispered something, and for an instant Clare assumed she was doddery and ignored her. Then, like a creeping rash: the realization that she herself had spoken first. Out loud, to no one. Like a crazy person. She clenched her hands and whispered "Nothing" and "Sorry," and the woman next to her smiled primly. She turned to Margaret, the real person, preparing to carry on with her service. Then she darted glances at the solemn, staring faces of the congregation and felt the truth like a slap. These things that went on in her head — the hijacked voices, the imaginary playmates — were not simply weird or pathetic, a quirk that others would chuckle at. They needed to stop.

Desperately she tried to blank out her mind. She listened unfalteringly to Margaret's announcements about the Women's Guild and the Tanzania Mission Project. She followed the closing hymn note by note and let the solid words of the benediction fill her. She read from Ecclesiastes until the woman next to her had left. And at last, when the pianist had dispatched his recessional hymn and there remained just a few stragglers chatting in the pews, she joined the dwindling line of people waiting to shake hands with the minister. It didn't matter whether or not their conversation led to Patrick Locke; it most certainly wouldn't. What mattered, what she needed, was something real.

Stationed at the doorway between the chapel and the main sanctuary, Reverend Biggar moved graciously but efficiently through her greetings. Clare inched her way along behind a hunchbacked man with a walker, impatient for her turn, ready to be drawn into whatever pleasantries her mother's friend would choose to exchange. As the old man shuffled away, she hoisted the straps of her bag — a straw market bag Emma had bought in Guatemala — and fleetingly pictured her friend bargaining in her mangled Spanish, not caring how she sounded. Then she stuck out her hand and summoned a smile.

"Hi — I'm Isobel's daughter. Clare."

Margaret extended a plump, pale hand. "Margaret Biggar. Very nice to meet you."

"You too."

"And did you enjoy the service?"

"Yes ..." Briefly Clare struggled to remember something — anything — to comment on, but Margaret, eyeing her expectantly, seemed only to want her approval. "Yes," she repeated, "very much."

"Well, that's good." Margaret fingered her purple stole and glanced at the three women still talking and laughing in the pews.

"The church is beautiful," Clare said. "How old is it?"

"Oh, yes. It's lovely. The cloisters are twelfth century. Other parts have been restored."

The minister jumped awkwardly from phrase to phrase, as if she were walking barefoot across hot asphalt.

Clare called up a look of astonishment. "Twelfth century. That's incredible."

"Yes, yes it is."

"So ... your father used to be minister here?"

"Yes. Until 1974. Then it was Simon Deeks."

"And when did you start?"

Margaret looked off to one side. "I transferred here from Glasgow in 1980. Simon and I worked together until he retired. In 1989 that was."

"Are you the only minister now?"

"No, no. There's Janice Murphy as well."

"And ... so ... do you take turns conducting the services?"

"Usually, yes. She's on holiday just now."

"Oh? Whereabouts?"

"Greece."

The stragglers were making their way over, so Clare stepped back. Her conversation with Margaret was more pointless that she'd expected, the minister herself a larger-than-life mirror of Clare's own awkwardness. Again she felt the cold slap of truth: this was what others experienced in her company. Emma, Adam, even Markus. She wondered how they'd tolerated such awkwardness. How they'd tolerated *her*.

The three women disappeared into the abbey proper. Fidgeting with her stole, Margaret turned back to Clare. "Will you be joining us for coffee or tea?"

Clare forced a smile. "Thank you, but I think I'll head off." She took a step into the abbey then hesitated. The awkwardness circled them, a catlike creature, feeding off their silence. She met Margaret's grey-blue eyes and took a breath. "There's another of my mother's friends I need to visit," she said, and her bold words echoed in the vast sanctuary, nudging the creature away.

Almost imperceptibly, Margaret frowned. "Oh? Here in Stanwick?"

"Yes. On Farrell Road."

She held Margaret's gaze, urging her to ask the next question. But Margaret looked down at her hands.

"It was a surprise to hear from your mother after so long. I wrote her a few letters after she went away to Canada, but ..." Again her eyes met Clare's, and the awkwardness slipped farther away. It was the quality, the intensity, of her expression. It conveyed not a lack, Clare now saw, but an abundance. A failure of language to carry the load. So easy to understand. "We did have lovely times together," Margaret added, meaningfully, then she brushed past Clare, into the chapel. "I'll just get my things, then I'll see you off."

Clare nodded. She wanted to start over, to go to the hall for coffee and chat about ordinary things, but it was too late.

Margaret returned to the pulpit, her stride a little lopsided. "Isobel mentioned in her note that you're a pianist," she said.

"Yes. I mean, I don't play professionally; I work in a music store." Clare drifted past the rows of empty chairs, toward the piano. "Used to work, I should say. I quit recently."

"Really? What are your plans then?"

"I'm not sure. I have a few ideas."

She stood at the piano, an upright of dark mahogany, old but well-maintained, and stared down at the keys. There was no shortage of possibilities: looking for work in London, travelling until her money ran out, going back to school, calling Markus and telling him she'd made a mistake. Each prospect seemed as viable, and as arbitrary, as any other. The only one she was certain about was moving to Vancouver — she wouldn't do it. She struck middle C with her index finger.

"Actually, I have no idea."

Margaret gathered up her papers from the pulpit and tapped them into a neat stack. "Well ... that must be frightening and exciting at the same time."

"Yes ..."

Clare struck another note. She wondered what Margaret would suggest. She wanted to ask her advice, to have a sensible outside voice counsel her. Instead, she played a final note and lowered the heavy fallboard. But Margaret, stepping away from the pulpit, flapped her papers at the piano.

"Would you play something before you go?" she said with surprising ease. "If you don't mind, that is. I'd love to hear a song."

Clare frowned. "You want me to play for you?"

"Something by Bob Dylan maybe?"

She realized even as she puzzled over Margaret's request that her reaction made no sense. She was a musician; playing for others was part of the role — a part she'd once fantasized about. And yet, no one had ever done this. Made a request of her this way. Spontaneously, hopefully. Twenty years at the piano, and no one had ever said *Could you play such-and-such for me?*

"I know 'Blowin' in the Wind,'" she finally said. Her grade seven class had sung it at the spring concert. She'd asked Mrs. Aroutian if she could learn it, and for several months it had been her favourite.

"That would be great," Margaret said. "I've always wanted to hear him in concert, but it's just never happened."

Clare sat down and lifted the fallboard. It had been more than a week since she last played — longer, perhaps, than she'd ever gone since the day of her first lesson with Mrs. Aroutian. Poised now over the stretch of keys, she was struck by their familiarity, their invariable arrangement of white and black and the precise tonal ratios locked within that arrangement. She played a few chords, tested the pedals, with which the black-robed pianist had been too enthusiastic, then turned to Margaret, who'd settled herself on a front-row chair.

"I can't really — I mean, this won't sound much like Dylan's version."

"Oh, I'm sure it'll be just fine. Go on; give it a try."

She began, and the intervening years closed up. She was back in the den, her father's room, where the piano used to be. She played the song the way she'd learned it, without variation or improvisation, the way it was scored in *'60s Folk Classics for Piano*, her thirteen-year-old hands tense, correct. *How many roads must a man walk down before you call him a man?* For a transcendent moment she rediscovered the solitary, introspective girl that she was, perched on her piano stool in denim cut-offs and a striped halter top, passionate about the mysteries contained in her music. Then she glanced at Margaret and saw the same thing. Her enormous body was slowly swaying, her cassock like a wide, white sail. Her eyes were closed, and she was smiling. There was no doubt she knew all the lyrics and was hearing Dylan's wheezy tenor in her head, so Clare played every verse. She played to the teenage Margaret, a rosy-cheeked idealist with a record player in her room. It was so easy to imagine her.

At the end of the song, Margaret clapped noisily. Clare looked down at her own hands and noticed how they'd aged.

"I haven't played it in a long time," she said. "Sorry if it was a bit rusty."

"No, no, it was perfect," Margaret said. "Just wonderful. Thank you so much. I think our pianist would be delighted to retire and have you take over here." She laughed.

Clare picked up her bag. "I should get going. They'll be wondering what's happened to you."

Margaret didn't protest. She pushed herself out of her chair and led the way back to the chapel entrance. In the main sanctuary, Clare tried to recall the greeting her mother had asked her to pass on. She looked at the floor and cleared her throat. Then Margaret touched her arm with a light but meaningful pressure.

"By the way, Clare," she said, "which of your mother's friends are you away to visit? It could be someone I know."

Clare's hands clenched. Back at the piano, she'd forgotten him, forgotten why she was here. She made herself look up.

"Patrick Locke."

"The lad who worked with her father, you mean?"

"Yes." Her insides quivered — a sensation more like swimming eels than butterflies. He was real. "Do you know him?"

"Oh, not well. I haven't seen him in years. Isobel's stayed in touch with him then?" She sounded puzzled.

"Not really. No. I just wanted to track him down ... for some personal reasons." Clare held her breath.

"Oh?"

She believed that Margaret would understand. She suspected the whole story might be something her mother's friend deserved to know. The words were in her head. But her too-brief relationship with Margaret didn't warrant the uttering.

"My mother thinks he's done a lot of travelling," she said. "I wanted to talk to him about it."

Margaret nodded. "Aye, I seem to remember him leaving on some grand adventure. Seems he and your mother both had itchy feet."

"I guess so."

Margaret nodded toward a distant door. "The hall is through there. Are you sure you won't join us for coffee?"

Clare smiled and shook her head. She needed to return to the phone box across from Hobbs and Sons before her courage failed her. "No. Thank you. I'll be off. It was good to meet you." She extended her hand. "My mother sends her love. She'll write again."

Margaret gave a sharp squeeze. "Lovely to meet you, Clare." She turned to the hall then turned back. "I think his house is out of town a wee bit. You may want to ask for directions."

"Thanks. I will."

In the phone box on the high street, Clare gripped the black receiver in one hand and stared at the slip of paper on which she'd written P. Locke's telephone number. She thought of Adam, struggling to get back to his roots. His voice came to her weakly, but she shut him out. This wasn't a homecoming. It was a departure, an irreversible transformation. She deposited a coin in the slot and entered the number. At the first double ring, her heart struck up a riotous pounding, and her hand clenched the receiver tighter. She hoped he wouldn't answer, but knew at the same time that that wouldn't solve anything.

After the third ring, a woman's voice said hello.

18

THE PATH TO THE SUMMIT became steeper, narrower, wetter. The rain, angled by wind, rustled through the leafy shrubs and skinny trees and splattered the ragged flagstone steps. Rudy still had no sense of the peak as a whole. He'd imagined himself climbing the benign, two-dimensional hill of Uncle Ernie's painting, but this was something entirely different. He followed his uncle blindly up the slippery ascent, stopping regularly to shake water from his hair and pluck small leeches from the legs of his trousers. Since their last stop, in a tiny clearing with sodden planks for benches, the pain in his pelvis had reached deeper, tightening its grip, so that his progress was now hindered by a limp. To carry on was foolish. Still, they climbed in silence, and gradually Rudy found himself anticipating the summit, allowing himself to believe that the red pavilion in Uncle Ernie's painting would actually be there, warm and welcoming, when they arrived.

His optimism was dampened by the return of the teenage brother and sister from Toronto. Their T-shirts and sweatpants were smeared with dirt and soaking wet. They'd made it to the top but were clearly unimpressed.

"There's, like, no view at all!" the girl complained, as if, despite the weather, she'd been expecting the glorious panorama of the tourist brochures. "It's totally clouded over. But at least you get a workout."

"Are there any buildings up there?" Rudy asked, aware that he sounded desperate.

"There's some, but they're all closed, I think," the boy said. "You can see the footprint, though."

His sister elaborated. "Yeah, it's just, like, a big slab of concrete, though. It's in a little temple thingy, but the whole place is locked up. There's a guy up there with a key, and he lets you in. I don't think he speaks much English, though. He kept speaking to us in Sinhalese" — she glanced at her brother — "but I can, like, hardly even speak Tamil anymore. Oh, and you have to take your shoes off! It's, like, freezing! But the guy won't let you in if you don't. I mean, I understand we should respect the culture and everything, but that's just a little extreme." She rolled her eyes. "Don't you think?"

Rudy gave a noncommittal smile and wondered if Kanda would acknowledge these Canadian kids as his kind. They could have been any of the hundreds of teenagers Rudy had taught back in Toronto, and he could easily have chatted with them at length about "home." Even their talk about Sri Pada was steeped in subtle cues that identified the three of them, like a password or a secret handshake, as members of a particular club. It was comforting, but the very fact of the comfort, the reminder of what it signified, left him anxious to get away.

"How far is it to the top?" he said.

The girl widened her eyes and turned to her brother, who deliberated a moment in silence. "Uh, not too far," he said. "I think we left there about half an hour ago. Maybe a bit more. I'm not too sure."

"It gets super-steep near the end, though," the girl added. "But there's railings for that part, and you're pretty much finished by then, so it's not so bad."

Rudy glanced at his uncle, who seemed not to be paying much attention. He considered asking the brother and sister, diplomatically, if they thought the climb would be too difficult for an elderly man, but decided that their judgment on that matter wasn't likely to be any more reliable than their sense of distance.

"Well, we'd better get going," he said instead, adjusting the straps of his knapsack. "Enjoy the rest of your trip."

"Yeah, you too!" The girl waved, then she and her brother carried on down the steps, quick and agile as mountain goats.

"Are you still up for this, Uncle?" Rudy said. "We could turn back."

In answer, Uncle Ernie jabbed the end of his walking stick into the uphill slope and took three of the steps at once. Rudy limped behind, scanning the forest for a stick of his own. As they climbed, neither able to see the face of the other, he imagined himself in a confessional. Ernie was the aging priest, familiar, but mysterious nonetheless; Rudy himself was the muddled confessant, struggling at that moment to sort out the peculiar restlessness that his conversation with the teenagers had fuelled.

"You know, Uncle," he began, "I expected that moving back to Sri Lanka would be different than it's actually been."

"Is that so?" Uncle Ernie said, his tone appropriately neutral.

"I think I expected that coming back here would give me a sense of who I really am. But it hasn't really worked out that way."

"Hmm. You're having what they call an identity crisis then."

Rudy couldn't tell if his uncle was making fun of him or not. He gave a short laugh. "Yeah, I guess that's what it is. It sounds pretty corny."

"Not necessarily. What were you hoping would happen back here?"

"I'm not sure. I guess I thought I could slide back in where I left off when I was six. Become an older version of that kid."

"Ah. Well. Picking up where one left off isn't so easy. Too much water under the bridge, as it were."

"Yeah. I suspect that kid I left behind drowned ages ago." He sighed noisily, partly in disgruntlement, partly in pain. "I never really thought about it this way when I left, but I actually believed I'd step off the plane and there'd be some kind of mystical Sri Lankan vibe connecting me to everything." He paused, recognizing in his words the very thinking for which he'd criticized Kanda. His tone became mocking. "I thought I'd be in my groove."

"And I take it that didn't happen? Your groove?"

"Well, obviously I didn't feel like a complete stranger. But no, it hasn't been what I was hoping for."

As if in affirmation of what he'd been saying, Rudy lost his footing on the steps and fell forward onto his hands, shaving his palms on the wet stone. He swore at the sudden cold sting and the jolt to his wrists. Uncle Ernie turned around.

"All right?"

Rudy wiped his palms down the front of his trousers. "I'm fine. Just clumsy."

He squinted ahead at the point where the muddy stairway was swallowed into the cloud mass; he massaged his hip. He suspected that if he were to plead fatigue, or pain, or wimpiness, Uncle Ernie would agree to turn back. But stubborn pride, and a niggling fear that he'd regret the retreat, prevented him from making the plea himself.

"Are you still sure you want to continue, Uncle? From what those kids were saying, it sounds like we're still quite far from the top. I don't mind turning around."

Uncle Ernie pulled a handkerchief from his pocket and shook it out vigorously.

"Stop worrying about me, Nephew. I'm not an invalid." He mopped the rainwater from his face, muffling his words. "In fact, I'm jolly glad we're coming up here out of season. I'm all for this kind of thing. Man against the elements. No modern conveniences to dull the senses. I'm telling you, Rudy, this is better than battling hordes of drunken pilgrims for a full night. Builds character."

Listening to his uncle's litany of clichés, Rudy stared at the ground. He tried to imagine what had happened to the sensitive, quirky artist of Aunty Mary's recollections. He wanted to tell Ernie that he understood, that there was no need to pretend; he wanted to tell him about Adam. And yet the possibility remained — not entirely absurd — that Ernie wasn't pretending. That somewhere along the line he had changed. Or perhaps, Rudy considered, the young man who'd been capable of giggling and prattling like a village woman at the market was also capable of blustering like an old army general.

"I'm up for it if you are," he said, and they carried on.

The rain let up a little, and for a while the voice urging him forward, as clear and real to him as the dripping vegetation, was his grandfather's. *To climb Adam's Peak is to conquer one's demons,* the old man was saying, but

Rudy found that the words, on him, were lost. If he had demons at all, they were of a fat, indolent breed that neither chased him down nor haunted his soul, but rather clung to his skin like leeches. He recalled that the entry in Grandpa's diary hadn't actually referred to demons at all but to "weaknesses," a more suitable term. Demons had no interest in him; they were for people like Alec Vantwest.

His thoughts began to drift, back to Morgan Hill Road, but Uncle Ernie cut them off.

"You were saying you feel out of place here."

Rudy stooped to pick up a discarded walking stick, a slender tree trunk trimmed of its branches. It was on the short side, but it worked well enough. "Oh. Yeah," he answered absently. Like the rain, his confessional mood had subsided. If he couldn't ponder in silence, he wanted Ernie to talk, to start clearing up some mysteries.

"But what about you, Uncle? What was it like moving to England? Did you feel you belonged there?"

"So you know I was in England?"

"You mentioned it when you came to the house." Rudy planted his stick rhythmically, pleased with the momentum it gave him. "And Aunty Mary told me. She said you were a teacher there."

Uncle Ernie gave a quizzical grunt. "I conducted evening classes in painting. She must be thinking of that. No, I worked for the Ministry of Agriculture. Government job."

Rudy hesitated, flustered by the implications of each perfunctory piece of information, wondering which thread to pursue. "Was it the job that took you to England?" he said at length.

"In part. There were boatloads of us ex-colonials returning to the homeland after independence. The British were offering passports."

"The homeland? But it wouldn't have seemed like home, would it?"

"No less than Ceylon," Uncle Ernie said, matter-of-factly. "I had a good job, a decent flat in London. The country was a mess, I'm telling you — decimated work force, end of the empire and all — but very interesting. England had to be rebuilt from the ground up, like a new civilization if you will."

Ernie's progress up the mountain had slowed. Pausing, Rudy tore through a clump of dark, leafy vines with the end of his walking stick.

He suspected his uncle had fascinating stories to tell about post-war Britain, but it wasn't the sort of thing he wanted to hear.

"Why did you come back?" he said.

Ernie looked skyward. "Got fed up with the weather."

"The weather?"

"Damp, cold. Like this. I put up with it while I was there, but you know, Rudy, chaps like you and I simply fare better in the equatorial climate. The English are miserable here, but you and I, we thrive. It isn't just a matter of skin pigmentation either. I've seen the same characteristics in very fair-skinned Burghers, chaps as pale as the English. Yes — there's something else we've acquired over the generations, something in our metabolism."

They'd reached another clearing, an abandoned tea stop probably, and Rudy, grateful for the distraction, shook off his knapsack and took out his water bottle. While his uncle relieved himself behind some shrubs, he lifted the lid of a rough wooden crate in the futile hope of discovering some food. They'd not yet finished off the package of tea biscuits, but the dry, bland rectangles served only to stir up wistful thoughts of cousin Bernadette's beef inferno and coconut sambol. Predictably the crate was empty, and there was nothing to be found in the mess of planks scattered next to it. Rudy took a swig of water and turned his attention to a blue plastic tarp covering part of the clearing. The tarp, which had apparently served as a barrier between the now-dismantled tea stand and the tangle of vegetation behind it, was strung at one end to a scrawny tree that had fallen across the clearing. Massaging his hip in the drizzling rain, Rudy studied the incongruous sheet of plastic on the mulchy ground. He returned the water bottle to his knapsack. Then he crouched and began picking at the wet knot that attached the tarp to the fallen tree. Uncle Ernie's muddy loafers appeared next to him.

"What's this, men? What are you doing?"

Rudy looked up. "I thought I'd take this thing with us. Not that we'll — I mean, we can still turn back."

"You're expecting we might spend the night here?"

If anything, the old man seemed excited by the prospect.

Rudy grimaced. "I hope not."

He desperately hoped not. Sri Pada in the middle of night would be a thoroughly inhospitable place. And yet, as before, he was incapable of doing anything to avoid it, of breaking his inertia and making a decision that would prevent what would certainly be a miserable, even dangerous, experience. They would keep climbing, he supposed, either until they reached the summit or until progress became physically impossible.

Uncle Ernie went to the other end of the tarp, attached to a sturdier tree, and set to work on the knot. "Best to be prepared, though," he called over his shoulder. "This is good thinking, Rudy. We can rig a shelter out of this."

They folded the tarp, and Rudy crammed it into his knapsack. He sent his uncle on ahead, then he unzipped his trousers and urinated in the middle of the clearing, facing the trail, daring hypothetical strangers to make a sudden appearance. The sensible part of him wished they would. Some pilgrims or hikers heading back to the base would shake him up. *You're crazy*, they'd say. *No time to get up there now; come back down with us.* When he'd zipped up his fly and no one had appeared, he wondered vaguely if it would be most practical to set up camp immediately, right there in the clearing, while there was still light — fashion a tent out of the planks and the tarp, start scouring the forest for edible plants, drying some sticks to make a fire. The sort of things they must have taught in Boy Scouts. But the Boy Scout ethos, Rudy decided, wasn't designed for circumstances such as his. With a sigh, he picked up his walking stick and carried on, up the interminable steps.

For a stretch of time that might have been two minutes or twenty, as he fell farther and farther behind his uncle, he managed to think of the climbing itself as the objective. He discovered a quiet satisfaction in the measured, meditative planting of his feet and his stick, while even the pain in his hip took on a necessary and gratifying role. *We must imagine Sisyphus happy*, he repeated to himself every few steps, like a mantra. But the final steep approach, for which chain-link railings had been installed, broke his trance. He jettisoned the stick and took hold of the iron chain. If the Toronto girl's recollections could be trusted, they were almost at the summit, though apart from the railings there was nothing to signal an impending climax. The cloud mass was thicker than ever — they'd actually entered it — while wet branches drooping across the stairway gave the impression that they were being swallowed into the mountain. Hauling himself forward, Rudy tried to recreate the sense of triumph his grandfather had experienced in February 1944. When that failed, he remembered, almost too late, the true purpose of the climb: he was here for Adam. The gruelling ascent was an act of atonement. He couldn't have talked himself out of it if he'd wanted to.

To compensate for his negligence, he concentrated all of his attention and the remainder of his energy on his brother. He pictured Adam in his hospital bed, rested and serene, and imagined that with each near-vertical step he took, he was dragging his brother up from the depths of his languor, up through the enigmatic recovery levels. He started at level one, to be thorough, and gradually advanced, through stages marked by particular degrees of "confusion" and "agitation," toward level eight, that peak of "purposeful — appropriate" behaviour, according to the Rancho Los Amigos scale. It was hard to know how many steps to allot each level, for the end of the stairway remained stubbornly out of sight. He devoted several to the first five, then, worried that he'd reach the summit before he was done, he decreased the allotment. Between five and six, he slowed down to wipe unexpected streams of sweat from his face. He saw Adam out of bed, walking and conversing. Approaching level seven, he gripped the railing tighter and planted his feet with leaden purpose, while in his imagination Adam steered Zoë like an airplane through the rooms of the house. At level eight, he wasn't yet at the summit, but the mist had thinned, and he'd spotted a small building up ahead. It wasn't the fanciful pavilion of Uncle Ernie's painting, but it was enough.

"Come on, machan," he whispered. "This is for you. Adam's Peak."

As he climbed the remaining steps, he returned to the day of the last afternoon tea on his grandfather's lawn. Not the time he spent listening to Grandpa read from his diary, but what came after that: sitting on the lawn next to his father while his sister and cousins squabbled on their makeshift cricket pitch; the news, delivered quietly, without fuss, that Mum was to have a baby, and the parental good sense with which Dad allowed him to choose the baby's name. In the rain and the dark grey gloom, he took a final step, and he was there. He leaned his forehead against the locked chain-link gate at the end of the route and caught his breath.

But as his lungs calmed and his legs went rubbery beneath him, the rest of him — creepingly, insidiously — mutinied. His stomach cramped and his throat strained; his eyes stung. He couldn't have imagined how it would be when he started out on his pilgrimage, but the reality now was glaring: his achievement was meaningless. He'd made it to the summit of Adam's Peak, was undeniably planted there, thousands of feet high, but what did it matter? For all the formidable exertion, his brother was no better off. Nothing had changed; nothing had been proven. The climb was useless. Even worse, this uselessness that now poisoned the very contact between the soles of his shoes and the final step of the ascent was merely a symptom of something bigger. As a brother, as a son, a teacher, a lover ... he'd failed. The top of Sri Pada might just as well have been the middle of a deserted, frozen plain. Rudy himself might just as well have been lost in his brother's mysterious world. Confused, agitated, exhausted, he coughed and gasped and struck his forehead against the gate.

∞

IN THEORY, THERE WAS JUST ENOUGH TIME for a fit young person to get back to the base before nightfall. Uncle Ernie might even have made it, on his own. As things stood, though, Ernie had engaged the gatekeeper in a conversation, in the hope that the man would make his tiny shed available as an overnight rest house. Rudy slouched on a bench in the shed, staring out at the darkening sky, under which his uncle and the gatekeeper talked and smoked in the fog, like film noir characters. The inside of the wood plank hut was plastered with newspaper and magazine clippings. Most of them were in Sinhala or Tamil. The few English ones seemed to be about the peak itself, though one rogue article featured the headline "Dozens Killed in Jungle Battle Near Trincomalee." Rudy dared not read it. Turning away, he concentrated on his own agonies.

His hip was throbbing, and the hot pain radiated down his thigh and across his lower back. Stopping for tea in the gatekeeper's shed had done it. Given a taste of immobility, his body had packed it in and refused to go on. If the gatekeeper proved unable or unwilling to give them shelter, he and his uncle would be spending the night under the plastic tarp, in less hospitable conditions than the clearing down the mountain had offered. Or Rudy would, anyway, for there would be nothing stopping Ernie from returning to the car.

It did seem likely, however, that the gatekeeper would oblige. It had to be a lonely post, guarding the sacred footprint out of season, and the man had appeared pleased, in a quiet way, to have visitors. When they arrived, he'd escorted them, barefoot, to the pavilion that housed the print, which was marked, as the Toronto girl had described it, by a large stone slab, vaguely shaped like a foot. "Real footprint is underneath," the gatekeeper had informed them. The stone was strewn with coins and marigolds, hints of a devotion that Rudy could scarcely imagine. But though the relic held no spiritual meaning for him, he found the entire scene moving. Fierce gusts of wind now tore through the fog and drizzle, and when he rang the heavy bell hanging outside the pavilion — once, for his sole ascent of the peak — he imagined himself and his two companions as the only survivors of some destroyed civilization, banished to this harsh outcrop of land and charged with the responsibility of carrying on as best they could.

The fantasy was fleeting, though. When the gatekeeper touched his arm and said, "You like tea?" Rudy could have hugged the man. He took a last look at the grey nothingness beyond the bell, then he limped hurriedly back to the gate, where he and his uncle had left their shoes and socks.

The gatekeeper's shed was furnished with two wooden benches, which formed an L around a small table. Another table was cluttered with magazines, mugs, tins of tea supplies, and a Primus stove on which water was boiled. The tea was good strong Ceylon stuff, and the longer Rudy had sat drinking it in the unexpected comfort of the shed, the clearer it had become that he'd never make it back down the mountain without a very long rest. He'd explained his predicament to his uncle, at which point Ernie and the gatekeeper had gone outside to smoke, leaving the rickety door ajar.

When Ernie ducked back inside, his expression was nonchalant.

"Well, Rudy, everything is arranged," he announced. "We're welcome to spend the night in here. This chap has a house of some kind up here. He says he'll fetch us some blankets."

Rudy wondered if his uncle were disappointed not to be camping out under the tarp.

"Thanks for fixing that up," he said. "Sorry for wimping out on you."

Uncle Ernie waved his hand dismissively. "Who knows? The way this wind is blowing, we may actually get a view in the morning. Make it all worthwhile, no?" He rubbed his collarbone. "At any rate, I'm going to go with this chap to get the supplies. You'll be fine here on your own?"

Rudy nodded. "Tell our friend I appreciate his help."

When his uncle and the gatekeeper had left, Rudy hoisted himself up and hopped awkwardly to the magazine table. There was nothing in the stack that he could read, but he selected two fashion glossies with plenty of photos and tossed them onto the other table. He then fished his journal and pen out of his knapsack.

July something or other. I made it, barely. The top of Adam's Peak. Closest thing to the end of the earth I've ever experienced. Where are you right now, Clare? I wish you were here. I'd make you a cup of tea. This is really good stuff (better than arrack, although I wouldn't mind a swig of that too). Have you ever had decent tea? I guess Scottish people are probably as crazy about it as the English, so I suppose you have. Do you know how it gets made? I could tell you. It's a family business, sort of. The fermenting of the leaves is the most important stage. It's not as exciting as the rolling or the heating, but that's what'll make or break a batch. Goddammit, Clare, I wish you were here. I wish I had some fucking aspirin, and I wish

He gave up. In the fading light, he closed his journal and began flipping through one of the magazines. A long section on wedding wear

featured women in glittering saris and white dresses, posing in front of
exotic backdrops. There was a feature on office wear, which seemed to
be endorsing East-West combinations. An English-titled "What's
Hot, What's Not" section gave Rudy pause as he recognized a version
of his sarong and T-shirt combination in the "not" column. He was
absorbed in a series of hairstyle makeovers when his uncle and the
gatekeeper returned, laden with blankets, a kerosene lamp, and a card-
board box that looked promisingly to contain food.

"Well, we won't go cold or hungry," Uncle Ernie announced,
depositing the box on the table, and again Rudy suspected that the old
man might be itching with a frustrated desire to rough it in the bush.
Rudy himself, however, could only sink back in immeasurable relief as
he noticed, wedged between a basket of hoppers and a comb of
bananas, a foil packet of painkillers. Dumbly smiling his gratitude, he
made a mental note to write down the angelic gatekeeper's name and
address so that he might send a gift when he returned to Colombo.
He would have liked to chat with the man for a while; it seemed the
least he could do. But the gatekeeper didn't stay. His armful of blankets unloaded, he lit the kerosene lamp and hung it from a hook on
the ceiling, said a few words to Ernie, then left, closing the door
behind him.

In addition to the bananas and hoppers there was a container of
cold chicken curry, two boiled eggs, a few rambutans, plastic plates,
and cutlery. Picking through these luxuries, Rudy shook his head.

"This is incredible, Uncle. I don't think I would have been as generous as this with complete strangers."

"Oh, I paid the chap," Ernie said flatly.

Rudy looked up, embarrassed that a gesture he'd thought to be
generous and authentic had in fact been formulaic, even crass. But on
the other hand, an awkward weight of indebtedness had been lifted.

"I hope it wasn't too much," he said. "Not that — Don't worry
about it, though; I'll pay you back. I mean, it's all because of me that
we're stuck here."

"We'll settle it when we get back to town," Ernie said. "Let's eat,
shall we? I'm famished." He reached into the box. "Here, take some
paracetamol."

The hoppers were gluey and the chicken curry salty, but they ate greedily, until there remained only a banana and rambutan each, reserved for breakfast. It occurred to Rudy that if he'd known the food and accommodation were to be paid for, he would have inquired about some booze as well. But he abandoned the idea straightaway. On a full stomach, his belief in the gatekeeper's goodwill had been restored, for, really, the fellow could hardly have been expected to give up essential supplies without some form of compensation.

When the table had been cleared, Ernie lit his pipe. Rudy sat with a thin, itchy blanket wrapped around his shoulders. Above him, the kerosene lamp hissed; outside, branches whisked against the shed. The silence between him and his uncle was awkward.

"This must be different from other nights you've spent up here," he finally said.

Ernie sucked on his pipe. He sat with one bony leg crossed over the other; his right elbow rested in his left palm. "Hmm? Oh, yes. It's certainly quieter."

"My dad has an old photo of you taken up here. It's hanging in his study." Somehow he had to bring up Alec.

"Is that so?"

"Yeah. You're posing next to the bell with another guy. One of Grandpa's employees, I think."

"Hmm. Yes."

Rudy shifted his weight onto one buttock and reached for the packet of paracetamol. "I think it was the same climb Grandpa wrote about in his diary." He pushed a tablet through the foil and swallowed it with a gulp of cold tea.

"That could be," Ernie said. "Your sister's child is deaf, isn't she?"

Rudy straightened up, surprised and confused. "Zoë? Yes."

"And how does your sister cope with that?"

"Uh, with difficulty ... usually." He searched his uncle's calm expression then carried on. "Susie's kind of a high-maintenance person herself. She's terrific; I love her. She just gets very stressed out. And she and her husband have just split up, so things aren't great." He ran his fingers along the splintery edge of the table. "She's done everything to make Zoë's life good, though. Zoë'll be okay."

Uncle Ernie nodded thoughtfully and smoked his pipe, punctuating the silence with tiny clicks and aspirations. Rudy tightened the blanket around his shoulders. He imagined he should say more about Susie and her life. Uncle Ernie seemed interested. And eventually the conversation would lead where he wanted it to, gradually, naturally. But thinking about his sister's life had made him uneasy. He charged ahead.

"Uncle, why did you and my father lose contact? Was it because of him?"

Again Uncle Ernie nodded, and Rudy braced himself. But the nod was not an affirmation of that sort.

"Yes, I thought you might get around to asking that," he said. "What does Alec have to say about it?"

"Not much. Nothing very specific."

"Well, there's nothing very specific to be said." He lowered his pipe. "My father and I had a final discussion that more or less marked the end of things. It was quite innocuous by our usual standards, but the estrangement had been building for years. I was jolly glad to leave, and I'm sure they were happy to see the tail end of me." He stopped briefly and frowned. "Except Mary. She probably disapproved of me most of all, but I was her brother and that was that."

There was little sense in pressing on, Rudy suspected, but he'd come so far with the old man — all the way to the summit of Adam's Peak — that the story he'd constructed about this long-lost relation begged a climax of its own.

"What was the disapproval about, Uncle? Why the estrangement?"

Uncle Ernie uncrossed his legs and rested the heels of his hands on his knees. "You're an intelligent chap, Rudy." He lifted his pipe to his mouth. "Let's just say I didn't suit the tea planting life."

And that was that. Rudy fixed his eyes on a magazine photograph pinned to the shed wall — an elephant draped with red velvet blankets and strings of lights, for the Kandy Perahera. "Festival of the Sacred Tooth Relic brings together Sri Lankans of all ethnic backgrounds," the caption read. When he and his sister were children, Rudy recalled, Susie used to place tiny elephant figurines on the turntable of their grandfather's phonograph and give them a ride.

19

F ARRELL ROAD WASN'T DIFFICULT TO FIND, though it was, as Margaret had said, out of town a wee bit. Past the enormous Safeway, it branched off the main road, a narrow, dead-end lane banked by rolling fields and hedgerows. Most of its scattered houses were of brick; number seven, at the very end of the lane, was a light brown pebble-dash box. Approaching it slowly, Clare rehearsed her part — the greeting, pleasant but formal; answers to questions she would no doubt be asked; questions she herself could ask if the conversation lulled. She carried a bunch of flowers, which she expected to give to Patrick's wife, Anne. So far she'd spoken only to Anne, an easy person to speak to.

"Yes, yes, I'm sure I've heard of your grandfather, Clare," she'd said. "I've probably heard about your mother, too, but I'm getting a bit wandered in my old age." She laughed. "And so you're here on a visit?"

"Yes. Just for a few more days, then I'm going to France."

"Ooh, lovely. But listen, Clare, you must come and visit. Do you have plans for lunch?"

"You mean today?"

"Aye. Right now. I'm experimenting with a new Moroccan dish. Lamb tagine. Do you like lamb? Why don't you come and join us?"

"Uh, sure. Thank you. But is it okay with your husband? Will he mind?"

"Mind? Ach, he'll talk your ear off!"

Two houses away, Clare slowed her pace even more and repeated to herself the significance, the potentially life-shattering magnitude, of what she was about to do. The essential fact was there in her consciousness: *You're about to meet your biological father.* But somewhere between the phone booth and Farrell Road, the words had lost their texture and weight. They were just words, as stubbornly flat and mundane as the midday light. She concentrated, tried to make herself feel. Then she decided that her subconscious was protecting her. She would go to P. Locke's door in this numbed state, afflicted with only the mildest of awkwardness, so that when the startling realities hit — an unmistakable physical resemblance, an identical mannerism, a mention of Patrick's other children — she wouldn't be entirely paralyzed. It made sense.

Number seven was one of the plainer houses on the lane, but the brass door knocker was impressive — an elephant head with enormous ears and a curled trunk, which served as the knocking mechanism. Clare shifted the bunch of flowers to her left hand, breathed in, and knocked. At the sound of footsteps approaching, a hint of the significance she'd been searching for materialized. But it wasn't anything she would have expected. Not the magnitude or the melodrama, but rather a bizarrely acute awareness of her own weight. The pressure of her feet on the rubber doormat, the heaviness of her arms. She lifted one foot a few inches off the mat to intensify the sensation. Then the door opened.

"You must be Clare," the tall, wiry man said, extending his hand. "Glad you could come. No trouble finding the place?"

"No. Not at all."

So this was him.

"Aye, Anne's good with directions. Well, come on in." He stepped back into the dark entrance hall, craning his neck to look over Clare's shoulder. "I'm just looking for the cat. Did Anne warn you we have a cat? We forget sometimes. To warn folk, that is. A friend of ours is allergic, you see, and the minute he's inside, he comes down with sneezing fits. Muffy! Here, puss!" He scanned the tiny front yard then closed the door. "You probably won't see her; she's skittish. But her fur's all over the place."

"It's okay. I'm not allergic."

She had his chin and jaw, perhaps. Not his nose, thank God. His coarse hair had a bit of brown remaining. The top of his head was almost entirely bald, but the rest needed a trim. He wore green corduroys and a scruffy denim shirt.

"Well that's good, then. But we have some antihistamine tablets, if you need them."

"I'm sure I'll be fine."

And his eyes — that was where resemblances were often most striking, Isobel once said. His eyes were blue and large. Indeed, there was little doubt about the eyes. But then again, Alastair's had been very similar.

"Those are lovely flowers."

"They're for you and Anne."

She handed him the bunch of flowers and watched him trace his finger along the underside of a purple iris petal then plunge his long, lumpy nose into a yellow chrysanthemum. She shifted her weight and tucked her hair behind her ears. She had a place here, she told herself. A claim to this man's attention.

She followed Patrick from the entrance hall into the living room, a bright, high-ceilinged space at the front of the house. She called it a living room, but it was more like a museum. The various shelves and end tables were crowded with travel artifacts: wooden carvings, clay pots, lacquerware, baskets. The two couches, dark rattan with red velvet cushions, one of them covered in long, grey fur, were separated by a flat-topped steamer trunk piled with books and *National Geographic* magazines. The shorter of the couches was flanked on one side by a wooden giraffe and on the other by a water pipe, its long hose snaked around the orange glass base and the gold neck. On the walls were masks, batiks, a green and yellow flag, a pair of papier-mâché puppets, and a zebra skin that reminded Clare of the Vantwests' crocodile — though next to Patrick's things, the Vantwests' crocodile seemed ordinary.

"You've travelled a lot," Clare said.

Patrick nodded thoughtfully. "A wee bit, aye. I worked on ships, and Anne used to work in West Africa. She's a nurse, you see. We met in Ghana."

Anne appeared then, drying her hands on a tea towel. Small, fit-looking, she wore jeans and a faded red sweatshirt, no makeup, and her silver hair was drawn from her face with a headband.

"You found us!" she announced. "I hope you're hungry!"

Clare nodded and smiled. She hadn't noticed till then, but she was famished. "It smells delicious. Thanks again for having me."

"Never turn away a guest," Patrick said. "That's wisdom from the Bedouin."

They ate in the dining room, a much more Scottish-looking room, with sturdy sideboard and lace tablecloth. The walls featured dozens of photographs of children and teenagers, who sparked in Clare an anxious curiosity. But none of the motley array belonged to Patrick. They were Anne's nieces and nephews, her son from a long-dead marriage, and a collection of foster children from different countries, supported by Patrick and Anne over the years. The current one was Shyamala, an eleven-year-old girl from a village near Mysore, India. She wore a navy blue tunic and a white blouse, and her pose was stiff and serious. Over the course of lunch, Clare's attention drifted repeatedly to the snapshot of the little foster girl, remaining there long enough at one point that she missed much of Patrick's account of a hunger riot in one of his ports of call.

He didn't seem to notice. His demands on the listener were minimal: an occasional nod, a smile or a frown, as the subject dictated. He had a wealth of stories to tell, and he seemed determined to get through as many of them as possible. Occasionally Anne spoke up, to corroborate or to steer Patrick in a particular direction — it was Anne who eventually asked about Isobel and the McGuigan family, a topic that soon fizzled — but the conversation, if it could be called that, belonged to Patrick. The last remark Clare had made was a vague question about Shyamala's living conditions. Now Patrick was off and running about India, describing the place in terms that would make Isobel cringe and Alastair blush.

"Nothing's hidden away there, you see. The whole fantastic stinking lot is right there in the street for anyone to see. Defecation, celebration ... It's a bloody teeming cesspool, India is." He leaned forward. "My first time in Bombay, I got myself lost wandering about a vegetable market. I wandered into an alley, but all I found there were open doorways with these young lasses. Prostitutes. Aye. Some of them not much older than wee Shyamala there. They saw me looking, so I went closer. But when I got within spitting distance I was in for a nasty shock, so I was." He jabbed the air with his fork. "These girls weren't ordinary prostitutes, you see. One of them had no hands; another was missing half her face. They were lepers, you see. Aye. First time I'd seen such a thing. I thought I was in hell. Folk decomposing before my eyes, the whole place reeking of sewage. I nearly spewed right there on the pavement. Then they started yelling at me to bugger off. A lass with no nose hit me in the head with a rock. I was mortified, so I was. But her aim was fantastic."

He paused to eat a piece of lamb. Anne was picking idly at the salad. Clare stared at her almost-empty plate and tried to imagine her mother listening to such stories.

"Aye, India's a cesspool and a carnival all in one," Patrick mused, settling back in his chair. "But it works. It runs." He looked at his wife and nodded. "Shall we take a wee stroll before the sweets? Out to the pond and back?"

Anne shook her head. "You two go on. My knee's still jiggered." Turning to Clare, she added, "We climbed Ben Nevis last week. It was really spectacular, but coming down was murder on the knees."

"Oh, aye. First time in ten years we've had a view up top," Patrick said. "So it'll be just me and the young lassie out to the pond, then?"

Clare smiled and wondered anxiously if Patrick had put two and two together and figured out who she was. If his biological fatherhood had, like some sixth sense, recognized her as his lassie. She wondered what he might possibly do about such a thing. Take her in his arms and vow to make up for lost time? Make sure she had no awkward intentions — matters of inheritance and whatnot? Offer to exchange Christmas cards and leave it at that? As he led the way back through the living room, chattering about Ben Nevis and calling to Anne to look for the hiking guide, it seemed unlikely that he suspected anything at all. But when they stepped outside and Patrick dug his hands in his trouser pockets and pronounced the name "Isobel McGuigan," as if he were calling forth a witness in court or summoning a ghost from the afterlife, Clare's hands clenched. She said nothing, waiting instead for Patrick to elaborate.

At the front gate, he went on: "I admired her, bolting off to Canada like she did. Aye, it was Isobel who inspired me to get off my own backside and see the world."

He turned toward the dead end of Farrell Road, where a narrow path cut into the field. They took the path, Patrick in the lead, and Clare wished she'd worn sturdier shoes. Through her flimsy sandals she felt all the lumps and stones underfoot. But if Patrick planned to introduce extra discomforts along the way, he was in no hurry to do so.

"I had my sights set on more exotic places than Canada," he said, "but I hadn't done anything about it, you see. I was just marking time, havering about my big plans, waiting for something to happen on its own. But when Isobel left, I thought to myself, there you are, you big windbag; there's somebody actually doing something." He paused. "So what did your mother do after Canada?" It was the first question he'd asked her.

"After Canada? I'm not sure what you mean."

Patrick pointed across the rolling, grassy field to a clump of trees on a hill a few hundred yards away. "That's the pond over there. I mean did she travel? Work abroad? Anything like that?"

"No. She and my father pretty much settled down."

"Right away? House, kiddies, the whole lot?"

She wondered if he were testing her out, confirming his suspicions.

"More or less. There were no other kids, besides me. But they bought the house right after they arrived. And I was born soon after that." She held her breath and waited. If he were going to confront her, now would be the time. When he didn't, her hands relaxed. "My mother's a pretty traditional housewife. She worked at my dad's store sometimes, and she's started doing some accounting from home. But that's about it." There was a comfort in these certainties.

"No travelling then?"

"Not the kind you've done. She and my dad went to New York a few times."

The path had widened, allowing them to walk side by side. Patrick rubbed his stubbled chin.

"I have to say, it's not what I expected. Isobel leading the quiet, domestic life like that. She was such a fiery, get-up-and-go lass. All sorts of dreams. I thought she'd travel all over America at least."

Clare shot a glance sideways. He was confronting her after all, it seemed.

"I don't think that's what Mum had in mind," she said, aware, even as she spoke, that her claim was hollow.

"Oh, I don't know about that," Patrick mused.

Clare frowned. She marched on in silence, then, without meaning to, she stepped on a smooth, fist-sized rock, turned her ankle, and pitched forward. Patrick caught her by the arm. With a firm, gentle tug, he pulled her up straight.

"Are you all right?"

She clenched her teeth and nodded. The injury wasn't serious, but the sharp shock of pain stirred up her irritation, and she looked at the ground, avoiding Patrick's eyes.

His hand remained on her elbow as she circled her foot slowly in the air.

"Is it sprained, do you think? Can you walk on it?"

She took a cautious step, considering again what he'd said. "It'll be fine. Let's keep going."

"You're sure? We can turn back."

"No, it's fine. Really. I'd like to see the pond."

She walked on, slowly at first, and for a few steps Patrick kept his hand just behind her. He was quiet. But his words echoed in Clare's head. *A fiery, get-up-and-go lass. All sorts of dreams.* A young woman who'd gone out with her father's apprentice and exposed herself to all the wonder and terror, the pain and nervous ecstasy and slimy wetness of sex. And who then covered it all up, covered herself up, with a smooth domestic mask. A conscientious suburban housewife who would cringe at stories of what goes on in the alleyways of Bombay.

"Did my mother talk to you about her plans?" she said at length. "I mean, what she wanted to do with her life?"

"Ah, well ..." Patrick stalled.

In the strange silence, she looked out over the rolling landscape and struggled to call up an authentic image of her mother. An expression of delight, or confusion, or regret. But nothing came. She could picture the person, the unchanging basics of eye colour and nose shape, but the rest was out of reach. It was more than a passing *sentiment d'étrangeté*, a quirky moment of turning to a loved one and being suddenly struck by that person's absolute otherness. This feeling was more banal, but more difficult to shake. It was the realization that something possible had been missed out on. She glanced at Patrick, scratching the back of his head. It was a version of herself that had been lost. Clare Fraser, the daughter of a fiery get-up-and-go lass with a hippy friend and a loquacious lover, had never come to be. She fixed her eyes on the treacherous path and limped ahead. More than the loss of her blood tie to Alastair, more than the fact that she'd come into the world unbidden, this realization orphaned her.

Again she looked to Patrick, hungry now for his reply.

"What were my mother's dreams?"

But Patrick, at the end of his silence, only waved his hand dismissively. "Ach, I should quit my blethering, is what. I only knew her for a wee while. I remember the two of us planning all sorts of fantastic escapes from the Scottish doldrums, but it's probably my own plans I'm remembering." He chuckled. "I tend to talk a lot, you see."

Clare took a breath and forced a smile. "I noticed that," she said.

∞

THE POND THEY FINALLY CAME UPON hardly justified the trip. It was cloudy and tangled with weeds. Small too. With a running start, any athletic young man could have jumped across it. A youthful Patrick Locke, for instance. Still, they'd come a fair distance from the town, gently climbing most of the way, and the view from the clearing where they now stood was impressive.

Patrick was talking about ports: how it used to annoy him that he rarely saw the middles of countries, the heart and guts so to speak, until he discovered the advantages of port cities.

"Folk in a port city are more cosmopolitan, more tolerant," he said. "They understand that civilization doesn't stop at the border between their country and the next, you see." He nodded his head toward the town. "There's folk out there never been as far as Glasgow their entire life. They think the universe begins and ends in Stanwick."

Clare, crouching to massage her ankle, pictured the map on page seventy-two of her father's atlas. Colombo was a port city, she recalled. A boldface dot on a pale green blob.

"Have you ever been to Sri Lanka?" she said.

"What's that?" Patrick was distracted, looking back at the pond.

"Sri Lanka. Colombo. Have you ever been there?"

He turned slowly and rubbed his chin. "Ceylon? Aye."

It was the pond. In a sudden, perfect tableau, Clare saw them, Patrick and Isobel, sitting next to the water, fantasizing about the places they would go. Perhaps Patrick had done all the talking, but Isobel had paid attention; she'd remembered. Clearly enough that in the years that followed she'd gone, over and over, to page seventy-two of her husband's atlas, so that the book came to open naturally at that place. Clare eyed the thick, long grass that surrounded the murky pond, inviting as a soft bed, and for an instant felt a tingle of connection.

Still crouching, she met Patrick's eyes and saw that he knew. He knew in the way she herself had known for so long, perhaps always. Knowing without knowing. He was trying to transform her in the way she'd attempted to transform herself, and it wasn't working. She lowered her gaze to the flat, dark surface of the pond, the thick bed of grass. With sparkling clarity, she pictured the young lovers — Isobel's hair long and fiery, her face anxious; Patrick waxing lyrical. She watched them fall back into the grass, slowly, floatingly. Laughing at some private joke. She tossed a pebble into the water. Then she let them fade. Their thoughts, their lovemaking, their very existence.

"What was it like?" she said, standing. "Ceylon."

Patrick scratched his head helplessly. Clare picked up another pebble and tossed it.

"I was just wondering," she said. "My neighbours back home are Sri Lankan. I think it'd be an interesting place to visit."

Patrick smiled faintly and pointed toward the field beyond the pond. "Look. We have visitors."

Two shaggy Highland cows, an adult and a calf, were watching them through a wire fence.

"They look docile," Patrick said, "but you don't want to get between the wee one and its mother." He eyed the cows steadily and silently, then he turned back toward the town. "Aye, it's a coincidence you should mention Ceylon. I was just thinking about it, when Anne mentioned Ben Nevis. The strangest climb I ever did was up a sacred mountain there, with a Ceylonese lad from the ship. One of the only times I saw the middle of a country."

"What was so strange about it?"

Patrick checked his watch and set off down the path. Clare followed, her limp almost gone.

"Well, for one thing, we climbed all night," he began, nestling back into his familiar rhythm. "The idea, you see, was to be up top for sunrise, which was really spectacular. One of the grandest views I've ever seen."

"Really?"

"Oh, aye. Tea fields and rivers and lakes, as far as the eye could see. Really spectacular."

"Is it a hard climb?"

"Not too bad. The last stretch was a wee bit hairy, but it was mainly just long. Aye, bloody long. The Ceylonese lad and I started climbing just after midnight — the two of us and a few hundred others as well." He kicked a stone off the path. "That was the other peculiar thing: going for a hike with a whole mob of strangers. Some bits were so crowded we could hardly move. Aye, it was nothing like hiking up Ben Nevis, out in the wilderness. Ach, I couldn't even see the bloody wilderness."

"Why all the people?"

"It was a full moon festival, or something like that. A few of the lads were just young neds, out for a good time, but the rest were serious, right enough. They had wee shrines set up all along the way. Something Hindu or Buddhist. They've got both in the country, you see."

"I know," Clare blurted. "I mean, my neighbour's told me a little about it."

"Aye, well, the whole to-do of climbing up the mountain is a religious custom. I remember when we finally got to the top there were folk lined up to visit a wee temple. I couldn't have told you what it was all about, but I reckon it didn't matter."

"What do you mean?"

"Oh, as far as I could see, all the climbing and the praying were just an excuse to bring folk together."

Clare gazed across the fields to Stanwick Abbey, solitary and grey. Ignoring Patrick's voice, for he'd pushed on with his story, she looked down at her sandalled feet navigating the narrow dirt path and was once again struck by the weight of her body and the solid contact between the soles of her shoes and the ground beneath them. She imagined herself sovereign — neither Fraser nor McGuigan, nor Locke. Not even woman, perhaps (though her suitcase contained a well-hidden vibrator, put to use twice since her departure). She concentrated on her perfectly gauged steps, on the insensible energies that activated the whole process, until, the intensity of her self-awareness threatening to paralyze her altogether, she forced herself to think of something else.

Was there a place in Stanwick to buy hiking boots, she wondered, or would it be necessary to wait until she returned to London? She'd packed running shoes and Birkenstocks, but nothing suitable for climbing. A silly oversight, really, for anywhere she might go there would be scenic hikes. Scotland, France, the north of Spain. And if she were to climb a sacred mountain, she would need decent boots. Her right hand clenched, and she rubbed her index finger with her thumb. It wasn't such a strange idea; it was something people did: travel to a place for the purpose of climbing a mountain. Unlike Patrick, she would avoid the full moon festival. She would climb alone, in the daytime.

Patrick again pointed across the fields. "There's another couple of cows over there. Do you see them?"

They'd stopped next to a low stone wall. Clare squinted in the direction Patrick was pointing but could make out only a distant smudge of brown.

"Why did you and Anne come back to Scotland?" she said.

Patrick looked around, as if to confirm that he was indeed in Scotland. "It's home," he said. "We're not strangers here."

∞

IN THE LATE AFTERNOON she returned to the abbey and sat in one of the back pews of the main sanctuary. There were a few tourists strolling silently around the periphery, but the cavernous space was otherwise deserted. Leaning against a stone arch, she extracted a stack of postcards and a pen from her bag. A hard-covered New Testament gave her something to write on. She cast her eyes down the empty aisle, down the choir, to the distant altar, admired the afternoon light shining feebly through the dark rose window, then she selected a card — a photo of a living room furnished in the style of Charles Rennie Mackintosh — and began to write.

> Hi Markus. I'm writing this from my parents' hometown of Stanwick, not too far from Glasgow. The weather has been very Scottish. So far I've mainly been visiting, but I'm hoping to get more adventurous in the next few weeks. Don't think I'll make it to Germany, but thanks for the recommendations. Tell Peter I'm going through with Plan A after all (after France, that is). He'll explain. I hope all's well at the shop. Say hi to everyone for me. All the best, Clare

She imagined Markus sitting at his desk under the composer calendar, reading her card. For the first time in a long time, perhaps ever, she imagined him happy. She added a smiling face to the bottom of the card and went on to the next one.

> Salut Marielle! J'espère que tout va bien. Je suis en Écosse (non, je n'ai pas encore vu de beaux hommes en kilt, à part ces gars sur les cartes postales!). J'ai hâte de voir la maison en Normandie. Merci encore une fois à tes parents. Le festival de jazz a-t-il été bon? C'est la première fois que je le manque depuis je ne sais pas combien d'années. Bon été! Claire

> Dear Emma, the church on the front of this card is where I'm sitting right now. I have the place pretty much to myself. It's

amazing to think that some of these arches were constructed 400 years before Shakespeare. Some of the lighter coloured stonework is obviously

She stopped, reread what she'd written, then tossed the card aside. From the remaining ones, she selected a photo of a purple heather shrub and began again.

I did it, Emma. I found him. Didn't want to say anything on the phone (it was a little overwhelming, I guess). Anyway, he's a perfectly decent, interesting person (probably a better match for my mum than Dad was), and we got along fine. I had lunch with him and his wife (no kids). He talks nonstop, which made things easy. Saying goodbye was a little strange. I suddenly realized I might not ever see him again, and I felt kind of weird and out of sorts. He did invite me back, though. So we'll see. Will write again soon. C.

Hi Ma. Thought you'd appreciate this scene of the high street as it's looking these days, video shop and all. I went to Margaret's church this morning and talked with her for a while after. She got me to play "Blowin' in the Wind" for her. Remember that? I told her you'd write. And yes, I found Patrick Locke. His wife took a photo of the two of us, which she promised to send. He's worked on merchant ships most of his life. Says you should look him up next time you're home. I'm going to spend some time in London before France. Thought I'd check out some other travel possibilities while I'm there. Running out of room; will call soon. Love, Clare

She shook out her hand and looked around. The tourists had gone, leaving her alone in the massive, magnificent sanctuary. From her place at the back, it was easy to imagine that this abbey had been inspired by God. Except for a few colour variations in the masonry, everything — nave, transept, choir — seemed gloriously unified. But the impression was apparently misleading. The guidebook Clare had picked up at the shop where she bought the postcards treated the abbey's haphazard evolution as a point of pride. "English invaders, accidental fires, structural failures, zealous Reformers, and equally zealous renovators of every persuasion from High Gothic to Abstract Expressionist have inscribed themselves on the sacred space," the book boasted, before concluding that the history of Stanwick Abbey was as random and contingent as that of the country itself.

Leaning against the cool stone arch, tapping her pen lazily against the stack of postcards, Clare attempted to recall Patrick's recounting of Scotland's Wars of Independence, of which she'd known absolutely nothing before the topic came up over tea and dessert. Patrick was something of a Scottish nationalist, he'd said. A mess of invasions and vaguely familiar names circled her head, accompanied by a rogue voice — not Patrick's, strangely — insisting that this was really fascinating stuff. The voice was clear and distinct, yet it took several repetitions before she recognized it as Mr. Vantwest's. "Fascinating stuff" he'd said of British history, the afternoon Clare and her mother went for tea.

Again she looked around. Mr. Vantwest would be in his element here. He would pore over the faded stone inscriptions, make sense of the stained glass battles, populate the cloisters with medieval monks. She picked up the postcard with the photograph of the abbey and wished she hadn't wasted it. It would have been perfect. There was no obvious reason to send her neighbour either of the remaining cards; still, she selected a Glasgow street scene and wrote "Dear Mr. Vantwest" on the back. The rest was more difficult. She wanted to write; it seemed suddenly important. But the writing needed a pretense. Chewing her pen, she considered the possibilities.

Dear Mr. Vantwest, I hope you're well. I'm visiting my parents' hometown . . .

Dear Mr. Vantwest, greetings to you and your sister. The streets here in Scotland are certainly different from Morgan Hill Road . . .

Dear Mr. Vantwest, I thought you would be interested to know that I've decided to take a trip . . .

Dear Mr. Vantwest, I've just had a very unusual experience. It turns out my father —

This last thread was impossible, of course, but it gave her what she wanted. Not even a pretense, but a message she should have delivered long ago. She returned to the Glasgow street scene, studied her opening greeting, then dropped the card onto the pew, on top of the wasted photo of Stanwick Abbey. Her last remaining postcard was a picture of two Highland calves.

> Dear Alec, ever since I visited you the day you found out about the bombing in Colombo I've been wanting to tell you something. You spoke to me about Adam and his feelings for you. I don't know Adam well, but on the day of his accident he gave me a ride to the shops, and he talked about you. He knows you love him, and he loves you too. You talked about being responsible for all the misfortune in your family, but I don't think Adam would believe this. I think he'd say that things are much more complicated than that. I hope you don't mind my writing to you like this. I thought it was important, and I'm sorry it's taken me so long to do it. Yours truly, Clare Fraser

At the post office she bought an envelope for the card. She'd left no room for the address, and in any case the message was private. She also bought a stamp for the Stanwick Abbey card. Writing quickly, to make the last pickup of the day, she completed the description of the church, signed and addressed the card, then scratched out Emma's name and wrote "Joanne" in its place. Mrs. Skinner would be pleased.

20

Despite the pre-dawn chill and the hardness of the bench, Uncle Ernie slept. Rudy listened to the steady rise and fall of his breathing and envied his uncle's adaptability. His own night had been spent shifting from one awkward, cramped position to another, all the while tugging and stretching the blanket to keep it both under his body as a flimsy mattress and on top of him for warmth. It was possible he'd slept, but not much more than a fitful hour in total. Now, as the darkness began to thin, he lay on his back with his legs bent and stared up at the cracks in the wood plank ceiling. Resigned to wakefulness, he found it easier to be comfortable, even to appreciate the silence and the faint cooking-fire smell of the air.

Yet the company made him uneasy. His uncle's presence was a little like that of a one-night-stand lover he hadn't meant to wake up with. Their relationship didn't justify being alone together in such a close, dark space. To distract himself from the old man's gentle snoring, Rudy began a letter in his head. His time with Ernie had fostered a new sympathy for his father, and he was eager to act on it before the feeling disappeared.

He'd start with the easy stuff. *I hope you're well and that the summer is turning out as hot as you like it. Sorry I wasn't there to work on the garden with you this year. I always enjoy our expeditions to the nursery.* As soon as it was light enough, he would leave the shed and find a place to sit at the summit, where he would write the letter out on a back page of his diary. *You may be surprised to hear this, but I'm at the top of Sri Pada with Uncle Ernie — with your brother, Ernie. Aunty Mary convinced him to look me up, as I'm sure you know, and we decided to come up here together. It's obvious that Adam takes after him. Would it be fair to say that Ernie is at the root — No, scratch that. Forget I mentioned it. It doesn't matter. Ernie's an interesting guy, but I think he'd get on my nerves after a while. The person he reminds me of most is Grandpa. Of course, Adam looks a lot like him, but that doesn't mean much. How is Adam doing? Look, Dad, I'm sorry I haven't been around the past few months. Next time you're with him, could you tell him that I climbed the peak for him? God, I'm a self-centred prick. Don't tell him that. I mean that I climbed up here for him. You can tell him I'm a prick, though. Be my guest. And you can tell him I say he has to get better, because we all need him. You know that, right, Dad? How's Susie doing? I've been thinking about her and . . .*

He squinted toward the door. His imagined letter had spun out of control, and the ache in his pelvis needed to be walked out. Slowly, stiffly, he pushed aside the blanket and sat up. His clothes were wretched — grimy from the climb, creased and rank from having been slept in while damp. Eager now to be out of the shed, he slid his feet into his hiking boots but didn't bother tying them. He groped for his knapsack then crossed to the door in a single, silent step. Outside, the sky was indigo and clear; the air was bracing. He limped to a clump of bushes behind the shed and unzipped his fly, praying that the chicken curry he'd eaten the night before would hold its peace until he'd returned to civilization.

At the entrance to the compound that housed the footprint, there was no sign of the gatekeeper, but the gate had been left unlocked. Rudy swung it open, then he remembered his boots. It would be especially boorish, he supposed, to flout custom after the gatekeeper had been as accommodating as he had. Nevertheless, it was damn cold out, and the idea of wandering about barefoot was more off-putting now than it had been the previous afternoon. As a compromise, he removed his socks — stiff and filthy anyway — then slid his feet back into his boots. If the gatekeeper appeared, he could pull them off speedily enough. Stuffing the socks into his jacket pockets, he entered the compound.

The bluish haze and quiet expectation of the near-dawn gave the place an otherworldliness. Whether it was Shiva's or Buddha's or Adam's, the compound had a presence, which Rudy confronted with a sharp sense that he himself was crass and out of place. Legs plodding, feet chafing and sliding in his boots, he made his way to the enclosure that housed the footprint. The stone slab was barely discernible in its gloomy shelter, though the flower petals and coins strewn across it reflected speckles of light drawn from somewhere. He rubbed his arms and thought of Robinson Crusoe — spotting Friday's footmark in the sand, being blown away by the discovery that he was not alone on his island. Then he carried on to the stone wall over which the bell hung.

Where the day before he'd seen nothing but thick masses of cloud, he was now able to make out the broad contours of the hilly landscape that extended from the base of the peak. The sunrise would be spectacular — like the fated climax of some exotic quest-romance, Rudy thought. Only he didn't feel like much of a quest hero. More a tourist than anything. He rested his forearms on the wall and squinted into the murky distance. Then he looked back at the shed. According to his grandfather's diary, Uncle Ernie had missed the sunrise at least once as a young man. Surely he'd want to see it now. And so, from a sense of duty more than from any desire to share the spectacle, he hurried back across the compound.

Outside the shed door, he coughed loudly, but when he peered inside, he found the old man still asleep.

"Uncle," he said, "the sun's coming up."

Uncle Ernie was lying on his side, facing the wall. "What's that?" he mumbled.

"The sunrise. The sky's cleared up quite a bit. It should be good."

"Alec?"

Rudy held his breath. Was it merely a slip-up, the kind that Aunty used to make all the time? Or was his uncle away in some unreachable place?

"It's Rudy."

Uncle Ernie stirred but remained on his side. "Let me sleep, then we'll go," he said, like a parent to a young child.

Rudy listened to the steady rhythm of his uncle's breathing. He
studied the curled-up position, in which he himself had lasted no
more than a few minutes.

"Where are we going?" he whispered.

Uncle Ernie grunted. "Nuwara Eliya."

"Okay."

He closed the door softly and stood outside the shed, scuffing his
shoe into the pebbly dirt. Then he returned to his lookout.

Already the compound was losing its otherworldliness. Within
minutes, in stark daylight, it would be an ordinary place, its surfaces
marred by cracks and grime. Beyond the peak, however, the landscape
was emerging from the darkness. Rudy leaned over the wall and witnessed the transformation: the symphonic eruption of chlorophyll
greens, the sudden brilliance of streams and lakes and crystal waterfalls, the bold rising of the peak's own shadow, whose black form
accented the surrounding radiance. The light was pure, and thin patches of mist hovered here and there, as if the wizard who'd zapped this
miracle into existence had only just vanished with a poof. Rudy marvelled at his luck. The scene was far more beautiful than he'd expected, more magnificent than his grandfather or James Emerson Tennent
had managed to convey — an Eden.

He looked about for a place to sit. Eyeing the chest-high wall, he
thought of his brother. He knew what Adam would do. A young man
with no qualms about climbing on the roof to hang Christmas lights
or riding his motorcycle in spring slush wouldn't think twice. *What are
you waiting for?* he would say if he were here. *Get up there!* Rudy peered
over the edge. A fall would hurt him, but it wouldn't kill him. He took
his journal from his knapsack and rested it on top of the wall. Then,
with his pen braced between his teeth, he planted his hands, hoisted
himself up, and manoeuvred his legs to the other side. The procedure
was clumsy and painful, and for an instant, hanging headfirst over the
menacing drop, he saw his sister teetering on the edge of Aunty's well.
But he got himself up.

Heart still racing, he took in the splendour and again imagined
himself at the climax of a quest, on the verge of an epiphany. For if
such a thing were possible, then surely this was the place and the

moment for it to occur. Yet. as he watched and waited, the scene, by imperceptible degrees, became familiar. It became the assortment of trees and lakes and rocks that happened to be in front of him. Like the compound that housed the footprint, his Eden lost its power, and he was left perched on a stone wall, looking out at a tropical hillscape, all his uncertainties still intact. He opened his diary to a back page and wrote "Dear Dad."

Balancing the book on his lap, he wrote about the weather in Montreal, and the garden, and even mentioned Uncle Ernie and Sri Pada before his ideas, and his will, dried up. He tapped his pen a few times then turned to a new page and wrote "Dear Adam." He'd learned somewhere, or perhaps just imagined, that brain injury victims could benefit from being read to. It made sense. But there was so much to say to Adam that he got nowhere. He turned back to his unfinished entry to Clare. It ended with "I wish," but he couldn't remember how he'd intended to complete the sentence.

"What the hell do I wish?" he muttered to the valley beneath him.

Peevishly he flipped through previous entries, snapping the pages, catching fragments of ideas and hints of old moods. Words whispered to an audience miles away. But to what purpose? Eyes fixed on the green hillscape, he took a thick wad of wordy pages in his hand. Slowly, raggedly, he tore them from the book. He wasn't convinced it was the thing to do; it wasn't an epiphany. He ruffled through the torn entries once more, noticing only the pen strokes and blots of ballpoint ink and the regular repetition of a woman's name. Then he flung the pages down the slope of the peak. Some got caught in the shrubs right below him; others dropped out of sight. He tore more pages and flung them away, until all that remained were the empty ones at the back. He felt sheepish about the mess, but not terribly so. The loss of his letters would take time to assess.

Overhead, clouds had begun to gather. Most of them were white; the more distant ones were thick and grey. Anchoring himself with one hand, he looked over his shoulder toward the gatekeeper's shed. His uncle had missed the best of the show, again. Turning back, he dated a fresh page.

Dear Susie,

It's been ages since I've written. Sorry. I heard the news about you and Mark, and I'm sorry about that too. I don't know what you'll think of this idea (feel free to turn me down), but I thought I'd run it by you anyway. I'm thinking of going back to Toronto after this term is over, and I'm wondering if you and Zoë would mind having me as a roommate (a paying one, of course). I could find a place of my own, but I was thinking that we could maybe help each other out by living together for a while. I could take on the cooking and the cleaning, and I'd be happy to look after Zoë while you go out, if she's comfortable with that. You can't have had much time to yourself, or with friends, these past few months. As for me, I'm still not altogether sure what I want to be doing with my life.

He paused here and reread the last sentence. The words suggested that his life hadn't yet started, that it wouldn't begin in earnest or have any meaning until he'd streamlined it into a governing design. That his year in Colombo had been a waste, a botched design. He reconsidered his proposal to Susie. He had no intention of living with his sister forever. Was he simply staving off commitment to the elusive something he was meant to be doing with his life? He stared at a meandering stream far below him and tapped his pen.

As for me, he imagined writing, *I'm at the top of Adam's Peak with Uncle Ernie, who doesn't seem too bothered that he and Dad haven't seen each other in decades, and who thinks that the Tamils should have their own homeland . . . and I haven't forgotten the look on your face when I pulled you down from the edge of Aunty's well . . . or how you taught me to read, that awful week we spent at the Pereiras' . . .* Just So Stories *or something like that . . . and maybe I just want to pull you down again, feel like a hero again . . . I don't know, but you're my sister, goddammit, and I think that having me around could be good for you and Zoë, and maybe for Dad and Adam too, but even though I want to help them, I just can't do it the right way . . . or maybe I just don't want to.*

It was complicated. He left the sentence as it was and carried on writing.

Right now, though, I'd really like to help you out if I can. I'll
go back to work in the dreaded 'burbs (and hope for something more central, eventually). I don't know if I'll be able to
get a full-time gig for September, but I'm sure the board will
take me back as a sub. I'll give you some time to

"Rudy!"

At the sound of his uncle's voice, Rudy closed his flimsy diary.

"Morning, Uncle. You missed the sunrise."

Uncle Ernie shot a look over the wall then leaned back against it
and fished for his pipe.

"To be honest, I always found it overrated. Not as interesting as
all the goings-on on this side — during the season, that is. Pretty to
look at, though." He pointed with his pipe. "How's your hip?"

"Stiff, but I'll make it." He glanced down at his uncle's bare feet.
"Was the gatekeeper around when you got up?"

"I didn't see him, but I imagine so." Uncle Ernie unzipped his
tobacco pouch and set about filling the pipe. "If we're efficient, we
should stay ahead of those rain clouds over there."

Taking the hint, Rudy manoeuvred his legs to the other side of
the wall and slid to the ground.

"There's some fruit on the table," Uncle Ernie said. "I've had my
fill; you're welcome to the rest."

Rudy put his diary in his knapsack. He stepped out of his boots
and wound the laces around his hand, then he hobbled across the cold,
damp cement on the outsides of his feet. Back in the shed, he found
that his uncle had eaten only one banana and left the rest for him. He
picked up a rambutan and briefly admired its extravagant design before
piercing the spiny skin with his thumbnail.

21

S HE WAS AT ONE OF THE airport book shops, flipping through an issue of *Marie Claire*, when she spotted Rudy Vantwest. He was in a coffee shop, sitting at a high, round table and writing. At first, it seemed to her a miracle that he should be there, an astonishing coincidence, and she stared, delighted and amazed, as each slight shift in his position confirmed that it was indeed him, made him more *him*, even. What were the chances? In a couple of hours she would be boarding a flight to his homeland, a trip that, for now, was embodied in a flimsy paper ticket and a gate number. And now here he was, across the concourse, scratching his head and squinting into the distance, perhaps at the massive, flashing departures board hanging from the ceiling. Chance meetings do happen, she told herself. There was the time she and Markus went to the symphony, and the woman in the seat next to Markus's turned out to be his grade two teacher. "You always had such a tidy desk," the woman said, as if to confirm that she still knew him, had known all along what he would be. But this particular meeting was more striking than Markus's, for the Vantwests had been on her mind. She'd thought about Rudy Vantwest as recently as half an hour ago, when she checked in for the Colombo flight, so that to have him right in front of her now was extraordinary — more extraordinary, surely, than the presence of any of the other people at the coffee shop, or the duty-free store, or walking up and down the gleaming concourse, trailing suitcases and children. Emma once said that airports were otherworldly, detached from place and time. They were exciting, she said, for you never knew who you might meet by chance. And it was true.

But then it occurred to her that the meeting might be fate. Not the nasty, vengeful fate that Alec Vantwest believed in, nor the fate to which Isobel deferred when she insisted that things happen for the best. No, the fate that had put Rudy Vantwest in that particular Heathrow coffee shop was, if it existed, a sort of inexorable energy that organized circumstances a certain way — not for the best, or for the worst, but simply in ways that made sense. Over the past few months, the Vantwests had woven themselves through her life, and she, perhaps, had woven herself into theirs. It was a pattern that had worked itself out, beginning with the evening she returned from Vancouver — maybe even earlier — such that now it was perfectly logical that she should find herself in exactly the same place as Rudy Vantwest. It was the energy, the momentum, of the pattern. They were meant to be there together.

She watched him write — a diary, it seemed, though it was hard to tell. Perhaps a letter. He was a little oddly dressed. Nobody wore shirts like that anymore, and the shorts reminded her of the ones he'd been wearing the day he stood on his front lawn, scrawny-legged, carrying two miniature suitcases. Still, he had pleasing qualities: the way he twirled his pen then held it in his mouth like a pipe, the curve of his calf muscle (no longer scrawny) as his foot perched on one of the crossbars of the stool, the tidiness of his hair and the strong line of his jaw. If he were indeed writing a letter, it was possible he had a partner, but Clare dismissed the possibility. She pinched the Celtic cross at the base of her throat — a souvenir from Stanwick — and slid it back and forth along its chain.

Her thoughts jumped ahead, following this new pattern. She and Rudy Vantwest would stand together in line to board the flight to Colombo (he'd been home visiting his brother and now was returning). They would try to switch seats in order to be next to each other, but

the man checking boarding passes at the gate would smile apologeti-
cally and say it couldn't be done. At the airport in Colombo, however,
they would arrange to get together. A walk through the city; he'd show
her around. They would plan to climb the sacred mountain together.
She pictured the ascent, up the steep path, past the shrines — she and
Rudy talking briefly, dutifully, about their shared past, the way Isobel
and Alec had done, then leaving Morgan Hill Road behind and con-
centrating on themselves. Their conversation unfolding without awkwardness. But it wouldn't be conversation alone connecting them. She
saw Rudy stop near the summit of the peak and step in very close to
her, brush her hair from her face, rest his hands on her shoulders. She
saw her own hands press against his hips and pull him closer still. She
imagined, and even felt, the fluttering arousal, so different from anything Emma's gift had yet delivered, for it would derive from a real
touch, a connection with the thrilling mystery of another. And she
imagined the powerful conviction she would have of this relationship
making sense. For such a relationship could not happen out of the blue.
The motorcycle ride with Adam, the visits with Alec and Mary, even
her decision to find Patrick Locke — all had a place in this particular
design, this fate that was now announcing itself through the presence
of Rudy Vantwest at the coffee shop across the concourse.

Of course, this fate meant an unsettling of her new plans. She'd
decided to return to Paris. Marielle's cottage had been a disappointment — the rooms were chilly and dark and scantily furnished — so
she'd left the place for a three-star hotel in the Marais, a nineteenth-
century establishment from which she went on long walks, studying
her reflection in windows and cultivating feelings of being at home in
the great stone city. Her plan was to return there and study music
again, at the Sorbonne, or wherever it was that one studied music in
Paris. Her apartment building would be old. The sitting room would
have a worn Persian carpet, and the window would look out on Notre
Dame, or the Eiffel Tower, or anything at all that would be out of
place in a Montreal suburb. There'd be a café and a *boulangerie* in the
same block, a second-hand bookstore around the corner. She would
get to know the owners of the shops; she would introduce herself to
her classmates. So she'd thought. But this encountering of Rudy

Vantwest could not be ignored. It had to be lived out — the walk across the concourse, the greeting. The energies of fate must be permitted to have their way, to change her plans even.

She went to the cashier's desk to pay for the magazine.

It was this shift in her perspective that caused her to notice the plastic duty-free bag on the floor next to Rudy Vantwest's table. It was white with red lettering, and she recognized the design, having seen it on her own ticket envelope, as Air Lanka's. Clare stared as its implications sorted themselves out. She'd assumed that Rudy had been home visiting his brother and would soon be making his fateful way to the gate from which their shared flight would depart. But what of the duty-free bag? Did Air Lanka even have flights from Montreal to London? It didn't seem likely. What was likely, in short, was that Rudy had not just come from Canada after all. In all probability, he'd been on a flight out of Colombo — perhaps the very same plane that Clare would board, in two hours, for its return journey. In an utterly banal way, this explanation made the most sense of all: she and Rudy Vantwest had been brought together by airline timetabling. He wished to leave Colombo; she wished to go there. The possibilities for carrying out those choices were limited.

Clare slipped the magazine into her bag and slid the silver cross back and forth along its chain. There was a voice in her head, quiet and unfamiliar. More of a loose consciousness than a particular arrangement of words. It was telling her it didn't matter. How Rudy had come to be there — coincidence, fate, choice — didn't matter. The presence in her head was gently persuading her that she needed to pick up her belongings and go to him. That it would be foolish not to — he was her neighbour.

Across the concourse, Rudy Vantwest was again squinting into the distance. He seemed bored, in need of companionship. Clare hitched the straps of her bag up her shoulder, ran her fingers through her hair, and started walking. He looked over before she reached him, and their eyes met, just as they had years before on the day of Adam's birth.

JUNE 2002

Dear Claire,

Thanks for your last letter. Great to hear from you, as always. And is the new version of your name official? (I like it.) I thought you'd like a copy of the enclosed photo. As you can probably guess, it was taken at Adam's graduation, which was on May 21st. I took the train out with Susie and company.

That's Sue standing next to Adam. The guy on her other side is Lawrence. They're still going strong. I fear I'm going to get the boot any day now (I've actually been scouting out condos around the Annex), but I told Sue and Mark I'm holding out for collective custody. I think they'll be willing to indulge me. But to return to the photo, the beautiful young lady next to me is Zoë. People have started mistaking her for my girlfriend when we go out together, which makes me feel really creepy. She's only thirteen! Fortunately she's got brains to go with her mature looks. I think she's absolutely brilliant (not that I'm biased or anything), and hilarious too, often at my expense. Everything's fair game: my clothes, my receding hair-line, my cooking, my clumsy signing. (My latest faux pas was to sign "orgasm" when I meant "mouse." What I want to know is how the hell my thirteen-year-old niece learned the word orgasm!) But anyway I guess I'm just a big schmuck, 'cause I let her get away with it.

As you can see, Dad's getting on. He doesn't usually look quite this wrecked though. The ceremony was very emotion-al for him. When Adam walked across the stage, he (Dad that is) had tears streaming down his face. I'd never seen my father cry before, even when Mum died. It was strange and kind of freaky. Sue and I each took his hand, and the three of us just sat there watching. Anyway, he continues to ask about you whenever we see each other, and he wanted me to pass on his good wishes. So here you go: Alec sends his best.

And of course that's your mum standing next to him. It was really nice of her to come to the ceremony. Apparently she did Dad's taxes for him this year, and he was so chuffed with the refund she got him that he's been recommending her to all his old work cronies. She and I chatted for a while after the cer-emony. She was telling me about her real estate fiasco and pass-ing on some helpful advice. Sounds like she's happy in the city, though, and the apartment is a classic (I saw some pics).

I can't remember when I last updated you on Adam. He's still kind of irritable and more unpredictable than he was before the accident (I imagine those things might be perma-nent), but he managed to finish his thesis, which he dedicated to Mum. He got the defence waived (that whole scene would have been too much for him), and I gave him quite a bit of help with the writing. The ideas are pretty insightful, though, which makes me think the essential Adam is still there. Oh, and the thing he's holding in the photo isn't his diploma; it's a plane ticket to Colombo (a grad present from all of us). Finally he's going to go, next month, with Dad. I told him this is a lousy time of year to climb the peak (as you know!), but he's psyched. And of course my aunt can't wait.